PRAISE FOR *Mayflower Chronicles:*
The Tale of Two Cultures

"Haueisen narrates a historical saga that captures the heart,
mind and faith of the Indigenous Pokanoket and the English
settlers, and their struggle to understand each other in a
way that leads to mutual respect, friendship and peaceful
cooperation."

—The Rev. Dr. Jay Alanís, Lutheran Seminary
Program in the Southwest

"Since my doctor of ministry emphasis is in intercultural studies,
this comes as an interesting foray. I heartily recommend this
book. It is an easy-to-read story of flowing prose."

—Gulf Coast Synod (ELCA) Bishop Michael Rinehart

"As a retired Advance Placement American History teacher with
a Master of Arts degree in History. I know most all the facts
about the Pilgrims, but my knowledge about the Pokanoket
Nation was limited. *Mayflower Chronicles: The Tale of Two
Cultures* has broadened my knowledge base. I would recommend
it to anyone interested in this period of time."

—Glenda Hayes, retired AP American History teacher

"*Mayflower Chronicles* explores not only the treacherous trek
across the Atlantic, but the equally dramatic and surprising
conflicts that occurred on both European and North American
soil to make the arrival of the new settlers possible . . . includes
enlightening and much needed representation of the Native
American men and European women."

—Roger Leslie, PhD, author, retired librarian

T0170303

"This is definitely a book worth reading as it can be a way to bring healing and reconciliation between the two cultures."

—The Rev. Larry Johnson

"The reader enters the life of each culture and feels the tensions that naturally arise when they encounter one another. The movement of the story line keeps the reader engaged. The writer did considerable research to make the story real and alive. The encounter of the two cultures illustrates how human lives have parallels and value reflected in the Creator's intention from the beginning."

—Paul J. Blom, Bishop Emeritus, Gulf Coast Synod, Evangelical Lutheran Church in America

"Perhaps the most remarkable thing about this classic, foundational story is realizing that for so many of us, the story we've all been taught has been boiled down to a teacup sized account of the 'first' Thanksgiving at Plymouth Rock in 1621. Haueisen gives a detailed yet refreshing backstory [about] those moments of intersection where Indian and Anglo cultures came together four hundred years ago. This story is for anyone who enjoys engaging in the twists and turns of a very complex and comprehensive historical account brought to you by an incredibly accomplished author. Besides the general reading public, I highly recommend her book to historians, to descendants of William and Mary or other Mayflower passengers, and to members of the Pokanoket tribe."

—*Story Circle* Book Review by Shawn LaTorre

MAYFLOWER CHRONICLES

MAYFLOWER CHRONICLES

*The Tale of
Two Cultures*

KATHRYN BREWSTER HAUEISEN

GREEN PLACE BOOKS | *Brattleboro, Vermont*

Green Writers Press is a Vermont-based publisher whose mission is to spread a message of hope and renewal through the words and images we publish. Throughout we will adhere to our commitment to preserving and protecting the natural resources of the earth. To that end, a percentage of our proceeds will be donated to environmental activist groups and The Southern Poverty Law Foundation. Green Writers Press gratefully acknowledges support from individual donors, friends, and readers to help support the environment and our publishing initiative. Green Place Books curates books that tell literary and compelling stories with a focus on writing about place—these books are more personal stories, memoir, and biographies.

GREEN
PLACE
BOOKS

Giving Voice to Writers & Artists Who Will Make the World a Better Place
Green Writers Press | Brattleboro, Vermont
www.greenwriterspress.com

ISBN: 978-1-950584-59-8

COVER DESIGN: ASHA HOSSAIN DESIGN, LLC
BOOK DESIGN: DEDE CUMMINGS
Typeset in Adobe Caslon

FOR MY MOTHER,

ELIZABETH J. BREWSTER ROSS HIEBER (1914-1992),

WHO INTRODUCED ME TO THIS STORY.

MY BROTHERS, ROSS (1940-2019)

AND BRUCE, WHO SHARE THIS HERITAGE WITH ME.

AND MY DAUGHTERS, CAROL AND KAREN,

AND THEIR CHILDREN:

CHRISTOPHER, SARAH, ERIN, JACOB, JONATHAN, AND LAURA,

WHO CARRY THE STORY FORWARD.

Contents

Where today are the Pequot?

Where are the Narragansett, the Mohican, the
Pokanoket, and many other once powerful tribes of our people?

They have vanished before the avarice and the oppression of the White
Man, as snow before a summer sun.

—TECUMSEH SHAWNEE LEADER (1768–1813)

WHERE are the Pokanoket? We are still here. We are here—even when diseases brought from foreigners almost wiped out our people. We are here—even when the very people who we helped turned on us during our time of need. We are here—even when some of our own betrayed us. We are here—even when after the war they took our people, dispersed us, tried to run us off our land, sold us as slaves, and told us we could not identify ourselves as Pokanoket. We are here—even when history tried to write us out of it. We are here—even when opportunists tried to take our identity. Yet we still remain.

Who are the Pokanoket? We are a proud people. The Italian explorer Giovanni da Verrazzano encountered our people during his navigation of the Americas in his letter to King Francis I of France in 1524. In 1675, John Seller created a map of New England which he dedicated to King Charles II of England that clearly identified that the new land they colonized was known as "Pokanoket Country." Even Daniel Gookin, a colonial settler of Massachusetts during King Philip's War, recognized Pokanoket as a "great people" in his writings. When the Mayflower came to our shores in 1620, Massasoit Ousa Mequin was the acknowledged

Great Leader of the Pokanoket and the many tribes that paid allegiance to him.

It was only after the King Philip War that the word 'Wampanoag' came into use. And even then, it was reserved for those who fought in the war—not for those who did not. Warner F. Gookin writes in *Massasoit's Domain*, "Is 'Wampanoag' the Correct Designation?"—something to the effect of why there are tribes mostly of the "Cape and the Islands that are known by the name used for the tribes whom they refused to aid in 1675."

For generations, our ancestors have struggled to keep our identity because society was conditioned to call us 'Wampanoag.' We are most fortunate that we have not forgotten the history that our ancestors so diligently held on to and passed from generation to generation. We are the people of the Massasoit, we are Pokanoket.

For generations we were shamed when we talked about who we were and the story of our people. The Sagamore's maternal great grandmother, Susan Simons, was stoned as a girl but survived for the sake of retaining our people's memory. Even when the Sagamore was a little boy, he was called in the house and reprimanded by his mother for telling people about who he was. The fear of being Pokanoket was still in her blood and she feared for her son. We acknowledge Eliza Jane Weeden Congdon, Hannah Glasko, Princess Red Wing of the Seven Crescents, and many others who were faithful in passing the oral history of our people in light of the many barriers they faced from society.

We are grateful that now is a time when people are seeking true history, and because of the age of technology in which we live, that information is readily available in a way that was not obtainable in the past. It is amazing that the history that we have been told for generations is being backed by the findings of forensic historians. We are more than happy to share our rich history, and many people have come to help us with correcting and setting back on track the truths that have been hidden for so long.

Now is the time, for in this generation we have no fear. We will be known by the name the Creator gave to us. We are POKANOKET, we are still here!

On a final note, we want to express our heartfelt gratitude to Kathryn Haueisen. It has been the beginning of healing for our people. We are honored in how she has reached out to the Pokanoket people and respected our history as she has written this book. We truly believe that this book has been written in good faith in holding to the renewing a dream that our ancestors aspired to, that both our people can prosper in this land in peace and fellowship.

Aquene,
Sagamore *Po Wauipi Neimpaug*
Sachem *Po Pummukoank Anogqs*
Tribal Historian *Po Menuhkesu Menenok*

Dear Reader,

In 1620, a group we call the Pilgrims sailed to North America on the *Mayflower*. About half came in search of religious freedom, the others seeking a better economic life. A year later they hosted a three-day harvest celebration with the area Natives. That is the classic story I learned about the history behind Thanksgiving.

I was never taught that shortly before the *Mayflower* arrived, the Pokanoket were dying in droves, from diseases introduced by earlier European explorers and traders. Their population declined by around seventy percent prior to the arrival of the *Mayflower*.

Nor was I ever taught the English settlers could communicate with the Pokanoket only because the Native kidnapped by a European in 1614 ended up in London, where he learned English. Commonly known as Squanto, Tisquantum's knowledge of English enabled him to help leaders from two cultures work out a treaty.

I never learned their Massasoit (his title) Ousa Mequin opted to come to the settlers' aid, enabling them to survive, even though earlier Englishmen kidnapped his people, even though some of his men watched these Englishmen rob graves and help themselves to Native stored food supplies.

The English believed God wanted Christianity to spread to North America. For them, that explained why they discovered the Natives' food supplies, which kept them from starving, and the deserted Patuxet village where they established their new Plimoth Plantation.

Mayflower Chronicles: The Tale of Two Cultures is based on historical events, chronicled in accounts listed in the bibliography, and interviews with historians and Native descendants of both the Pokanoket and Wampanoag. The book was in production before I met three descendants of Massasoit Ousa Mequin. From them, I learned I had a few details wrong, which I have corrected. I then asked their Sagamore, his daughter, a Sachem, and her son, the Pokanoket historian, to write the forward as a token of my earnest efforts to build bridges between our cultures and make amends for centuries of conflicts. Being a middle child, I want people to just get along. Naïve, I'll admit, but still a centering principle on which I base my daily decisions.

Native heritage is a sensitive topic today. It has taken generations for Natives to find their individual and collective voice. Some of what appears in this story may seem offensive, and if so, know that was not my intention. It is always a risk to presume to know the perspective of a culture not our own. Yet, unless we try to walk a mile in the foot wear of those from a different culture than our own, how can we ever learn to understand and respect one another? Any factual errors are my sole responsibility.

William and Mary Brewster are my ancestors. William most likely sat with the Massasoit and other leaders from both cultures that March afternoon in 1621. Three of my grandchildren have Native heritage. Their bicultural heritage prompted me to more closely examine what I've been taught. Until these grandchildren joined our family, I'd never questioned typical assumptions Anglo people often have about non-Anglo people. Now I question Eurocentric assumptions that the white way is the right way.

I filled gaps in the recorded history with my imagination. For example, we do not yet know what English family raised Mary Brewster. For the sake of telling the story, I've gone with the Wentworth theory, though I do not claim it to be true.

History does not tell us how Tisquantum got from Spain (where his captors took him) to London, where he learned English. That part of the story is all my imagination.

Finding conclusive dates for births, marriages, and deaths in the 1500s and 1600s is a challenge. Names and places are often spelled multiple ways. In that era, the new year started in March, not January, so dates can be confusing. I chose to use our modern dating system. Multiple people have the same first or last names, spelled in a variety of ways, making it difficult to verify who is referred to in a document. Some data is missing. Records either don't date back that far or have been lost over time. I've endeavored to be as accurate as possible, but this book is not intended for use in genealogical or historical research. I wrote it to honor the people from two cultures with a thought-provoking story about their struggles.

I used the term "savage" only because that is what the English settlers considered these sophisticated Natives to be. Realizing the term is offensive, I use it only where the settlers would have, to jolt us into reconsidering common, erroneous assumptions about indigenous people.

As you read about the desperate plight of the settlers and their impact on the Natives, I hope it cultivates a more charitable attitude towards today's desperate refugees, and respect for the thousands of indigenous people who were here first. A portion of the proceeds from this book are being donated to the Pokanoket Nation, Pilgrim Hall Museum, and Plimoth Plantation. Thank you for coming along on the journey that changed a continent.

Kathryn Brewster Haueisen
JANUARY 2020

PROLOGUE

For thousands of years, two distinct cultures evolved unaware of one another's existence. Separated by what one culture called the Great Sea and known to the other as the Atlantic Ocean, the course of each culture's future changed irreversibly when they encountered one another along the shores of what is known today as Cape Cod. This is the story of what drove the English across the ocean and how the Pokanoket people responded to them.

MONTAUP (RHODE ISLAND)   1580

The time for Magnus to deliver would arrive soon. Last spring her brother's woman, Sokanon, went alone to the birthing place he built for her. A couple of days later Sakonon returned with her sleepy new infant wrapped in fur.

Though this was not her first baby, she felt more secure once her sister, Tatapanunum, and sister-in-law, Sokanon, agreed to accompany her to her birthing place. Men built the birthing places far from village wetus, but even so, sometimes birthing cries reached the village. Magnus thought, *It is good to have others with me.*

Far into the night, the women talked. Every few minutes, Magnus felt her baby stretch and push against her swollen belly, then be still again while the women resumed telling their stories. The black night sky slowly yielded to the grey of predawn, then pastel peach, and finally bright orange. The baby stirred more often now. Whenever another sharp pain ripped across Magnus's lower back, she grabbed the birthing strap hung over a sturdy pole supporting the birthing structure. She gritted her teeth until the pain relented. Each pain began like a low wave gently washing to shore, increasing in intensity until it became a crescendo of agony. As the pains began to come one on top of another, she tightened her grip on the birthing strap and squatted, waiting with hope and pain comingled together.

Each time another contraction rolled across her lower abdomen, Tatapanunum gently rubbed Magnus's shoulders and sang a soothing melody. Sokanon wiped the sweat off her brow and kept reminding her, "Breathe in. Push the breath out. Long. Slow. In. Out. Slow. Slow. There. Good. Good."

Tatapanunum rubbed her back and crooned, "Soon, sweet sister. Soon." She repeated this over and over as Magnus pulled on the strap and pushed with her all her strength. She cried out again, and this time Tatapanunum clapped with delight. "I see the top of the head! I see the head!"

Sokanon reminded her, "Take in a deep breath now, and push." Magnus clenched her teeth and panted.

"I see the head!" exclaimed Tatapanunum. "A head of thick, silky hair."

A moment later, the baby slipped from her body onto a soft, woven cattail mat beneath her. The infant, covered with milky residue from his mother's birth canal, landed with a soft thud on the mat. He pumped his tiny arms and legs and looked around.

Tatapanunum swooped him up, still attached to the umbilical cord, and gently tapped him on the back. He sputtered and spit out what was in his mouth, then cried in protest at being suddenly exposed to the cold. Magnus delivered the placenta, let go of the birthing strap, and sank down onto a fur blanket. She reached for her son and clutched him to her bosom. With her free hand she gently touched each tiny finger and toe. Sokanon handed a knife to Magnus after she lay the baby across her outstretched legs so she could cut him free from the placenta. Sokanon picked it up and gently set it aside.

Exhausted from labor, Magnus leaned against the center pole. With tears of gratitude, relief, and joy washing her cheeks, she watched Tatapanunum clean her baby and place him in the birth sack. A few weeks earlier, sensing the time to deliver was near, she'd sewn a beaver pelt into this sack, with the soft fur turned to the inside. The baby filled his tiny lungs and let out an ear-piercing cry.

All three women laughed with relief that he was alive and healthy. Magnus held out her arms to receive her baby. Elated at the sound of his cry, she snuggled him in her arms, gently pressed his mouth against one swollen breast, and nudged him to take his first suck of milk. As the baby nursed, Sokanon buried the placenta in the earth as a gesture of gratitude for this gift of new life. Then she left to inform We Meika his wife Magnus had safely delivered his son.

So it was that Massasoit Ousa Mequin made his entry into the Pokanoket community. He and his brother, Quadequina, grew up together in strength and stature during the time when disturbing changes disrupted their ancient ways. The English would eventually think of these brothers as the Two Kings.

The Mid-Atlantic Ocean – 1620

The howling wind grew even more intense, making it impossible to hear Master Jones yell out orders to the crew. Jones waved his arms in a wild arc, motioning everyone to get below. William and Mary Brewster rushed down into a hold full of women and children screaming or crying. Men shouted all at once; no one could decipher who said what.

Two sailors tossed coils of ropes into the crowd. "Tie yourselves down. It's gonna get worse. Nothing we can do but ride it out. Go on, now—do it quick, before someone breaks their bones."

The wind whipped waves up over the ship's railing, pouring icy salt water into the lower decks. Dark replaced what little light they'd had at the start of the storm. William huddled with Mary and the children. He prayed. "Lord, deliver us! Let us not have forsaken all to be buried alive in this watery grave that surrounds us."

He and Mary held fast to their children as icy seawater drenched everyone and everything. Anything not tied down was rolling back and forth, bruising anyone in the way.

Then their precarious situation got worse.

PART ONE

England

CHAPTER ONE

TWENTY-NINE YEARS EARLIER

SCROOBY, ENGLAND – 1591

"WILLIAM, do stop your incessant pacing! You shall wear out the floor beneath us. How can it be that you went off alone to Cambridge, then traveled all the way to Holland, but now you pace among people who have known you since before you could walk?"

William Brewster stopped pacing and turned to look at his younger brother, James. He'd been so deep in thought, he'd lost track of time. "Is it time to go?"

"It is beyond time. You must put on your jacket, and we must go."

"Yes, I suppose we should." William pulled back his shoulders and took in a deep breath. With a slight trace of a smile, he added, "I would rather prefer Mary not think I am not coming."

The Brewster brothers crossed the yard from Scrooby Manor to St. James in a few long strides. A few minutes later William stood at the altar with the priest, waiting for Mary to join them.

The priest studied his prayer book and waited for everyone to be seated and quiet down. Parishioners murmured among themselves. One woman whispered to another sitting next to her, "Weren't we all proud as peacocks when Sir Davison took our lad with him in service to Her Majesty? But he don't say much about what brought him home so soon."

"He'll talk when he's ready," the other woman whispered back. "He came home to a heavy load, what with his mother gone and his father in such poor health. Poor lad's had more than his share. Some days he looked lower than a thief sneaking away under a bush, if you ask me."

The first woman nodded. "Such a pity his father didn't live to see this day. Well, today is a happy day, and I'm glad for it. He deserves to find some happiness in this life. I pray his fortune is better from this day on. Such an intelligent and decent young man to know such sorrow so soon."

A man seated in front of the two women turned, glaring at them to be quiet. Mary Wentworth seemed to glide down the aisle as she took her place next to William in front of the priest.

The priest cleared his throat and began the service.

※

Will I? The priest had asked if she would take this man to be her lawful wedded husband. Mary thought about her answer as she stood holding William's hands and gazing up into his handsome face. The few years since he'd returned home from service to William Davison had been full of both hope and sorrow.

She hesitated before answering, not because she had any doubts about William, but because she was still trying to take it all in: that she was really here, standing at this altar at St. James, exchanging vows with this man. *Will I? Why yes, of course!*

William smiled down at her, his blue eyes bright with excitement and anticipation.

"I will," she said softly. William squeezed her hands. She squeezed back.

With those two simple words, their fate was sealed. The priest looked past them to the friends and family gathered to witness their vows that sunny June day.

"I pronounce William and Mary to be man and wife together, in the Name of the Father, and of the Son, and of the Holy Ghost. Amen."

The congregation followed the young couple out of the ancient stone church across the short distance to the Manor House. Mary's family presented the couple with a beautiful green silk pillow, large enough for them to sit on together by the fire on cold evenings. Prudence, William's stepmother, presented the couple with a looking glass. Others gave them food items for their pantry. Soon, all were enjoying ale and feasting on the roasted peacock friends had prepared in honor of the newlyweds. The bird's colorful feathers adorned the platter.

⁂

The next few days were a blur as Mary moved her few dresses and other personal things into the Manor House. She began taking her turn in the kitchen helping William's stepmother and the other women with preparations for the frequent guests who spent the night at the manor. The manor's location on the North Road connecting London and Scotland meant that nearly always at least some of the dozens of guest rooms were occupied.

William seldom spoke of his time away at Cambridge or his service to the Queen's secretary of state in the Netherlands. He seemed content to come home to assist his father with the bailiff and hosting duties for the Manor House. Now that his father was gone and he was the bailiff, he seldom had time to dwell on those days traveling with Secretary of State Davison.

Yet Mary sensed William struggled with something more than taking over his father's position in the community. One quiet afternoon a month or so after their wedding, they were together on their usual afternoon walk. With only a few hundred residents in the village, they easily traversed the lanes around Scrooby in a leisurely hour-long stroll. These walks soon became Mary's favorite part of the day.

Once they were alone, Mary hoped William would tell her more about his brief service to William Davison, yet she hesitated to prod him directly. "I thought you wanted to stay in the Lowlands. Did serving with William Davison not bring you satisfaction?"

William looked away. He wanted to be truthful with Mary, but he also believed it his duty now, as her husband, to protect her. *I might be in serious danger. I might endanger her, as well. These are precarious days. I was closely associated with Secretary Davison. Though I am safe enough here for the present, perhaps I have not heard the last of that nasty business.*

Mary tried again. "William, dear. You seem troubled. We are one now. Your afflictions are mine as well. Please, do trust me to understand. I beg you to tell me. Not knowing what troubles you tortures me."

He sighed and looked at her for a long moment before answering. "Ah, well, dear one, then I shall tell you."

William clasped his hands behind his back, pacing back and forth, looking down at the ground.

"I was rather pleased that Sir Davison chose me, a young man from such a little village, to serve him in his service to Her Majesty. Though it meant traveling far, it was thrilling." He glanced up to confirm Mary was still listening. "Mary, I saw the most amazing sights, and overheard astonishing conversations."

"You speak of them with such excitement. How could that trouble you?"

"Some events were rather troublesome. Secretary Davison was doomed the day he was appointed to that bloody commission to try Queen Mary."

"And that is what troubles you? That they beheaded Queen Mary?"

"Not just that. It was what Sir Davison was compelled to do. When they sentenced her, they entrusted Davison with the warrant for her execution. It was his horrible duty to obtain the signature of Her Majesty."

Mary sat down on a low stone wall. William stopped pacing and combed his beard with his fingers. He sat down next to Mary with his elbows on his knees, forehead resting on cupped palms. He spoke so softly, Mary leaned in to listen. "They declared Parliament should be petitioned to execute Mary."

Neither spoke for several moments. Finally, Mary said, "Her execution was all people talked about for months, but dear William, what has all this to do with *you?*"

He couldn't look up. "Queen Elizabeth signed the death warrant and gave it back to Davison. He took it immediately to receive the royal seal. I went with him and waited while he gave the instructions."

Mary sat so quietly that William glanced sideways to be sure she was still there. He combed his beard again before continuing. "When it was ready, Davison delivered the sealed warrant to Lord Burghley. Burghley sent it forward to Fotheringhay Castle. They carried out the execution."

Mary said nothing, but twisted a few loose strands of hair, then looked up to see him clenching his teeth. His eyes had grown moist.

"I suppose it was rather fitting they beheaded Queen Mary. Who can count all the Protestants she condemned to their death for the sin of not being Catholic?"

Mary winced. *Yet another head severed from yet another neck.* In her mind's eye, she saw Queen Mary's blood splattered everywhere. She'd heard stories about how the queen had gone bravely and serenely to the chopping block. She gave an involuntary shudder. *More senseless violence—because civilized people cannot agree on what the Good Lord meant when He said to go forth and make disciples.*

William noticed her shuddering. "Yes, I, too, feel my bowels lurch at the thought of it. When Queen Elizabeth learned of the execution, she feigned indignation. She claimed she had told Davison not to seal the warrant. Perhaps she thought she could have changed the order, or delayed signing it. The signed and sealed warrant arrived at Fotheringhay Castle before she could send another order. Burghley acted on the death warrant that *she* signed."

"So, she might have changed her mind and spared Queen Mary?"

"Our queen can be rather fickle at times. I believe she was hoping someone would assassinate Queen Mary and spare her having to order it done. It was a rather delicate situation."

"I am beginning to feel grateful you are now far removed from all that goes on at court."

"Yes. It is a bit quieter here, among our crops and cows. In any case, she ordered Davison arrested!"

"And you were loyal to him." Mary dabbed at tears with the backs of her hands, then stood up.

William nodded, still seated. "I worked for him, so I was without employment. That brought me home, Mary—to the Manor House, and to you. That is rather fortunate, I think." He smiled at her and stood up. *I suppose I should warn her I might yet be in trouble . . . but right now, I prefer to savor our time together without worrying her.*

William embraced her and whispered, "Enough of this. The day is too beautiful to dwell on yesterday's sorrows. Let us think more uplifting thoughts, and continue our walk. I am here now, where I can be with you. Family and friends surround us. We have one another. The Good Lord has surely watched over my going away and my coming back. That is enough to know for this day."

CHAPTER TWO

SCROOBY MANOR – JULY 1566

Sir Henry Killigrew turned to his young clerk, William Davison, as their carriage bounced along the North Road. "Do you see it now? Just up ahead. That is Scrooby Manor. I am weary from the dust and ready to stop for this day."

"That truly is a welcome sight," agreed Davison. "I wonder if I shall ever be rid of the taste of dust. The sun begins to feel as hot as a fire in winter."

"Soon you'll be in out of the sun. I'll introduce you to the bailiff, Thomas Wentworth. The gentleman does what he can to keep the place going. I hear in days of old it was quite specular. Now it seems in need of a bit of repair. No matter. Here we are. Down you go to rest for the evening."

A servant approached to collect the horses. Killigrew inquired where they might find Bailiff Wentworth. "You shall not find him here this day, sir. He is off to York on business. Master William Brewster and his new wife shall be at your service this evening."

"Brewster is here at the Manor?" Killigrew turned to Davison and explained, "Though Bailiff Wentworth has business away, I suppose he thought we might welcome a little company in his absence. Perchance the messenger ahead of us gave word we would soon pass through here. Ah well, I do not know the man well, but I suppose his company will provide diversion enough from the rigors of travel. Reason enough to rest a spell and learn the local chatter."

To the servant awaiting instruction, Killigrew said, "Put the horses up and tend them well. These beasts have well earned their rest."

He and Davison headed toward the main entrance where another servant showed them into a large room with chairs arranged around a fireplace. Mercifully, it did not contain a fire on this toasty day. She left to inform William Brewster that the expected royal messenger from London had arrived.

When she left, Killigrew said, "Well, now my lad, we shall see what comforts this neighbor William Brewster has in store for us. I heard he has married John Sympkinson's widow since I was last here. We will soon know what difference a woman's touch makes to the health of the man. Though if it be true she brought three children with her to their marriage, she might not be able to do much to add a bit of comfort to his life."

"If they offer us drink in a place out of that relentless sun, I shall be pleased enough," responded Davison. He soon felt more comfortable as the cooler temperature inside the manor's thick stone walls brought welcome change from the oppressive midafternoon sun.

William Brewster approached to welcome them on behalf of Bailiff Wentworth. "Usually the business comes here, but there was some dispute about some confounded thing or another. He was called to York and thought it best to go see the affair was put to rest properly."

Brewster then called to his wife to join him. When she stepped into the room, Davison and Killigrew tried not to stare at her protruding stomach. Brewster introduced her. "This is my wife, widow of Sympkinson.

"Ah, then it is true. You did wed the widow Sympkinson. And got three children in the bargain."

William's young stepdaughters, nine-year-old Margaret and seven-year-old Dorothy, peeked at the guests from around the corner until their mother spotted them. "Margaret! Dorothy! You should not be pestering our guests. Go now, tend to your chores."

When the girls left, Brewster continued. "It shall not be much longer now 'til we have a wee one of our own." He tenderly patted Mary's belly and smiled. "Mary was John Sympkinson's widow. Did you know of him?"

"Aye, I should say so. He earned much respect during his time as mayor over in Doncaster. Is it true his funeral was on Christmas morning?" Killigrew asked Mary.

"Indeed, it was. God rest his soul. He left me with four young ones. It wasn't but a year before our youngest son died, too. Those were my sorrowing years. But then the Lord brought me to the house of this kind man."

"And now we await the birth of one of our own to join Mary's three. The Lord taketh, and the Lord giveth; blessed be the name of the Lord."

Mary blushed and reached out to squeeze her husband's hand before retreating back to the kitchen.

When Mary was out of sight, William told Killigrew, "Should the Lord Almighty see fit to bless me with a son, I shall name him after me: William Brewster." He grinned and held up a tankard for a toast.

"To good health, safety in birth, and a son of your own," toasted Killigrew in return. Davison held up his tankard to join them, but added no well-wishes of his own.

Killigrew explained, "We're on our way to Edinburgh to deliver Queen Elizabeth's official royal congratulations to her cousin Mary and Lord Darnley. She gave birth to a son in June," began Killigrew. "They named—"

"It is so thrilling! Queen Mary's baby James might someday inherit the throne of Scotland!" interrupted Davison.

The older statesman glared at Davison. "You would do well, young man, to know your proper place and stay well within it. Though I suppose no harm comes from your impetuousness here, it cannot be tolerated when we are presented to her Royal Highness Mary."

Davison's cheeks flushed scarlet red. He bowed his head and scooted further back in his chair, examining his fingernails as Killigrew continued. "Though my young assistant spoke out of turn, he spoke rightly. Queen Elizabeth wishes to show she holds no jealousy toward her cousin. It may gall her that her rival bears a son when she has yet to have a husband, but she will never let her subjects know of it. The royal vanity grows a bit strong at times."

Mary Sympkinson Brewster moved in and out of the room, supervising staff while straining to hear the men's conversation. She managed to sneak several glances at the handsome twenty-five-year-old Davison. With a serious expression and silky voice, he was a welcome guest at the Manor House. It seemed to her too many of the men she observed stopping at the manor were stodgy, ill-tempered, arrogant old clergy, or royal messengers eager to be on their way. This one appeared excited to be here, though she sensed his good spirits somewhat dampened from the way he kept his head down. He had not spoken since the older man's rebuke. *I like the looks of that one. He's the sort of gentlemen I fancy for my daughters when they are ready.*

Davison studied his surroundings. Still smarting from Killigrew's reprimand, he left the conversation to the two older men and began to daydream. *I like this place and these people. I hope I may find my way here often in my service to the court.*

Chapter Three

Scrooby, England – 1575

Young William listened to his parents talking from the safety of his favorite hiding place in a closet. Hiding was one of his favorite pastimes. He loved the drama when people missed him and searched high and low for him. It became a game, timing his reappearance just as their worry began to turn from exasperation to anger. He listened carefully to gage when the timbre of his mother's voice changed toward annoyance. Then he would come strolling out into plain sight as though he had no idea why she would be upset with him.

He especially loved overhearing conversations that revealed information adults thought children need not know. He almost gave himself away this day when he heard what Father was telling Mother.

"Then is it true?" exclaimed Mary Sympkinson. Her voice raised in delight and excitement.

"True it is. Confirmed and signed. This very day. I shall assume the duties formerly held by the recent Bailiff Thomas Wentworth, God rest his soul. We are to take up residence in the manor immediately."

"Oh my. Dear me. So much to do. I must put the children to work at once. Have you seen William anywhere?"

"He's not outside with the others?"

"Not when I was there but a few minutes ago. Where *is* that lad? I've never known a boy what could hide so often as that one."

She scurried out of the room, calling for her wayward son to come to her, immediately.

William Brewster senior assumed duties as bailiff and postmaster at the Scrooby Manor in 1575. Young William spent his older childhood years exploring the manor inside and out whenever he wasn't away at school in nearby Doncaster. He soon found new hiding places where he could overhear news delivered by the many royal messengers who stopped by to change horses or deliver official documents.

Chapter Four

THE women bumped into one another in the kitchen. They were busy tending to tasks for the morning meal for young William. No matter how many logs they put into the fireplace, Mary Sympkinson Brewster still shivered in the early December chill. She longed for the warmth of her bed, but insisted on overseeing every detail herself. "This is going to be his last meal with us for a very long time," she said to no one in particular.

Mary fussed at her daughters Margaret and Dorothy to be quick about setting out the pewter plates and cups. "Can you not rejoice with us at the good fortune of your brother to have such a glorious opportunity! This will surely will bring honor to us all. Hurry, now. William will appear at any moment."

It was not the first time Mary had reminded her blended family that William's acceptance at Cambridge University's Peterhouse meant good standing in the village for all of them. She wanted everything to be just so before sending young William off on his three-day journey.

"Fifteen years old, he is. Old enough to go, yet I shall miss him terribly. On his days away in Doncaster, he was often here. I won't be laying my eyes on him much after this morning."

"Yes, Mother. We all know this," said Margaret. "It is an honor indeed for young William, and for all of us. The Lord was surely watching over us when you married Gentleman Brewster. I can hardly remember Papa."

"It's a wonder you remember him at all, being you were but five that Christmas when we buried him at St. George in Doncaster." Mary felt the familiar lump in her throat as she recalled the bleak Christmas Day when the priest led her reluctantly through the funeral service. "That was many years gone by. Now we have this wonderful home and one of our very own off to Peterhouse. The wonder of it makes my heart sing."

Young William walked in and gave his mother a peck on the cheek. He went over to a pot of simmering porridge, poked a tentative finger into it, then put it into his mouth. "William!" admonished his mother. "You are old enough to know better. For shame!"

William grinned while maneuvering his tall, lanky frame onto the long wooden kitchen bench. He put his elbows on the table and rested his chin in one palm. With his other hand, he scratched at the youthful start of a light brown beard. It was finally visible on his narrow face.

Mary and her daughters placed the food on the table. Father joined them. Mary nodded that all was in place. Father offered a prayer. Young William thought the prayer covered every contingency that could possibly occur on his journey to Cambridge. He quickly finished eating then impatiently waited for the others to finish. It was all he could do to give civil answers to the endless questions.

"Did you hide your money in a safe place?"

"Yes, Father, I did as you showed me."

"Did you pack plenty of warm clothes? It is a very long journey, and who knows where you will find shelter along the way. You must be prepared."

"Yes, Mother, I have taken all the clothes I have. I am prepared."

"Do you have parchment so we may expect to receive word of your safe arrival?"

"I do. And I promise I shall post a message to you as soon as I possibly can. But have you forgotten? I made arrangements with our neighbors to travel with them as far as Lincoln. We shall find shelter there. Surely, someone from there will be traveling toward Cambridge. And if not, I have the musket you gave me, should any thieves come upon me."

William's father nodded consent and looked pointedly at Mary. "He's a grown lad now. I suppose it would do no good to bid you not worry, but he is as ready as ever he shall be. Let us send him on his way with our blessings, and commend his fate to the good Lord who watches over us all."

William's father bowed his head to indicate another prayer. As soon as he said "Amen," young William sprang up from the table, ran to his room to gather his things, and returned to say one final farewell. He dashed out of the manor and quickly mounted Good Fortune, the horse the stable boy had waiting for him.

William's father reminded him again, for the tenth or perhaps the twentieth time, "This horse helps put food on our table. Treat him well, and return him to me so that I may lease him out to those who will pay to have such a fine steed."

William promised again. "Yes, Father. I shall take excellent care of Good Fortune. I pray he is rightly named."

⁂

William joined up with three neighbors taking bags of seed to sell in Lincoln. When they were a few hundred yards down the Old North Road, he turned. As he had hoped, his parents stood watching. He waved to them, then turned to stare straight ahead. *I am glad I travel with others. It forces me to pretend I feel as confident as I should hope to be.* As they rode along, William let his mind drift back to a conversation between his parents he'd overheard months earlier. He'd long since grown out of his childhood passion for hiding in the closet to listen. Yet, he still liked to be near, but out sight, when he thought they might discuss something of interest to him.

That day his mother's voice had been both firm and pleading. "His cousin will be there. It is not charity, William. It is an opportunity. We know not what troubles may soon come our way. My brother John only wants our son to have the same chance as his own son Thomas."

William strained to hear his father's reply. It seemed long in coming. "I do not like being obligated to John Smythe and his money from the Hull Port."

"Dear William, do be reasonable! What opportunity has he here? Think of it. Cambridge! John said he might invite William to join him in his merchant trade. Imagine all the places he could go. Poland. Norway. Even Spain! And my brother John will provide the money."

William heard something slam—perhaps his father's pewter mug on the worn kitchen table. "That is exactly what I do not want! *I* should be able to provide for my own family!"

There was silence for what seemed a long time. When his mother spoke again, she spoke so softly William was not sure what she said. It sounded like, "Could you not see this as the hand of our dear Lord reaching out to bless our son for something great? You *do* provide for us. And I thank you for it. Aye, I thank God for it every day. But William, a chance like this is too wonderful to turn aside."

William smiled at the way his mother convinced his father to accept the offer from Uncle John Smythe. He suspected John's brother, Uncle Frances, may have had a hand in the plan to enable him to enroll with his cousin. *Uncle Francis seemed determined that either his own son or I would follow in his footsteps as a priest. Perhaps that dream will be fulfilled when little James grows a few years older. We shall see what things the Lord Almighty has in store for me. I am on my way to Cambridge, praise be.*

Chapter Five

England – 1580

WHEN Samuel Witherspoon called out, "William. William! Have you suddenly gone deaf, Lad?" William realized he had been lost in his thoughts. He prodded Good Fortune with his heels, and for the next few minutes, they trotted along the well-traveled North Road in silence.

As they approached Lincoln, Witherspoon pulled in his horse's reins. "We come to the end of things now. William, you will have to find your own lodging for the night. My men and I will go to the mill and see what we can get for our efforts. Then we start back. We'll camp in the woods. Surely you can find someone here to give you a place to sleep in exchange for chopping a bit of wood or some other chore. God be with you now."

I will not let them know I am worried. Surely, God's goodness and mercy travel with me. William rode on alone for another half hour until he spotted a house at the edge of a forest. Smoke rising from the stone chimney gave him hope this might be where he and Good Fortune could rest for the night. A dog barking announced his approach. William stayed mounted as the barking spaniel ran circles around them. Good Fortune moved back and forth and side to side to dodge the dog. Mercifully, the horse didn't rear up.

An elderly man approached, calling the dog back. Amazingly, it obeyed. The loud barking subsided to low growls. An old woman appeared and stood behind her husband, resting on a walking stick.

William tipped his hat. "Good evening. I have traveled far this day. My horse needs water. We could both use somewhere to rest the night. Might my horse and I rest in your barn until morning? I need nothing more than water for my horse and a place to rest.

I have provisions enough for myself. The horse would be happy to graze a while in that field."

Both the man and woman looked him over from the tips of his boots to his now bare head. "Where have you come from, and where do you go?" asked the man.

"I hail from Scrooby, Scrooby Manor, on the North Road," he said, pointing the direction he had just traveled. "Cambridge is my destination. I must be there day after tomorrow."

"Cambridge!" exclaimed the woman. "Can you prove it?"

"I can if I dismount." William swung his right leg up over Good Fortune's hindquarters, slid to the ground, and nearly collapsed after so many hours of riding. He reached into one of the leather pouches slung over the horse's rump to pull out his acceptance letter from Peterhouse.

The farmer looked at it briefly and passed it to his wife, who quickly returned it back to William. He suspected neither could read since they barely looked at it. The farmer said, "You seem honest. And young. And strong. Answer my question correctly, and you may join us for supper. That is, if you'll help with the firewood. You're welcome to sleep by our fire for the night. Your horse can have some hay. But first, tell me this, be you Catholic or Protestant?"

William felt sweat forming under his arms. If he answered wrong, he wondered if he'd have time to mount and ride away before they came at him with the pitchfork leaning against the house. He took in a deep breath and answered truthfully. "Sir, as you may know, our manor has frequently been the resting place for priests and bishops in service of the Holy Established Church of England. My father is trusted with both the sacred and royal mail. Would he be allowed such an important duty if we were not Protestant?"

"Well, then you are welcome here. There's the wood to chop before supper." The man pointed to a large pile of logs behind William. By the time he chopped his way through the stack, his arms and back ached. Supper was simple but plentiful. He thanked his hosts and made a bed for himself against the wall, next to the fire. Before settling in, he added several of the logs he'd chopped barely two hours earlier. William rested with his back tucked into the corner, where the stone fireplace met the wood wall. As this was his preferred position, he dozed off sitting up, barely an hour after the sun went down.

CHAPTER SIX

ENGLAND, DECEMBER – 1580

William was up with the sun. He shivered as he tossed aside the quilt the woman had provided, and put on the two layers of clothing he'd taken off the night before. He found the woman with her arms full of wood to add to the fire. "I'll feed you soon. I'm glad you're up and about. I need the fire now to warm the porridge."

"Thank you, but I'd best tend to Good Fortune before I eat. Shall I bring in more wood?"

"It would be a blessing if you would," she said, turning away to add two logs to the smoldering fire.

A blast of bitter cold caught William's breath the instant he opened the cottage door. It had snowed overnight. He left footprints on his way to the barn. Good Fortune whinnied as he entered. William looped a rope around his neck and led him over to a trough to drink. The water was frozen, so he looked around until he spotted an axe. With little effort, he broke through the half-inch-thick layer of ice, tossing sheets of it onto the frosty ground. He rubbed his horse's silky neck as the animal lowered its nose into the ice-cold water.

William led the steed back to the stall, tossed in some hay, and braced himself for the brisk walk across the yard to the house. After finishing some piping hot porridge, William thanked his hosts, and departed. *Imagine it! Going to classes in Peterhouse! Founded by Bishop of Ely three hundred years ago! What must it be like?*

Eager to get there, William urged Good Fortune to trot. A couple of times he nudged Good Fortune into a canter as they crossed open fields. The horse's steamy breath reminded William that working the animal so hard in such cold weather might endanger its health. He reluctantly slowed to a walk.

At the end of the day, William saw a proper inn. After settling Good Fortune in for the evening, he found a place near a roaring fire to warm himself and listen to conversations between other guests. Mugs of ale in hand, guests were discussing the news of the day. Francis Drake and his triumphant return from his three-year voyage was the main topic of conversation. "Mark my words," said one man, "that one'll be a knight before long."

"Do you think she'll ever marry?" another asked when the conversation turned to Queen Elizabeth's marital status. "The poor Duke of Anjou. So close, but no success. I'm bloody well grateful I don't have no privy council telling me who to marry." He raised his mug high before polishing off its contents in one long gulp.

"Don't know about that," said another. "Do you think it's true Drake claimed a place called California for England? Now ain't that something? To have land so far away it takes a three-year journey to get there and back?"

William was fascinated. *Think of it. Sailing across the world. I should like to do that someday.* His ears perked up even more when the conversation turned to the ongoing battle between the Protestants and Catholics.

"It's not safe to be a Catholic now, I tell ye. Her Majesty's on a hunt to rid the whole country of every bloody one of them. There's sure to be trouble soon. More trouble than we already got."

William was well aware of Queen Elizabeth's determination to remove Catholics from England. He momentarily tuned out, lost in his own thoughts. *And why would the good queen not do so, after Pope Pius sided with the Rising of the North plot to depose her? Long live our Queen!*

When he realized they were still talking about Her Majesty, he tried to interject some bits of information he'd overheard from her messengers as they sat by the fire at Scrooby Manor. *I like it when one of them stays the night. I never tire of hearing the story of how she put her cousin Mary in prison to keep her from letting the Catholics back into England.* After several failed attempts, William gave up. *What care they about the words of one my age? If only they knew the stories these ears have heard. Pity. Well, it be their loss.*

The boisterous conversations, the warmth of the fire, and several mugs of ale made him sleepy. He slipped away unnoticed.

CHAPTER SEVEN

CAMBRIDGE – 1580

It was barely daylight when he mounted Good Fortune and urged the horse into a lively trot toward Cambridge. By mid-afternoon, William saw the magnificent three-hundred-year-old university buildings on the horizon. His pulse quickened. He clucked for Good Fortune to pick up the pace. *I can scarcely believe my own good fortune to be here.*

The December sun cast long shadows across snow-covered fields. After a few false starts, William found the front office just inside the gate to Peterhouse. He edged the door open and peered inside. A high wooden counter loomed only a few steps away. Three men in long wool coats stood behind it making notes in ledgers.

One glanced up as William stepped inside. "Are you a new student?"

"Yes, sir. I am William Brewster. Of Scrooby."

The man nodded. "Chancellor Lord Burghley will be pleased to learn you have safely arrived. And without encountering a robber eager to separate you from your tuition and board money, I dare say."

He finished writing something in his large ledger and walked around the counter, opened the door a few inches, and pointed down the walkway, along a snow-covered courtyard. "Just down there. That'll take you to the residences. Someone will show you what to do next. Supper is served promptly at five o'clock. If you're hungry, I advise you not to be late."

William led Good Fortune though an archway opposite the one he'd just entered. It opened into a small garden, where he tied the horse to a hitching post with enough slack to reach the water trough and hay. William found the room assigned to him. The door was closed, so he knocked in case he was in the wrong place.

"Enter!"

When he opened the door, a young man about his age was sitting on the edge of one of six beds in the small room. The fellow looked up from his book. "Greetings. I am John Slaney. And who might you be?" William introduced himself, and Slaney asked, "What place do you call home? I come from London. My father is preparing me to follow in his footsteps as a merchant. How far have you come?"

"From Scrooby. On the North Road."

"Where is that?"

"Not far from York. In Nottinghamshire. Do you know of it?"

"No, I can't say that I do. Well, did they inform you supper will be served in the Great Hall at five?" William nodded, but before he could say anything, his roommate continued talking. "This is my second year, so I can show you about. Here, we sleep. And there," he said, pointing to the wall across from where he was sitting, "is where we have our own room for study."

The Great Hall refectory adjacent to the kitchen was the last stop on John's introductory tour. Through the open kitchen door, William noticed another door that he assumed opened onto the garden where he left Good Fortune. Girls only slightly younger than himself stirred the contents of large iron kettles hanging from cast-iron rods over an open fire. Whatever they were cooking made his stomach growl. His mouth watered at the prospect of it.

After dinner, William slipped away to check on Good Fortune. "You will rest here a day or two," he said to the horse. "Then I will find someone to take you home." He rubbed Good Fortune's velvet nose, resting his cheek against it. "Truly, I cannot remember ever being as happy and excited—but with a bit of nerves, as well," he confessed aloud.

Chapter Eight

O ne of the older students told William Queen Elizabeth herself had spent nearly a week here only a year or so before
William's birth. Other students told him about when Vice
Chancellor Edwin Sandys was sent to the Tower for being on the
wrong side of a dispute with the Crown.

William remembered how, after the imposing Edwin Sandys
became Archbishop of York, he arrived at the manor from time
to time to check on Scrooby affairs. *And now I am in the very place
where he was once Vice Chancellor.*

New friends talked with William until their candles burned
low and flickered out. The loud clanging of the morning bell startled him. Six young men groaned and reluctantly put their feet on
the frigid floor. Groggy and longing to linger under the covers,
each pulled on thick hose, knickers, and woolen shirts in layers.

"Come on, Brewster," called out Slaney. "That be the five o'clock
bell calling us to lecture. Best hurry. The professors give no grace
for being late." William's stomach rumbled, but food would have
to wait.

Mid-morning, he joined his fellow hungry young scholars in
the refectory. William cautiously poked a spoon into the bowl
waiting for him at the table, tasted it, and groaned. *Porridge again!*
He swallowed his portion in half-spoonfuls until he couldn't bear
another mouthful. William pushed the bowl away and ventured
out into the courtyard.

The cold felt like a slap on his face. Hugging himself and rubbing his hands briskly up and down his upper arms, he scurried along the cobblestone path that surrounded the rectangular courtyard. He took in every detail of the two-story stone buildings, located on three sides of the courtyard. A high brick wall at the front of the courtyard closed the college off from the rest of Cambridge. The cold made it hurt to breathe. William was sorely tempted to cut across the grassy courtyard to return to the refectory more quickly. However, the registrar yesterday had warned against it. *Had that really been only yesterday?*

William took long quick strides back around the courtyard. The refectory was already empty except for a few girls clearing away dishes. He raced to the lecture hall and took his seat. The professor had not yet arrived. He was grateful for a moment to catch his breath. Turning to the student next to him, he introduced himself to John Penry, a Welshman soon known for his quick wit. In turn, Penry introduced him to John Greenwood. William listened as they railed against the restrictions of the church. "Here, we learn what is the truth," Penry told William.

"Aye, the bishops think they are gods. Most of them are drunk on power. You shall soon enough find out for yourself," added Greenwood. "Before long your head will be so full of new ideas, you shall struggle to hold it upright. Right, John?" Penry agreed, and the two friends continued talking as if William were not there.

They speak so boldly of their disdain for the Established Church. I sometimes wonder about some of the things they demand of us, but Father said it is best to keep such thoughts to myself. William remembered his father's advice: "To speak all you think, lad, is a good way to shorten your life. We live on land owned by a bishop. Be careful what you say."

The professor entered; the young men stood to honor him. He waved permission to be seated. The room wasn't much warmer than the courtyard had been, so William rubbed his hands together in a futile effort to warm them. *I see now why they call this place The Little Ice Age.* He opened his notebook and readied a quill to take notes. The room was so cold he feared the ink might freeze before the end of the lecture.

William's Latin and Greek studies had prepared him well for the rigors of this new academic life, and now he wanted to absorb everything. That evening, he found a quiet place adjacent to the sleeping room. William lit a candle and wrote his first letter home.

> *6 December, 1580*
> *My beloved Father and Mother,*
> *I greet you this evening from my room at Peterhouse. I have a fine fellow for companionship. Esquire John Slaney hails from London, where his father is a merchant. John is training to someday assume the duties of caring for the family business. He fills me with tales of ships coming into the harbor on the Thames filled with wondrous things, some from as far away as America! I can scarcely believe the stories he tells. He has even seen the strange-looking men the ships bring back from the New World. Oh, to think of it. What must it be like to travel so far?*
>
> *Lectures and reading fill my days. Already, I have been tasked with reading the works of the Italian humanist Stefano Guazzo. For the moment, this is a challenge, as* The Civile Conversation *is only available in Italian. Mercifully, our professor translates his thoughts into English. It is to be published in English next year! I pray you will approve my great desire to obtain such a book for my own collection. I can think of no better treasure than to have a collection of such books.*
>
> *Professor tells us Guazzo believes gentility and civilized behavior ought to bring as much to bear on a man's status as his wealth or lineage. Would that not be a better way to order our community? I wonder if such a thing is possible.*
>
> *I am so inspired here. I thank you for your part in bringing this to pass. I assure you I am well. The trip was pleasant enough. Good Fortune did, indeed, bring me safely to my own good fortune. For now, he is safe here at Cambridge. As you bid me, I shall search out a fellow who needs a mount to ride through Scrooby and send Good Fortune back to you when I find such a fellow.*
>
> *My candle burns low now, so I bid you a fair day, with my deepest affection and gratitude.*
> *Your grateful and loving son,*
> *William*

So busy was William with reading, studying, and exploring Peterhouse and Cambridge beyond the college, he was surprised when Christmas festivities started unfolding all around him. "Well, now it is time to enjoy some merriment," announced Slaney. "How do you honor the Twelve Days of Christmas, Brewster?"

"We know little of the games you propose. We attend Christes Masse, as do all my family and our friends. The priest tells us Christmas frivolities are not of God, but of the devil, who seeks to pull us away from our Lord."

Slaney laughed heartily at such an idea. "Not celebrate? Why, it is the very birth of the Lord that we honor with the festivities. So dour. Join me and others this evening for a bit of winter cheer. It will do you good, and warm you through and through."

William wasn't sure. He suspected the priest could explain clearly why this was wrong, yet John Slaney had been only kind and helpful to him. *I am here now. Should I offend my new friends by judging them harshly? Yet the priest was so passionate on this point.*

"I am grateful for your graciousness. I shall give you an answer when we gather for our evening meal."

Slaney clapped him on the back and left their cold, tiny room.

In the end, William decided he must at least go to see what others did to make the birth of Christ so festive. His eyes opened wide and his jaw dropped low when he stepped into the refectory hall. Evergreens hung from every pillar. If he could count all the candles, he supposed there would surely be hundreds. A table, perhaps fifteen feet in length, was piled with more platters of food than he had ever before seen in one place. Hogs on long spikes were laid out next to calves, deer, partridges, and geese with feathers still in place.

Dozens of loaves of beautiful brown bread alternated with mounds of golden yellow cheese. All around the room jugs containing gallons of ruby red or light white wine were available. The music captivated William. Musicians wandered about with lutes and lyres. He was used to singing psalms at home, but they never had such lively music as this. The music reminded him of the elaborately decorated pipe organ at St. James. A wave of nostalgia washed over him, making him feel totally alone, though surrounded by people chatting and laughing.

His thoughts strayed back to conversations at home. Some of the people seemed concerned the organ was too beautiful or the sound too distracting. Psalms were part of God's word, but the rest were not. A classmate rushing to refill a tankard bumped into

William, interrupting his reminiscing. Strolling minstrels passed by within a few feet. William nodded his head in time to their tunes and surveyed the luscious food choices. He pictured his family, all together at St. James, this year, for the first year ever, without him. He felt a lump forming in his throat as he thought about his family.

CHAPTER NINE

PETERHOUSE AND SCROOBY MANOR —1583-1584

"Are you not feeling well, William?" Slaney saw William sitting on the edge of his bed staring down at the floor, holding a letter on his lap. Slaney had to touch him on the shoulder to get his attention.

William looked up. His eyes were red. His cheeks moist with fresh tears. "Did you say something?"

"I asked if perhaps you are not feeling well. You look a bit peevish."

"Oh. No. I am not sick. It is this news from home. Father says I must return. Mother is not well."

Slaney sat down next to William. He put an arm around his friend. The two sat together in silence for several long minutes. Finally, Slaney said, "Tell me how I can help."

"I must prepare to go. I shall tell the office. Will you tell the others? After I am gone? I do not think I could bear to tell them myself."

Slaney agreed. William folded the letter and put it away. With a deep sigh, he pushed himself off the bed and began gathering books and garments. John slipped away unnoticed to let William pack and prepare to leave.

Young William returned to Scrooby Manor in late 1583. Cambridge was wonderful, but duty came first. When he saw his mother, he gasped. "Mother, what has happened to you?" The vibrant woman who insisted on overseeing every detail of his last morning at home now appeared emaciated and weak. She was stooped over. Her color pale. Her skin hanging off thin arms.

"I have a bit of some sort of sickness. We all do from time to time. It comes with age. Do not fret about me. It is nothing for you to worry about. It pleases me greatly that you have come home at last."

Her words ran through William's mind over and over a few months later when he and the other young men carried the coffin from the church to the adjoining cemetery.

⁜

As the Separatist movement gained momentum, tensions within the Established Church escalated. William continued studying new ideas put forth by contemporary scholars he read while away at Peterhouse. His brother frequently found him hunched over a book, forgetful about everything except the concepts contained within.

"James, listen to this," he said, displaying the cover of *Concerning the Republic of the English* by solicitor Sir Thomas Smith. "This man thinks people prosper best when they are free to move up into a higher social class. Can you imagine that? All my life, I have been instructed to know my proper place and stay within it."

"As have I," replied James.

William pulled on his beard. "If Smith is right, Father could have been more than an errand man for the Archbishop of York."

"Father seems content enough with his lot."

"Perhaps. Or perhaps he believed he had no choice, so why not learn to be content? I rather wonder what this could mean for our own futures."

"I cannot fathom a future anywhere but here."

"Nor could I have imagined anything different, until I had the chance to study at Peterhouse. That rather changed my view of things. Now I realize there is so much more out there to explore and consider." William pointed through the window and sighed.

"You would do well to let go of such lofty ideas and focus on running this manor," James responded. "That is what is expected of you now."

"Perhaps. Even so, I am bound to learn more of these new ideas."

"Be careful, William. Already several men and women we know have gone to the gallows for such talk."

William was careful. Each time a delivery of mail came to the manor, he looked to see if there were any letters from his Peterhouse friends—Pentry, Greenwood, or the others—and if they looked as though someone might have opened them. He feared that if ever letters from these friends were intercepted, they might be charged with sedition.

Chapter Ten

Scrooby – 1584

William heard the clip-clop of a horse-drawn carriage pulling up in front of the stables. Even from across the yard, he immediately recognized Davison. Ambassador Davison had been a regular manor guest over the past ten years. Young William had grown into adulthood watching Sir Davison's career expand in service to Queen Elizabeth. Davison would sometimes quiz him on Latin and Greek. William beamed with pride whenever Davison commended him for his Latin exhortation letters. Sometimes, Davison switched from English to Latin in their conversations, just to challenge the young scholar. "You are doing well, my young friend. I understand your Latin as easily as I do our conversations in English. Continue your studies. They will serve you well."

William's father told him Ambassador Davison found such favor with Queen Elizabeth that she often turned to him to intervene in difficult political situations. "She relies on his diplomatic skills. That, along with his reputation as a godly gentleman, renders him a welcome guest all along the Great North Road. It is good you are here to see him again." Davison routinely brought the latest news from London and the court. He eagerly divulged juicy tidbits of gossip with a likable, trustworthy nature.

After dinner, William's father and Davison talked softly, making it impossible for William to make sense of their words. He wanted to join them, but his stepmother Prudence needed more wood for the morning and the horses in the stable needed their evening meals. *One day, it will be me sitting by the fireside engaged in such conversations.* William shrugged his shoulders and headed out to tend to his chores.

Long after sunset, the senior Brewster invited William to join them by the fire. In his eagerness to do so, William bumped a jug on the floor as he pulled up a chair, spilling what little remained in it on the floor. William blushed and quickly set the jug upright. His father and Davison chuckled at his youthful enthusiasm, but refrained from commenting on his clumsiness. Instead, they simultaneously took sips from their tankards. Neither thought to offer any to William. William Senior studied his son, as though seeing him after a long absence.

"Son, the years have flown by so quickly. I remember an evening some twenty years ago when our friend here first spent a night at the archbishop's manor. He was about your age at the time. Your beloved mother was yet protecting you within her womb. And now look at you. Your studies at Cambridge behind you. You have proven yourself a great help to me, but it is not right to keep you here when the world bids you to go explore and experience it." He pointed to Davison. "Our friend comes bearing exciting news."

Davison cleared his throat. William tightened his grip on the arms of his chair and leaned forward. Davison said, "I am in need of an assistant. Just as I was an assistant to Sir Henry Killigrew when first I came to this manor, so now am I in need of someone to assist me. I have spoken with your father. He has agreed to let me invite you to assume the position of my clerk. You will keep my papers in order, write official messages as I dictate them, carry out errands for me, and tend to other duties as I continue to serve Her Majesty. What do you say to that, young Brewster?"

William said nothing. He pulled at his beard, trying to think of something sensible to say. He thought back to the conversation just yesterday with his brother.

"Your father speaks often of how grateful he is to have you home. I suppose it was a disappointment to leave Cambridge so soon?"

William looked at the floor and mumbled, "I needed to be here." *But some days the slow pace here—after all the excitement at Peterhouse—has been a bit of a disappointment.*

"You are still so young," continued Davison. "You remind me of myself when I was young as you are now."

William's heart started pounding. He could feel his pulse quickening. Though he tried, he could think of nothing clever to say.

"Well, young Brewster?" asked Davison. "What do you say? Are we agreed?"

William began moving his head up and down. He wanted to jump up and run over to Davison, or his father, or both of them, but feared giving into that impulse would prove him unworthy for the position. At last he answered, "Yes. YES! I would much enjoy serving you. I shall be your faithful servant in whatever duties you assign me."

Barely in his twenties, the world of diplomacy and travel beckoned and he eagerly answered the call.

Chapter Eleven

Greenwich Palace – 1585

William jostled in the carriage seat as he and Davison traveled toward Queen Elizabeth's Greenwich Palace along the Thames, south of London. Davison passed the time filling William in about the unrest resulting from the July 10 assassination of William of Orange. "Her Majesty has been severely challenged on account of this nasty business."

"More than her own people plotting against her?"

"Quite so, I fear. The Catholics never tire of trying to remove her from the throne. They are resolute in their determination to put her cousin Mary in her place. They believe the Queen of Scots will turn our beloved England back to Rome. I fear that business with the pope was but a small pebble in the very large pond of her present problems."

"But if Her Majesty could resist the pope and all his sympathizers, surely she will prevail now?"

"She is of strong will; that is most certainly true. Did you hear what the pope wrote about her? Do they teach such things at Cambridge?"

"To be sure. The professors spoke often of the pope's letter, and one shared it with us. My professor said the pope wrote Her Majesty was a guilty woman, and the source of much injury to the Catholic faith. Professor Smythe said the pope even blamed her for the loss of millions of souls! Apparently, the pope told faithful Englishmen they could best demonstrate their faith through their *disobedience* to Her Majesty. If they valued their souls, they should swear allegiance only to the Holy Roman Church."

"That was what I heard, as well," responded Davison.

"Professor Smythe also told us the pope said that whosoever should remove her from power, by whatsoever means, commits no sin, but gains a reward for faithfulness. How can that be?" asked William.

Davison shrugged. "We humble servants are caught. Do we owe our loyalty to our queen, or to someone said to be appointed by the Lord Almighty to reign as head of the church? One controls life now. The other the rest of eternity. I suppose there have been many plots against Her Majesty's life. Mercifully, she has ears and eyes throughout her kingdom, and a good many more in Europe."

"We hear talk of such things sometimes at the manor," agreed William.

Davison nodded. "William of Orange's assassination shall either bring our queen good fortune, or thrust her into greater danger. The low countries are now split. The northern territories are sympathetic to Her Majesty, and fancy the Protestant faith. The southern ones defend the Catholics. So, the brutality continues."

"She sends you to plead her cause, then?" asked William.

"Yes. The Dutch remain undecided. They need help to rid themselves of Spain's occupation. But should they put their trust in England? Or France? The French might consider assisting the Dutch to discourage Spain's increasing influence there."

William's body ached from persistent jarring over ruts, but his mind was hungry for more. He squirmed in his seat, trying to find a position less uncomfortable. He stroked his chin, drifting into daydreaming. *I am soon going to actually see Her Majesty. I pray I do not embarrass myself. What do I know of how to present myself in court?* William gave his head a quick shake to refocus when he realized Davison was still talking.

"Her Majesty sent me a message urging me to nourish hope in the Dutch and give assurances that, should France reject their need, she would never abandon them."

"Is this why we travel to Greenwich now?"

"It is."

Without thinking, William rubbed his derriere, sore from the relentless jostling of the carriage.

They arrived for their first audience with Queen Elizabeth in July, a few hours ahead of the Netherland Commissioners. William could barely contain his excitement. He stared at dozens of flags snapping in the breeze, tapping his feet in time to the fife and drum music filling the air with welcome. William thought it must be thrilling for the commissioners to glide along the Thames in their royal barges.

As they entered the palace, William strained his neck to take in the opulence. *I was foolish to be anxious about how to present myself to Her Majesty. With so many all about, she'll take no notice of me at all. There must be several hundred here!* Never before had he seen such luxury on display. His eyes gravitated to the queen's golden crown. *Oh my, how the diamonds and emeralds sparkle in her red hair.*

William's stomach fluttered as he studied her. Even now, in her fifties, she cast a spell of regal bearing. He was too far back to see her face clearly, but thought she must surely cover the remnants of smallpox with makeup, for her complexion appeared fair and smooth. He gawked at dozens of bean-sized pearls sewn into her velvet dress. Then he looked around the enormous hall and estimated that fifty or more men stood guard around her throne, each with a gilded battle-axe. *How very different from our simple lives in Scrooby. What must it be like to always be surrounded by so many—and to constantly wonder if any of them might be plotting your demise?*

A hush fell over the crowd when the Dutch envoy's spokesman approached the throne and bowed low to honor Queen Elizabeth. He raised his face. "Pleased were we with the kindness and good offices extended to us by Sir Davison following the death of Prince of Orange." He nodded toward Davison near the back of the room with William and other staff. The Dutchman turned back to Her Majesty, who offered a tight smile in response. The Dutchman pressed on. "If it pleases Your Majesty, I speak on behalf of our envoy, and indeed, all our people, when I humbly offer Your Majesty sovereign control of our modest province."

Queen Elizabeth turned to her advisors. Though neither Davison nor William saw a change of expression on any of their faces, apparently they had somehow conveyed their opinions to her. When she again turned to the Dutch dignitary, she said, "That shall not be necessary. We shall pursue our negotiations shortly, when we have completed our move to Nonsuch Castle." The

Dutch envoy was astute enough to understand this meant she was dismissing them for the time being.

※

Within the hour, William and Davison found a corner table in a pub. With ales to quench their thirst and bread and cheese to quell their hunger, they continued a conversation about Davison's diplomatic duties. William asked, "Why did she not want to accept their offer to become sovereign of their province? I thought that was precisely what she did want?"

"The queen wants many things. She is wise, and has enough experience to know that in order to obtain one thing, she must decline another. She fears that should she accept their offer, she would make more enemies, and she is amply supplied with those already. So, she declines this honor to control the impulses of those who would see her unseated from the throne."

William shook his head in disbelief and stared into his ale. "I dare not hope to ever understand the currents in the river of diplomacy."

Davison chuckled. "It does take many moons and more than a few missteps to begin to know when to speak and when to refrain, with whom to speak and who should never be trusted. You do well enough for one with so few winters behind you. Did your father ever tell you how the queen wanted to lease out the manor in Scrooby just two years ago?"

William's jaw dropped. Davison continued, "While you were away at Cambridge, she thought she might exercise her right to secure the property as a favor for her cousin Robert Dudley. I suppose because they have remained close since childhood. He is the Earl of Leicester. Neither man nor beast can be safe once members of royalty set their heart on something. I believe it was her intent to let him use it as a hunting lodge. The good Lord Almighty only knows what should have happened to your family had Bishop Sandys not intervened."

"The Bishop of York has always treated us kindly," said William. "When I was a lad, he would often bring a treat for me when he came to inspect the state of things."

"He certainly did right by your father in this affair. The good archbishop told her it would have been be a serious deprivation for him and the bishopric he oversees."

"I can well imagine he would feel that way, after he went to all the trouble to complete renovations to the manor," said William. He put both hands around the tankard of ale and swallowed what remained in one gulp.

Davison leaned in, lowering his voice. "His Holiness went so far as to write the queen a letter. I believe it read something like: *It would be too much, most gracious Sovereign—too much to pull from a bishopric inferior to many in revenue, but superior in charge and countenance.* I thought it quite bold of him, but apparently he believed the importance of his position within the Established Church of England would protect him from her scorn."

"Is that the reason he so eagerly leased the two parks and the mills and the forest to his son?"

"I believe it well could be," agreed Davison.

William stroked his beard. "How fortunate for Father. How else would he provide for us should he lose his position as bailiff and postmaster? It is a wonder how many suffer for the whims of the few. How has God ordained it that the few control the many?"

Chapter Twelve

Nonsuch Palace – August 1585

After weeks of negotiations in London, William and Davison followed the royal Court to Nonsuch Palace, a day's ride outside London.

"Why do we move to another castle?" William asked.

"She likes to move about to keep her enemies guessing where she'll be next. That, and because with all the resources she has, she can."

William shook his head. When they entered, he gaped at the palace's splendor. That evening, he wrote in his journal:

> *I've never seen such opulence. Outside, the sun nearly blinds me shimmering off white stucco and gilt. I am unable to count the number of statues everywhere I turn my eye. Some I recognize as Roman emperors we studied in school. Some I recognize to be beasts from Greek mythology. To think this is but one of a dozen such palaces. I respect her for her tolerance toward different points of view, yet I cannot believe our Lord, born himself in such humble conditions, would think this necessary to rule wisely and rightly.*

Davison was energized and jubilant when the Treaty of Alliance was finally completed. "She has committed our English troops to the lowlands! Think of it! Our own countrymen will be aiding those whose sympathies are akin to my own thoughts. It is superior to the Church of Rome, yet still, the Established Church of England is sorely in need of purification. As for the Church of Rome, we must do all within our power to keep it out of England."

William wondered about the wisdom of this. "Won't that be dangerous for us? We do well to protect our own island, but are we prepared to put our men in the way of Spain? And perhaps France? Is that not too great a risk?"

"It is a risk. The King of Sweden has said as much: 'Queen Elizabeth has now taken the diadem from her head and ventured it upon the doubtful chance of war.' But the situation is desperate," explained Davison. "Antwerp fell to the Spanish on August 7. Her Majesty chose Sir John Norris to command the English troops in the low countries."

"John Norris?" asked William. "Isn't he a veteran of the area?"

"He is, indeed, and Her Majesty sent word ahead she is dispatching me, as well. I saw the letter. 'Our faithful and well-beloved Davison comes to represent to you how much we have your affairs at heart, and to say that we are determined to forget nothing that may be necessary to your preservation.'"

❧

William forced himself to slow down his writing that evening so the words would remain legible.

October 7, 1585 – Flushing. My dearest family: I pray the length between my correspondences has not unduly concerned you. Since I last wrote you some two months ago now, I have been rather active from early morning to late evening. Ever since I crossed the Channel with our friend Sir William Davison, we have been either in meetings with officials or traveling to the location of our next meeting. The Queen has charged dear Davison with receiving, on her behalf, formal authority over two Dutch towns and a fortress. Though they were uncertain about it, they could see the benefits to their well-being in providing a fortress as security for the Queen's promise to send troops. She has committed to send horses and money for the troops.

I do not know when I shall next be able to get word to you. I pray this shall not cause you concern. I travel with one who is well received in the Low Countries. I am confident that being with Davison shall ensure my own well-being.

Davison tells me the Queen sent a message to the Dutch insisting she be repaid to the last farthing after the war. Our Queen is a stern mistress. She insists she be given one town in every Province as a pledge against her support. They are known as the Cautionary Towns. Now the ports of Flushing and Brill, along with Fortress Ramikins, are under her command.

I will soon arrive at Hague, where Sir Davison will meet with the Dutch officials to discuss how they shall carry out the Treaty of Alliance. We will visit each of the Cautionary Towns, and one of our people shall officially receive each town in the name of Her Majesty.

All this is quite exciting for a young man from our quiet region.

Your faithful son,
William

Prince Maurice, wearing mourning clothes and still grieving his father's assassination three months earlier, received Davison, Brewster, and the rest of Davison's staff. They watched with the general-in-chief of the Dutch army as English troops marched with perfect precision from their quarters into the church for the diplomatic ceremony, swearing loyalty to Queen Elizabeth. Next, they marched in formation to several fortifications where Dutch troops transferred responsibility for security to the English soldiers before retiring.

William's neck was getting sore from so much turning this way and that to take it all in. His ears rang from the drums and trumpets.

Davison received the keys on behalf of Her Majesty. When they were alone, he handed them to William, saying, "I confer these to you for safekeeping. Guard them well."

After Davison left him for the evening, William looked around the tiny room, opening each drawer and cupboard door, looking under the bed and behind the curtains. Finding no place he considered sufficiently secure, he slipped the keys between his bedding and pillow. William tossed and turned most of the night, recalling visions of officials strutting about in elegant coats of satin trimmed with jewels and ribbons. He saw their swords dangling from thick belts, and the way they gleamed in the sun whenever pulled out as a ceremonial show of strength.

⚘

A few days later, Davison pulled William aside and read him a section of a letter from Secretary Walsingham.

I see not her Majesty disposed to use the services of the Earl of Leicester. There is great offense taken in the carrying down of his lady.

William scrunched his forehead as Davison put the letter away. "Her Majesty would rather her troops continue on without a true leader than allow her cousin to bring his wife with him? Isn't this the same cousin she wanted to give Scrooby Manor to for a hunting lodge?"

"Yes, the same man. The queen can be contrary. Her distain for Lady Lettice knows no bounds. I dare say, our beloved queen may be jealous, knowing Lettice lies with the man she counts as one of her closest confidants—if not more than that." William, still young enough to live in a world consisting of equal parts idealism and naiveté, had no response.

"Kings and queens wield much power. To get and keep that power, they are forever engaged in an international game of draughts. All of Europe is the board upon which the game is played. Each monarch wants to take control of the squares occupied by the others. The goal is to control as many squares as possible while surrendering none of their own."

William rubbed his chin. "Is our queen very good at draughts?"

"Indeed she is. I once saw her outwit a cocky man whose pride was likely bruised beyond repair when she made her last move. But I fear this time she lets passion overcome her thinking. The Dutch have great respect for her cousin, the Earl of Leicester. So do our English troops. He could be a true aid to our presence here."

"I should think she'd be glad for his presence, then, with or without his wife."

"You have the gift of thinking with your head. I sense Her Majesty is engaged in a battle between heart and head. Jealously makes her want to keep Leicester close, where she can know more about his business. Yet her longing to strengthen the Netherlands to prevent Spain from becoming any more powerful requires his services here. Let us pray her fear of Spain attacking from across the Channel is greater than her jealousy of Leicester's Lady Lettice."

William wrinkled his nose and scratched at his beard. "Do you suppose she might change her mind?"

"I pray she will. Enough of this. Let us walk about a while and see what happens in the streets."

CHAPTER THIRTEEN

THE NETHERLANDS – 1585

They soon came upon another Huguenot being led to the stake. Two men witnessing the grizzly scene rendered their opinions. "I heard they found the books hidden under the floor of his house," said one.

"Foolish to keep them where he eats," said the other.

"Seems they followed him. That's how they learned he was making them available for anyone wanting to read the Holy Scriptures in French."

"Foolish heretic. Why can't they be content to accept the teachings of the church that Christ himself established?"

"It's a wonder any are left to read anything. Peter Titelmann won't rest until he's burned every last one of them."

William pulled Davison's sleeve and pointed to an alley where they could talk privately. "Does this happen even here, in the low countries?" he asked.

Davison nodded slowly. "It does. Though there is more freedom here to do as one pleases than many places, it's still dangerous to be on the wrong side of the battles between the monarch and the bishops. They wield tremendous power. Cross one of them, and that's likely to be the outcome," said Davison, pointing back to the place where three men were wrapping ropes around the Huguenot to secure him to the pole. Others pitched straw around his feet. Two more men approached, each carrying a lit torch.

Smoke and fire rose high over the heads of the crowd. The man's screams filled the air. William's blood ran cold, his stomach lurched. He turned away, unable to bear seeing the man's life pass away in such agony. The smell of burning flesh made the bile in William's stomach rise. He turned to leave, but Davison grabbed his arm and held him in place.

"You must know how desperate each side is to exterminate the other. God may have mercy on their souls, though they show no mercy to one another."

As long as I live, I shall never be party to such cruelty, thought William. *This cannot be the way of God.*

Davison led him away from the crowd. They walked along a narrow cobblestone street in silence. Neither found words suitable for conversation after what had just transpired. It was the first burning at the stake William had witnessed. William felt weak in the knees and was grateful when they stopped walking and paused at the convergence of several streets. He leaned against the rough brick building as they considered which direction to go. William noticed a small print and bookshop across the street. "I would like to go in there. Perchance they have a title recommended to me by one of my friends from Cambridge. I long to read Martin Luther's *On Christian Liberty.* Several of my professors were enthralled with it."

"Are you sure you want to do that now? Printing religious books is a risky business today. First, they come for the books to burn them. Then they come to burn those who dare print them."

"It is a risk I am willing to take. My soul cries out for more understanding of the things explained by Luther and Calvin. Where else might I gain such knowledge? Where would we be today if Luther had forsaken printing his letters and pamphlets? There is great power there. I will avail myself of a bit of it."

"Very well, then. I shall wait here. Be quick. If I come in, let that be a warning that you must purchase no book with any religious theme. Indeed, as I enter, you must exit. We shall meet . . ." he looked around for a suitable rendezvous spot. "There, in that pub with the Brown Fox sign."

CHAPTER FOURTEEN

NETHERLANDS – DECEMBER 1585

William came out of the bookshop less than a quarter of an hour after entering. "Judging from your smile, it appears you procured what you sought," Davison said. William showed Davison his purchase over a tankard of ale. When he finished, he excused himself to write a letter home about this horrible day. New developments were unfolding daily. He climbed the narrow stairs to his room and got out his quill and fresh parchment.

December 1585
The Low Countries
Beloved Family,

At last, I have time to tell you all I have seen and heard. As astonishing as it sometimes is to hear the news from court, it is many times more marvelous to observe it in person. Though some of what I witnessed today is too horrible to tell. I saw a man burned at the stake for possessing books. The sight of it shocks me through and through. Perhaps I shall tell you of it when I return home. Truly, I cannot bear to write of the details now.

The queen's affection for her cousin, the Earl of Leicester, has finally caused her to set aside her intense distain for his loathsome wife, Lettice. Whether it be her affection for her childhood companion or her fear that the Spanish might grow too powerful and close for her royal comfort, I am unable to judge. In either case, she has changed her mind. She is sending Leicester back to us to the Low Countries.

He arrived a few days ago. What a triumphant procession it was. He brought many aides with him, including his stepson. You may remember he is the Earl of Essex now. Do you remember we were at Cambridge together? Imagine my thrill at seeing him again under such lofty circumstances.

There is so much more I long to tell you, but Master Davison and I are to attend the banquet this evening. I must put great care into my appearance. It is such an honor—and for you, as well—that I have been asked to attend such an affair. I am grateful to have a bit of diversion to distract my mind from the cruelty I was compelled to observe earlier this day.

With greatest of affection,
Your loving son, William

Davison and William made their way among the crowd at the banquet. "It's a wonder the tables don't break under the weight of so many platters of food," observed Davison as he led the way to the back of the room. Musicians strolled about playing lyres and flutes. The odor of roasted goose mingled with mulled wine and wassail. The room buzzed with lively conversation. Dozens of lit candles in the chandeliers overhead and torches hanging along the walls rendered the room nearly as bright as broad daylight.

William looked all around the room in wonder.

Davison seemed not to note his excitement and spoke of work as the grand feast began. "We shall travel with Leicester and his entourage as they journey through the Netherlands. After this banquet, we attend the military review in Middleburg. Then we travel on to Hague for a week of more banquets, and whatever other manner of welcome the Dutch shall confer upon Leicester's party."

CHAPTER FIFTEEN

LONDON – 1585

JOURNEYS with the Earl of Leicester ended abruptly when Queen Elizabeth called Davison back to London to give an account of what was transpiring in the Low Country. William was pleased to later learn how Leicester had written to Queen Elizabeth's minister, Baron Burghley, about Davison:

> *You shall find him as sufficiently able to deliver the whole state of his country as any man that ever was in it, acquainted with all sorts here that are men of dealing. He is a credit. Additionally, he is known for keeping a very good table.*

However, as Davison and William made preparations to return to London, the Earl, Robert Dudley, defied the queen's orders. He accepted the title of Supreme Governor-General of the United Provinces that Dutch leaders offered him as a token of their gratitude for his leadership. It was a diplomatic blunder of elephant-sized proportions. The queen had specifically instructed him to decline any titles. When he learned about it, Davison confided to William, "She will not receive this news well. She plays a delicate balancing act among these people. She wants their respect, and wants to protect their rights for religious freedom. Yet even more, she is determined nothing shall give the impression she is insulting the Spanish. After all, the King of Spain is still their lawful sovereign. I fear we shall encounter a storm of words as fierce as any gale wind from Her Majesty when we return."

Before leaving the Netherlands, Davison and William attended an elaborate farewell event in their honor. The Dutch presented Davison with a gold chain, which he gave to William for safe-keeping. William beamed when Davison handed it to him. He gently touched it, turning it over and over to inspect it thoroughly. He felt new energy coursing through his veins as they left of the canal-laced city for London and the court. William could not pull himself away from admiring how the sun sparkled on the gold links. As they journeyed, William composed the next letter he wanted to send home in his head:

> *Your son has returned to our beloved England a changed man. I left as one unaware of the complexities of international politics and practices. I return triumphant, and my heart is overflowing in gratitude for the opportunities I have experienced. I have so very much to tell you and long to be with you in person. Yet I also rejoice to be here. It is all so alive and full of intrigue.*

Davison and William walked around the palace gardens anticipating what the queen would have to say. Evergreens all around them made their walk pleasant, even on a dreary February Sunday morning. Along the way, the queen's secretary, Sir Francis Walsingham, caught up with them. "I bid you be forewarned. Her Majesty is frightfully upset by the Earl of Leicester's acceptance of the honor from the people of the low countries. She is furious he has done so, and considers it a betrayal at the most severe level. Furthermore, she expected you to dissuade Sir Dudley from accepting the title. She holds you accountable."

William never wrote that letter home. Without so much as a "Welcome home," the queen launched into a furious tongue-lashing. She unleashed a tirade with nary a word about the glowing reports of their successful tour of duty on her behalf for the past six months.

William had walked with Davison into the queen's receiving room, but when she began her outburst, he retreated back to the garden with stomach tightening and skin prickling. *I do not wish to further embarrass him by listening to his thrashing.* The queen's fury followed him and the garden now seemed as dreary as a sunless late winter afternoon. He had never heard anyone—especially a woman—speak such violent, abusive words. The sound of it made him feel physically sick.

Davison was a veteran of Her Majesty's many rapid changes in countenance. William was yet naïve enough to believe she'd value their work and weigh that more heavily than her cousin's transgression.

When William thought enough time had lapsed for her to calm down, he returned inside. As soon as William entered the castle, he heard ranting, "How dare you! How dare you come to me with this report? You *knew* my wishes on this matter. And still, you did nothing to dissuade him? What sort of a fool do you take me to be that I would ever approve of that stupid, foolish, traitor? You both knew that I expressly commanded him to never allow such a thing."

Davison stood silent before her wrath. William stayed out of sight while Her Majesty spewed more venom. "The earl accepted this title from the Dutch? Very well, then. He must renounce it. He must renounce it publicly. He must do so at the very spot he received it!"

Davison turned pale. He tried to conceal his horror at this turn of events. He wanted to speak, but dared not interrupt. She continued, "I shall send Sir Thomas Heneage at once to inform the earl of my decision." She stopped speaking and began rotating her thumbs in small, slow circles. Davison recognized this meant she was thinking more about the matter.

He took advantage of the pause to pull the letter from the Earl of Leicester out of his pocket. He inched forward to give it to her, but she swiped his hand away. "I have no need to read his limp justifications for directly disobeying me." She waved Davison away. He left with William only a few steps behind him.

***

William had never been this close to a royal temper, and did not know what to think or expect. He listened as Davison considered options for handling the situation over some ale. "You see," he told William, "if she goes through with this, she shall undo all the good we have accomplished. More to the matter, she will tarnish the good name she has established among the Dutch. Yet if I cross her, I endanger my very life. If I do not encourage her to reconsider this matter, I fail in my duty to present the queen to the people in the most flattering manner."

William made no comment, but thought, *How fortunate I am not to be the one to determine the right course of action. There seems to be no good path forward.*

Finally, Davison decided he'd seek another audience. "Surely, when she has had time to reflect upon the gravity of her position a bit more, she will see what a disaster her current course of action would bring. It would do no good, and could do much harm, should she force the Earl of Leicester to publicly renounce the honor the Dutch wanted to bestow upon him—and through him, all of England."

❧

The queen agreed to receive Davison the next day.

Before he went to see her, Davison told William, "I know not if she perhaps has had a change of heart. Perchance she holds a sliver of appreciation for our efforts. Or perchance another has spoken on our behalf. I bid you pray for me as I go to her again."

William stayed in the gardens while Davison tried again to persuade her not to do as she had threatened. He went down on one knee, tears forming in his eyes. "Your Majesty, I implore you, consider the message such an action will send to those who are our friends, our advocates against those who threaten us. Dare we offend them by so blatantly rejecting what they perceive to be a show of gratitude for Your Majesty's generous and gentle intervention in their affairs?"

She was not persuaded, though this time, she did accept the Earl of Leicester's letter when Davison again offered it to her. She read a few lines, then stuffed it in a pocket. "I cannot abide the thought that Sir Dudley is to be called Your Excellency. This is totally unacceptable. What must the King of Spain think? The earl could have claimed the substance, had he not accepted the title."

Davison bowed low before daring to speak again. Without looking up, he suggested, "Perhaps the King of Spain is unable to distinguish between the name and the thing."

She glared. "I am no longer confident I am able to completely trust you to carry out my wishes to my satisfaction."

"Then, my most sovereign Majesty, I implore you, release me from my duties that I may no longer offend you, but rather spend

my days in prayer for your welfare and salvation. For I fear that
if you continue on this present course, your very salvation is at
stake."

Davison left and caught up with William. "She is offended that
one in whom she has entrusted so much would disobey her. Yet
even more, she fears the consequences from Spain. The Spanish
are well able and eager to invade England. Though she did treat
me sorely, yet I have compassion for the delicate game she must
play."

"Yea, but what manner of things is this that one person should,
by her very delicate state of emotion, bring to ruin those who serve
her best?"

Davison sighed deeply. "It is the way of the world. True justice
and fairness are rare on this earthly pilgrimage. We must thank
our Lord that we have, now and then, the opportunity to experience them in our fellowship among the true faithful."

The situation was salvaged when Lord Burghley came to the
defense of the Earl of Leicester by limping into court (recovering
from gout) giving a concurring analysis and threatening to resign.

When Davison learned Burghley had succeeded where he had
failed, he told William with a hint of a smile, "Perhaps I should
have limped in. She sent a scathing letter to the earl. I know not
what was in the letter, but it did convince Sir Dudley to find a way
to mollify Her Majesty."

William chuckled at the idea of Davison feigning a limp to
solicit sympathy.

"He did so in a most unusual turn of events," continued
Davison. "He became gravely ill. This returned Her Majesty to
her earlier warm affection for him. Diplomacy takes many forms."

"How mercurial she is," said William.

"That is most certainly true. Though she reigns over lands near
and far, and subjects wise and not, she is still a woman with deep
feelings and longings. I do not envy her the power entrusted to
her. What a lonely life it must be, when all is said and done."

✠

William wrote in his journal:

> *How precarious is the position of one who sits on the throne.
> And yet how vulnerable are all we who must abide by their
> ever-changing moods. What a wonder it would be to live in a*

place free of such perils at the hands of the court. What a wonder to live where we can worship the Lord in peace and prosperity among others who believe as we do, and to govern ourselves according to our own good instincts.

CHAPTER SIXTEEN

ENGLAND – SPRING 1586

Davison re-read several times the letter he'd just received from his cousin, Sir Philip Sidney, then read it out loud to William.

"Perhaps diplomacy is a family trait," Brewster told Davison when he paused reading for a moment. Davison was still smarting from recent rebukes, especially Leicester's cruelty toward him when it had been Leicester's own actions that incurred the queen's wrath. Davison had tried to defend Leicester. He picked up the letter and continued reading.

"Well, Cousin, these mistakes sometimes breed ill effects, but I know he, in his judgment, loves you very well, whatever the passion with which he has written. And so, I end by assuring you I am still one toward you, as one who knows you and therefore loves you"

Davison was relieved, encouraged, and grateful for the letter. He carefully folded it and tucked it inside his shirt to savor again later.

It helped that Davison now had the chance to rest with family at his country home. He encouraged William to also take leave, telling him, "My young friend, you have seen that although we may be tasked with diplomatic service in foreign lands on behalf of our queen, more often, our diplomatic skills are needed here at home with Her Majesty herself. It is quite an adventure you and I have had. As for me, I am in need of rest. I am retreating for a while to my home in Stepney. You would do well to tell your family in Scrooby of your adventures in person. Surely, you have much to report."

William arrived back at Scrooby Manor on a balmy spring day in 1586. Stepmother Prudence peppered him with a barrage of questions, along with his brothers and sisters, and even the household servants. When he finally settled at the kitchen table with a mug of beer and platter of cheese, he told his tales of adventure.

"And there I was, right in the midst of it all. You would not believe the luxuries I beheld. Plates lined with gold. Crystal glasses for wine. The finest linens covering the tables. Tapestries and exquisite paintings on every wall. Truly, it was more than I could take in."

"And did you take a fancy to it all?"

William turned to see who had addressed him from the doorway. "Mary Wentworth! How quickly you have learned of my return. I was hoping I would see you soon, but I have been kept here answering more questions than the queen has jewels."

Mary smiled shyly. Prudence Brewster suspected William might prefer to answer Mary's questions with fewer people listening. "Before you answer, the two of you go away now. We shall have plenty enough time to hear more. I must see to getting our supper ready, and you are sitting precisely where I need to be working. Now, off with the both of you." Prudence winked at Mary. "For now, do take him away somewhere until all of this energy and information of his has quelled a bit."

When they were alone, William kept Mary enthralled with more stories about the astonishing things he'd witnessed. Mary pressed her first point, "Yes, but tell me, do you fancy such things? Do you long for a life like that?"

William combed his growing goatee with his hand and answered, "I tell you truthfully, Mary, I know not what I think. I do rather enjoy the splendor of it all. But the cruelty—I do not understand it. Surely, our Lord did not suffer, die, and promise to return only so that those who profess to follow him should torture and kill one another for worshiping differently!"

"I suppose fervor for one's faith prompts one to punish those who disagree."

"Yes, I rather think that is possible. Yet how strong could that faith be, that the faith of another drives him to torture and kill? It does trouble me. I cannot bring myself to tell you of some of the horrors I have witnessed. Thinking of it, I feel queasy even now."

"I do not understand, either," responded Mary. "Mary Queen of Scots' own son, King James, is Protestant. Yet she is determined we all should be Catholic. Even here, while you were far away, I overheard of plots to unseat our queen and force England to return to the Roman Church."

"Is it not written that Jesus came not to bring peace, but that son would turn against father, and mother against daughter-in-law? It does seem these words will prove true. Even those who support the queen are themselves in trouble if they dare suggest the Established Church of England could use a bit of reformation. This cannot be what our Lord wanted."

"I suppose not. But William, sometimes I do wonder, how are we to know what is truly God's will for any of us? So, I ask again, do you fancy this life of visits to court and travel to exotic places? Is this the future you envision for yourself?"

"I think it may be, for a little while. Though I do love it here, and I so missed my family, and . . ." William looked at the ground, where he noticed he had unconsciously been drawing in the soft dirt with his right foot. He looked up and continued, "I missed you too, dear Mary."

Mary's cheeks turned bright pink. She gathered her skirts and stood up abruptly. "I fear we will start tongues wagging should we linger alone any longer. Let me walk back to the manor with you, then I must be on my way."

※

After a few weeks at home William was called back to London. At supper he told his family he'd soon be off again.

"And how shall you be letting Mary Wentworth know of this?" asked his father, barely able to conceal a smile.

William did not disappoint. He turned red instantly and began furiously pushing mashed peas around his plate. "I suppose I should tell her myself," he said, as soon as the others quit laughing at his embarrassment.

"I suppose you should," said Prudence. "Shall we wait up for you?"

William stood up and began walking out of the room. "No need. I do believe I am able to find my way home, and I doubt her family shall allow me to tarry long."

After William left, the senior Brewster told Prudence, "It is time I spoke with the Wentworth family. They must surely be worried about Mary's future with no father to watch over her and arrange a proper marriage for her. Should William continue on this course I wonder how she will fare. Would she go with him so far away?"

"How could she not if they were wed?" asked Prudence.

"Perhaps he will decide to come home and eventually serve here, even as Mary's father did before me. In any case, I believe it is time to make the arrangements."

※

"And now I must leave again."

"What do you mean?" asked Mary.

"Ambassador Davison beckons me. Though I dread parting from this place I do love, I have committed to serve him. So, I must depart."

"You could decline, could you not?"

"I suppose I could. But what sort of man would I be to back out of an agreement so eagerly made barely two years ago?"

"That is my dilemma," sighed Mary. "The very trait I so admire about you is the one that will take you from me."

"And what trait might that be?"

"Do you seek flattery, dear William?"

For the second time in less than an hour William's cheeks turned red. "I seek only to do honor to the position I have accepted, and to leave the one I shall miss the most in the hope that she may miss me, as well, in my absence."

"She will. She will, very much."

CHAPTER SEVENTEEN

LONDON – 1586

Davison helped William settle into a room he'd rented for him, then took him to a pub for shepherd's pie and ale. "The queen has gotten over her fury at the Earl of Leicester. She sent word I am to come the day after tomorrow for an audience. She has received good reports of my service on her behalf in the lowlands."

"You are forgiven, and back in her good graces, then?"

"It does appear so."

After his audience Davison nearly skipped from the palace to where William was waiting under the shade of a flowering Redbud. "Young William, we are sure to have adventures now. She has appointed me to her privy council! Do you know what this means?"

"I believe I do. It means you are now one of twenty people she trusts more than all others to give her council and carry out her wishes for all of England's affairs."

"Yes, yes, indeed! Truly, it was worth enduring her wrath to now have her trust."

Queen Elizabeth named Davison her secretary of state on September 30, 1586. Davison often met with Sir Francis Walsingham, taking William along. "His health is a concern, William. Though Her Majesty does completely trust him and relies on him greatly, he is often unable to do her bidding due to one illness or another afflicting him."

The next letter William sent home contained all good news.

Dearest family,

I can barely believe all that has happened in the few weeks since I most reluctantly bid all of you farewell. Our queen has forgiven Ambassador Davison and appointed him to the privy council. And more than that – he is to be her Secretary of State! He has switched from disgraced to one of the most important people in all of England! And I, his humble servant, am often at his side, taking notes or fetching whatever is needed. From early morning until late at night, I accompany him from one meeting to another. In between, I record what he needs for the official records.

We are to work closely with Sir Walsingham, but his health is poor. On several occasions Sir Davison has gone in place of Sir Walsingham.

How very grateful I am to our Lord above that dear Father holds the position at the manor so I might have occasion to know Davison. Providence has surely blessed me.

I beseech you to carry my greetings to Miss Mary. Father, I honor your right and duty to arrange for a proper bride for me. But if I am not too bold to suggest it, perhaps you could approach her family about joining our families through wedlock. It does occur to me that this would be proper since you possess now the position her own dear father claimed as his own when he lived and you were not yet servant of Bishop Sandys. I hesitate to cor-respond with her directly for fear I may, in some way, tarnish her good reputation. I know it is not my place to do so; yet I long for her to know how well her friend does here, among royalty and the queen's advisors. Dare I hope that would make me a suitable candidate as her future husband?

We will be off again early on the morrow.

All my affection,
William

CHAPTER EIGHTEEN

ENGLAND – FALL 1586

Davison and William were resting between meetings. William noticed Davison's melancholy mood, encouraging him to disclose the source of this sadness. Davison sighed. "Though I am pleased to be so honored by Her Majesty, the responsibility weighs heavily on me at times. Last night, when sleep would not come, I made a list of assassinations I've lived through. The list is long. Sometimes I have a feeling of foreboding our beloved Queen Elizabeth may be added to the list. It seems there is always a plot underway somewhere to remove her from the throne, by any means necessary. I suspect King Philip of France is plotting to put Queen Mary on the throne. I even heard the new Pope Sixtus V said it would not be a mortal sin to assassinate Queen Elizabeth because it would return England to the one truth faith."

William shuddered. "Surely, that cannot be!"

"It could happen. Look at my list." Davison reached into his vest pocket and pulled out a sheet of parchment. William frowned as he read.

~Henry Darnley, husband of Mary Queen of Scots, murdered 1567
~Earl of Murray, charged with the care of her infant son James, King of Scotland, murdered 1570
~William of Orange, murdered 1584.

Davison folded the list and put it back in his vest pocket. "We live in treacherous days."

"Surely, the queen has guards protecting her?"

"Of course she does. And with her cousin, the Queen of Scots, now imprisoned, it would seem she is safe enough. Yet somehow, Queen Mary manages to correspond with her allies in France. It is really quite maddening. Queen Mary is under guard at all times, yet plots with those who want her on the throne."

"What has this to do with us?" asked William.

"Would that I could answer that. For now, we listen to the gossip and carry out the wishes of Sir Walsingham and Her Majesty. I did learn the new guard at Tutbury Castle took away her official cloth of state. They say that until this most recent move, that symbol of royalty hung over her chair wherever they confined her. I suppose it was part of a plan to treat her more harshly."

"Hasn't she been imprisoned since the year after her husband was murdered?"

"Aye. Indeed, nearly twenty years. The woman who would be the queen of France *and* England a prisoner—nearly your entire life. Her son reigns over Scotland. Her husband murdered. Her cousin sits on the throne of England. Queen Mary's life has been a tormented one."

"Do you think she shall ever be free?"

"Not as long as our queen lives. And that is exactly what concerns me, dear William. There are those who have the desire and the means to put an end to Queen Elizabeth's life and reinstate Queen Mary as Queen of England. Should that happen, we shall all need rosaries."

"Is there no one who can do something?"

"I am confident a great many people are doing many things. Some to ensure Queen Elizabeth's safety, others to ensure Queen Elizabeth does not continue her reign much longer. One of Sir Walsingham's servants heard him discussing the matter with a messenger. Apparently, Queen Mary's new guard was charged with putting a stop to her secret correspondence with her supporters."

"If it is secret correspondence, how does Walsingham know about it?"

Davison patted William's arm and smiled. "You are too trusting for your own good, young friend. Servants often serve more than food and drink. For the right price they also serve a great deal of information. Sometimes, they can be bought rather inexpensively. At other times . . . well, at other times, rather unpleasant methods are used to extract information. Let me tell you how Gilbert Gifford, a loyal Catholic, was convinced to help in the effort to protect our queen. Gifford came to England from Paris after one of Queen Mary's agents, Thomas Morgan, told him to reestablish the secret communication network between the queen and her French supporters.

"Apparently Walsingham's people intercepted him and brought him to Walsingham, who told Gifford he knew of the various plots to assassinate our good Queen Elizabeth and Gifford's role in the plot. Walsingham gave Gifford a choice. Continue on that course, and be dead long before Queen Elizabeth, or help put an end to this nonsense. Then Walsingham explained his own plot. He said that Christmas Eve, his men would move Queen Mary from Tutbury Castle to Chartley Hall in Staffordshire—the Earl of Essex's manor house. Gifford was told to go to the French ambassador and volunteer to deliver letters for Queen Mary that had been accumulating for the past year or so. Since Chartley Hall adjoins the property of Gifford's father, that would be easy enough to accomplish.

"And that, my young friend, is how Gifford agreed to become a double agent. For the next several months, he took all incoming and outgoing letters first to Walsingham's agents. A man who could decode them then carefully copied them, then sent them on their way to the intended recipient."

"How did they get the letters in and out with such tight security?" asked William.

"They were hidden in waterproof containers and sent in and out in beer barrels. Gifford bribed the local brewer to cooperate. As I said before, sometimes cooperation is purchased. And sometimes it is acquired in other ways."

William shook his head. "Did you know about this?"

"No, not at the time. Only six people knew: Sir Walsingham, of course, since it was his idea. Gifford, who cooperated for fear of his life. The bribed brewer, the guard Walsingham assigned to watch over Queen Mary, and the man who broke the code in the letters. And, of course, our beloved Queen Elizabeth."

William shook his head in disbelief. "All this was transpiring while you were resting at Stepney and I was at home in Scrooby?"

"Yes. All that and more. Anthony Babington is a young, very rich, and very faithful Catholic. He knew Queen Mary when he was a page. Babington appealed to six of his friends to assassinate Queen Elizabeth, but that wasn't enough for them. Walsingham himself was also on the list, along with the queen's chief advisor. Mercifully, I was not on the list. While these men were busy ending lives, Babington and a few others planned to rescue Queen Mary from Chartley."

"Yet our queen lives. What happened?"

"I believe Queen Mary became overconfident. She boldly wrote her approval of this plot in a letter in July. Sir Walsingham read about the plot."

"Will Queen Elizabeth have Queen Mary executed?"

"That I do not know. It would be a terrible precedent for one queen to execute another—and her cousin, at that. It would not sit well with the other heads of state in Europe. There are already rumors that Spain plans to invade us again. I cannot know the future. What I do know is that I am weary of talking about this, and wish to retire for the night."

William stared into his near-empty mug of beer. *Maybe this life of diplomacy and high-level planning and plotting is not the life for me after all.* He said nothing further other than to beg Davison's pardon, saying only that he was ready to retire for the evening.

CHAPTER NINETEEN

ENGLAND – SEPTEMBER 1586

News about Sir Anthony Babington's plot spread across London faster than beer from a broken pitcher. In pub after pub, people talked about Babington's capture.

"They executed six more bloody traitors with him," the Black Swan Tavern host told William and Davison, who sat at a small table in a dimly lit corner.

After the host moved on, Davison told William in a low voice, "I've heard they intend to hang seven more tomorrow. The city's aflutter with rumors. Most are horrified anyone would dare to plot to assassinate our queen. I've heard a few conservative Catholics are disappointed, but act shocked to protect themselves."

William stared at Davison. "The threat against Her Majesty is that close?"

Davison nodded. "Soon, a group of Her Majesty's enforcers will travel near your home in Scrooby. The privy councilors, along with others she appointed, set a trial for Queen Mary on October 11. Any reservations they had before Babington's assassination attempts are gone now."

"Will they try Queen Mary for treason?"

"Indeed, they will. In spite of rounding up and executing over a dozen men caught in the assassination plot, Her Majesty does not feel safe. Can you blame her?"

"No, of course not," agreed Brewster. He combed his beard, then shook his head back and forth. "What torture it must be to constantly worry that anyone around her might wish to do her harm."

"She carries a heavy load, to be sure. Come with me. I must now assume the duties that Sir Walsingham and Baron Burghley normally carry out. They will, of course, be part of the trial at Fotheringhay. I must finish this note and get it to them before they leave."

Davison wrote, *Your Lordships, I may, in my poor judgment, do a necessary deed in imploring you to persuade Her Majesty to become more circumspect of her person, and spare showing herself publicly until the brunt of the business now at hand blows over.*

When Davison finished, he put down his quill and asked William to read the note before sealing it with wax. "What you think?"

William pursed his lips. "Do you think she will listen to them, if she will not heed your good counsel to be less visible during these dangerous days?"

"I cannot know, but I must do all I can to preserve her safety. She appears to have the support of nigh on all of her subjects, but still . . ." Davison trailed off.

"Still, how can anyone be certain they have captured all those who would murder her?"

"Right. I heard some Catholics still worship in secret. They pretend to be faithful Protestants even as they smuggle in French Catholic priests—and maybe some from Spain, as well. It is good to take extra precautions. Our beloved queen cannot be safe as long as Mary lives, yet I fear for her future—indeed, that of all England—if she carries out the execution of another queen."

"I had no sense I would encounter such dangers when I accepted your offer to come away with you."

"And do you now regret that you have?" asked Davison.

"Surely not! How else would I acquire the education I receive with you?"

CHAPTER TWENTY

LONDON – FALL 1586

Queen Elizabeth sat still as a marble statue as Davison reported Queen Mary's denial, claiming lack of proof as nothing in her own writing could be produced. She sat silent, teeth clenched for so long Davison was about to ask if she'd heard his report.

She asked, "What do you think is the best course of action? If we execute her, we will suffer the wrath of France. And even though King James is a strong Protestant, she is, after all, his mother."

"A mother he has not known since he was too little to speak," Davison reminded her.

"Even so, how could a son approve of the execution of his own mother? Even worse, what if he should use this as an opportunity to muster supporters to invade England to place himself on my throne?"

Day after long, agonizing day, such conversations took place between Davison and the queen. Then, on October 29, Davison again asked William to look over a letter he intended to send to Walsingham.

William shook his head. "I am very grateful I was born in the quiet countryside, and not a son of royalty. I marvel at how you listen to her concerns, and yet also somehow persuade her toward a different course of action."

"Or, rather, how I am able to persuade others to persuade her," said Davison with a wink. "Truly, the workings of royalty, yoked as they are to matters of faith, require great tenderness as well as toughness."

"I do not envy you the delicate dance between offering sympathy and soliciting cooperation, however you go about achieving it."

"At times I feel sorry about the circumstances in which she finds herself. I cannot imagine the horror of growing up knowing her mother, Queen Anne Boleyn, was beheaded before her third year. Then her stepmother, Queen Catherine Howard, when she was not yet ten. She has reason to behave erratically."

A messenger entered to announce the queen wished to see him again. He sighed, and left to respond to her bidding.

※

"I want you to write a few hastily scribbled lines for a stay of sentence."

"Yes, Your Majesty. As you wish. Are you certain this is what you wish?

"Do you dare question me?"

"No, Your Majesty, of course not. It's only that . . ."

"It's only that what?" she snarled.

"Your Majesty, I pray you know how tenderly I hold your well-being in my every thought and action. I inquire only because this is such a precarious situation. It does seem as though we will not be rid of these problems unless the court moves forward to find Queen Mary guilty of the charges brought against her."

"Deliver the message."

"As you wish."

When he was back with William, Davison admitted he had done as directed, but hoped the letter would not reach Fotheringhay before the commissioners finished the trial and announced a verdict.

Chapter Twenty-One

Parliament convened on October 29 and prepared a petition to Queen Elizabeth, requesting Her Majesty set the death sentence for Queen Mary, as required for treason.

"Parliament can surely find another way to resolve this situation," Queen Elizabeth insisted.

Parliament held fast.

November – December 1586

"We are nearing the end of November, and still, no action has been taken," Davison complained to William one dreary evening. "How much longer can this go on? It saps my strength and afflicts my spirit."

William nodded, combed his beard, and sat mute.

Finally, in the first week of December, Queen Elizabeth agreed to proclaim the death sentence. "Burghley and Walsingham are writing up the order for Queen Mary's execution even as we warm ourselves by this fire." Davison announced.

"I cannot determine if I should feel relief, sorrow, jubilation, fear, or some other manner of response," William responded.

"I fear this is not yet the end of it, nor is there much cause for feeling good about how it shall end, if ever it does."

On December 10, they met at the Red Rooster Pub. "Burghley and Walsingham have sent orders to Queen Mary's guard at

Fotheringhay that our queen will order her to be punished for treason."

"Is that why the bells are ringing all over the city again?" asked William.

"That is why," confirmed Davison.

People lit bonfires to show their approval—and perhaps their relief—that finally, something was going to happen.

"Though the people celebrate, we are not through yet," continued Davison. "The warrant requires Her Majesty's signature. As you've seen, her mood changes more frequently than the seas surrounding our beloved island home. Now, she wishes to move to Richmond Palace. She prefers to spend winters there. Nothing more will happen until she and her court—and you and I with it—move again."

"I marvel that you want to do this work."

"I marvel at that myself sometimes. In spite of all her changes of course and her ever-shifting from praise to publicly humiliating her servants, I find it a suitable calling. I count it as a privilege in this life to serve my Lord by serving my queen. I dare hope and believe that in some small way, I am contributing to bringing peace and harmony to our people."

"I had not thought about it that way. It does seem, then, a rather pleasant way to spend one's days."

"I am off now, my friend, to meet with Baron Burghley. Perhaps finally we shall come to closure of this whole affair."

"I want you to take this executive order that we have drawn up . . . the order that Her Majesty herself told us to prepare," Burghley told Davison. "Have it engrossed. When it is ready, deliver it to the queen yourself. Entrust it to no one else."

It took several days for the official court recorders to carefully transcribe the orders onto parchment. When it was done, it would be preserved as an official document of Parliament—that is, it would be official once the queen signed it. If ever she would. When the engrosser finished his handiwork, Davison took the warrant to Queen Elizabeth as instructed.

"I cannot sign that!" She waved the document away, clenching her teeth, straightening her back, and enunciating each word for emphasis. "Do you not understand? The Spanish and French ambassadors have petitioned me to *save* Queen Mary's life. What should happen to me if I were to decline their pleas? Save the warrant. There will be a more convenient time."

She dismissed Davison, and the waiting lingered on.

***

"Today is a double burden for me, young William. We wait for we know not what with regard to the fate of two queens. And now, I have also received word that my dear cousin, Sir Philip Sidney, has passed on to his eternal reward. He is the one who showed me such kindness when the Earl of Leicester blamed me for the trouble he brought on himself."

"It is sad when those we love depart," acknowledged William. He thought back to the last time he saw his mother and felt his throat closing and his eyes starting to water. "But we are assured of the consolation of our Maker and Great Redeemer. Surely, your dear cousin is, even now, seeing one of the many mansions promised to all who remain faithful in this earthly pilgrimage."

Davison nodded. "Your words comfort me, my friend. You have a greater gift for theology than diplomacy. Though I am most certainly thankful for your help and companionship in this business with Queen Mary, which seems as long as eternity."

"Whatever the outcome shall be, it has been my good fortune to watch these affairs unfold with you."

"And here is the rub: Sidney's dear wife is now large with the baby he will never see. She is Sir Walsingham's own daughter. I fear her husband's death will dim her father's passion for dealing with Queen Mary—and Queen Elizabeth's ever-changing mind. He must now worry about his widowed daughter's future."

"How hard life can be at times."

"Yes, and it seems Sir Sidney left behind not only a wife and unborn child, but also a rather long list of people expecting to be paid. Sir Walsingham must sort all that out which will postpone the funeral until February. Surely, by then, this whole dreadful business will be resolved!"

"How does Sir Walsingham fare through all this?"

"Not well. More and more, I tend to duties which would usually fall to him. Between his grief and family responsibilities, I fear he is not well."

CHAPTER TWENTY-TWO

LONDON – 1587

The year 1586 closed without Queen Elizabeth's signature on the death warrant for Queen Mary. January 1587 opened with yet another plot against her life revealed, this one led by a French ambassador. As the threats against Queen Elizabeth's life increased, so did the demands from her subjects to execute Queen Mary. The privy council summoned a meeting with Queen Elizabeth.

"Your Majesty, you must pay heed to the demands of your people. They fear for your life, and will not be reassured so long as Queen Mary lives."

"I suppose you are right. Tell Davison to bring me that warrant."

Davison and William were walking about in the palace garden when the Lord Admiral caught up with them. "The Queen has agreed to sign the warrant!"

Davison dashed to his room to retrieve it. Thinking the queen might more readily sign it were she to first sign other documents, he slid the death warrant into the middle of a stack of papers. He took a few deep breaths, and left to see her.

She greeted him warmly, asking about his health and well-being. "Have you been out this fair morning?"

"Yes, Your Majesty."

"Good. You ought to do that more. Exercise benefits us all, don't you agree?"

"Yes, Your Majesty."

"Well, what have you brought me this day?"

"Different warrants and other things requiring your signature, Your Majesty."

"And the warrant for the execution of the Queen of Scots? Were you not instructed by the Lord Admiral to bring that to me, as well?"

"Yes, Your Majesty. And here it is." He handed it to her and stepped back.

She read it several times. With a deep sigh, she commanded, "Bring me my quill and ink." As Davison turned to get them, he heard her mutter to herself, "You'd think by now, *someone* would have taken care of this matter for me! Cowards, all." With a clenched jaw, her back arched and hand steady, Queen Elizabeth signed the death warrant. She set down the quill. "I have hesitated due to regard for my reputation. The world may perceive, no matter how justified I might be in responding to Queen Mary's many offenses against me and England, that I could have pursued other means of protecting the security of the throne."

She twirled her thumbs in circles. "How very difficult it is to take the step that will bring an end to another's life. Are you not sorry, as well, to see the warrant signed?"

"Yes, Your Majesty. It is sad, indeed, that a woman of her station should be put to death. Yet, my beloved queen, it is no doubt also true that without this course, your own precious life would continue to be in grave peril. You have done only what is justified to preserve your life and protect the sovereignty of the country we love. Surely, it is better that the guilty one die rather than one who is innocent."

This seemed to please the mercurial queen. She inquired, "What more have I to sign?"

Davison stood by silently as she signed the remaining documents. William, waiting for Davison out of sight around the corner of the entrance to the room, edged a few steps closer.

He heard the queen tell Davison, "Take the warrant immediately to receive the Great Seal, and as privately as possible. I fear if any learn I've signed the warrant before it is delivered, the danger to my life shall increase."

She arranged her skirts and stood up. "Now, I am through with this dreadful business. I wish to hear no more about it until the execution is complete. I forbid you to trouble me with this again until then. Queen Mary shall be executed quietly and quickly in the hall of Fotheringhay. There shall be no public viewing."

"I shall take the warrant for the seal immediately," said Davison.

"No, let it wait until this afternoon. You have other business to handle on my behalf. Oh, and do call upon Secretary Walsingham at his London home where he is recuperating. Tell him I have signed the warrant. I hope the news shall not bring his own ailing life to an end."

Davison gathered up the papers and promised to inform Walsingham. With long strides, he left the throne room without looking back. William scurried to catch up, his heart thumping. An icy finger of dread came over him. However, the man carrying the death warrant walked away so briskly, talking was out of the question. William discreetly moved away when Davison approached Baron Burghley, but remained close enough to hear Davison inform Burghley that the warrant now bore Queen Elizabeth's signature.

Then, as was their habit, they ate their midday meal together. Davison talked of every topic imaginable except the one William most hoped to discuss. When they finished, William retreated to his room with a book and Davison called on Secretary Walsingham. Not only did the man not die from the news, he promised to immediately honor Queen Elizabeth's request to instruct Queen Mary's guards to carry out the execution.

Davison left Walsingham to deliver the warrant to the Lord Chancellor for the official seal, which it bore by late afternoon. Meanwhile, Walsingham composed his letter laying out Queen Elizabeth's instructions. It was addressed to Queen Mary's guards. Tactful it was not.

> *She does note in you both a lack of care and zeal for the service she expects at your hands. You have not, in all this time, without other provocation, discovered some way to diminish the threat from Queen Mary, considering the great peril she is subject to hourly so long as said queen shall live.*

※

The messenger delivered Walsingham's letter to Fotheringhay the next day. Davison and William spent the night in London. A

court messenger woke Davison before dawn with a new message
from the queen.

*If you have not already taken the warrant for the Great Seal, do
not go until you speak with me.*

Davison finished a pot of brisk breakfast tea and told William
about the message. "Her constant turning away from the direction
in which she was headed, only moments before, gives me great
cause for consternation!"

William felt sorry for his master and teacher. He sipped his
tea and stroked his beard while Davison poured out his perpetual
frustration at Her Majesty's incessant alteration of plans. When
Davison stood up to return to court, William went for a stroll in
the chilly February morning. As he walked, he prayed this would
all soon be over. William concentrated so hard on his prayer that
he tripped over a tree root and fell to the moist ground. He stood
up, rubbed his knees, and turned back to wait for Davison to return
from his meeting with the queen. The book he carried helped calm
his nerves a bit.

※

"I delivered the warrant as you instructed, your Majesty," Davison
informed Queen Elizabeth. "It has been sealed."

She exploded. "Why were you in such haste?"

"Truly, Your Majesty, I did only as I understood you to instruct
me. I believe this affair is so consequential for your well-being—
indeed, for the security of England—that I thought it best to
proceed. Is it still your intention to go forward with the matter
according to your former directions?"

"Yes, of course." She began twiddling her thumbs. Davison
thought he saw tears forming in her eyes, and her voice was lower
and softer than usual. "Yet I continue to think it would have been
better for all of this to have been handled in a different manner.
Now the full weight of it rests upon me."

*I presume she still hopes the guards will take matters into their own
hands and murder Queen Mary without the death warrant,* thought
Davison, keeping that thought to himself.

Chapter Twenty-Three

England – 1587

February 3 started with the kind of grey, damp sky that makes a good profit for those who sell coal and ale. The privy council gathered in Baron Burghley's chamber. Davison instructed William to wait by the fire in the sitting room while they met. Burghley had prepared the letter that would go to the two officials who would personally oversee the execution of the rogue queen. One by one, the members of the privy council agreed to forward Burghley's letter without further troubling Queen Elizabeth about the matter.

"She did sign the warrant. And she did instruct Davison not to tell her more about it until the business has been completed," pointed out Burghley.

The privy council clerk left for Fotheringhay with the signed and officially sealed warrant for Queen Mary's execution. He also carried the letter of instruction signed by the nine privy council members who'd gathered for the meeting. Walsingham added his signature from his sickbed.

Davison scarcely ate any of the bangers and mash he ordered for supper that evening. William attempted to draw him into conversation, but he seemed too distracted to participate.

The next morning, Davison again went to court, where he found Queen Elizabeth and Sir Walter Raleigh deep in conversation. She turned to Davison. "There you are. I had such a dream last night. I dreamed the Queen of Scots had been executed." She shuddered. "To think it. I further dreamed how incensed this made me. Why, I believe that in my dream, I could have done anything to you for it."

Davison took a step back. The blood in his face drained. He held his breath and inquired with trepidation, "Does Your Majesty now regret her decision?"

"No, no, of course not. Yet I still think all of this could have been tended to in another way."

Davison started breathing again, but felt prickly sweat forming in his armpits. "I think you were wise to have handled it according to the method provided by the law."

On Sunday, the bells of St. Paul's Cathedral pealed loud and clear as Davison handed Queen Elizabeth a message from fellow diplomat, Sir Amyas Paulet.

> *I am so unhappy to have lived to see the day I am required, according to the direction of my most gracious sovereign, to commit an act forbidden by God and the law. My life is at Her Majesty's disposition, and I am ready to lose it, should it please her. I acknowledge that I hold it as a result of her most gracious favor, and do not desire to enjoy it without her Highness's good blessing. God forbid, I should make so foul a shipwreck of my conscience, or leave so great a blot upon my poor posterity, to set blood without law or warrant.*

The queen marched up and down the great hall, sputtering, "It is all well and good for them to show such concern for my safety when they do nothing, NOTHING, to secure it."

Davison tried to disappear against the tapestry covering the wall. When the queen was still pacing and fuming a quarter of an hour later, Davison slipped out of the gallery and found William strolling among the evergreens.

"She is in a mood now. I cannot imagine how this will end. She is not safe so long as Queen Mary breathes, yet she will not accept the duty of her office to secure her rival's death."

Monday passed with no further action.

Tuesday dawned damp and dark. "I will call upon Her Majesty this morning about other matters. Perhaps she will disclose her plan without any need of mentioning it to her," said Davison to William as they emptied a pot of tea and nibbled on scones.

The queen quickly reminded Davison that she lived in constant fear for her life. "It is past time that this bloody affair is finished. It is shameful that you and the privy council, in negligence of your duty, leave me in such peril. Have I not done all the law requires of me? Have I not?" she demanded to know. Davison only nodded in agreement. "Write a short letter to that spineless Paulet to hasten the warrant's execution."

With as much caution as he could muster, Davison suggested, "Your signature, with the Great Seal and the warrant, should be sufficient, Your Majesty."

"Send the letter anyway!"

A servant interrupted to discern her wishes regarding another matter. Davison left.

⁂

The executioner beheaded Mary Queen of Scots at Fotheringhay Castle on Wednesday, February 8, 1587. A small group of her servants attended her as she calmly said her prayers and lowered her head for the fatal blows.

CHAPTER TWENTY-FOUR

ENGLAND – 1587

Queen Elizabeth found horseback riding in the parks of Greenwich Palace as one of the few times she truly ever felt at peace. She rode there the morning after her order to execute her cousin had been carried out.

When the people heard the news, they lit bonfires and tolled bells throughout the city. When he heard the bells, Davison said, "It is finished. I dare to hope that we will once again know calm and return to our regular duties on behalf of Her Majesty."

The next morning, Davison arrived at court to find the privy council members meeting in the Earl of Leicester's apartment. "She is furious with us all," one of the members told Davison. "Sir Hatton, tell him how your meeting with her unfolded."

"She said she had never commanded, or intended to command, that the execution be carried out." Pausing to look at Davison, he continued, "Further, she said that you betrayed her trust by sending the warrant to Fotheringhay."

Davison's mouth dropped open. He gripped the back of a chair to steady himself, but still, his hands trembled. His stomach felt as if he had swallowed rocks. When Davison thought he was steady enough to walk without falling, he begged to be excused and departed for his own home.

William ran after him. "You look as pale as a ghost. What happened?"

Davison was still shaking as he answered, "I had hoped that given enough time, Her Majesty's temper might calm—and that when I saw her again, she would understand the necessity of it all."

"Any who serve her know her moods swing. Doesn't she always come back to a place of reason, given time?"

"I do not think that will happen now." Davison summed up his brief conversation with the privy councilors. "I hoped a day or two to consider the wondrous response from her subjects would calm her anxieties so that we might all continue on with other matters of state."

Bells continued to peal all over the city. Bonfires burned bright in any available open place, lit by subjects celebrating the end of the Catholics' persistent attempts to overthrow their queen. Saturday, February 11, Queen Elizabeth summoned the privy council. Davison, still feeling ill and shocked, stayed home. After the meeting, one of the privy council members told Davison the queen's temper had grown worse. "Most of her anger was aimed at Burghley, but that is only because you were not there. She absolutely condemns you, my dear Davison. Indeed, she is even now arranging for you to be sent to the Tower. We pleaded with her, even on our knees, but she is set in her course."

When he overheard the conversation, William's stomach lurched; his bowels threatened to humiliate him. After visiting Davison to see how he might be of service, William spent several anxious hours alone in his London room. He turned to one of his books, but after reading the same page several times without comprehending, he resorted to pacing back and forth. He visited Davison again. As he approached, he saw Lord Brockhurst leaving Davison's home. William's heart sank when he saw his friend, employer, and mentor. This dear man who had been vibrant, eloquent, gracious, and eager to confide in him and coach him on the ways of diplomacy now looked old and feeble.

"She sent Lord Brockhurst to take me to the Tower," Davison explained. "But by the grace of our Lord above, he had not the heart to do so when he saw the sorry state in which I lie."

The queen had a tender side for those who suffered ill health. She waited a few more days for Davison to feel better. Then, one day short of a week after Queen Mary was beheaded, Lord Brockhurst returned to escort Davison to the Tower.

That night, William started to write a letter home, but decided not to send it just yet. The situation seemed to change course every few hours. What had been true at breakfast could be completely wrong by supper. He couldn't find words to describe the shock of it all. The enormity of it was all too much. William decided to stay in London, hoping Her Majesty's temper would cool and Davison would be released.

While he waited, he did what he could to assist Davison's wife and children. Occasionally, he received permission to visit Davison to deliver books and other things of comfort. Various privy council members attempted to intervene on Davison's behalf. The queen would hear none of it. Burghley even offered to resign in a letter defending Davison's character. It did no good. Davison lost his place on the privy council as well as his health and freedom. William feared his friend and mentor might also lose his life before the queen's anger played itself out. William's own demeanor turned toward despair when he visited Davison after several weeks in the Tower. Fighting back tears, he told his friend, "I lack words to know how to console you."

"No words can aid me now. Where once I hoped for another assignment in the Lowlands, now I only hope to live to join my family again. I fear she may be plotting with my friends about how to execute me for treason."

"This is so unjust. You have done only as she has asked—no, as she commanded you to do on her behalf."

Davison nodded but didn't look up. He rubbed his hands against his knees until William thought it a wonder he didn't rub a hole through his trousers. Davison slowly lifted his face toward William. "My young friend, I know not what will become of me. I think it best you depart. I may be left here for months, or even years—or I may be dead by the end of the month. It is not right that you should stay on in such uncertain circumstances."

William stayed in London several more weeks, as did other members of Davison's staff. William continued to visit him while others petitioned his case with Her Majesty. Days turned into weeks. On March 28, 1587, Davison had his day in court. The verdict was determined before the trial began. If the queen conceded that Davison was innocent, she would be implicated as the sole cause of Queen Mary's death. That could not be.

Davison, to his credit, did not betray Her Majesty, though she felt no compulsion about betraying him. The strain took its toll. Davison's once firm and confident speech was now soft and barely audible. His left arm had such tremors he was obliged to put it in a sling. He sent a note about the trial to William.

March 29, 1587

I must thank my remaining friends and allies that she ultimately decided to settle for fining me 10,000 marks and keeping me here in the Tower for as long as it suits her. One of my former colleagues on the privy council said that even Archbishop Sandys tried to intervene on my behalf. Apparently, he said he was sorry for me, and that I acted not wittingly or willingly, but rather in good conscience in my effort to rid us of our common enemy. Yet even he concluded that no honest or wise man would have done what I did. So here I shall remain, for I know not how long.

William walked for hours along the Thames after reading that note. Davison's diplomatic career was over, and with it, his own. He wrote in his diary:

I have done all I know to do, and it has not been sufficient. I leave this city of power and passion deeply saddened. I remain grateful for the people I have met, the sights I have seen, the conversations I have heard. Indeed, I am a more well-rounded and educated man for it all, yet I mourn that the politics of the court and the temperament of those in power have inflicted such sorrow upon such a good and decent man.

A few days later, William started the long trip back to Scrooby Manor.

Chapter Twenty-Five

WILLIAM returned to Scrooby just as spring began to color the pastures yellow, blue, and pink with wildflowers. Children ran through meadows, dogs chased squirrels, and the trauma of London seemed like another world. His first days home were a blur of visitors, meals, and more visitors. At first, he had trouble sleeping. He'd grown accustomed to the busy city sounds and constant activity. Chirping crickets provided such a sharp contrast that he struggled to sleep. When he did, he dreamed of Davison enclosed in the Tower, emaciated and defeated.

As days turned to weeks, William spent more time helping his father manage the manor, and less time thinking about those last days in London. Though his neighbors were cordial, he soon learned they hesitated to question him about his time in diplomatic service. Rumors about Queen Mary's execution reached Scrooby before he did, claiming William's employer had betrayed Queen Elizabeth. People William had known since childhood now stopped talking as he approached. Some greeted him stiffly, but kept moving to convey that they did not wish to speak.

Prudence overheard two neighbors whispering. "Well, I say where there's smoke, there is sure to be a fire. No wonder he don't talk much. He must be ashamed to work for the likes of a man who would betray Her Majesty."

Prudence was furious. She called for William as soon as she got home. "Now, you must tell me everything that happened. I will not have you the center of rumors and gossip."

William sank into a chair and told the entire tale. "I still hope she will see the folly of her ways and release Davison. And if that is to come to pass, I would gladly return to work for him. He is as honest and forthright a man as I have ever known."

In 1588 a courier passing through Scrooby delivered a letter from Davison:

> *Though I am now free to walk about as I please, I have no plan for each day without reinstatement by Her Majesty. I am blessed with friends who intervene on my behalf, yet she is resolute in her determination that I shall not be at court again. It confuses me, for my friend Essex claims she has given me many praises.*
>
> *I tried to regain her favor and a place in her court by sending a letter via a friend. She refused to accept the letter. It seems all attempts to return to my former life are proving futile. I shall now retire to my home at Stepney. At least she has not ended my pension, so my family will not endure the indignity of the poorhouse. If ever you should pass this way, know that I would cherish your companionship.*

William longed to see his friend again, but hesitated to leave Scrooby. Day by day, his father's health was worsening. As the weeks passed, the problems of Davison and the court faded.

Life in Scrooby was pleasant and calm with the exception of concerns about the health of William's father. Young William and Prudence functioned unofficially in the roles of bailiff and postmaster, doing what they could to always have horses ready for couriers so riders delivering the royal mail would maintain their expected speed of seven miles per hour. William eagerly greeted each messenger, eager to receive whatever meager news they had the time and interest to share.

In April 1590, a courier brought news that Secretary Walsingham had died. Though few people in William's village knew or cared about such a thing, William dared hope that perhaps this might mean Her Majesty would reinstate Davison to the court. If that happened . . . maybe William could return to the diplomatic life. But what would that mean for his father, step-mother, and the others now looking to him for guidance?

A letter from William's Cambridge friend, the Earl of Essex, ended that speculation:

> *I petitioned to name Davison as successor to Walsingham, but alas, Her Majesty would have none of it.*

Spring yielded to summer. William focused even more on tending to his father. The senior William was showing the effects of many winters. Consequently, Prudence was doing more manor work than was good for her health.

One sultry June afternoon in 1590, William senior sent for his son to come to his sickroom. "I will not have many more days in this life. I am counting on you to take care of the family . . . and the manor." He started coughing and motioned for William to stay longer. The coughing subsided and he continued, "About your marriage."

"What about it, Father?"

The older man, propped up on pillows, his color as pale as the sheets, struggled to continue. "I want you . . ." Out of breath, he paused again and pulled the bedding up to his chin, even though it was warm in the room with bright afternoon sun streaming in. In a raspy voice, coughing every third word, he continued. "You marry the Wentworth girl. Only proper thing to do now. It's a good life here."

The coughing stopped him again. With effort he kept going. "Not like Cambridge. Or with Davison." He gasped for breath. "But honest, decent work."

"I will do my duty, Father."

The senior William coughed harder and couldn't seem to stop. William left to fetch a mug of water. He returned and held his father's head in one hand while gently tipping the mug against his lips, then gently eased his father's head back onto the pillow. His father closed his eyes. William heard him snoring softly as he walked down the hall. A week later, the senior William slipped from this life into the next, leaving his son to manage the house-hold and the manor.

A few weeks later, Prudence started fussing at young William. "I am grateful for all the help, but truly, I am fine by myself for an afternoon now and then. I think you should spend time with Miss Mary Wentworth."

Similarly, Mary's mother asked almost every evening, "Mary, shall I set out a plate for William?" Mary hesitated. Though the Wentworth family frequently set out an extra plate for William, assuming he would join them seemed presumptuous; yet not doing so might indicate they had grown weary of his regular presence.

"As you wish, Mother," Mary replied. The plate appeared moments later. Hints about William's future with the Wentworth family grew less subtle as his appearances grew more frequent. Though the senior William Brewster died before he could make final arrangements for his son to marry, both families understood this was the plan.

"Do you think you shall settle down now, William?" asked Mary's mother. As a widow, she was eager for her daughter to marry. She particularly liked the idea that the man might be young William Brewster. After leaving the manor when her husband died, she was eager to see her daughter live there now.

William's face turned bright pink. He studied the peas and potatoes on his plate. Without looking up, he said, "I suppose I shall, when the time is right."

"Tell me, lad, how are you to know when the time is right?"

William shuffled back and forth on the bench. "To be truthful, when I have a bit of security about my future financial situation. I do not know what will happen now that Father has gone to meet the Lord. I must do what I can to tend to his estate without a will to direct me."

"Bless his departed soul," said Mrs. Wentworth. "My own dear Thomas died while bailiff at the manor. Do you remember him? You were ten or so, I think, probably off to school in Doncaster. That was when your own dear father was appointed."

"Yes, of course. One does not forget moving into the Manor House!"

"Your father was as good a bailiff and postmaster as my dear Thomas. Those rumors about his indiscretions with maidens are the idle talk of those who envy his position. One does not assume responsibility in this world without also attracting the envy of others. You seem to know all that is necessary to carry on in his place, if you are willing."

William looked at Mrs. Wentworth. "My future is not so clear. I must be appointed to the position. The man who knows me— and to whom I should have applied while Father still lived—has now also died."

"Oh, dear," said Mary. She clasped her hands over her mouth. When she dropped them, she added, "that does put you in a peculiar situation."

"It does, rather. The new man has already appointed his cousin, Samuel Bevercotes, to become postmaster here." Silence followed. People generally assumed that young William would inherit his father's position. Mrs. Wentworth stood and began clearing away the plates. A few minutes later, she sat down again.

"You must go talk to Sir Davison. He has been released from the Tower, so surely he has some diplomatic influence left to use on your behalf."

"He can no longer even get a letter through to Her Majesty. He certainly would not be granted an audience."

"Surely Her Majesty does not get involved in the appointment of every postmaster throughout her kingdom? She surely has staff to oversee such matters for her."

William nodded. "Yes, of course, she does. In this case, it would be Sir John Stanhope, who just appointed his cousin to the position." Mary asked to be excused. She made it to the garden behind the house before the tears began to flow. She sat on a fallen log and twisted a strand of hair, gazing across the meadow, watching the sheep grazing and a Spaniel sniffing the ground in search of something to catch.

Each day since his father passed away, I've thought, this will be the day he will ask me to be his wife. I remember it, and I've always wondered what it might be like to live there again. But that cannot be if he loses the position at Scrooby. How would we live? Where would we live? What will become of him? He's suffered so much already. And then, what will become of me? There is no other in all this area I would want to be with for the rest of my life.

The next morning Mary's mother told her William had left early for a trip to London, hoping to yet save his position. "If he goes at the pace the royal messengers do, he'll be back before the week is ended."

Mary tried to concentrate on sewing, but often had to undo what she'd just done and start over again.

CHAPTER TWENTY-SIX

LONDON – 1591

With no human to hear his case, William talked to his horse as they headed south. "I doubt Stanhope will see me, but perhaps I can at least call on Thomas Mills. He manages the payroll for the postmasters and reports to Stanhope." With a plan in place, William pushed his mount into a trot.

Mills received William, then spoke to Stanhope, who complained, "And why would he trouble you with this rather than come straight to me?"

Stanhope wrote to Davison.

I never heard one word from young William. He neither came to me, being in town, nor sent for me, but, acting as though I were to be overruled by others, made his way according to his liking. I know my interest, and think him worthily displaced for his contempt in not seeing me at all.

Davison sent a note to William, chastising him for his tactlessness but also assuring his young friend that he would do what he could to salvage the situation. On the back of Stanhope's letter to him, Davison wrote a list of reasons William ought to be appointed. Before sending the note to Stanhope, he added:

Young William served in the position long before his father's death; indeed, ever since I was removed to the Tower and he returned home to Scrooby. His name is on the rolls among other

posts, and he has been receiving payment for his services for the
past year and a half.

Stanhope conceded. The job was William's now, for as long as
he should remain in Scrooby. With that settled, William focused
his attention on Mary. His stepmother's health was also starting
to fail, and though he spoke of it to no one, he hoped he and Mary
might be married while Prudence was alive to witness their union.

✠

Prudence insisted she did not need William's help, that he could
best help by going for a walk. "Your constant fretting about my
well-being is what prevents me from being well. Out with you.
Leave an old woman to a bit of peace and quiet."

Not quite by coincidence, William caught up with Mary in her
garden. She was looking for any early spring vegetables she might
use for supper.

"Have you time for a walk?" William asked.

"Why, William, I always have time for you."

They walked for a few minutes, commenting on birds they heard
or saw, the signs of spring in the changing leaves, and what they
planned to enjoy for supper later. "With all you've been through, is
this truly what is on your mind, William?"

He stared at his feet and pulled on his beard. "No, to be truthful. I have so much on my mind, I hardly know how to manage it
all. It seems rather peculiar how the plans we make are often not
the plans we live. Does it seem so to you, Mary?"

"I don't know that I have ever thought about it much. My life
is a simple one. I tend the house. I work the garden. I help with
the village children as needed. I have few plans, and there is little
opportunity for them to change."

"I see," William replied. He walked a few feet ahead of Mary,
then turned back to look at her. He suggested, "I suppose it is
different for a woman. He again walked a few paces away from
Mary, and stared at the ground before looking at her. "I cannot
describe the wonder of it all. London was so exciting! Then that
came to an abrupt end like my Cambridge days." William looked
away and dabbed at his eyes.

"I've heard bits and pieces of that. I do hope the day will come
when you will tell me more of it."

"I suppose the day may come, but it will not be this day. I am still so unsettled by it all. It seems to me a gross miscarriage of justice." Neither spoke, but they continued to walk. A few minutes later, William spoke again, as though there had been no lull. "I nearly lost my position as postmaster. I truly do not know what I would have done. Prudence and the others depend on me for that income. Thank our dear Lord above that in the end, I was able to keep the post."

"I do, indeed, thank the Lord, for I am glad you will now stay in Scrooby. Though I am pleased for you that you've had such grand adventures, I rather like having you here."

"Do you, now?"

"I do, William. I do."

"Perhaps, then, you like it well enough that you would consent to live with me? To be my wife?"

Mary laughed. She rushed toward William and reached for his hands. "I can think of nothing that would bring me more pleasure."

William put his hands in hers, dropped them, and put his hands on her shoulders. "There. I've done it. I've made the one plan I trust will not change course. We must tell everyone. We must make our plans for our wedding." He embraced her, and she did not pull away.

Prudence was told of the latest plans over their simple midday meal. She was speechless. Even though she rarely showed physical affection to her family, she gave William a tight hug and planted a kiss on his cheek. Then she sat down to finish eating as though nothing spectacular or life-changing had just happened.

✺

"Dust to dust, ashes to ashes." The priest made the sign of the cross over a simple wooden coffin, and backed up so the gravediggers could lower it. William walked away as they began shoveling dirt over his stepmother's final resting place.

Mary walked up beside William and took his hand. They walked for a long time without speaking. When he thought he was sufficiently composed to do so, he turned to Mary. "I had so hoped she'd live to see us wed. Perhaps she will anyway, but from a different place now."

✺

Three months later, William and Mary walked out of St. James with their futures irreversibly linked. Once the priest had declared them husband and wife, there was no going back. Neither of them wanted to go anywhere but forward together, whatever the future might bring.

The first event the couple weathered was assuming full responsibility for all the manor duties. "And now I alone am left with the responsibility of all Scrooby Manor and our family," William remarked wistfully.

"You are not alone, for I am by your side. I shall help you when I can, and pray for you when that is all I can do."

William smiled at his bride. "You can never know the depth of comfort I draw from your presence with me."

CHAPTER TWENTY-SEVEN

SCROOBY, ENGLAND – 1593

In February 1593, Mary asked William to pause his work to walk with her. "Dear Mary, I treasure your company, truly I do. But I must look after affairs here while I have light to work."

"I need only a few moments of your time. What I have to tell you is too urgent to wait." William set aside his work and went outdoors to walk with Mary around the manor garden.

"Tell me now, what news could you have that cannot wait until the sun has set?"

Mary's smile grew from a slight lifting of the corners of her mouth until all of her front teeth showed. "Sometime next summer, we shall welcome a baby to join us."

William stopped abruptly and stared at her. "Are you sure? How do you know?"

"Women have ways of knowing such things. I assure you, it is so."

Their son was born on August 12, 1593—a hot summer morning. "What shall we name him?" asked Mary.

"I have thought much about that. A name is so important for setting the course of a child's life. What do you think about Jonathan? Was another Jonathon not the brave son of King Saul? Was he not the most loyal friend to mighty King David?"

"Yes, I like it," said Mary, savoring the soft touch of Jonathan's silky hair against her cheek.

William welcomed the courier and led his horse, breathing heavily from exertion, to water. The two men had just settled in with tankards of ale in the shade of a giant chestnut tree when the courier blurted out, "Such a bloody shame about poor Penry."

"What about him?" asked William. "I know him from my days at Peterhouse." After hearing what happened to John Penry, William stood abruptly and excused himself.

Mary looked up from chopping vegetables. "What happened? You look like you've seen a ghost."

"You have often heard me talk of my friend John Penry."

"Yes, I remember. What about him? Is he sick?"

"No. Dead. Last May."

Mary gasped. William continued in a stilted voice. "He was executed. As a traitor. Accused of writing the Marprelate Papers." Mary stared, but said nothing.

"He was such a good friend. Always cheerful. I enjoyed his Welsh voice, though we made fun of it often enough." He smiled at the memory. "And now, he is gone." They were silent for a long while.

Finally, Mary gently asked, "These Marprelate Papers . . . I've heard of them. I've heard they are as humorous as they are critical of the Established Church."

"What you heard is true. Penry was affiliated with people in London who openly criticized the Established Church. Puritans continue to campaign to clean up the excess, but some, like Penry, think that is not possible. They say the only resolution is to completely separate."

"And do you agree?"

William chewed his lower lip and tugged at his beard. He wasn't quite sure how to respond. "I think I do, Mary. I withhold some of what I know to protect you, and now our son."

"Surely our queen does not execute people for religious musings?"

"She is more tolerant than most, but will not tolerate flagrant criticism of the Established Church of England. Rather, she thinks any criticism of the Established Church is criticism of her."

"Do the Marprelate Papers do that?"

William nodded. "They do. A courier told me that before they dragged off poor John, he managed to publish one last paper and smuggle it out. It was his farewell. In it, he urged supporters to prepare to go into exile so they could stay together."

"Exile! Is that not a bit extreme?"

"It may seem so now, but perhaps it will be necessary in the future."

"William, what are you telling me?"

William looked at Mary through red, swollen eyes. "John Penry was certain we would find no room in all of England to enjoy religious freedom. I fear he may be correct."

That night, William prayed a long time before turning to his journal. Lately, he'd started keeping it tucked away in a bag, covered with assorted items of clothing.

I know not the way to turn or which direction to take. I do not like withholding from Mary the extent to which I have begun to engage in conversations with others—conversations some would consider treason. Yet now, with the execution of John, my fears for her well-being are confirmed. Should she be found complicit in the course of action some of us are considering, she could be in mortal danger. How could I allow that? Especially now, with our new baby at her breast depending on her for his very life.

SCROOBY – 1600

It was one of the first warm days in months. The couple strolled around the manor, savoring the warm sun on their backs and filling their nostrils with fresh air. Birds chirped overhead while a dog barked at some cornered prey in the corner of the garden.

"Soon, Jonathan will have a playmate."

William clasped her hands. "Do you think it will be a girl?"

"We will have to wait, now, won't we?"

"A man can hope, though, can he not? Jonathan will make a fine big brother. He is old enough now to help when he is not at his studies. And you will be wanting a little one to keep you company when he is."

Patience was born a few months later.

Mary sat outside one warm March afternoon in 1601. The air was chilly, but if she sat in the sun, it was warm enough to be outside for a spell. She was working on mending an outfit for Jonathan. She'd learned that a young boy could go through britches faster than a dog devouring leftovers. Patience slept in a cradle nearby, covered with layers of woolen blankets.

Mary heard the clatter of horse hoofs on the packed dirt road and looked up to see dust rising in the distance on the North Road. A few moments later, a carrier slowed his lathered horse to a walk, stopping a few feet away. He dismounted, shouting, "Where's the bailiff? I've news to tell!"

Mary rushed off to get William. As soon as the courier saw him, he called out across the yard, "She had him beheaded!"

"Who?" asked William as he took giant steps to reach the courier.

"The Earl of Essex!"

William gasped and protested, "But he was one of Her Majesty's favorites! How could that be?"

"It is true. I was there," insisted the courier. "The earl led a small band of men through the streets of London, and not for the first time. I suppose he thought she'd gone too far in her determination to rid England of any who dared challenge her authority over the church and the affairs of her subjects. She ordered him beheaded in the courtyard of the Tower."

"She has seen nearly seventy winters now. Perhaps she is going mad, as others before her have?" suggested William.

"Mad or jealous, only God can know. All I know is that she ordered him put to death even as she wore the ring he gave her as a token of their friendship."

William looked down and noticed his hands were shaking. He clasped them together to stop the trembling. "It appears no one is truly safe from her ever-changing moods."

CHAPTER TWENTY-EIGHT

ENGLAND – 1602

William enjoyed watching the children in the garden. Jonathan was often away at school, following in his father's academic footsteps. When home, he was proving to be rather helpful with Patience. The little girl followed Mary everywhere, until she thought she'd never get any work done. Mary stopped picking peas when the pouch she'd made out of her apron was full. William followed her into the kitchen.

"I was thinking I might rather enjoy going to Babworth next Sabbath. I could hear Pastor Richard Clyfton for myself. In my reading, I find more and more evidence that the Established Church leads people astray. Friends tell me Pastor Clyfton has insight on this. There are others with passion and zeal, as well. There's a Pastor John Smyth at Gainsborough, but I would only need to ride an hour to hear Pastor Clyfton. Some travel many miles to hear him, many more than the seven or so I will travel. I have even heard there is a young orphan boy who attends worship at All Saints whom Richard Clyfton treats like a son."

"Why, William Brewster! Are you suggesting you would risk the security of our pleasant life missing worship at St. James? You, of all people, will be missed. Neighbors would surely report seeing you on the road to Babworth on a Sunday."

"All Saints is still a congregation of the Established Church. Do I not have the right of a freeman to go where I choose? We may not even have a priest at St. James. If anyone asks, we can tell them I chose to go where it was certain there would be a priest present."

Mary dumped the peas from her apron into a large wooden bowl and began to shell them. "Do not the books you read recount the fate of others who have done similar?"

"You remember me telling you about John Foxe's *Book of Martyrs?* It is true, many Protestants paid for their faith with their lives under bloody Queen Mary, though things are rather better under Queen Elizabeth. Even so, Protestants and Catholics continue to turn one another in. Some take great satisfaction in helping the authorities arrest those who stray from whichever group has the upper hand in their community."

"And knowing this, you still want to venture away from us to hear this . . . this . . . whatever his name is, preach?"

William stepped closer to put his hands on Mary's shoulders and whispered, "I would never intentionally bring harm to you or our children." Mary stiffened, but did not pull away. She continued shelling peas.

"Yet, Mary, I must follow where I believe God is leading. Does it not say in the Scriptures that anyone who loves anything—or anyone—more than God Himself is not worthy?"

⚜

William Brewster bid his family farewell and rode the seven miles to Babworth. He listened spellbound as the Reverend Richard Clyford opened the Scriptures for him in ways he had not heard since those exciting days at Peterhouse.

"Are we not mismatched with those who proclaim sovereignty over that which is rightly sovereign only to our Lord?" thundered Clyford. "Does it not say in the Holy Scriptures, 'Do not be mismatched with unbelievers. What partnership is there between righteousness and lawlessness?' We know many claiming to be our Lord's representatives on earth are lawless. They torture true believers. They hang them or behead them. They fornicate. They indulge themselves in riches our Lord would want them to give to the poor."

William nearly rose to his feet, but since those around him sat spellbound and motionless, he leaned forward a little instead. Clyfton jammed one long bony finger into the Bible he held open and read, "What agreement has the temple of God with idols? For we are the temple of the living God; as God said, 'I will live in them and walk among them and I will be their God, and they shall be my people. Therefore, come out from them, and be separate from them, says the Lord, and touch nothing unclean, then I will welcome you, and I will be your father, and you shall be my sons and daughters. That is what the Lord Almighty tells us."

William urged his horse to go faster on the way home. He found Mary in the yard plucking a chicken while Jonathan occupied Patience watching baby lambs in the pasture across the road. "Mary, it was so exciting! Surely, what Pastor Clyfton says is the true meaning of the Scriptures. It cannot be about priests making themselves rich by taking the land peasants need for food, or the endless slaughter of people who only want to be closer to God."

Joining with others who believed as he did became the most important focus of William's life, second only to family. He shared his excitement with Mary. "The elaborate ceremonies that are still part and parcel of the Established Church make them Protestant in name only. Substitute King James for the pope, and you have the Roman Catholic Church in English rather than Latin. These things bring us no closer to God, but rather, drive us further away. We must restore the church to the ways of the earliest followers of Christ."

Mary sighed. "I admire your zeal, William. But I worry about the outcome. Please, do exert caution. Be circumspect when you speak with such passion."

"I speak with passion with you because I must talk about it, and waiting a week between gathering times is more than I can bear. When I am about in the village, I am careful to be silent about many of the things I tell you."

Legal or not, gathering with others who shared these new ideas was a chance William was willing to take. The fellowship of friends, combined with Clyfton's powerful preaching, drew the Brewsters to Babworth as surely as a Labrador is drawn to water. It required extra work to prepare for a day away from the manor, but soon, both William and Mary found the fellowship and fresh ideas at All Saints worth the effort. Six days a week, they tended to the needs of their children, the manor, and the guests who happened to be with them. On Sundays, they bundled their children and food for the day, hitched a horse to the wagon, and made their way to All Saints.

There, William met a young lad named William Bradford. Bradford was an orphan. His uncles had begrudgingly taken him in as a small child. By the time William met him, he was a teenager searching for someone to care about him. William, now in the prime of life, was ready to bestow upon him the sort of friendship he'd received from William Davison. The two struck up a conversation after worship.

"Is it true you came by yourself when you were but twelve years old?"

"That is partly the truth," admitted Bradford. "I came with a friend, but the walk is long, and my friend no longer wished to make it."

"But you have continued? What brings you here without your family?"

"Pastor Clyfton. He gives me things to read. He asks me what I think. He shows me affection." The boy's voice began to quiver, so he stopped talking.

William walked with him in silence for a few moments. "I was much older than you when my father died. I still keenly feel the loss. Surely, your uncles help you?"

"They feed me, and give me work to do. They make sure I get to school, but they are not much interested in things of the spirit."

"Then I certainly understand why you walk the eight miles each way to worship here. When a man is starving and he knows there is food up ahead, he will keep going as long as he has breath." Bradford shrugged, but said nothing.

In speaking to others about the boy's situation, William learned that Bradford's uncles had forbidden him to continue the trips. Apparently, they feared Clyfton was corrupting the lad. "And I suppose they fear the consequences to themselves if their nephew should be found defying the authority of the Established Church by listening to this kind of preaching," someone suggested.

"Yet he comes," observed William. "He is quite brave. It must be that God, in His mercy, has ordained that Bradford be fathered in some way by Pastor Clyfton. The pastor's long white beard gives him a fatherly look."

PART TWO

Pokanoket

Nation

Chapter Twenty-Nine

Dawnland - Patuxet Nation - (Massachusetts) – 1603

USING hoes constructed by binding the shoulder bones from deer to sturdy sticks with rawhide, the Patuxet women worked the sandy soil under a warm spring sun. In each new hole, they placed one of the herring the men had caught in the spring herring run. One woman stood to stretch her stiff back. She looked around and saw her son, Tisquantum, walking past with more herring tied over a pole balanced on his shoulder.

"My son, come here with those. Stay long enough to let me use what you carry. Then you can go back to help get more." Tisquantum's tanned arms and torso gleamed with sweat from working to catch herring and carry them to the field. He helped his mother take the fish off the pole. The Sagamore passed by, observing how the planting was progressing. He approved. The people had made good use of the long winter evenings around their fires in the long house. Their tools were ready for the planting season at hand.

The Sagamore thought back to evenings spent with his own family in their birch wetu. That, combined with the sight of people working together in the fields, gave him a sense of immense well-being. Though he ruled over hundreds of people along the Cape Cod coast, his own home was also functional and modest.

Tisquantum looked up to glance at robins flying overhead. The sight of them made him glad. Summer was coming soon. The sight of robins combined with the croaking of frogs at night indicated winter was fading away, making room for longer and warmer days. His father and grandfather taught him the frogs croaked when their muddy hiding places were disturbed. That is how they knew when to start the spring planting season.

He could still hear his father's voice teaching him about the annual cycle of life. Plant, harvest, use some, store some. Between the gifts from the soil, fish so thick one could nearly walk across the bay on them, an abundance of deer in the forest, and plenty of fowl flying overhead, they had a good life.

Tisquantum pulled the last herring off his pole and left the planting to the women, returning to the stream to reload. He knew his mother would be expecting many more, just as other sons were bringing their catch, as well. Other women followed behind those putting a fish in the ground, covering it with a little earth and adding seeds that would yield another harvest.

The Patuxet Sagamore would have happy news to report to the Massasoit when they met again. Though only a little older than many of the people he governed, Massasoit Ousa Mequin carried out his responsibilities for thousands in the Pokanoket lands with dignity and wisdom. His people lived and worked together more or less in peace. It took him many days to walk from one end of the Pokanoket lands along the Cape Cod Bay into Canada, but he enjoyed the journey and the numerous conversations with those along the way.

He was grateful the people had sufficient resources for themselves, and more to share with the pale newcomers. For many years now these hairy-faced people had been finding their way across the sea to this land. The lucrative beaver trade with them brought good fortune for the Pokanoket people; they brought useful items. Their huge cast iron pots proved especially useful for storing corn. And they liked to adorn their jackets with the glass beads acquired in the trades.

Tisquantum and his neighbors filled their days hunting, fishing, harvesting bark to repair the wetus, or going out to select the best tree for a new canoe. Men and women worked together to set small trees into the holes around their home site to keep small children safe and discourage animals from wandering in.

Massasoit Ousa Mequin often conferred with other saga-mores about the hairy-faced men. So many were coming now in enormous boats that it became cause for concern, but hearing good reports about the progress of spring planting gave him confidence.

As Tisquantum and the others worked at the herring run, they passed the time with talk about the weather and gossip. "The clouds carry the promise of rain soon. This will reward our efforts," observed Tisquantum. Several others looked up to study the clouds overhead and murmured agreement.

"Yes," said one. "And even more, our Massasoit makes good trades with the strange-talking white men. The tools they offer in exchange for our beaver and corn have helped."

"That is true," said another worker. "The Massasoit says little. He always looks concerned. But he keeps peace. He is wise."

"And strong," said another.

"And clever," said Tisquantum.

While Tisquantum and the others planted, a father and son were fishing at the shore. They spotted a ship far out on the horizon. Though it was still only a bobbing dot, they knew that soon enough, they would see an enormous wooden structure. When it was close enough, they could see what looked like large white flags flapping in the wind. As many as two hundred ships had come and gone in recent years. Still, sighting one was both a thrill and cause for caution. These strangers sometimes brought them metal tools, cloth, and trinkets. But they also brought trouble.

The Sagamores and Massasoit Ousa Mequin passed along reports of missing men after a visit from these strange men. Men now grey of hair and stooped with age passed along stories they had learned from their grandfathers. One told of an explorer from across the sea who captured fifty or more people from Pennecook many seasons ago. "They come to trade, and we learn to trust them. Then they turn on us, and sometimes steal our young."

The fisherman told his son, "Run as fast as the wind. Tell the field workers to get the Sagamore. Tell him to come quickly."

Dozens of Natives watched as Martin Pring and his crew of forty-four set up their camp at Patuxet. Tisquantum nudged the man standing closest to him. "Do they bring dogs?" The sight of the explorers' two enormous mastiffs awed the Natives.

"I have never seen any dog the size of a deer before," responded his companion.

Days passed and trade and talk seemed relaxed.

"They make a good camp. I like visiting them. I like hearing them make music on their strange boxes with strings. It sounds so different from our drums, flutes, and rattles," said one of the Natives.

"I like it, too. And I like watching their expressions when we show them how to dance and make music. But I wonder if there will be a single sassafras plant left in all the forest when they are done. All day, every day, all they do is pluck the plants up and carry them away to their big wooden house on the water."

"The Sagamore says sassafras is valuable where they come from—over the horizon."

After Pring and his men had been rooting for sassafras for several days, a group of a hundred or so Natives strolled toward where the hairy-faced men were taking stock of the plants they'd gathered that day. Suddenly, there was an explosion that sent them running for the woods. "What *was* that?" several cried out at the same time.

"It is smoke, but fire does not make such noise."

"I think it comes from that big black thing. See, smoke comes from it."

Several Natives crept toward the edge of the woods for a better view. They retreated quickly when the two mastiffs came loping toward them, mouths open, tongues hanging out. There was no cultural exchange that night, or any other night after that.

The Sagamore consulted with several elders of the Patuxet village. "It is time for these people who pluck up plants and send their giant dogs to chase our people to return home. We will encourage them to go now."

One evening, at the start of Pring's seventh week in Patuxet territory, an army of one hundred and forty Patuxet men circled Pring's encampment. Pring and his men didn't get the hint.

"They do not understand our message. We will send another," decided the sagamore.

The next day, the Patuxet men set fire to the woodlands where the English were collecting sassafras. Two hundred Native warriors gave them a strong yet bloodless farewell send-off a few hours later.

A mother was singing softly to her young son. She dipped a cloth in cool water and gently dabbed at the child's forehead. Still, the boy moaned in pain. He grabbed the sides of his head and begged for the pain to stop. "Shh, shh, my son. I have sent for Pau Wau. He will know how to make the pain stop, and the blisters that cover you go away."

But the Pau Wau's medicine, made from his carefully combined mixture of herbs, was powerless against the headache and fever. Never before had he seen anyone covered with blisters that oozed and itched. Though he danced and sang throughout the afternoon, the boy continued to groan. He died two weeks later, in pain and misery.

Hardly had they buried him when another fell ill with the same symptoms: headaches, blisters, fever, and pain, and lots and lots of pain. Again, the Pau Wau's treatments were futile. Mothers barely had time to mourn the death of their children because there always seemed to be another falling captive to this strange disease.

❈

Mutually frustrating and disappointing encounters between Europeans and Natives paved the way for the capture of Tisquantum and the others in 1614. That kidnapping set off a backlash of fury that dampened the People of the First Light's enthusiasm for continued trade with Europeans. The Massasoit was furious.

"We must call our people together," he declared. "We cannot tolerate more of their conniving and cheating. We trust them to trade with us, and they thank us by stealing our young."

His brothers, Akkompoin and Quadequina, agreed. Massasoit Ousa Mequin continued, "We will show our strength and disapproval to the people from the other side of the great water."

CHAPTER THIRTY

ABENAKI NATION (MAINE) – 1609

Sagamore Samoset from the Abenaki region stood on a hill overlooking the scene below. In the spring warmth, he wore only a deerskin breechclout. Long black locks fell down beyond his shoulders in the back with the hair in front cut shorter. His face was smooth, for now free of any paint. A quiver full of arrows rested over his shoulder. He observed a small group of odd-looking pale-skinned people wandering through the forest. The way they stomped about warned any deer within a mile that they were coming.

They will never find food that way! These people are so strange with many layers of clothes, blue eyes, and hairy faces. They don't know the most basic things about providing for themselves. I see the value of the iron kettles they bring, and it is true their knives cut faster and easier than our flint ones, but their smelly, loud, strange ways make me glad I don't have to live with them. As long as all they want are fur pelts, fish, or plants in exchange for what they bring, I suppose there is no harm in letting them tromp through the woods. The land gives us all we need.

Sagamore Samoset lived up to the meaning of his name, He Who Walks Over Much. In his nineteen years, he had probably walked hundreds of miles through the forests and along the rocky coast, and sometimes far beyond. His people, the Abenaki, had lived in this rugged land for more time than anyone could measure. Since Sagamore Samoset spoke one dialect of the Algonquian language, the Nauset and Pokanoket could communicate with him as he moved in and out of their villages to trade products and information.

Sagamore Samoset often encountered both French and English explorers. They appeared far out near the horizon, with white sheets flapping in the breeze. They came more often now, searching for things to take away beyond the horizon. None of them spoke any of the Algonquian languages. At first, he could not understand any of their French or English, but over time, he learned enough words to trade with them. His father, and his father's father before him—and all the elders—had stories about these strange light-skinned people who wanted to trade with the Abenaki.

The Sagamore knew from Nauset neighbors that sometimes these strangers brought trouble with their trade deals. They took Natives away across the sea. He knew, too, that his people some-times died from diseases the white ones brought with them. It was odd how the white men could make people sick, but not get the sickness themselves.

Another Abenaki interrupted his thoughts. "A runner from Powhatan's people arrived this morning. He tells of war between his people and the white ones. He says many more white ones have come, but none of them know how to make a good life from the bounty of the land."

"I have observed this for myself about the pale ones I have seen. How many of these strange floating houses do they have that they can come to the land of Powhatan?" asked Sagamore Samoset.

The Native reported, "Powhatan's people say they seem to know only how to fight, cheat, and steal."

The Sagamore gritted his teeth. "Did Powhatan come seeking help?"

"No, he came to warn us. He told me the white ones do not know how to prepare a field for planting, so they make trouble with their fire sticks. They burned his people's villages and chased them far away from their fields. Some they captured. Now, they are making them work for them, and will kill them if they do not. All this trouble because the white ones are lazy and don't know how to work for themselves."

Sagamore Samoset frowned. The companions gazed out over the peaceful calm of the early morning. The ocean gently lapped against a rocky beach in the distance. Still looking out, Sagamore Samoset murmured more to himself than his companion, "For many seasons, we have lived here, mostly in peace. When we do have troubles, our men and their arrows protect us. We must come together now and find a way to deal with these strange people."

They stood together in silence for several long minutes, each lost in thought. Finally, the Sagamore asked, "Do you think the white ones will come here and burn our fields?" He did not wait for an answer. "We must be sure they do not. Though their tools and weapons make things easier for us, we cannot let them burn our villages and take our crops. Tell Powhatan's runner we thank him for his warning. See that he gets what he needs to prepare for his trip home. We must be vigilant."

The Sagamore heard about trouble in some of the villages not far away, but so far, most of the hairy-faced explorers seemed content to trap beaver, hunt in the woods for sassafras, catch fish, lobster, and a few waterfowl to take back to their big boats.

Because the white men also took people, the Natives made sure the invaders from beyond the horizon stayed close to the shore to explore and trade. If they didn't, there were plenty of warriors ready to convince the light-skinned people to retreat to their own lands. But now, Powhatan's messenger had traveled many days from a place the white men called Jamestown. Someone told him they named their village after their leader. The news Powhatan's messenger brought was troubling. *The more we trade with them, the more people come. No matter how much we swap with them, it never satisfies their appetites. Their numbers grow greater with each passing season. We cannot fight their fire sticks with arrows. If we cannot trade in peace, I do not know what will become of us.*

Sagamore Samoset looked out over the ocean again. He strained his eyes in search of any more ships on the horizon. Seeing none, he made his way back to the long house where people were busy with morning chores. The warm sun, birds chirping, and the scent of pine needles underfoot gave him a sense of tranquility. For now.

Chapter Thirty-One

Patuxet Nation (Massachusetts) – 1614

Explorer John Smith was satisfied that he and the men under him had thoroughly identified the many Cape Cod harbors on the maps he was drawing to take back to England. "Yes, this will make a good place to establish a trade association. And I know just the man to put in charge of trade with these Indians."

"I am grateful to you, Master Smith, for your confidence in me to see to the trade. Patuxet, Nauset, Pokanoket—strange names, but how rich we will all grow trading with them," said Thomas Hunt.

"Right you are, Thomas. This is good fortune for many of us. Do not do anything to bring it to ruin," warned Smith. "Think of the fortunes to be made back home from such a bountiful supply of cod and beaver furs. I see no end to the profits to be made from these. Return home with your hold full of dried cod and pelts, and merchants will be eager enough to invest in trade here."

Master Hunt assured Master Smith that he would. However, Hunt had an additional agenda. He intended to put cargo even more valuable into his hold before he set sail.

Tisquantum and his companions watched as Hunt instructed his crew to keep loading cod onto his ship. Eventually, Hunt turned to the Natives. He waved, and they waved back. Hunt signaled to them to come closer. They cautiously took a few steps forward. Hunt held up a large mirror and several knives. The mirror glimmered in the sun, as did the blades of the knives. Tisquantum and the others came closer still to look at the objects. Hunt pointed to his ship anchored in the harbor. He held out the items in his hands, "I have more of these, there." He pointed to the ship again, and waved for them to come closer. The men took a few steps, but kept their distance.

Hunt called to a couple of the crew closest to him. "Pull the long boat up on the beach. Get the trinkets and bottles of rum, and bring them here." When the men returned with the bottles, Hunt took a swig from one and extended it toward Tisquantum. Tisquantum reached for it and took a sip. He made a face, but took another. Then he passed the bottle around to his companions. Hunt again pointed across the bay to his ship. "More there," he said, pointing first to the bottle, then to the ship.

He turned to his crew again. "I will get them into the long boat. Go ahead of me to the ship in the other boat. When they're all on board, distract them with more of these." He showed them the items he had in his hands. "Lead them into the hold."

As they followed the sailors, Tisquantum, trusting they could not understand any of their Algonquian language, told the others, "These strange hairy-faced men bring many new things to us. Our elders will be pleased when we return with so many good things. They want our fish and beaver skins. We have more of those than we will ever need. We cannot so easily get the things they bring. Let us see what else they have in their big boat."

As they drew near the ship, one of them pointed at the rigging. "Look! So many ropes and poles."

"And there!" said another, pointing to the barrels lined against the railing. The sailors grinned, pointing to the opening of the hold. One gestured for them to come closer. He backed down the ladder and returned a minute later with more knives, glass beads, and bottles of rum. Pointing to where he'd just been, he motioned for them to come see for themselves.

One by one, twenty-seven curious Natives followed the sailor into the dark hold. They were barely able to see in the flickering light from the lantern the sailor was holding on a pole above his head. The sailor waved his arm around the cramped quarters, pointing to a few open barrels. He pulled out some trinkets from one and handed them to Tisquantum. Then, with a wave of his arm, he encouraged the men to dig through the barrel for themselves.

"Quick, now, lads. Bring down the ropes. They won't be distracted for long, and they look to be strong." A dozen hefty men, each with lengths of rope coiled around his neck, descended the ladder in seconds. They had ropes around the Natives' arms and upper torsos before they could react. Though they kicked and yelled, they were no match for seasoned sailors who shoved the men onto the floor and left them to prepare for sailing.

"We are betrayed!" howled Tisquantum in Algonquian. Nothing in his thirty-odd years prepared him or his companions for this. They strained against the ropes, but were helpless against the treachery of these men.

"Where are we going? What will happen to us?" called one.

"We may never see home again. They will take us with them. We must stick together and try to find a way out," said another.

Escape was impossible. It was dark. The hold stank with the smell of dried fish mingled with rotting food. Soon, the ship started to rock back and forth, up and down. The kidnapped men bumped into one another. With their arms tied to their chests, they were helpless against the pitching of the ship.

Tisquantum couldn't tell how much time passed, but he knew it had to have been many hours. The ship was still rocking. He thought about people searching for them. *They will search until they are too exhausted to take another step. Then what will happen? Will there be revenge? Will I ever see my home again?*

THE ATLANTIC OCEAN AND SPAIN – 1614

Bright sunshine flooding through the open hatch door nearly blinded the captives. Three crewmen climbed down into the hold. They carried pots, yelling out orders Tisquantum and the others could not understand. They got the message though when one of the crewmen started kicking at the man closest to Tisquantum.

"Move, you savage beast!" The man scooted back as far away from the crewman as he could. Soon, all three crewmen were kicking the terrified Natives until they huddled together in a tight group against one side of the ship. When they were as far back as they could get, one of the crewmen tossed an empty pot at their feet. He grabbed at his groin and pointed to the pot.

The Natives understood. They weren't leaving the hold. The pot was their best option for answering calls of nature. Another crewman swung another pot back and forth in front of them. He set it down and pretended to take something out of it to put in his mouth. Tisquantum scooted toward it to examine the contents. It looked like some kind of meat. Two crewmen stood glaring at the Natives with swords gleaming in the sunlight that streamed through the open door of the hold.

A third sailor motioned for Tisquantum to come closer. As he approached, the crewman cut away the ropes wound around his chest, grabbed his wrist, and pushed it down into the bucket. He growled, "Your dinner. Don't waste it."

One of the crew stood waving his sword back and forth in front the captives. He chimed in, "We barely git enough for ourselves, and now we gotta share what little we have with the likes of you. Master wants you alive when we get there."

One by one, the crew undid the ropes around the Natives' chests, replacing them with long ropes around their waists and securing them to poles that ran up through the deck.

Two guards waved their swords so they clashed and made loud, clinking sounds. Keeping their eyes on the prisoners, they backed up to the ladder. After the third one climbed it, they quickly closed the hatch with a thud.

In the nearly dark hold, the Natives heard a scraping sound that signaled they were once again locked in. Small slits in the sides of the ship near the deck above them provided barely enough light to find the food pot. They emptied it in less than five minutes.

Things continued in this way, one monotonous day after another, until the captives had no idea how long they'd been imprisoned. Once a day, the scraping noise indicating another visit was imminent, then a burst of daylight would flood through the opening and a crewman would toss down an empty pot. Later, another unfortunate sailor would come down to take away the full pot and toss the contents overboard.

The captives shared a daily allotment of salted meat, hard cheese, and occasionally hunks of bread so hard it was a wonder they didn't break their teeth trying to chew it.

The back-and-forth pitching never let up. Occasionally, it was so bad that they all had to find a pole to wrap their arms around to keep from flying into one another. Nights and days were so blended, it was hard to tell them apart.

Tisquantum joined in on the conversations with the others. "We outnumber them. We could take them."

"Perhaps. But what would we do when we did?"

"What do you mean? We would be free of their tyranny."

"We would be free to drown. We know nothing about a boat such as this."

"We could make them teach us."

In the end, it was all talk—something to do to pass the endless hours of tossing back and forth with no idea of how long this trip would last.

The journey ended six weeks after it started. One day, when the crew opened the hatch, ten men scurried down the ladder. Eight carried lengths of rope, and two came with guns. They went to Tisquantum first. Tisquantum turned and twisted, but he was no match for the two men. The rope dug into his wrists but he refused to cry out from the intense pain. The sailors quickly wrapped another rope around his waist and tied it so that it became a leash, tying the Natives together with ropes while the two men with guns pushed them toward the ladder. One by one, the crew led the men up the ladder. One went in front, pulling on the rope around a prisoner's waist while another pushed from behind.

"What is this?" cried out one of the Natives in Algonquin. "So many floating houses! So many people!"

Tisquantum listened carefully before speaking. "That's not the same tongue. These people look different from the others." He nodded his head toward the crewmen who were pulling them along the deck. They watched as other members of the crew scurried all over the ship. Six climbed high to release the sails so they dropped into piles. Four others lashed the sails tight with ropes. Six men, three on either side, hoisted a large wooden plank, inching it over the side until it rested on the dock. Four more tossed ropes as thick as a man's wrist across to the dock, where two more men wrapped them around poles.

Master Hunt appeared, walking up and down inspecting the Natives. "*Hmm.* The voyage didn't seem to do them harm," he said to no one in particular. "Take them off. Off to the auction house with them. Be quick about it."

Two men walked ahead and stood on the dock with guns aimed at the plank. Sailors pushed the first Native man in line onto the plank. Soon, all were standing on the dock.

People gawked at them as they were marched along then into a large brick building. Tisquantum kept his eyes on the ground in front him. Step by step. When all twenty-seven of the young braves were inside the building, one of Hunt's crewmen came down the line. One by one, he swiped his long sword across the ropes connecting the men. As each was released, a captor would push the man into a small space with bars forming one wall. It took four such cells to contain all of the men.

The accommodations were barely an improvement over the ship's hold, but here sunlight came through a barred opening about ten feet high. Trusting that Hunt's men couldn't understand them, the group began speaking in Algonquin. "What will they do with us?"

"Put us to work," answered one.

"Perhaps that is so," chimed in another. "If they meant to kill us, they could have easily done so already."

"I hear they sometimes take our people around and collect money to let people look at us," said another.

"Our Pau Wau says that sometimes they trade us to work for others," speculated Tisquantum.

Nothing happened to them for the rest of the day . . . or all the next day. The monotony was interrupted only when someone came along with meager rations of strange food they could not identify. Other than that, they were left to move about in the cramped cells as best they could while wondering about their fate.

CHAPTER THIRTY-TWO

SPAIN – 1614

Tisquantum woke up when one of his fellow jail mates bumped into him while turning over on the rotting straw that served as bedding. The acrid odor of urine caused him to wrinkle his nose. He rubbed his arms, which itched from the straw, and tried to stifle a sneeze. He could just make out the outline of the window, and heard birds chirping in the distance, announcing the arrival of a new day. *What will happen to us next? I miss the forests of home. What horrible place is this?*

He didn't have to wait long to find out. After a miserable meal of hard, dry bread and cheese, the guards took away six prisoners from an adjacent cell. Tisquantum couldn't see anything through the high window, but he could hear the commotion. A loud voice kept repeating words he couldn't understand. Then others would yell all at the same time. After several minutes, he heard one word he did recognize: "Sold!"

Sold? Are these strange people selling us? Tisquantum leapt to his feet and peered between the iron bars of the cell, which was only a few hands wider and longer than he was tall. With six men inside, there was barely room to move without stepping on someone. He turned to the others. "I have heard of such things. Sometimes, there are ways to escape."

The others looked at him in disbelief. "Do you know some magic that can melt these bars?"

"No, but I will not go with them to be treated like an animal. I will find a way." Before anyone could say more, two men with swords swinging at their waists took three more Natives from the cell. Again, Tisquantum heard the strange volley of words back and forth. And again, he heard the word "Sold!"

Tisquantum was contemplating various ways he might escape when three men approached and stopped in front of him. They looked even more peculiar to him than Master Hunt's men. These men wore long, brown robes that covered them from head to foot, leaving only their faces, hands, and toes exposed to reveal the same pale skin as the men on the ship. Even the backs and tops of their heads were covered with the same brown cloth. They wore ropes around their waists, and around their necks, each wore a shiny piece of metal dangling from a chain.

Unlike any of Hunt's men, these men smiled at Tisquantum and the others. One even extended his hand through the bars and tried to touch him, but Tisquantum backed away before he could. Though Tisquantum did not understand his words, he felt strangely comforted by the man's gentle tone. "Friend," he said, pointing to himself and the other two with him. Repeating the word "friend," he pointed to himself, then to Tisquantum and the other two braves still in the cell with him.

Tisquantum could not comprehend their words, but he sensed they did not intend harm. The one who had tried to touch Tisquantum spoke to the other two. "This is wrong. These men look ghastly. We must secure their freedom."

The other two nodded. One of them asked, "But how? We have so little money in the purse. It will be weeks—maybe months— before we will have wine ready to bring to market."

"I set aside a little in case of an emergency. Brother Samuel, I think we have enough to purchase the freedom of these three. They seem the youngest and healthiest of the lot. We cannot undo all the wrong in the world, but perhaps we can do our Lord's will for these few. Who knows what good our Lord Jesus may yet bring about from our modest effort." With that, he turned and stalked out of the building. The other two softly sang music the Natives had never heard before. Tisquantum found it soothing.

Eventually, the first man returned with two guards follow- ing him to unlock the door to the cell. The leader of the men in brown entered and again extended his hand to Tisquantum. With his other hand, he gently patted Tisquantum on the back of his shoulder. Tisquantum turned to look at his fellow cellmates. Their eyes revealed the same confusion he felt. The man in brown gently pushed Tisquantum forward, out into the open space between cells. "Friend, come," he kept repeating while indicating with his hand that he wanted the men to follow. They did.

When they were clear of the prison, the men in brown linked arms with the Natives and led them outside, taking them over to a cart full of colorful fruits and loaves of golden brown-crusted breads. One of the men reached inside his brown cloak to pull out a leather pouch. It contained some round metal objects. He handed these to the man on the other side of the cart. In exchange, he got as many pieces of fruit as he could hold.

Tisquantum bit into the orange the man in brown gave him, and its juice squirted him. He winced and made a face, making the men chuckle. One reached over to take it away, but Tisquantum was not about to let it go. One of the men in brown picked up another orange, pushed his thumb into it and tore away the orange skin before tossing the peelings on the ground. He pulled apart the pieces, popping them into his mouth and rubbing his stomach to pronounce them good.

Tisquantum imitated him. When he tasted the sweet pulp and juice, he smiled. Then he smiled more, telling his companions, "This is good. It's sweet. Try some."

One of them responded, "This is our best day since we trusted that traitor to go onboard his ship."

"Who are these men?" asked another.

"I do not know," said Tisquantum. "They appear to be friends, though." That night, they treated Tisquantum and his companions to more food—and wine. They showed them a room with water where they could wash themselves, and another room with beds covered with soft, straw-filled mattresses.

I like these strange men, thought Tisquantum. *They are kind.*

Tisquantum was fascinated with the way the morning light shone through the window. Something blocked his hand when he tried to reach through it. He was in the process of examining it when the leader of the men in brown entered the room. Nodding at Tisquantum, he said, "Good morning. I am Friar Francis. We will help you. Do you understand?"

Tisquantum did not understand, so he gave no response. The friar came closer, patted Tisquantum on the back, and continued, "Come with me. We will feed you. Then we will decide a path for you."

He speaks softly, like my mother and sisters. I can easily overcome him. This may be my chance. Maybe I can sneak onto one of those big boats and go back some way. Tisquantum stared at the man without speaking, but followed him out of the room. They descended steps and walked along a covered portico into a large room. Tisquantum quickly counted how many were at each table, and how many tables he saw. He guessed there must be fifty men sitting on long benches, each bending over a bowl and slowly eating the steamy contents with a wooden spoon. One man held something in his hands and stood at the end of the table. He looked at it and said words to the others that Tisquantum did not understand. *How strange are the ways of these people.*

Friar Francis led Tisquantum and his two companions to empty seats, where they found bowls on the table in front of them. Tisquantum cautiously dipped a sample the size of a walnut onto a spoon. It was hot, and smelled good. It tasted even better. As the Natives quickly gulped down the food, the three friars stood in the corner of the room, talking.

"Now that we have procured their freedom, what are we to do with them?" asked Brother Samuel. "I spoke with Abbot John. He forbids them to stay here. He fears their presence might draw danger to us. Master Hunt will not easily be persuaded to leave them alone for long, even though we did pay for them."

"Many are served well by their slaves," said Brother Andrew. "And fortunate indeed are those slaves who are likewise served well by their masters. Did not our dear Lord Jesus himself instruct masters and slaves on how to serve one another? But that Hunt is a cruel one. He treats them worse than strays begging for scraps in the market. Hunt could get a pretty purse for strong ones like these. He'll be prowling around soon enough looking for a way to steal them back and sell them again."

"I fear you are right, brother," said Brother Samuel. "But Brother Francis did what was necessary to save at least these three from Hunt's clutches. We must find a way to get them out of Spain. I worry their lives are in danger here. Ours may be, as well. If Hunt can increase the weight of his purse by capturing them, he'll not spare his sword to take them a second time. What does it matter to him how they suffer, as long as he prospers? He has chosen his master, and it appears not to be the One we serve."

Friar Francis scratched a spot on his cheek, then looked at the other two. "I believe I may have the answer. Do we not have cheeses and breads ready for market today?"

"Yes, that is so. How might that help?" asked Friar Andrew.

"We will hide these men in the wagon and cover them with straw and blankets. Then pile our breads on top and use the cheese wheels to hold down the blanket. We shall go back to the docks. Surely there will be ships ready to sail. We can offer their work to a master in exchange for passage away—anywhere away from Master Hunt. How rightly named is that monster of a man."

"But how are they to survive? No master I know of will keep them for long. Then what will be their fate? We have no more money to pay their way," said Friar Samuel. "Perhaps, in our good intent, we have only postponed their predicament."

"*Hmm,*" said Friar Francis, scratching his cheek again. "We shall have a few coins after we unload our cart. We must implore a master to let them work for their passage, and entrust a small purse to the master for his trouble. I have found that a few coins placed in the right palm accomplishes a great deal. If only we had some way to explain all of this to them. Poor lost souls. So far from home, and no way for us to talk with them."

Brothers Samuel and Andrew nodded. When they told Abbot John their plan, he reminded them they did know someone who could speak a little Algonquin. "Brother James went on a mission trip to the Americas twenty or so years ago. Though he is now weak in the eyes and limbs, his mind is still alert. Perhaps he can help us talk with these lads."

Brother James was dozing in a chair, a tattered Bible open on his lap. Brother Francis gently tapped the old man on the shoulder and explained their urgent need. The two headed toward the refectory, with Brother Francis trying to slow his gait to match the older man's shuffling pace. They found their Native guests gorging themselves. Brother Francis winced at the sight of them stuffing handfuls full of bread, cheese, and sausages into their mouths as fast as they could swallow. He tapped Tisquantum on the shoulder to get his attention and motioned for him to move over, asking Brother James to sit also.

Tisquantum complied, keeping his full attention on the food. Explaining the plan through the elderly friar made for tedious conversation since the young men were focused on food and the friar knew only basic words.

Finally, Tisquantum nodded and turn to his companions. Speaking rapidly and hoping Brother James couldn't follow Algonquin that well, he said, "They call that one 'Friar Francis,' and I do not know how they call the others. The old one speaks our language like one just learning to speak. He tells me they bought us from the sagamore of the floating house. He says they worry that the sagamore will hunt us and take us away again. They want to put us on another floating house and send us away. He tells me they will take us there today."

The others murmured. "Do you think it wise for us to do as they say?" asked one.

Tisquantum crossed his arms and looked around the room. "I do not know," he answered. "We are much stronger than these men, but we do not know where we are or what to do if we run now. I say we go with them and see what there is out there." He nodded his head toward the door that led to the courtyard.

Tisquantum turned to Brother James and, speaking as though to a two-year-old, said, "We go now. All done here." As he spoke, he pointed to his companions, then to the plates on the table. He pushed them away and stood up. The other two did the same.

Brother Francis motioned to Tisquantum and the others to follow him. Using various hand motions, and with a bit of transla-tion help from Brother James, Brother Francis convinced the three to follow him into the courtyard, where someone had brought in an open wooden wagon. He gave each Native man a brown tunic and showed them how to put it on. He indicated they should lie down on the wagon floor. When they did, he covered them with several more tunics and a couple of blankets before pitching straw over them. Next, the friars placed a wheel of cheese on top of each man and covered it all with more straw. The friars carefully stacked dozens of freshly-baked breads around the cheese. The fri-ars stepped back to survey their work. Brother Francis nodded his approval. Brothers Samuel and Andrew smiled. This part of their adventure was complete.

Tisquantum was startled when the wagon started moving. *This feels much like being in the floating house.* "Perhaps these men will betray us, as well," he said, loudly enough to be heard over the clatter of wagon wheels on the cobbled pavement.

One of the others called out, "I think not. I sense they mean to be friends."

"We thought that before, when the light-skinned men showed us their knives and the things that reflect like a still brook."

"I do not see that we have any choice but to go and see what happens next," the other responded.

Tisquantum grunted. "I am going. But I am not liking it."

When the wagon finally stopped, the smell of salt water, fish, and sweat filled their nostrils. Tisquantum cautiously moved the tunics and straw away, just enough to raise his head and survey their surroundings. He could see very little, but heard the commotion of dozens of voices all calling out strange words all at the same time. Friar Andrew pulled back the tunic covering Tisquantum, brushing away the straw until he was half-exposed to the brisk morning air. He put his right forefinger against his mouth, whispering, "*Shh.*"

Friar Andrew looked all around to confirm no one was paying any heed to them, then motioned for Friars Francis and Samuel to help. The Native men climbed out of the wagon, adjusting the tunics so only their faces and hands showed, and began walking among the many people milling around the crowded market.

Friar Francis walked away, leaving the others to unload the wagon. One by one they carried large wheels of cheese and baskets full of beautiful loaves of fresh bread to a nearby stall. The man at the stall pulled out a book, wrote something in it, then counted the wheels of cheese, then wrote in his book again. He also counted each loaf of bread, and by the time he was done counting and writing, Friar Francis had returned.

Friar Francis reviewed what the man had written. "You have done well to be honest with men who live only to serve our Lord. That bodes well for you."

"I would be afraid to cheat men of the cloth such as you." He pulled out a leather pouch and handed a day's worth of wages to Brother Francis. The coins clinked as Francis dropped them into his own leather pouch.

Friar Francis waved for the others to follow. They stopped in front of an enormous galleon bobbing gently alongside the dock. Tisquantum glared at it. He looked stern to aft, then craned his neck to see the tops of the bare masts. His friends did the same. "This is what we just left. I will not go on one of their big boats again without a fight this time." Without realizing it, Tisquantum began to rub his wrists where the marks from the rope still showed.

Friar Francis put up his hand to indicate that they should wait where they stood, and walked ahead to approach a squat man looking over a ledger of some sort. The odor he emitted suggested he'd probably last bathed or changed clothes several months ago. He snarled a greeting at Francis, revealing a mouth several teeth short of a full set. Tisquantum understood only a couple of words as they spoke: "England" and "Master James." The man growled more than he talked and seemed to spit out his words.

Francis nodded, pointed to the Natives, and said, "Good workers," while making shoveling motions. Master James narrowed his eyes and stared at the Natives. He looked up at his ship and back at the Natives before turning to one of his sailors. "We could bloody well use the help," he said to no one in particular. The crusty shipmaster turned back to Francis, and the two men shook hands. Francis opened his pouch and pulled out a handful of coins. Master James counted the coins, then shoved them into his pocket.

Tisquantum's stomach did flip-flops. He was scarcely breathing. Every muscle was tight as a drum. He was about to make a run for it when Francis slowly walked up to him and put one hand on each shoulder. *I could easily push him away and run—but where? I see no forest where there might be animals to hunt. I have no arrows. I see no gardens.* He heard the friar speaking slowly, carefully enunciating each syllable. It all sounded like so much noise to him. The one word he did recognize was "friend." The friar was pointing to the squat, foul-smelling man as he said it. Tisquantum was confused. *I should run while I can, but this man has been kind to us. He got us out of that stinky place. He gives us good food to eat. He gave us these strange things to wear. He has kindness in his eyes.*

Before Tisquantum could decide whether to run or stay, the friar stood in front of him with three of his right-hand fingers extended. He made an up-and-down and side-to-side motion in front of Tisquantum, and then the others. Tisquantum had seen other pale ones do this.

The friar placed one hand on Tisquantum's shoulder and made the same motion with this thumb on his forehead. Though it felt very strange, Tisquantum found it strangely comforting. He watched as the friar did the same for his two companions. He then indicated they should take off their tunics. As they did so, Master James approached carrying three outfits like the ones his sailors wore. Friar Francis imitated putting on the new clothes.

Still unsure, Tisquantum put on the strange sailor clothes over what little clothing of his own he was still wearing. "Let us do this, and see what happens next. If we must run, we have a better chance looking like them."

After Tisquantum and his friends were dressed like the sailors, Friar Francis looked up at the sky, then back at Tisquantum. "God bless you, my son," he said. With that, he motioned for Friars Andrew and Samuel to follow him. The three walked briskly away from the dock.

※

The short man pointed to the gangplank of the ship and yelled for two of his men to come to him. "Take them aboard. Be easy with them. The friar said they just got off Hunt's ship. Show them where they'll sleep. Give them something to eat, something that'll warm their innards. And drink. That should calm them a bit," he said, and winked. "Then ready the ship for sailing."

On board, Tisquantum and the other two looked around. "We can run fast, but what good does it do us if we have no idea where we should run?"

The other man chimed in, "The men in brown treated us well. Perhaps we should trust them. I say we go and see what happens next."

"I will go," decided Tisquantum. "But I will kill anyone who tries to put a rope on me again."

With no idea where they were going or who they were traveling with, Tisquantum and his two companions sailed away to an unknown destination and future.

CHAPTER THIRTY-THREE

LONDON – 1614

As the *Leicester* sailed along the Thames, Tisquantum and his companions stood on the deck gawking. Though the sailors had eventually begrudgingly accepted their brown-skinned, muscular passengers, they did not trust them or want their help with the intricate maneuvers needed to guide the merchant ship safely to the dock.

With nothing else to do, Tisquantum and his companions took turns pointing and commenting on what they passed. Wooden buildings huddled together along the shore with nary enough space between them for a stray cat to pass, some large enough to house several ships the size of the *Leicester*.

"Home at last," yelled one of the crew. "Weren't she made in that place over there?" he asked the master.

"That she was. Warms the cockles of my heart to see that sight again. No place like home, is there, fellas? Be quick about getting her tied properly."

Tisquantum spotted a man tied to a post on the far side of the river with water up to his waist. Tisquantum pointed and yelled, "He will drown! Someone help the poor man!"

He grabbed one of the crew and pulled him over to the rail, pointing to the scene. The sailor nodded, grunted, and went back to his task.

Tisquantum turned in shocked dismay, "What kind of monsters live here to do such a thing? Have they brought us all this way to do the same to us?" he shuddered and looked away. The crew didn't seem to notice as they called out back and forth and the captain inspected their work.

Though it was a sunny afternoon in London, Tisquantum felt a chill come over him. Not knowing what to expect next, his anxiety spiked. *If they care so little for their own people, how much less must they care about us?* "Maybe this is where we run away," he said to his companions.

"Do we have more here than we did all the other times you thought that?" challenged one of his companions. "We still have no way to ask for food or find shelter. We would do better to wait and see what happens. If they wanted to kill us, they could have dumped us into the sea long ago."

Tisquantum reluctantly agreed they really didn't have much choice. "I will wait, but I am ready to fight."

"Me too," agreed one of his companions. "So far, they have treated us better than that first bunch. Look, we have clothes— strange as they are—to warm us."

"And firewater. It burns, but it makes me warm," said the other companion, rubbing his stomach.

"I know some of their words," said Tisquantum. "We need to learn more soon. Then we can find our way when we get the chance." By listening carefully and asking once in a while, they had gradually picked up a few basic English words such as "ale," "bowl," and "spoon." The crew made sport of teaching them earthier words, howling with laughter when they repeated them, having no idea what they meant. Their English tongues struggled to say Tisquantum's name, so they renamed him Squanto.

Squanto is not my name, but at least they bother to speak to us. More than the other men did. All they did was yell and shove.

One of the sailors waved to Tisquantum and his companions to follow him. Soon, the three were standing on the dock, watching the sailors move back and forth with heavy barrels balanced on their backs. Tisquantum watched, feeling utterly lost and confused. His borrowed clothes were too big and felt strange compared to the simpler attire he usually wore.

It was colder here than where the men in brown had arranged for the voyage. Every sight, smell, and sound reminded him of just how far away he was from home, and how much danger he might yet face.

Tisquantum kept checking his shoulder to adjust the bow and quiver that weren't there. The harbor was full of ship masts, so full he couldn't see the sun, and thus had no sense of direction.

Tisquantum turned when he heard Master James call out to a middle-aged man walking toward them. "Hello, Mr. Slaney. Good to see you. Out inspecting your ships today, are you?"

John Slaney waved at James and came closer. He stared at Tisquantum and the others. "What have you brought this time, Master James? They look like that Indian woman Master Smith was showing around the other day. Where'd these odd fellows come from?" As he spoke, Slaney stared at their bronze skin, and long, silky black hair. "Why are they with you?"

"Sir, I bid you not be angry. Some friars in Malaga offered me a pretty purse to give them safe passage. They said that snake Thomas Hunt beat 'em and pitched 'em into the hold of his ship—these three and two dozen more. Them and a load of dried cod. Eager to sell it all in Malaga, he was."

Slaney nodded. "Master Smith told me Hunt decided to fatten his purse selling a bit of human flesh along with fish. That man is a greedy one."

"That he is. Guess the friars paid for these few. 'Spose they thought to save their souls I reckon, but none of them speak more than a word or two of Spanish—or English, for that matter. They put these three to me to bring here. Don't know what's to become of 'em. No family here. Don't speak our tongue. Know nothing about a place like London, that's for sure."

"That Hunt will be the ruin of us all," muttered Slaney. "What little progress we make establishing trade in the New World, he undoes with his reckless greed."

"Aye, sir. These three were a bit of help to me and my crew, when we could make them understand what was what, that is. They were willing to learn, I'll give 'em that. Didn't know nothing about rigging and sails, but they carved up fish better'n anyone I ever saw. What now? I can't keep 'em. I can hardly keep my own crew working between runs to Spain."

Slaney rubbed his palms together and studied the foreigners again. He slowly made a circle around the three of them, huddled together and standing as stiff as statues. "*Hmm.* Well, I can take one of them home to help there. I shall speak with a friend or two about taking the others. Do they have their own clothes? Likely I could earn some of their keep letting others take a gander at them, were they dressed the same as in America."

"None I've seen. The friars brought them to me in tunics. Figured they were trying to hide 'em in case Hunt came 'round looking for his lost 'cargo.' I gave 'em some of the crew's clothing."

"Ah, well. So be it. I shall find a way to get them settled. Now, back to work with you to unload my cargo. Be quick about it. The sun will not shine much longer on our labors this day."

※

Slaney led Tisquantum away who was craning his neck to keep his friends in view as long as possible, but they were soon out of sight. Icy fingers of fear curled around and within him as he watched his friends being led away by other men. He wanted to know where they were taking them, but lacked sufficient English to ask. Slaney kept a firm grip on Tisquantum's upper arm, but spoke gently. Nonetheless, Tisquantum tried to pull away. Slaney smiled and pointed to an open carriage pulled by a horse.

Slaney gently but firmly led the reluctant man to the carriage. He climbed up himself, then turned to offer Tisquantum a hand up, before picking up the reins and snapping them on the horse's rump. Where they were off to, only God and Slaney knew.

Tisquantum sat with his back erect, hands stiff on his lap and his gaze fixed firmly ahead. Slaney's tone was kind and reassuring, though Tisquantum understood none of his words. As the dock disappeared from view, Tisquantum began to relax a little.

"You will live in my home. Bit by bit, you will learn our ways. My wife and staff will tend to your needs. We will teach you how to do tasks. You will help us, and we will provide for you. My people travel often to your land. I know some of your ways. Soon, you will know some of ours. All shall be well. My wife and I are God-fearing Christians. We are compelled by our Lord to aid those in need. Indeed, you appear to be in great need this day."

※

Never an hour passed that Tisquantum did not wonder what was happening back home. He saw letters come and go from the house with words that had the strangest effect on those who looked at them. Some of these resulted in laughter, some in tears, some in angry outbursts. It was all very strange.

After he'd been with the Slaney family for several months, Mrs. Slaney handed him a slip of paper. By now, he understood enough English to follow her instructions. "Take this to the dock. Ask for Master James. Deliver the letter to him. Wait for his response. Do you understand?" Tisquantum nodded his head. "You will need to take this sack with you, and Master James will put what I need in it. Then you are to come directly back here. Understand?"

Tisquantum nodded. He understood the word "understand." He heard it many times each day. He sensed these people respected him. That didn't make him long for home any less, but at least he wasn't tied up, ate on a regular basis, and slept in a place that didn't pitch back and forth all night. After all that had happened before, being here wasn't so bad.

Occasionally, when one of the Slaneys or one of their servants took him into the city, he spotted others who looked like him. They never gave him a chance to speak with any of them. He never saw the men kidnapped with him and still considered running away to search for them. But since he had no idea how he could accomplish such a thing, he stayed. As long as he received food on a regular basis, staying seemed the better option.

Tisquantum was pleased that Mrs. Slaney trusted him to venture out into the streets of London by himself for an afternoon. It was so different from the woods and brooks where he used to wander, free to go as he pleased. The warmth of the sun on his face and chest and the sound of birds overhead gave him some sense of normalcy.

He was so focused on all the strange surroundings that he didn't notice people staring at his brown skin and the long braid trailing down his back. He was almost back to Slaney's Cornhill neighborhood when he heard horrible screaming nearby. As he followed the sound, acrid smoke filled his nostrils. People were rushing toward the screaming.

Tisquantum rounded the corner and stopped abruptly, gagging and nearly vomiting. The crowd was jeering at a poor fellow tied to a stake, screaming and howling as fire licked up his legs and torso. The desperate man strained against the ropes that bound him, but it was useless. His screams filled the air. Tisquantum hurried back the way he'd come, trying to erase the image, but couldn't. The memory of the man tied to the pier flashed before him. *These pale ones deal harshly with any who displease them.*

He was still trying, unsuccessfully, to shake the sight and sound when he reached the Slaney home two hours later. Slaney had just come home from a day of bargaining and planning for his next business venture. As treasurer of the Newfoundland Company, his days were filled with paperwork and arrangements for upcoming trading expeditions.

"Well, Squanto, I have news to share. Today, I have procured the services of a tutor for the children. You will sit with them as they do their lessons. It will be beneficial for both of us for you to increase your understanding of our language."

Though Slaney spoke slowly and deliberately, pointing to himself and Tisquantum and then to the open pages of a book, Tisquantum did not understand. Nonetheless, when Slaney finished with, "Understand?" Tisquantum dutifully nodded that he did.

His life in London settled into a routine. Early the morning he reported to the kitchen to learn what tasks he might do that day. The family sometimes expected him to join them for morning devotions and prayer, though he hardly understood what they did or said. Some days he sat for an hour or two with the tutor and Slaney children, Edward and Abigail. Abigail participated during lessons in penmanship and reading, but then left to learn the requisite feminine skills of running a household. Tisquantum preferred the days when he too was dismissed to do some chore for one of the family.

After the noon meal, Mr. Slaney sometimes invited Tisquantum to go along for his rounds of meetings with other merchants and investors. He heard the names of places near and dear to him, but the businessmen never included him in their conversations.

Chapter Thirty-Four

London – 1615

Tisquantum's command of English grew at the rate of dozens of new words each day. Slaney's wife and children made a game of teaching him new words. In turn, Tisquantum taught them a few words of Algonquin. He learned English much faster than they learned Algonquin; but then, they didn't have to speak his language, and he had to learn theirs to function in this strange place.

Tisquantum especially enjoyed watching the process of meal preparation in the kitchen. It was so different from the way his mother and sisters prepared meals. The first difference he noticed was that here they left the house with empty baskets and came back with bread, meat, vegetables, and fruit, though he saw no garden anywhere, and never saw the men take bows and arrows to hunt. He never saw a whole carcass, only a shoulder or a leg. They looked different from the deer and fowls he used to bring home. The meat tasted different too: not bad, but not familiar.

Tisquantum longed for his people, and for the woods and fields of his homeland. He walked the streets of London, always searching for the faces of his companions—or anyone who looked like him. He never saw his lost companions and rarely anyone who looked like him. At least these people treated him decently. He slept in a tiny room at the top of the house, and usually ate alone at a small table in the kitchen, or with the servants after the family finished their meal. He preferred the company of the servants and felt more at ease with them than with Slaney and his family.

The servants were kind enough, but it was obvious they'd never really befriend him. *They talk openly as if they think I cannot understand them. I'm glad they think that. I learn more this way.* After nearly a year in the Slaney household, Tisquantum understood far more than he let on. He nodded whenever Mrs. Slaney asked if he understood what she wanted. This occasionally caused him trouble when he did not, in fact, understand.

Mrs. Slaney generally laughed, but he found nothing humorous about the language barrier. *She thinks I should know what she says when she does not bother to learn any of my words. She treats me like one of her children. I'd like to see how long she'd survive in my land. All of them would starve, or be devoured by wolves.*

Thinking about wolves stirred another wave of longing. He hadn't seen one since the kidnapping. Indeed, he rarely saw any familiar animals here. *I am expected to know all about their culture while they care nothing about mine except to stare and mock it.*

The next day was sunny with a warm spring breeze, which caused everyone to feel energized and alert. Mrs. Slaney sent Tisquantum with a written list. "Your English gets better each day, but this way, we won't have a repeat of yesterday's mistake," she said, smiling and handing him the basket. He took it, but said nothing.

On the way to market, he thought, *I am weary of this. I must find some way out of here.* The warmth of the afternoon sun, combined with the sounds of busy city streets, cheered him some. He was glad to be away from the house, if only for an afternoon. Again, he searched the faces pressing all around him, longing to see one that looked like his own, but saw none. A twinge of anguish came over him. He let his mind wander back to two years earlier, when he had roamed along clear, babbling brooks through sunlit woods. He could recall every detail of the fateful afternoon when he and his companions spotted the hairy-faced men at the edge of their woods.

He tried not to remember. It was still painful. But remember he did: long weeks in the dark belly of the ship. His stomach crying for food. Nearly gagging from the stench of the mixture of human waste and the salted fish packed in barrels. He remembered tipping from side to side whenever he tried to stand up in the cramped quarters. The memories set off a wave of nausea; the intensity of it startled him. *No! I will not think on that. Maybe today I will see the others. I fear they have not fared as well as I have. I long to know. But I do not know where they are.*

A scream brought Tisquantum's memories to an abrupt halt. He stopped to listen. Someone behind him bumped into him and cursed. "Out of my way, you barbaric heathen. What right do you have to be out here?"

Tisquantum took several steps to his right and waited. The man kept walking. Tisquantum leaned against the wall of a shop and tried to determine the source of the screaming. Screams kept coming, one on top of the other, each louder than the previous one. Someone was in very great trouble. He knew he could do nothing about it, but as if caught in a riptide, he was drawn toward the sound. He saw a crowd walking that direction and followed. He still couldn't see anything, but heard someone's screams mingled now with the sound of people cheering and clapping.

He slowly worked his way around the crowd until he could see. What he saw made his blood turn cold. The crowd was cheering because a man was being torn to pieces by ropes tied to his arms and legs. Each rope was tied to the saddle of a horse. Four men sat on four horses. Another man counted, "One, two, three, pull!" The men prodded their mounts forward, pulling the poor man's limbs from their sockets. Then the riders backed their horses a few steps, dropping the tortured man to the ground.

Tisquantum quickly made his way to a narrow passage between two buildings. Out of sight of the crowd, he gagged and spilled the contents of his stomach. He wiped his mouth with the back of his hand, then spotted weeds growing in the crack between the building and the cobblestone street. He pulled some out and began chewing on them.

After a few minutes, he felt a little better. He didn't hear the screaming anymore. The poor man was probably dead, or dragged off to jail. He'd heard of such things. The servants seemed to delight in recounting stories of men, even women and children, caught worshipping the wrong way and paying mightily for it. He didn't understand any of it, but had learned to hide his shock and disgust when they spoke of these things. He didn't want them to suspect how much he understood of what they said. If they suspected, they might not talk so openly in front of him. He didn't want to become even more isolated.

The crowd was breaking up and moving on with their afternoon affairs. Tisquantum pushed his back against the cool, shaded stone of one of the buildings and waited. He understood enough to be terrified by what these strangers were saying.

"Serves the heretic right!" said a man in a green overcoat and high hat. "We don't need none of those heretics going against Her Majesty. Burn in hell, I say."

"Bloody right," agreed the man walking beside him. "First the bloody Catholics, and now these confounded Brownists. The country cannot be rid of them fast enough, if you ask me."

Tisquantum could tell from their tone of voice they approved of what he'd just seen. *How is it they fight about how to worship? Because of their god? How strange. We learn about our Creator from our elders. When we are ready, they teach us. These people seem lost. The men who sent us here showed us kindness and friendship. But here I see so much cruelty. I wonder why.*

If only there was someone to explain the strange ways of these people. He knew not one person he trusted, and besides, he didn't yet speak their language well enough to ask such questions. *To hear my own tongue again. To hear Pau Wau sing his chants, and ask Manitoo for blessings. These people do not seem to know the land is sacred. They do not seem to know the land is our mother, the source of all life. They are foolish.*

The breeze picked up, and the spring sun moved behind a cloud. An involuntary shiver ended his reminiscing. He finished the errands and returned to the safety of the Slaney home.

"You look ill, Squanto. Are you feeling sickly?" inquired Mrs. Slaney when he put down his basket on the worktable in the kitchen. He nodded. He didn't really feel sick, just shaken and shocked by what he'd seen—but he relished the thought of being alone in his little attic room.

"I'll have one of the servants make you some hot tea. A good cup of strong tea always helps bring an end to troubles. That's what my mother taught me. Go to your quarters, and I'll have it sent up to you shortly."

Tisquantum was grateful to be alone for the remainder of the afternoon. Again, his thoughts turned to his village across the sea. *Tea. What these light-skinned people drink is nothing like what we have. I miss the pine-needle brew my mother made for me when I was little—or, if I really was sick, her flag root drink. She seemed to think that could cure anything.*

Tisquantum daydreamed the hours away until his stomach reminded him it was past time for an evening meal. That evening he sat alone in the kitchen, eating what the Slaneys and their servants had not finished from their own meals. The Slaneys sat at another table, sipping tea and sharing the stories of the day. The servants were busy scrubbing the heavy cast iron cookware and dinner dishes. From his perch, Tisquantum could hear the Slaneys without being seen. John Slaney was recapping the day.

"I do not know what is to become of this country. I will remain loyal to the Established Church of England, but surely it cannot be God's will that those who wish to worship in another way should be slaughtered and tortured. In public, yet, with the crowds cheering. Browne is to blame. Even though he realized the sins of his ways, we are still paying for the problems he stirred up with his nonsense."

His wife nodded in agreement and turned to the children. "Listen, now, to what your father tells you. You must be very careful. Listen carefully, and refrain from speaking to others unless you are invited to do so. Then answer only as you are asked, and do not add ideas of your own. It is impertinent for children to talk of things they do not fully comprehend. They arrest even those with as few years as you possess."

Slaney continued, "I do think it foolish the way some so boldly disregard the ancient traditions of the church, though I admire their commitment. I surely would not risk a flogging or worse for the chance to disregard ancient traditions. The bishops and their armies delight in arresting and torturing those turned in by searchers and enforcers."

"You are right about that Robert Browne, John. The priest was saying the same thing last Sunday when you were away. He asked how the man could publish such nonsense. He said so many hundreds, perhaps thousands, have had their minds poisoned by his foolishness. He told us the Separatists, or Brownists, or whatever name they call themselves, hide their sinning away in attics and barns out of town. If they are so sure they are right, why must they hide?"

"Why, indeed? It was bad enough when Queen Elizabeth sat on the throne, but King James shows none of the leniency she did.

I suppose when something takes place like what happened this very afternoon, not a ten-minute stroll from our own home, they fear for their lives. It's a terrible thing to be ripped from limb to limb for not worshipping in the one right and true church."

Neither spoke for a moment. When Edward and Abigail could contain their youthful energy no longer, Mrs. Slaney looked at them as if seeing them for the first time. "John, dear, perhaps it is time for our evening devotion, and to release the children for their evening rituals."

John stood and retrieved a well-worn copy of the *King James Book of Acts*. "Edward, where did we leave off last evening?"

"Chapter Thirteen, Father."

"Good. Here, son, you may read this evening. Read slowly, now, and loudly, so perhaps the word of God may penetrate the ears and hearts of those at work in the kitchen even now."

Edward took the book from his father and gingerly turned page by page until he found the portion he was seeking. "The same thing occurred in Iconium, where Paul and Barnabas went into the Jewish synagogue and spoke in such a way that a great number of Jews and Greeks became believers. But the Jews stirred up the Gentiles, and poisoned their minds against the brothers."

"Well done, son. You may stop there. Poisoned minds. That is what we face. The people do not know the truth when they hear it. It is a sad thing. Guard your mind carefully, lest you, too, be led astray. Stay alert, and do not fall into the trap of heresy that lurks everywhere. Now, Edward, if you would lead us in prayer."

When he had finished with a confident "Amen!," he and Abigail were sent off with one of the servants to prepare for bed. That night, when she was sure no one was paying attention, Abigail tiptoed to the room next to hers and inched inside. By moonlight, she could see her brother's frame huddled under heavy layers of quilts. He heard her come in, and sat up on one elbow, waiting. She often came to him at night to discuss assorted preadolescent questions and concerns. She was allowed to learn only the most basic reading and writing, and hungered to learn more of what her brother was studying.

"Edward, I do not know what to think. Father says it is wrong to worship anywhere but the Established Church, but he seems also to think that the church of the king is wrong on some points, as well. And did not that church begin because King Henry opposed the Holy Catholic Church?"

"You ought not concern yourself with such matters, Abigail. Adults say and do strange things. As long as we do as Father commands, and he continues to do well in his trading with the Newfoundland Company, we will be well. Do not let your mind be poisoned with such matters. Soon, you will be thinking of what manner of husband you should like. Heed what Mother tells you. Observe her manner. That is what should occupy the mind of a young woman. Off to bed with you. I am worn out."

⁂

Tisquantum sat alone by the fading flames of the kitchen fireplace until the moon was high and the stars filled the sky. *What a strange land this is. How I wish I could return to the land of my own people.*

CHAPTER THIRTY-FIVE

LONDON – 1619

FROM where Tisquantum sat, he could overhear John Slaney talking with three business associates. One asked him, "How much trouble did that rascal Hunt stir up when he took your man and the others?"

"Plenty enough. Our men have to tread with great care to appease the Natives now, or they won't trade so much as a fish skeleton."

"But you still send ships?" asked another man.

Slaney nodded. "Of course. This has proven too lucrative to let one rotten scoundrel like Hunt shut it all down. But it is a challenge. None of them seem interested in learning any English. Then again, I do not think many of our men know much of their tongue, either. Makes trading a challenge, but we manage."

"Could it be true what Master John Smith reports about so many of them dying?"

"I do not know for sure, but there have been reports of coming to communities with nothing left in them but corpses rotting for lack of anyone to bury them. Makes our efforts both harder and easier," concluded Slaney.

"How so?"

"Harder because they have come to be rather suspicious of any of us. Afraid, I guess, that we might make them sick, but easier to assert ourselves and work out good deals. Desperate people do not tend to argue much. It sure would be better if we could find a way to talk to them in their own language. It is so tedious to try to work out a trade with pantomime."

I speak two languages! Maybe there is a way to get home, after all.

Later that evening, John Slaney sat alone in his study looking through a stack of papers. Tisquantum silently slipped in and stood before him. Startled, Slaney looked up. Tisquantum had never before dared to come into his study without first being summoned, and Slaney wasn't sure what to make of this. Before he could speak, Tisquantum cleared his throat and said, "I speak good English now, yes?"

"You do well enough."

"I can speak for your people to my people. I can help make good trade with my people."

Slaney stared at him for a long moment before speaking. "Are you telling me you want to go on a trading trip to America?"

"Yes. I know the land and the ways of our people. And because of you, I know the language of your people."

Slaney set aside the papers he'd been reviewing and stood up. "You aren't happy here?"

Tisquantum lied and said, "You very kind to me. I will repay you by helping." He thought, *How happy would you be if someone ripped you away from everything you ever knew, and took you so far away, there was no going back? And now, I hear many of my people are dying, and I don't know who lives and who has passed on. Of course I want to return to my own people!*

Slaney crossed his arms and considered what it might mean for his business to send Tisquantum back to America. "Would you want to stay there? Or return here?"

Tisquantum debated how best to respond. Finally, he said, "I can stay there and convince my people and your people to make good trades. Then I will be there when more people come to trade."

"We will try it. As it so happens, I am sending Thomas Dermer on a trading voyage in a few weeks. I will speak to him and see if he might be inclined to take you along."

In the spring of 1619, Tisquantum and Thomas Dermer finished their trade negotiations in Newfoundland. Thanks to Tisquantum's ability to interpret, the Newfoundland Trading Company efforts proved more productive than previous trips. After their trade negotiations, Tisquantum and Dermer sailed south along the coast in a small open boat. Tisquantum sat erect in his seat, staring intently at every detail of the shore as they passed by. *I never thought I would see my people again. I will be there soon!*

Dermer documented what they saw in a journal as they sailed past where Tisquantum had been kidnapped in 1614: *We passed by ancient plantations, not long since populated, but now utterly void; in other places, we saw remnants of remains, but no place free of sickness. When we arrived at Tisquantum's Native country, all were dead or gone.*

Tisquantum stared in disbelief. Bones bleached on the beach. Weeds where crops should be. Two thousand family, friends, elders, and children—all gone. He walked around where there had once been homes and fields growing the three sister staples of corn, squash, and beans. What was left of the wetus hung in tatters or lay on the ground. Waist-high weeds now covered the fields. Everywhere he looked, he saw more bones baking in the sun. He bent down to retrieve a basket and clutched it to his chest. He clenched and unclenched his fists several times, then beat them against a tree.

His cry was part moan, part primal howl. He marched toward a brook babbling along the backside of what had been his village. Dermer stood silently by, afraid to speak, equally afraid to leave the young man alone.

I will overcome, somehow. I will survive. I did not endure that long trip and serve in Slaney's house—and learn his language—to give up now.

He turned to Dermer, "I must go tell the Massasoit what I have seen. We must go to Nemasket. We will walk toward where the sun goes away," he said pointing west. "There people may tell us what happened to my village."

They arrived late the next afternoon. Tisquantum exclaimed, "You live!" when he discovered a few of his family escaped the plague. He told Dermer, "If they live, others must also. I must learn the fate of the Massasoit and other Pokanokets. We will go now to Sowams to see about the powerful Massasoit."

Dermer and Tisquantum borrowed a dugout canoe and recruited a couple of Native men from Nemasket to go with them. They walked and paddled their way to Massasoit Ousa Mequin's village. They found him and learned he struggled to resist his enemies after the loss of so many thousands of his people. In spite of the devastation from the recent epidemics, Massasoit Ousa

Mequin and his brother, Quadequina, had gathered fifty warriors still healthy and strong. They had as prisoners several Dutch sailors they'd taken hostage in retaliation for the English kidnapping of Tisquantum and the others.

Massasoit Ousa Mequin inspected Tisquantum and glared at Dermer. Tisquantum assured him, "He is safe. He brought me back home. I learned his language while I was away. I helped him trade, and then he brought me back to Patuxet, but now, the village is empty."

Massasoit Ousa Mequin nodded. "Many are dead. Too many to count. Too many to bury."

The Massasoit and Dermer worked out a trade. The Dutchmen for Tisquantum.

After Dermer left, Tisquantum told the great leader about his incredible adventure. "After many days in the bottom of their big floating house, we came to a place with hundreds of people, all shouting and pulling carts full of things to trade. They put us in a dark place. It smelled like piss and mold. They took a few of us out at a time, and those they took away never returned.

"One day, three men came to talk to us. They wore long brown coats with heavy chains around their necks. They talked to us about their god, a man they call Jesus."

Massasoit Ousa Mequin nodded. "I have heard of this god man. Did you live with these men?"

"No. They sent us many days away, where it was cold and dreary, like it is here in the story-telling time. A white man took me to his home."

"You lived with this white man?"

"I did many things for him and his family. He was kind to me, but he made me wear their funny clothes. I learned his language. I was careful to make no trouble. I did whatever he asked. Then I told this white man I could help him make good trades because I speak our language and now, I speak their language too."

Massasoit Ousa Mequin nodded. "Continue."

"He sent me back here with Thomas Dermer. First, we were many days from here, where the white men traded their kettles, knives, and blankets for beaver furs and fish. Then Dermer brought me to my village. On the way, we saw places littered with bones and corpses. Then we came to Patuxet."

Tisquantum's words caught in his throat, and his eyes grew moist. His throat constricted as if invisible hands were squeezing it. Massasoit Ousa Mequin waited in silence. Tisquantum was describing a common sight all up and down the coast. Nonetheless, it never failed to raise the hairs on the back of his neck whenever he heard about another deserted village.

After a long silence, Massasoit Ousa Mequin said, "Tell me about this strange god man they worship."

"The men who sent us far to the north, they told me about him, but I did not understand. When I was in London, I began to learn. They say their Great Spirit came to earth as one of us, as a man god. They say he came as a baby, and grew up. They say he did many wonderful things. He made people who could not see, see again. He made people who could not walk, walk again. They say that once, he took a few loaves of bread and a few fish and fed thousands of people. He was murdered by hanging on a cross. Then, they say, he was buried, but came back to life."

"Impossible!" interjected the Massasoit.

"Many of them believe this happened. They have dolls that they say are images of their Great Spirit/Man. They put these on crosses. They hang them everywhere."

The Massasoit shook his head. "That seems peculiar. What else?"

"They go into giant houses made of stone or wood. These have crosses that hang high in the air. Their giant houses have openings along the walls that are filled with colors that let the light shine through them. These make pictures about their Great Spirit/Man.

"When do they do this?"

"They go every seven days to sing and talk to their God. It is very strange, I know. But they believe what they say is true."

The following spring, another English ship sailed into Narragansett Bay. Now emboldened by how well Tisquantum had fared at the hands of the English, some Natives boarded the ship when the English sailors invited them to do so. Once they were on board, the English sailors shot them all dead.

A few months later Dermer traveled north again, and passed through Massasoit's region. When the great sachem learned that Dermer was in the area, he prepared to send warriors to catch him and kill him. "This is not wise, Great Sachem," Tisquantum advised. "This Dermer, he is a good man. He did not catch any of our people, and he brought me back across the sea."

The Massasoit backed off and let Tisquantum join Dermer, serving him as part guide and part interpreter. Epenow, the sachem on Aquinnah Island (modern-day Martha's Vineyard), held only contempt for all white men, considering them all enemies. He and his warriors attacked Dermer's party in the summer of 1620. Dermer and one other man managed to escape, but Epenow took Tisquantum prisoner.

That night, while feigning sleep on the far side of the camp, Tisquantum overheard Epenow talking with his warriors. "I do not trust Tisquantum. He is too close to the white men. He is more like them than our people. He can say he knows what the English say, and then tell us something different."

"You speak some of their language," pointed out one of his advisors.

"Yes, but I proved my loyalty. I chased Dermer out and killed most of his men."

"We know you are loyal," said one of the others.

"Tisquantum is sly," warned Epenow. "He takes the name of the dark spirit—the spirit of death—for his own name. How do we know Tisquantum is not the reason the Great Dying continues?"

※

The great Massasoit shared Epenow's concerns about Tisquantum. In the fall of 1620, Epenow sent Tisquantum away to the Massasoit's territory, once again a prisoner. From where they confined him, he could hear the gossip around the fire at night. One night, he heard them mention Dermer's name, and strained to hear what they were saying about him.

"He ran away from Epenow, but not before one of his warriors' arrows found him. He did not travel far before the wound killed him."

This realization made Tisquantum more determined than ever to get his freedom back. He listened much and spoke little, always looking for a chance to escape. *At least I am among my own people, even if I am not yet free to do as I please.*

CHAPTER THIRTY-SIX

POKANOKET NATION (RHODE ISLAND) – 1616-1619

"ANOTHER five have died since you left early this morning." The Pokanoket Saunka, Massasoit Ousa Mequin's wife, reported the daily death count. He'd been out all day, hoping for some new inspiration. Not until his stomach began to rumble did he notice the sun nearly touched the horizon. Reluctantly, he returned to the wetu. He clenched his teeth, gazed at her, and with a barely detectible nod sat down. *I am too weary to bear it. Our warriors, our mothers and grandmothers, our little children, all die before this faceless enemy. Arrows are useless against this enemy. They look to me for help. I have no hope to give.*

Drawing in a deep breath, he said, "Day after day, they fall from life to death like beads falling from a broken string. I will look for someone to help bury them." He turned and left the wetu, his shoulders drooping and his gate unsteady.

Massasoit Ousa Mequin was the most powerful man for as far as one could walk in two days. But now, his spirits sagged as all around him people perished. *Perhaps our enemies, the Narragansett, have a spell over this invisible enemy. The silent stalker does not take Canonicus's people. Our enemies think we are their servants. Before long, my people will be gone. Were it not for our friends among the Nauset, I would be in utter despair. Though we are now small, yet together we remain strong. They will see. We will conquer this invisible enemy, then we will conquer those who think they rule over us.*

Massasoit Ousa Mequin withdrew into the forest. He wanted to be alone with Great Spirit Manitoo. Could what others said about the Great Dying be true? After that Englishman took twenty-seven warriors, another English ship crashed on the Cape Cod shoals. *Then we were so many, no one could count our numbers. We only did to them as they did to us. Yet one of the white men said their god was angry at us for this and would punish us.*

⁂

Massasoit Ousa Mequin walked again before the sun peeked over the ocean. He hoped walking might chase away his worries. The chilly morning breeze across the beach helped him better focus his thoughts. As layers of bright pink and orange began to fill the sky, his thoughts turned to Tisquantum.

Tisquantum brings me nothing but disturbing news. He says hundreds lie dead in his village. No one left to even cover their bodies with a blanket of dirt to prepare them to travel for their eternal rest with Manitoo.

More and more of these hairy-faced people come with their peculiar clothes and strange tongue. Tisquantum says they are but a cup of water from the whole ocean. He has seen many more of them in giant villages—as many as the grains of sand beneath my feet. Why do they come here when they have so much there? Massasoit Ousa Mequin scanned the horizon and prayed to Manitoo for protection. Seeing no white men, he started back to his wetu. After walking and meditating for two hours, hunger overshadowed apprehensions. He'd left that morning while his wife still slept. They'd worked together to frame their wetu with saplings bent and lashed together to form their dome-shaped home. The open center allowed smoke from the fire to escape. The industrious woman spent hours weaving mats out of cattail reeds, which she then laced together to cover the saplings.

Massasoit Ousa Mequin noticed that some of the mats were loose, and made a mental note to remind her to repair them. The aroma of corn cakes frying made him glad he'd come home. The Saunka was heating them in a cast iron pan acquired via trade with some English in the North Country.

His wife looked up and smiled, but when she saw his countenance, her smile faded. "Something is troubling my husband this day. What is it?"

"I cannot say now. Let us eat. I see a place over there—near the entrance, where the mat is coming loose."

"I will tend to it before I return to the fields. Perhaps as you visit among our people today, you will find a deer or turkeys that I will prepare for our village." She said no more. It would be pointless trying to pull talk from him if he preferred not to speak. *The Great Dying has brought many deaths, and also a shortage of wise people to lead us. He bears many burdens.*

She glowed when others praised her husband for his leadership as the Massasoit of the Pokanoket. She considered herself fortunate it was her wetu he returned to each night. She once treasured their daily discussions about their people, but these days he sought solitude more than conversation. She saw the weight of the Great Dying on his face and in the slump of his shoulders, normally held straight and erect.

He would consult her—and even more so, some of the elders—before doing anything; but for now, perhaps the company of food and his own thoughts would give him a bit of peace. Solitude was hard to come by in their busy village. Lately he spoke less and seemed to worry more. She realized there was little she could do to ease his tension, yet it concerned her.

When Massasoit Ousa Mequin left again to hunt in the nearby woods, the Saunka ate her own meal from the pan and cleared away the dishes, debating what to do next. The list of tasks only grew longer . . . never shorter.

The people had built a dozen wetu houses in a circle. The late afternoon sun made long shadows in the open area within the circle. Massasoit Ousa Mequin led hundreds of villages in the Pokanoket lands. He often walked among the people, conferring with village Sachems and delighting in their stories. He listened carefully to the people's concerns and addressed their needs as best he could. He'd barely reached adulthood when he assumed his role as supreme leader from his father, Meika. He knew his people were loyal to him, as they were when his father was the Massasoit before him, and would be with one of his sons who followed him.

He could rely on his men to come to his aid quickly should there ever be trouble with the Narragansett, of this he was certain. However, he had no experience that prepared him to deal with the current troubles. He listened for the voices of his elders to guide him, but their voices were silent. He prayed to Manitoo, yet Manitoo was also silent. He had to be bold and brave—that he knew—but how could he fight against the Great Dying? Or against these white people with fire sticks? How? There had to be a way. He would find it.

PART THREE

Exile in Holland

CHAPTER THIRTY-SEVEN

ENGLAND – 1603

COURIER after courier, year after year, the news was relentless. Criticizing the Established Church grew increasingly dangerous. One protestor after another was executed as a traitor, died awaiting trial, or left the country. Enforcers, eager to collect a bounty and certain they carried out God's will, combed the countryside, hunting for people to arrest.

In late March 1603, a messenger galloped into Scrooby with the latest news. "She died. Last week. March 24."

Mary and William gasped in unison.

"Queen Elizabeth died, still wearing the sapphire ring the Earl of Essex had given her many years earlier. She continued to wear it, even after she had him executed last year." William invited the messenger to rest a spell, but he insisted he only needed a fresh horse. "I must get the news to James VI. He is now our king."

As the messenger rode off, Mary said, "Now, we must get used to calling him the sovereign, King James I of England. Long live the King!"

"Long live the King," agreed William. "At least he is Protestant. We can thank God for that."

A few months later, another courier announced England's new king had admired the Scrooby manor when passing on his way south to claim the throne. "Said this manor might make a suitable hunting lodge, he did," the courier said. "But then, when he looked closer, he said perhaps it required too much work to make it suitable for a king."

When William told Mary that, she looked around at the many things needing repairs. William chuckled and said, "I often lament the fact that I lack the funds to do the all that is necessary to keep the manor in good condition. Today, I am grateful for our lack of resources. Our lowly station in life may have preserved our home. It seems that once each generation, we are spared the avarice of others who see here a place of sport rather than a home for faithful subjects."

ENGLAND – 1604

Persecution of religious rebels increased under King James. Nearly every courier who stopped at the manor delivered further reports of people jailed or executed for worshipping anywhere other than in recognized congregations of the Established Church. One of the guest pastors at St. James chastised William with a stern warning that he endangered the souls of his children if he became involved with anyone who disobeyed so blatantly.

Any hopes life under King James would be peaceful were soon dashed. Clyfton's Babworth All Saints congregants lived with chronic concern about their future. In January 1604, the king held a conference with a delegation of Puritan leaders. They presented him the Millenary Petition, signed by a thousand Puritan clergy.

As Martin Luther had done in 1517 when he boldly posted his Ninety-five Theses for discussion, these Puritan pastors petitioned their king for changes they considered crucial. They believed the changes they proposed critical for the future of the Established Church and the country.

"No! I am the king, and the head of this church. And I say no .. . never! How dare you defy me! I made it clear last year the priests in my church must either accept the prescribed ceremonies and other restrictions, or, by God and the authority invested in me by Him, they will be discharged from their pulpits!"

"What we lost in cooperation, we gained in clarity," sighed one of the priests as they left the meeting. In the following months, three hundred English clergy either lost their posts or resigned before they could be removed.

William and Mary, stunned about the outcome of the Puritans' meeting with King James, nonetheless continued to go to Babworth. They also occasionally traveled across the yard to St.

James, but their neighbors began to hold less and less regard for them.

"Even mild-mannered John Robinson was removed from his pulpit at Norwich, near the North Sea northeast of Cambridge," William told Mary. "I hear tell he will join Clyfton in Babworth. I hear good reports about him. I look forward to getting acquainted."

England – 1606

The year 1606 was a pivotal one for the Brewsters. William, a middle-aged man of forty, and Mary, in her late thirties, continued to worship at All Saints. Pastors Clyfton and Robinson now served there together. One Sunday, William and Mary arrived to find clusters of people gathered outside. William could tell from their raised voices and hands waving this way and that that there was important news to be gleaned.

"That was too close. We can't continue to worship here," they overheard a friend saying. "Enforcers were prowling around here looking for Pastor Clyfton. They would surely have taken him away, and perhaps Robinson as well, if they had found them." Apparently while enforcers hunted in Babworth, the two pastors were away visiting their colleague, John Smyth, some twenty miles away in Gainsborough.

The enforcers left behind a message. "Your so-called 'Pastor' Clyfton is no longer the pastor of this church. All Saints is the king's, and this 'pastor' is no longer welcome here."

William spoke to Mary on the trip back to the manor. "I cannot let our faithful pastor and spiritual leader suffer for proclaiming the truth. We must help him."

"Could we not meet at the manor? We have plenty of room."

William chuckled. "Would that not be the height of irony? To have forbidden worship services in the manor owned by Bishop Edward Sandys? I rather like the humor of it. We may try that, though it could prove dangerous. We never know when a courier might arrive, perhaps even as we worship."

Some of the All Saints members decided to cast their lot with Pastor Smyth all the way to Gainsborough. Others joined with the renegade congregation gathering in Scrooby, right in the bishop's own manor. Pastor Clyfton continued as pastor. John Robinson assumed a role as teacher. The group named William their ruling elder. Soon, a hundred or more were gathering for worship each Sabbath at the manor. Among that crowd, William was much respected and trusted. However, some neighbors distrusted him and those who associated with him. They looked upon William and his friends with contempt for defying the Established Church.

⚛

On a crisp fall day later in 1606, Mary came to William with little Patience skipping beside her. She implored him to set aside his work to walk with them in the afternoon sun. William smiled. His heart always warmed when his little girl swirled around or brought him a bouquet of lily of the valleys from the woods or dandelions from the fields.

He put away his books and grinned. "What is it, my dear wife? Do you come to tell me you are with child again?"

Mary swept Patience into her arms and blushed. "I believe I am." This news did not elicit the same happy reaction as her two previous announcements.

"I would offer you more enthusiasm, and I will surely welcome another blessed child from God. But Mary, I am fearful for the safety of you and the children. Every day now, the unrest grows more intense. Nearly every courier brings more unwelcome news of arrests. The hunt for people who defy the king on these matters has reached us here."

"I know, William. I know. Yet I feel such love from those who gather around us now. Surely God is watching over us. Perhaps this new child is a sign that our Lord approves of our efforts to make his holy church more like that of the early apostles."

"*Hmm*. And so, my wife presumes to correct her husband. Perhaps you are right. You rightly remind me that we must have faith and trust. Fear of the Lord is the beginning of wisdom."

Five months later, they named their new little daughter Fear, a reminder that the fear of the Lord was their guiding principle. The king could send spies throughout his kingdom; they would place their faith in the Lord.

⚛

Mary was at market one day with infant Fear tucked in a shawl wrapped around both of them to keep the chilly late winter at bay. When she returned home, she told William of an overheard conversation.

"One man was speaking of you, saying you have a cheerful spirit, are very sociable, and pleasant.'"

"That is pleasing to my ears," said William.

"Indeed, and they are correct in their assessment. But then I also overheard someone say, 'How dare they worship across the road from the true church?' What if they arrest you, William? What would happen to us?"

Robinson and Bradford warned William that it was a matter of time before trouble came to them all. Robinson pointed out, "How can the authorities *not* do something when we meet at the manor house—the Bishop of York's manor house? You offer us such great love, but you put yourself and your family at risk."

Bradford added, "When we are found out, and I have no doubt we will be, you will lose your position for certain. You may be put in jail. Or, dear God above forbid it, executed. I have lost one father. I do not think I could bear it if I were to lose the one who has become like a father to me in the absence of my own."

Chapter Thirty-Eight

By the fall of 1607, tensions were tangible, the situation for William and Mary unbearable.

"Mary, you must surely know some of our neighbors have already been arrested," said William. "Others have fled to hide with friends or families away from here. The Catholics are blamed—I think rightly—for the failed attempt by Guy Fawkes to end the life of King James and his whole Parliament with him. Some of His Majesty's anger spills over on us."

"What shall we do? We are too far removed now from the ways of the Established Church to turn back. We are no longer welcome at St. James."

"I have been praying for a way forward. The only path I see is for us to do what Mary and Joseph did with the baby Jesus. We must leave."

"Is there anywhere in England where we would be safe?"

"Unfortunately, I do not think so. Some have already gone to Holland. They would welcome us, if we can get there."

"It is illegal for King James's English subjects to leave without his permission. How could we get permission from the one who is the reason we leave?"

William took a deep breath and let it out slowly as he combed his beard with his fingers. "We must leave illegally, as religious refugees. When the laws are unjust, we must either change them or disobey them. We cannot change this one, so we must choose obedience to Christ the King over obedience to an earthly king. I recently learned that our brethren in Gainsborough have gone to Holland with John Smyth. We would be welcome among them."

"Then we must ask friends we can trust to care for our things until we can—if we ever can—have them shipped to us."

"And I must resign as bailiff and postmaster."

By September 1607, William left the position he had worked so hard to maintain when his father died. His timing was good. On September 15, Enforcer William Blanchard was commissioned to find and arrest William Brewster, along with another member of the Scrooby congregation. Thanks to an advance warning, Blanchard failed to find either man.

Not to be deterred, another of the many enforcers prowling around the countryside rounded up someone else. "They took him to the Castle of York," Pastor Clyfton told those who had gathered to discuss their emigration plans.

"For what?" asked Bradford.

"Membership in a Brownist sect, and maintaining erroneous opinions and doctrine repugnant to the word of God. That's what they said."

When a younger member of the group looked puzzled, Clyfton explained, "We think of ourselves as separatists—from Corinthians where St. Paul admonished us to come out and be separate from those who defile God's word and mission. Some call us after Robert Browne, one of our early leaders. He returned to the Established Church after one of his closest colleagues was executed as a traitor. That likely explains his religious preferences."

Clyfton's news prompted the group to make preparations to leave as quickly and quietly as possible. They now numbered around a hundred men, women, and children, and were determined to leave together, so travel plans proved challenging. One of the members hired a shipmaster to sail the group to Holland, who sent instructions to meet him at River Haven, near Boston on England's east coast—some sixty miles from Scrooby. Mary sighed. *Perhaps I shall never see this home again. How am I to know what to take and what to leave.* William found her packing things into bags, adjusting the weight of each so that one of the children could carry it.

"We will have to leave most of this behind for others to enjoy. It is a long journey and we must not allow ourselves to be bogged down. The scriptures tell us, 'Better a little with the fear of the Lord than great wealth with turmoil.' The Lord will provide what we need as we make our way."

Mary's lower lip began to quiver. William put an arm around her shoulder. "Come, come, now, all will be well. You shall see." They made their way to River Haven and waited. When no ship appeared on the horizon, they assumed they had been deceived. The sun set. They slept in the open with their young children and few possessions.

The next afternoon a ship sailed into view, and they gratefully settled in on board. "What's he doing?" Bradford asked William in reference to another passenger.

"He's waving to someone, but it isn't one of our group."

"Those are enforcers!" exclaimed John Robinson.

"Oh, my Lord, we've been betrayed," groaned Clyfton as the enforcers drew close to the ship.

"The shipmaster must have tipped them off," said William under his breath. The men were already rowing out to the ship. Gone was their chance to escape, along with all the money they had gathered to pay for their passage. Children started crying. Their mothers gathered them close. William and Bradford started to reason with the enforcers, but they cared nothing about their plight, only about money: the reward they would collect for bringing in so many in one arrest.

The enforcers loaded everyone into small, open boats. "Let me see what you have there," said one to William.

"Only a few coins," William assured him.

The man scoffed. "We'll find out for ourselves." The enforcers searched everyone individually, even the women and children, groping as they looked for anything of value the passengers might have tried to hold back. When they'd taken everything of value, the enforcer in charge sent a messenger off to the privy council in London to determine what they should do with so many runaways.

The Separatists waited.

William whispered to Bradford, "I was once in awe of the majesty and magnificence of the court. Now I wait to learn our fate from those I once served with pride. How life does twist and turn on itself."

Bradford responded, "We have friends here in Boston. They see hope we cannot see for reforming the Established Church. Even so, they would treat us kindly. We disagree only on the correct course to bring about change."

The local magistrate decided to assign the runaways to lodging in Boston area homes rather than sending them back to Scrooby. The Scrooby refugees were detained for a month before the privy council's decision reached Boston. "Keep seven of the principle men in prison until a trial at the next court. Send the others back home."

William's name was called. He spoke softly to Mary before his captors could lead him away to jail. "You will go with God, and so will all the others. Do not be concerned for me. God will take care of me, as well. Now, go and be brave, for the sake of our children. Jonathan is nearly grown. He will help you. I shall pray for you without ceasing, as I implore you to do for me."

Mary put her arms around William, biting her lip to stave off tears. "I am grateful for our children, for they force me to be brave for their sake. But I don't know how I will bear it without you. I will find a way to free you and bring you home. With God as my witness, we will be together again soon."

She sucked in her breath and turned to her children as they led William and the others away. Patience screamed, tugging and pulling to break free from Mary's firm grip and run to her father. Mary placed the child's tiny seven-year-old hand in Jonathan's. "Whatever happens, do not let go of her hand."

Mary clutched baby Fear in her arms. With Jonathan right beside her, and having no other choice, she joined the others for the sixty-mile walk back to Scrooby. Tears streamed down her cheeks as they made their way. They returned home defeated refugees. Assuming they'd never see Scrooby again, they'd sold or given away everything they couldn't carry. Now they were dependent on the generosity of extended family and neighbors.

Chapter Thirty-Nine

Scrooby England – 1607

Mary heard a knock on the door at the home where she and the children were staying with a cousin. Being the closest, she answered it. She nearly dropped the candlestick she was carrying as the door swung wide open. There stood William, looking weary but grinning at her.

"Might you, perchance, have something to give a traveler who longs for food and drink?"

Mary wrapped her arms around him. "I was so worried. I feared I might never see you again."

"But you see me now, and I am well. I am rather tired from the long trip, but otherwise, I am quite fit. Now, where are my children?" After everyone had exchanged hugs and tears, the children went off, leaving William and Mary to talk.

"The people seem not to know what to think of us," Mary explained. "They have asked few questions, and pretend as though it is normal for dozens of us to disappear and then return—some without our husbands."

"I pray we shall never be separated again, dear Mary. That was truly the worst of it. I can tolerate jail. I can manage with less food. I do not fear for my own life, but you cannot know how I suffered, not knowing whether you were safe."

"I am well enough. There are those who assist us, whether they approve of us or not. But what happened to you? Was there a trial?"

"No. Apparently, there were others stirring up worse trouble closer to London. They left us to languish and wonder for a while. Then, one day, they opened the jail and told us to leave."

"How odd," said Mary.

"Yes, but how grateful I am to be with you now."

⁂

William was now a wanted man in Scrooby. The April after their failed attempt at departure, Patience ran into the house her family still shared with a cousin, out of breath from running so fast. "Father," she gasped. "Father!" The little girl was sobbing and gasping for air.

"What is it, Patience?" asked Mary. "Are you hurt? Did someone hurt you?"

Patience shook her head. "Father! Father! They said they would hang Father! They said Bishop Sandys would hurt Father."

William came into the room and swooped Patience into his arms. He stroked her hair and sang her a little song she loved. Then he told her, "Archbishop Sandys isn't going to hurt me." He continued stroking her hair and turned to Mary. "I have stirred the Archbishop's ire; I believe he's had quite enough of our anti-Established Church congregation. He sent a message just yesterday to me and two others from our group. He said we are being fined twenty pounds each for failing to appear before a lawfully set court appearance for the twenty-second of April. Actually, Mary, I believe he is doing the best he can to protect me. Others have certainly fared much worse. I think he goes tenderly out of respect for the many years of service my family has given him. He certainly has the authority to arrest me."

"Even so, William. Twenty pounds! They might as well fine you an entire year's wages, if there were any wages anymore. We're nearly as destitute as a chimney-sweep orphan in London." She plopped down at the table and rubbed her eyes.

William set Patience down, went over to Mary, and began stroking her hair. "We shall not have to find the money. While some of us were in jail, a few of our men who stayed behind in Boston found an honest shipmaster who will transport us."

⁂

They walked the forty miles to the meeting place. The next morning, the Dutch shipmaster spotted them just as they were arriving after their cross-country hike. He sent a small boat from the ship to bring the first group aboard. "I want the strong men on board first, so they can help us load the women and children," the master told his crew.

A second group of men waited on the shore with the women and children. Out of nowhere, another gang of enforcers appeared and descended upon the exhausted refugees! Some rode horseback, others rushed forward on foot. They were all armed, quite pleased to come upon a group trying to sneak out of the country.

"Damn our luck," cursed the shipmaster. "They could seize my ship if I wait any longer. The wind is right. We have these few on board. We are sailing, now!"

He ordered the crew heading toward shore to return. William and the others waiting for the second boat stared in disbelief, helpless and stunned.

Some of the elder Scrooby men fled, but William stood firm with Mary and their three children, protesting to no one in particular, "And now, we have more women separated from their husbands as they sail away without us. Dear God, if ever we were in need of your help, now is that time!"

The men on the Dutch ship had taken with them only what they were wearing. What few other possessions they had remained behind with the second group that was stranded without them. Fourteen days after leaving their family and friends, they sailed into port in the Netherlands.

The armed enforcers surrounded everyone who did not go on the first group. With swords drawn, the enforcers herded their distraught prisoners into the nearest town like stray sheep. A middle-aged judge with a perplexed countenance stared down at them. He said nothing for several long minutes. Some of the utterly exhausted refugees fell to the floor in front of the judge. He turned to one of his officers. "Take them away to some other judge. How should I know what to do with this bunch of renegades?"

"What am I supposed to do with them?" asked the next judge. "What charges should one bring against them? These women are suffering merely for the sin of obeying their husbands. These men are too old to be the source of any serious trouble. Send them home."

Someone explained to the judge that they had no homes, that they had brought all they owned in anticipation of leaving the country. Not knowing what else to do with the pitiful band of women, frightened children, and older men, the judge agreed to let them leave the country as long as they did so quietly and in small numbers so as not to raise suspicion.

A handful decided trying to leave was worse than facing the consequences of staying. The rest departed over a period of several months on various ships sailing to the Netherlands. They found shelter in various homes of sympathizers in the community until their opportunity was at hand. William stayed in England until the last ship carried the rest of them to ensure all of the others were sailing to safe harbors.

On August 8, 1608, William clasped the hands of his dear friends William Bradford and Richard Clyfton in Amsterdam. "It drew tears from our eyes to see you on the shore as we sailed away," said Bradford. "Anything we had, we would have given to be ashore again."

"Again, our entire congregation gathers, now safe, in Amsterdam. We did it, my friends. We leave England behind. I pray we are at long last free to forge a new life for ourselves among friends," William said.

CHAPTER FORTY

AMSTERDAM – 1608

New problems replaced the ones left behind. In England, almost everyone made an adequate living as farmers or simple merchants in Scrooby. Here, they had no land to farm, no merchandise to sell, and no means to immediately make something to sell. Other than William, who'd traveled here years earlier with Davison, they did not speak Dutch. However, accustomed to hard work, the group gratefully took whatever jobs they could find.

For William, the Netherlands served as a flashback to a quarter-century earlier. The landscape, language, and buildings were all familiar. William helped the others adapt. The Dutch were thriving; Amsterdam had nearly doubled in population since William had been away. The country was now a major commercial center. Ships hoisting the Dutch flag sailed into ports around the world. The Separatists were eager to find their place in this new homeland. To their delight, they soon realized the upper classes worked with the common people. This attitude appealed to their belief that work was a gift from a gracious God.

William, Clyfton, and Robinson met to organize their transplanted congregation. Clyfton began the meeting with a report about his visit to his old neighbor, Pastor John Smyth. "Though he seemed glad enough to greet me and welcome us to Amsterdam," he reported, "I sense something may not be quite right."

"What makes you conclude as much?" asked Robinson.

"It seems there have been other Separatists from London looking for fellow English-speaking sympathizers. They now worship as one congregation, but John Smyth is reluctant to discuss how that is going."

"So, you conclude it is not going well according to what he is *not* saying?" asked William.

"That is, sometimes, the most accurate message. Would you agree?" asked Clyfton.

"I shall pray you have misinterpreted his silence," concluded William. "We've all gone through so much turmoil in order to be here at last. It would be such a senseless shame to bring conflicts across the channel."

A few days later, Jonathan Brewster confirmed Clyfton's suspicions. He told his parents over dinner about a conversation he had gotten into at work. "When they realized I was part of the Scrooby group, they wanted to know if what they had heard about the first Englishmen to flee England was true."

"And what did you tell them?" asked William.

"That I didn't know anything about it. But then they told me what they heard. It is peculiar that strangers know more about my fellow countrymen than I do!"

"Do not keep us guessing," prompted William. "What did they tell you?"

The next day, William told Clyfton and Robinson this news. "After all these years of relying on the Geneva Bible as the English word of God, one of his people told my son that he forbids them to use it for worship," said William. "Apparently, he claims it is but a translation, and they must use only the Greek and Hebrew texts. Then he tells the people that is not the authentic word of God, either."

All three men were shocked to hear what was happening among their English neighbors. "How can these people who have overcome such difficulties to get here now turn on one another?" asked Robinson.

"I had hoped we might reunite with them," said Clyfton, "but it appears Pastor Smyth has led them astray. It is little wonder that he was not more forthcoming in my visit to him."

Bradford added, "He is a man of able gifts, and a good preacher. However, his inconstancy and unstable judgment have overthrown him."

"What do you think, Preacher Clyfton?" asked Robinson. "I suppose we will worship with the faithful from London, though I am uneasy about their demeanor, as well."

※

The Brethren of the Separation of the First English Church of Amsterdam had grown to around three hundred members.

After several months of debate about how to respond to the dueling congregations, William suggested a new approach. "When I was here with Ambassador Davison, we visited other cities. Perhaps the Good Lord expects us to settle in one of them."

They decided to try their fortune in Leiden.

"I think it best that I remain here," said Pastor Clyfton during discussion of this new plan. "Perhaps I can be of some value in calming down the troubled waters in which the townspeople now find themselves. John Smyth and I were once friends as well as neighbors."

CHAPTER FORTY-ONE

LEIDEN – 1609

Leiden was a thriving city with good jobs readily available. The Scrooby refugees were excited about going there. However, they first needed to obtain permission from the Dutch authorities to relocate. The application was granted in February 1609. "Perhaps now, at last, we have arrived at our Promised Land," William said to Mary when it was all settled.

Robinson walked with William along a canal in Leiden. "Our little church will never grow to the size of Pieterskerk, but at last, we are free to gather in peace."

William agreed. "How we are blessed to now have our little house off Choorsteeg. It is so different from the Manor House in Scrooby, but at least here, we have a garden and all of you. What we lost in space, we gained in community. It goes that way, does it not? We lose a little here, and gain a little there."

Though the Dutch authorities were helpful and hospitable toward the new English residents, trouble from England continued. King James demanded that his ambassador mount a protest to the officials in Leiden. "They should not have been so quick to grant entrance to those bloody Brownist rebels. They are fugitives from English justice!"

The secretary of the City of Leiden wrote to the English ambassador. "Our decision to admit these newcomers was made without the knowledge that the petitioners had been banished from England and belonged to the Brownist sect. So long as they cause no trouble and incur no debts they cannot manage from their labor, they are welcome."

The Scrooby refugees gathered in Robinson's home to give thanks. Next, the fledgling community discussed how to organize themselves in Leiden. "Freedom and peace surround us like a fresh spring breeze. At last, we have settled in our spiritual homeland," proclaimed John Robinson.

"You must be our pastor," proposed Samuel Fuller. Fuller had joined the Scrooby refugees from the Amsterdam Ancient Brethren. "You are the most qualified, and the only one among us ordained to serve as pastor."

"I humbly accept this charge. And you, William, you must be our elder. With your knowledge of Leiden, you will help us to settle into our new home. You will assist me in my duties as pastor. And you, Samuel, will assist Elder William in the governance of our little community."

After years of uncertainty, their ecclesiastical affairs were in order and their new city had welcomed them. All that was left now was to find ways of supporting themselves. Bradford soon found a position in a factory making twilled fabric from cotton and linen. Because he was single, he roomed with William and Mary Brewster. He often returned to their home twelve or even fifteen hours after leaving for work. Nonetheless, he delighted in talking about his fumbling attempts to learn the skills necessary to please his supervisor. Finding housing for so many immigrants with so few financial resources meant that anyone with a place to live shared their home with others.

Now that Bradford no longer had Richard Clyfton as a surrogate father, he looked to William to fill that role. "We are glad we have room to accommodate you," William told him whenever the young man apologized for imposing. "Remember what the sacred texts warned us in Proverbs," William said when the community gathered to decide where everyone should live. "'Like the clouds and wind without rain is a man who boasts of gifts he does not give.' Though we boast not of our good fortune, we yet have the gift of a home, and we must share it."

Leiden was full of textile plants. Soon, sixteen-year-old Jonathan Brewster was working in one making ribbon. Others acquired new jobs weaving, combing wool, or tailoring. The pay was meager, and the Dutch guild system controlled the textile industry. Jonathan protested to his father, "We are at a double disadvantage. We must ask others to translate for us, and because we are not citizens, I cannot join a guild. This is all I am able to do."

"It is sufficient. God will take what little we have and make it enough. Son, how grateful I am for your efforts. It saddens me I cannot give you what I received in my time at Cambridge. Even so, God has blessed our family. We are together; we suffer no infirmities that would prevent us providing for ourselves. Mother tells me soon we will hear the cooing of another little one. What do you suppose we should name this child?"

Jonathan shrugged. "I think that is best left to you and Mother."

"You will not always work so hard for such a low reward. This is but one step along a long road. Thank you, again, for your help on the arduous journey from England to Leiden."

In June, a few months after arriving in Leiden, Mary called for William through gritted teeth, "I think you should summon Bridget Robinson to assist me. I think I am about to deliver. Send Jonathan for help. Do not leave me."

"So soon? Can it be time already?"

Mary winced and nodded. "Please. Send Jonathan, now!" She grimaced and wrapped her hands around her swollen abdomen. "Send the girls with him, and tell Jonathan to leave them with Pastor Robinson. They do not yet need to know the sounds of new life. It would surely alarm them. Please! Hurry!"

William paced throughout their small home, listening to Bridget and another woman she'd recruited trying to sooth Mary. Her moans filled him with dread. *None of the others took this long. There must be something wrong. Dear Lord, you give life and you determine when our lives should end. If it is your will, let her time of pain come to a close now, and deliver this child safely that we may dedicate him to you.*

At last, the moans and anguished cries stopped. The birthing room was silent for a quarter of an hour, according to the town hall bell. William knew before Bridget spoke. She dabbed at her eyes with her apron as she approached. "I regret to tell you . . . the child was born ready to return to our Lord. Mary calls for you. Shall I tend to the child?"

William hung his head and clenched his fists. "Yes, please, prepare the child for burial. We will tend to that when Mary is ready."

Bridget went back to find Mary holding the stillborn as if willing the infant to take in air and live. Bridget gently pried the still baby from her, wrapped him in a shawl, and slipped out of the room as William entered.

He approached to find Mary as pale as freshly fallen snow, facing the wall with a blanket pulled up to her neck. When she heard William enter, she slowly turned to him. He knelt beside her and took one of her hands in his own, trying to push a little warmth into her chilled body. Though it was June, the effort of delivery and the despair of a birth without life made Mary shiver. A tear slipped down William's cheek. They grieved together silently for another quarter of an hour.

"Forgive me, William, but I have doubts. How can our Lord allow such a thing to happen? Have we not been faithful? Have you not poured your life into leading God's people out of danger to safety?"

"It is not for us to know the ways of God, dear Mary. Job was a righteous man, and yet he lost all his family and everything he had, even though he was faithful. We have been blessed with three healthy children. We must not doubt. Though we cannot understand, we must yet trust."

"I know you are right, but sorrow fills me through and through."

"And I, as well. And I, as well. I will go for Pastor Robinson. We must prepare to return this little one back to his Maker."

✺

Though William did not complete his Cambridge studies, his time there enabled him to find a post at the University of Leiden. The university was considered one of the finest in all of Europe. It attracted students from many European countries, some eager to learn English. William soon used his expertise in Latin grammar to teach them English. He delighted in telling his young prodigy, Bradford, about this new university community. "Many come from Denmark and Germany. Some of their fathers are men of great importance and influence. It gives me such satisfaction to watch their English vocabulary grow day by day."

"And what of the children who are not your own who now reside here? How full this home grows."

"I am guardian to Ann and Robert Pecke. They have no parents and nowhere else to live, so they must come to us. I have already sent my older half-brother, Thomas Sympkinson, what money I could spare to pay their travel expenses. The Lord giveth, and the Lord taketh away. Blessed be the name of the Lord. Mary and I are blessed to be able to provide for these children. Did not our Lord say, 'Let the children come, and hinder them not?' I do believe they will help Mary recover from her grief at the loss of our baby. God's ways are not ours. We must trust and follow as nearly as we are able."

CHAPTER FORTY-TWO

LEIDEN – 1610

Pastor Robinson's prayer gave thanks for the health of the congregation, the weather, the birth of another baby, and the marriage of another couple. He also reminded the Lord to help people remain steadfast in their resistance to the temptations of the flesh lurking everywhere, before concluding with a loud, "Amen."

The congregants stood shoulder to shoulder in the home they'd selected for the day's Sabbath gathering. The routine was predictable. They crowded into someone's home to first thank their Lord for bringing them to this beautiful Dutch city, then petitioned God to help them find a more suitable place for their growing faith family.

It seemed that at least one woman was with child at all times. No sooner was a baby born than another woman let it be known she was expecting. Neighbors noticed the gentle way church members treated one another and wanted to join them. The original community of a hundred desperate refugees was now numbered nearly double. In contrast to the challenges in England, they now lived and worked together with contentment instead of fear and apprehension.

A year after settling in Leiden, William made an announcement: "Our prayers have been answered. Our Lord has heard us and found a place for us to worship as well as a home for our beloved Pastor Robinson and his family."

Combining their limited resources, the congregation purchased a home on Kloksteeg, near Pieterskerk Cathedral. It was a large house with a garden large enough to add a number of small dwellings for those still living with other families. The people clapped and cheered at the news. They built twenty-one small homes for their poorer members.

The new worship space was plain and simple, with no cross or crucified Christ, no pipe organs or any of the ornate trappings found in Catholic and Established Church Cathedrals. If something was not mentioned in the scriptures, it had no place among them. Women and children sat on benches on the right; men sat on the left.

The first service was equally simple. Pastor Robinson prayed and Elder William read a few chapters of scripture, applying what he read to their circumstances. The congregation sang psalms. They were grateful for benches once Pastor Robinson began preaching, as he typically preached for three hours. Each gathering included a collection for the benefit of the poorest among and around them.

❧

At the end of another long day, William sat with Mary. "We leave some troubles behind, and encounter new ones in their place. That is the ebb and flow of life. I am grateful you are by my side."

Mary smiled and reached out for his hand. "Do you remember when we were living at Scrooby Manor? How I would implore you to set aside your work for a moment so I could tell you something?"

"Surely, I do. And it seems that each time I did, you told me I would soon be bouncing another baby on my lap."

"Well, I do not think it proper for me to come to the university to ask you to take a walk with me. Yet I think you might want to know, that if I could, I would beg you take leave of work for a while and walk with me."

William stared at Mary. "Are you telling me you are again with child?"

"I am, dear William. I am."

They welcomed Love Brewster to their growing family at the end of 1611. "We shall call him Love for all the love we have experienced here in our new home among our dear friends and neighbors," announced William to the community when the baby was born alive and healthy. "The Lord has been good to us, and we are prospering in this place."

CHAPTER FORTY-THREE

LEIDEN – 1611-1615

"WE shall miss having you at table with us, Master Bradford," said Mary. "How wonderful for you to have a place of your own."

Bradford sat up a straighter and beamed. "I am as content as ever a man could be. You have been both parents and dear friends to me. Our church community is so filled with love. I believe our members come as close to the communities of the first churches as any other church in these later times."

William added, "Amen. It is so. Now that you are a grown man with your own place and honest work, it is also time for you to take a wife." He looked at Mary, who was busy moving from the fireplace to the table and back again. Using a ladle with a handle nearly as long as her arm, she scooped up a serving of steaming stew, poured it into a bowl, and set it in front of Bradford. He leaned forward to take in the full aroma of the vegetables and small pieces of lamb. "Today, you are twenty-one. You shall dip your spoon first."

William offered a blessing for the bounty Mary set before them. With a twinkle in his eyes, he added, "See what joys await you when you invite a woman to share your good fortune?" Mary waved the back of her hand at William's face, and quickly turned away.

William continued, "It is I who have been blessed. The Lord has given me a full quiver. We have the most loving and faithful friends and neighbors, and we live in the most beautiful city in the world. When I walk along the canals, it is exciting to imagine what treasures the men unload from the ships."

"I love the clatter of the horses' hooves on the brick streets," added Bradford. "Surely God has done marvelous things bringing us to such a fair place. I do not think I have ever been as content. Now that I am twenty-one, I can sell the property I inherited in England and that will provide sufficient funds to secure my own home near Pieterskerk Cathedral."

A week later, Bradford again joined the Brewsters for a meal. Though he was pleased to have his own home and even his own loom, he never turned down an invitation to sit with his friends. Meals at the Brewster home were lively, with the children competing for Mary's attention. They shared the latest news about neighbors and friends and discussed God's providence and plans for their future. Little Love was just learning to walk, holding onto one of his sisters or the edge of anything nearby. Patience and Fear, ages eleven and five, kept him away from the open fire. Ann Pecke joined them while her brother Robert followed Jonathan whenever he was home. It was a full house indeed.

⚜

William frequently served as witness to the many marriages among their growing congregation. The marriages meant Pastor Robinson generally baptized another baby within the next year. One of the weddings William officially witnessed was that of Jane White, Robinson's beloved sister, in 1612 to Randall Thickins, a looking-glass maker from London. The church rolls of the Leiden community recorded forty-six marriages.

One beautiful early summer day in 1613, Mary went to talk to William. The gleam in her eye made William suspicious. She confirmed his suspicions. "We are to be blessed yet again, William. I think we shall have another little one before the year has come to a close, or very early in the next."

"Mary, I am ever in awe of you. How you have blessed me. Though we have, at times, struggled, how many more times have we had cause to rejoice. I thank you now for the gift of life you will soon bring to us all."

⚜

In the fall of 1613, Bradford reported his good news. "I have committed to learn for myself the joys I have observed here. I shall soon have a wife!"

Mary gasped and covered her mouth. Jonathan grinned from ear to ear and clapped Bradford on the back. "Who is she?" asked Mary.

"I believe you may know her. Dorothy May, now sixteen and ready to assume womanly ways." Bradford's smile revealed every one of his teeth.

William raised his eyebrows in surprise and recognition. "Elder Henry May's daughter?"

"The same," confirmed Bradford. "Since her father is an elder in the Ancient Brethren Church, we shall be married in Amsterdam."

"In church?" inquired William with an edge to his voice. The Separatists respected and were grateful to the Ancient Brethren for the hospitality shown to them when they first arrived from Scrooby. However, they did not approve of church weddings. There was nothing in the Holy Bible that authorized the church to perform weddings.

"No, dear friend. Not at the church. But surely many from the church will come to celebrate our good fortune. You have many friends there from our brief time in Amsterdam. I had hoped you might consider coming as well."

"Oh, William!" said Mary. "Do you think we could? How I would love to see Pastor Clyfton and so many of our dear friends again."

"I shall see to the arrangements, if you are up to the trip when it is time to go."

William Bradford and Dorothy May were united in marriage in a civil service in Amsterdam on December 10, 1613.

Several months later, in 1614, Mary gave birth to another healthy baby boy.

While life in Leiden among the Separatists was congenial enough, reports of trouble throughout Europe persisted. William often wrestled with how to respond to the persistent senseless slaughter among warring religious factions. "I propose we name this new son Wrestling. What do you think?" he asked Mary.

"I think I am grateful to have another healthy son. Wrestling suits the times in which he will live."

In 1615, William and Mary marked the passage of their twenty-fifth wedding anniversary with the marriage of their oldest son,

Jonathan. "How God has blessed us. Friends as close as family surround us. Neighbors show us respect and goodwill. Our Dutch friends found work for our people before most yet speak their language. We are fortunate to have come here."

"You are right, dear William. Blessed we are indeed. Except for one tiny soul lost at birth . . ." Mary trailed off for a moment to compose herself. "And now, one son marries while another learns to walk.

"We share a good life here, Mary. I thank God every day for you and all we have together." They sat in silence together on a bench outside the town hall, savoring the beauty all around them.

⁂

The pleasant life the Separatists enjoyed was in contrast to events that unfolded throughout the rest of Europe. Conflicts, conquests, colonialism, and catastrophes continued throughout England, Europe, and beyond in the opening decades of the 1600s. French King Henry IV was assassinated in 1610, making his nine-year-old son King Louis the XIII. The fledgling Jamestown colony struggled to survive in the wilderness across the Atlantic. The French were establishing colonies along the St. Lawrence Bay. French, Dutch, Spanish, and English ships navigated the Atlantic with increasing frequency to trade with Natives in the New World. Shipmaster John Smith published his maps of the region, encouraging even more merchants to traverse the ocean in search of new sources of profits.

Religious tensions erupted into violence at regular intervals. King James railed against the Roman Catholic Church, rejecting any Bible except the one he'd commissioned in 1611. In Germany, princes and priests fought over the souls of the people, eventually declaring each kingdom must accept the religion of its ruling prince.

Puritans gained strength in England, but King James would tolerate no church but the Established Church of England, maintaining his role as the ultimate authority. "My church is not in need of purification," he'd thunder whenever anyone dared broach the subject.

⁂

Meanwhile, the Leiden community carried on their daily activities in peace and harmony. William and Pastor Robinson continued to cherish the intellectually rich environment of the university. Talk in local pubs often revolved around the latest reports of riches to be made in this strange new world across the ocean.

Some of the Leiden group who'd gathered at the Brewster home discussed what they'd heard about this exotic place. Robinson said, "How vast this place they call America must be. They talk of forests so dense, squirrels travel for miles without ever coming down to the ground."

Bradford added what he knew. "I have seen some of the Natives that merchants brought to Europe. They are tall, with long, straight, silky black hair. A sailor told me they hunt with bows and arrows, and need only one shot to take down an animal bigger than themselves."

Mary walked past the men on her way to see what she could gather from the garden for supper. She added, "I should like to see such a place. But it is so far away, I would not want to ever be so far from the ones I love here."

The men nodded. As exotic as this strange place sounded, they were content where they were. The years had unfolded through a series of weddings and births, mingled with the occasional sorrow of death. All in all, their people were content.

⚅

Robinson's respect and influence in the community was well established, in part due to several books he wrote about ethics and Christian behavior. "Think of it, young William," Elder William told Bradford one afternoon. "Our own Pastor Robinson has been invited to join the debate on theology at the university. I suppose it is on account of the essay he wrote to Puritan Bernard back home. It seems the faculty was rather impressed with his work challenging Pastor Richard Bernard's conclusion that King James might yet be convinced to free the Established Church from the excesses of the Catholics. Pastor Robinson contends it is impossible. The only way to be faithful now is to completely separate from such things, and return to the ways of the earliest followers."

The following Sunday, Pastor Robinson told his flock that he had decided to become a student at Leiden University. "I have been longing to again immerse myself in study. I pray that what I learn there shall enrich our Sunday afternoon prophesying times together."

CHAPTER FORTY-FOUR

LEIDEN – 1617-1619

The printing press emboldened thinking men throughout Europe. Martin Luther's pamphlets spread throughout the continent after he nailed his ninety-five talking points onto the Castle Church door in Wittenberg in 1517. Now, a century later, other reformers printed their protests and distributed them far and wide. Religious leaders railed against the privilege and corruption of priests and princes alike, correctly claiming they tormented the people they were supposed to help. Protests often took the form of anonymous books and pamphlets.

Robinson and William discussed the on-going protests. "When a few thrive while the majority struggle, unrest is sure to follow. The powerful will not readily descend from their places of privilege. Those who hold power will not tolerate any who threaten them. Punishment is sure to be swift," observed Robinson.

William nodded. "I cannot but wonder how many more must be martyred for their faith. Yet, if we are faithful, we must go where our Lord leads. Many suffered for their faith in the early years of the church. It must not surprise us that some suffer now."

However, for the Brewsters and their friends in their growing faith community, life continued on in a series of relatively peaceful days. Jonathan and his wife, Suzanna, settled into married life. Mary anticipated there might soon be a grandchild, but no announcements were forthcoming.

Patience had reached marrying age, but so far remained content to stay at home. Ten-year-old Fear helped make and mend clothing, shopped at the market, and performed other never-ending chores. The sisters kept their lively little brother, Love, from getting into too much mischief. Now that Wrestling was moving about more, Love got away with things his family overlooked. William put out word he was seeking suitable apprenticeships for the Pecke children: Robert to learn a craft and Ann to become a servant in a local household.

Though their lives now were peaceful, Mary vividly remembered when William was detained in prison, leaving her and the children to manage without him until he was released. As a consequence, if William was delayed coming home, she began to worry. Reports of unrest in other places occasionally invaded their tranquility like buzzing mosquitoes.

꧁꧂

"I feel pulled to do more," William confided to Robinson.

"What more would you do?" asked his friend and colleague.

"Perhaps what you do. Write more about the urgency to separate from the Established Church to more fully be our Lord's agents on earth. You write, perhaps I should as well."

"What would you write about? And how would you publish what you write? The university helps me, but I do not think they would be inclined to do the same for you."

William sighed. "No, I suppose not. I am welcome to teach English, but I cannot foresee them publishing any book I should write. Let us pray that if this is our Lord's will, he will also show us the way forward."

Not long after that conversation, William's printing business, Vicus Chorali Press, was born. One door of the Brewster home opened onto Koorsteeg (Choir Alley), and William chose the Latin version of the street for a name.

"Mary, it is a miracle. Pastor Robinson and I prayed for a way, and God has answered us." William picked at the roasted turnips and rye bread Mary set before him. Each time he picked up his spoon, he remembered another detail. Down went the spoon, and out came something about going into the printing business.

"Thomas Brewer—do you remember him, Mary?"

Mary murmured in affirmation.

"He said he believed the reason for his good fortune was to assist with the printing of religious books and pamphlets. And, Mary, he chose me! He is buying everything I'll need. The printing press. The type. The ink. All of it!"

Mary tried to match her husband's enthusiasm, but with a household already bursting at the joints with children and constant visitors, she could not quite pull it off. "Where will you put it?"

"Upstairs, in the garret."

"How will you get it up there? Is it not quite heavy?"

"Yes, of course. But we have many strong young men among our acquaintances, in addition to Jonathan. Did not Jesus say that with faith the size of a mustard seed, we can move mountains? I only need enough faith to move a printing press."

In 1617, William added publisher to his list of accomplishments.

The first book to come off Choir Alley Press was a translation of the Dutch *Tenne Commandements* by Dod and Cleaver. William proudly included a nameplate that read *Tot Leyden, Voor Guiliam Brewster, Boeckdrucker, Anno. 1617.* His fondness for Latin inspired him to use the Latin version of William. He published two books in Latin that year.

⚅

A member of their church community pulled Mary aside at market. "I must talk to you," he said. "I fear your William could bring great trouble to your home."

"Whatever are you talking about?" she asked indignantly.

"His printing press. Do you realize what heresy he prints in his garret?"

"I know well enough what my husband does. He prints in English things written by scholars who speak other languages. What is the harm in that?"

"If that were all, there would be no harm, but I fear it is not. I have reason to believe he also prints books that are banned in England. Books that stir up the wrath of the Established Church. I heard he smuggles these to England. I warn you, Mary, he will be in serious trouble if he is caught."

Mary turned away, pretending to examine carrots and radishes. When the man didn't leave, she snapped at him. "Have you said what you came to tell me?" She gripped a bunch of parsnips to steady her hands which had begun to quiver.

"I have done my duty. I have warned you."

Mary stood pretending to examine bunches of asparagus. Her stomach felt quivery, as it usually did during the first weeks of each new pregnancy. Her mind flashed back to the day the enforcers dragged William away. She began to shake and felt woozy.

"Are you alright, Mary? You do not look well."

Mary turned to see Bridget Robinson holding a large basket filled with yellow and orange blocks of cheese. She inhaled deeply and nodded. "It is nothing. I was just daydreaming a bit, I suppose."

Mary didn't know what to do with this information, but she wasn't ready to talk about it. "Perhaps I've exerted myself a bit too much in the afternoon sun. I think I shall finish my shopping when it is a bit cooler." She scurried home to sort out her thoughts. She didn't want to accuse William of wrongdoing. She considered him the most trustworthy man she knew. Yet a sense of foreboding hung over her like black clouds foreshadowing a thunderstorm. *If he prints such things, it must be for good reason. I have no reason to doubt him. I shall not speak of it. When—if—he wants me to know, he will surely confide in me.*

William and Robinson were in the garret one day in 1619 preparing for the release of another of Robinson's books. "I think perhaps we should publish this volume from the Choir Alley Press under my name," said Robinson. "While I see no harm in *The People's Plea for the Exercise of Prophesying*, it is perhaps best not to attribute it to you, as you are a lay preacher."

Mary interrupted them, calling up the stairs, "William, Jonathan has just come for help. Suzanna is ready. I must go. Patience will watch the children, but please be available should she need assistance." She told Jonathan, "Run ahead now. Boil water to wash the baby. I have to gather a few things. I'll be along soon."

Mary picked up the basket of supplies she'd set aside for this day. It contained towels, an extra sheet, leaves to make a soothing tea to sip between contractions, and an ointment to gently rub on Suzanna's swollen belly.

She found Suzanna sitting on a low stool, howling from the pain in her back. Mary knelt beside her and began massaging her frightened young daughter-in-law's tense shoulders. Then she gently began massaging her swollen belly. She could feel the baby's bony foot, or perhaps an elbow, moving from side to side.

"Shh, shh now, dear. Soon it will be over and you'll be holding your first child in your arms."

But it wasn't soon. The town hall bell marked off a quarter of an hour, then another . . . and yet another. Mary and Jonathan moved to either side of Suzanna and placed their arms under hers, hoisting her to her feet and helping her walk around the table in the center of the room.

Suzanna screamed in terror as another contraction began. Her face lost more color with each one. They managed to get her to the corner of the room and ease her down on the edge of the feather mattress. Mary handed Suzanna the cup of tea she'd instructed Jonathan to make, holding the cup to her lips as the frightened girl sipped a few swallows. "Here, sip a bit more. It will help ease the pain. It will be worth it. Soon, you will hold new life in your arms."

The town hall bell tolled again and again until nearly three hours had passed. Mary chased Jonathan away after he helped her ease Suzanna into a reclining position on the bed, which was now soaked with birth water and sweat.

She settled into the birthing routine she knew well from the six times others had tended to her own labors: Check the baby. Wash her hands in the warm water Jonathan brought. Let Suzanna squeeze her hand through the next contraction. Offer another sip of tea. Repeat.

Just as the church bells announced the start of the fourth hour since Mary's arrival, she told Suzanna, "I see the head. You are almost done now. Now a shoulder. Now the other one." Mary stopped talking. The umbilical cord was wrapped around the baby's neck. She desperately tugged at it until she could unwrap it. Then she grabbed the baby by the ankles. She held the baby up and tapped its back. No sound. She tapped harder. Still no sound. She ran her finger around the baby's mouth. She didn't feel any obstruction. She slapped the baby harder. Still no sound.

Suzanna reached to pull the baby away from Mary. She held the blue baby to her chest, willing the child to breathe, to cry. "No! No! No!" Suzanna screamed. "Nooooo!"

She sat up and clutched the still baby to her chest, rocking back and forth. Mary stood by helplessly. She felt again her own pain when she had worked so hard, only to deliver a lifeless infant. *But I had healthy babies waiting for me. This is her first. Why, God? Why?*

Jonathan came in and froze a few feet away from the bed. His eyes grew wide, his jaw dropped as color drained from his face. He latched onto a bedpost and looked first to his mother, then to his wife. Nothing in his experience with the birth of his siblings— even the death of one—had prepared him for this moment.

Unsure of himself, he inched closer to Suzanna. Mary had whisked away the placenta and was now holding Suzanna, who was still holding her stillborn baby. The women made room for Jonathan, and the three of them sat crying until the church bell rang again.

Pastor Robinson presided at the simple graveside service. His words rang hollow, yet they all wanted to believe him as he read from the Bible: "Weeping may last for the night, but joy comes in the morning."

Mary silently prayed, "Dear Lord, please let there be joy for Jonathan and Suzanna in the morning." It was not to be. A few days later, they were back at the church for Suzanna's funeral. An infection, begun with the delivery, raged out of control until the new mother joined her child in whatever followed earthly life.

Chapter Forty-Five

Leiden – 1619

William and Robinson were working on setting up the type for another pamphlet on proper conduct for Christians. William broke the silent concentration. "I believe our Lord leads us both to write and print the truth. The truth is what sets us free."

"True," agreed Robinson. "Our Lord has been leading us, but William, we must be careful. We may not be as free as you hope. King James's arm reaches easily across the channel. He has eyes and ears everywhere. He will not tolerate anyone criticizing his authority."

"Well I know it. I remember the filth and stink of the jail cell when first we tried to escape his reach. That is why Guiliam Brewster is not content to publish things of little interest." William chuckled at the absurdity of it. "Here, I have my own printing press, thanks be to God and the generosity of Thomas Brewer. Yet all it appears to produce are volumes likely to be used to keep papers from flying off tables when spring breezes blow fresh air through open windows. The real purpose of the press is to get the word of God into the hands and hearts of our fellow Englishmen who are languishing for lack of God's living water of life."

"On that, we are in agreement. How else should we give our friends who live far away what they need most? What work will you print next?" inquired Robinson.

"I believe it shall be *Concerning the True and Genuine Religion of our Lord and Saviour Jesus Christ.*"

"A fine choice," said Robinson. "Tell me, have you heard of the work of David Calderwood? He has written a response to the Perth Assembly. It tells the truth of the treachery of King James and the many bishops who cater to his unreasonable demands for total conformity to his will."

"Truly, I understand not the hold he has on men who profess to follow Christ, yet betray our dear Lord with allegiance to one who is so clearly not a Christ follower," said William.

"It is not for us to judge, yet there are times when it seems that judgment of another cannot be avoided. David Calderwood has heard of your print shop. He approached me about publishing a response to the 1618 *Perth Assembly* and King James's insistence all of the churches in Scotland succumb to the authority of the Established Church. They are not free to determine for themselves which church should be established in their own country."

William shook his head. "And to think King James was raised there and cared for by the Presbyterian community when his mother was taken from him before he could barely walk. I suppose he assumes that since he was raised there, he should now decide what all of Scotland must do." William pointed to his press and continued, "Perhaps he assumes incorrectly. I will do what I can to help Calderwood publish and distribute his *Perth Assembly* response. Is it true that he wrote from a hiding place?"

"That is what I have heard," answered Robinson. "God's servants must seek shelter to do His will. Paul wrote to his fellow Christians from prison in Rome. Luther hid in the Wartburg Castle, using his time in hiding to give his fellow German countrymen the Bible in their own tongue. Likewise, Calderwood must now hide from enforcers eager to turn him in for his leadership among Presbyterians."

"I shall stand with Calderwood," William declared.

He was wise enough to hide the extent to which he rendered assistance to Calderwood. The manuscript was smuggled out of Scotland, published in Holland, and returned to Scotland. The few remaining copies started a chain of consequences that eventually brought an end to the Separatists' peaceful years in Leiden.

⁂

"Mary, it seems to me every time you invite me for a walk, you tell me that I am about to have to bounce another baby on my knee."

"No, not this time," she said. "I am confident Wrestling shall be the last baby. Though Sarah, Hannah, and Elizabeth all bore babes when they were older than I am now, I do not think that shall happen to me."

William let out an audible sigh. "We have been blessed enough. What, then, is it, dear woman, that you would pull me away from my press?"

"Truly, I long for a few moments alone with you. It calms my fears and weariness to walk with you for a spell. It is so beautiful along the canal. You can come away for just a little while, can you not?" She debated telling him what others were whispering about his print shop in the garret. *Now that I have him to myself for a few moments, I lack the courage to broach the subject.* "It is so lovely here," she said.

"Indeed, it is. I ought to spend enough time savoring the peace-fulness and beauty of our fair adopted city. Thank you for getting me away for a few minutes."

William rarely thought about the workload his busy life imposed upon this woman who had stood by him through so many challenges. One of the children always seemed to have some problem Mary was resolving. The men who helped with the printing business came and went constantly, often needing food or drink along the way, and there was frequently a student or two from the university coming for an English lesson. Then there were the various members of their church who loved to confer with William about church affairs. Mary cherished the days when young Winslow brought Elizabeth with him when he came to assist with the printing work.

Elizabeth helped Mary with household tasks that lasted from before dawn until the moon was visible more often than not. Mary appreciated the extra pair of feminine hands to assist with the younger children, cooking, making and mending clothing, gathering what was ready from the garden, and the many other details required to run this busy household. Elizabeth was thankful for the female companionship and the chance to learn from a veteran wife and mother how to make everything run smoothly.

Mary depended on the support and encouragement of the other women in the Leiden community, especially when predictions William's printing press would stir up trouble came true. As it turned out, 1619 was the year the garret printing press brought an end to the Brewster family's peaceful life in Leiden.

17 July, 1619

Dear Secretary of State Sir Robert Naunton,

As your faithful servant and ambassador of our beloved King James, I must inform you that I have recently come upon a copy of a most odious volume by a certain David Calderwood with the title Perth Assembly. *I have endeavored to discover who is guilty of publishing this work, which so scorns our king and bishops. I have learned it was published by a certain English Brownist in Leiden. I shall obtain particular knowledge of the printer as soon as I am able.*

Faithfully yours,
Sir Dudley Carleton
Ambassador of His Majesty from England to the Dutch

At almost the same time Carleton was in Leiden tracking down the publisher of *Perth Assembly* response, other men in the king's service were confiscating all of the smuggled copies they could find in Scotland.

22 July, 1619
Dear Secretary of State Sir Robert Naunton,
I sent Your Honor a book entitled Perth Assembly. *Finding many copies dispersed in Leiden—and, from there, sent to England—I had reason to suspect it had been printed in that town; but upon particular inquiry, I remain somewhat doubtful. Yet in search of that book, I believe I have discovered the printer of another:* De Regimine Ecclesiae Scoticanae, *of which, if he was not the printer himself, he assuredly knows both the printer and the author.*

Carleton referred to William and enclosed the title page of another book that William admitted to having printed: *Concerning the True and Genuine Religion of our Lord and Savior Jesus Christ.* Carleton's letter to the Secretary of State concluded with:

*You will find that it is the same character. Since William openly
avows publication of the first, he cannot well deny printing the
second.*

Faithfully yours,
Sir Dudley Carleton
Ambassador of his Majesty from England to the Dutch

Mary was slicing carrots to add to the stew when several men
appeared on her doorstep. "We would like to speak with your
husband."

"He is not here."

"Pray, tell us, where is he?"

"I do not know. I only know he is not here."

"Then you will inform him that he is in violation of the Dutch
States General's edict against unlicensed printing. Since he has
printed books without proper license, we must enforce this edict."

The Dutch would have overlooked the small volume of work
produced in the garret print shop had it not stirred up the wrath
of the King of England. The Dutch were not inclined to dismiss
a king's rage. Dutch authorities felt obligated to close down
William's Choir Alley Press. They were sympathetic to the religious perspectives of their immigrant friends, but they dared not
challenge the authority of the king across the channel.

The men marched past a dismayed Mary and her children, who
quickly gathered around to show their intent to protect her—and
to be protected by her. The men marched upstairs, seized all of
the books they could find along with the type and other printing
equipment. To make sure the Choir Alley Press stayed closed, they
put a large green wax seal on the door before leaving.

A few days later, Mary met University of Leiden Professor
Polyander while out walking. When they were out of earshot of
others, he told her, "I regret we must do this. William Brewster is a
fine man and I considered it an honor to write the preface for one
of his books. But we Dutch cannot afford to disregard the wrath
of the English king. I am sorry, Mary. It must be so."

28 August, 1619
Dear Secretary of State Sir Robert Naunton,
With regard to William, I am now informed that he is on this side of the sea, and was seen yesterday at Leiden; but as yet, he is not there settled.
Faithfully yours,
Sir Dudley Carleton,

2 September, 1619
Dear Secretary of State Sir Robert Naunton,
I must now report that William Brewster has been seen in Amsterdam, but he is not, as yet, to be lighted upon. I understand he proposes to settle himself at a village called Leerdorp, not far from Leiden, thinking to be able to print prohibited books without discovery there; but I shall lay in wait for him, there and in other places, so that I may doubt not. Either he must leave this country, or I shall, sooner or later, find him out.
Faithfully yours,
Sir Dudley Carleton

William kept both Carleton and Secretary of State Naunton speculating about where they should focus their next efforts to locate him. Meanwhile, the authorities in Leiden concentrated on William's benefactor, Thomas Brewer. On September 9, they detained him for questioning.

He answered: "William has discontinued the printing business, in accordance with the proclamation regarding publishing unlicensed books. He is here in town, but he is now sick. Furthermore, the Choir Alley Press has published nothing since November of last year." In this way, Brewer discredited the theory that William Brewster published the inflammatory *Perth Assembly* publication.

10 September, 1619
Dear Secretary of State Sir Robert Naunton,
I have, at length, found out William at Leiden, whom the magistrates of that town, at my insistence, apprehended last night, though he was sick in bed.

Faithfully yours,
Sir Dudley Carleton

12 September, 1619
Dear Secretary of State Sir Robert Naunton,
I had advised Your Honor that Brewster was taken at Leiden;
which proved to be an error in that the scout employed by the
magistrates for his apprehension, being a dull, drunken fellow,
took one man for another.
Faithfully yours,
Sir Dudley Carleton

King James demanded Thomas Brewer report to London for further questioning. Brewer agreed to go, but only if the king paid his passage there and back. Brewer provided little information of any use, and was released after agreeing to do his utmost to find William upon his return to Leiden. Since the king refused to pay for his return passage, Thomas Brewer stayed in England for three years. William Brewster was no longer in Holland when Brewer finally returned to Leiden.

Because the Dutch liked and respected their English neighbors, they made only halfhearted efforts to find William in order to appease the British crown. Persecuting authors and printers for publishing books about religion was against their philosophy of tolerance. They took in David Calderwood, author of the controversial *Perth Assembly* response, when he fled England in August 1619. King James was furious. "That knave has now leaped over the sea, with a purse well filled by the wives of Edinburgh."

Though grateful for the warm Dutch hospitality and freedom to worship as they pleased, the Separatists had been wondering if they should continue to dwell in a foreign country. The trouble stirred up by William's garret press operation brought such conversations to the forefront.

CHAPTER FORTY-SIX

LEIDEN – 1619

"THINK of the hardships!" Mary protested when William told her of his most recent discussions with Robinson, Bradford, John Carver, and Robert Cushman.

Carver and Cushman, deacons in their congregation, also served their community as informal ambassadors to the Dutch and other English communities in Leiden. The men had been considering the possibility of moving their growing community once more—all the way to the New World.

"This is like a dream that cannot be, and yet will not go away," William said with a sigh. "Mary, what started as an interesting subject to explore has grown like the many tulips here that sprout from bulbs into beautiful flowers."

For the next few minutes, William recapped that fateful conversation with Robinson two years earlier. "We were talking about the new colony at Jamestown, ten years old already when we talked about it. I asked John if he knew about Sir Edward.

"John said he remembered that Archbishop Sandys and his son, Sir Edwin, were part of my childhood when Bishop Sandys was our landlord and my father his servant at the manor. But John didn't realize the younger Sandys had served in Parliament since 1586, when I was with Davison in diplomatic service. I told John how Edwin is now a knight with a fervor for exploring and establishing colonies across the Atlantic.

"John was impressed when I told him Edward is now the joint manager of the Virginia Company. That must mean he has his hands on the treasury for the colony. You should have seen him then, Mary. I believe his face took on a glow. He stopped walking and turned to me and asked, 'And you believe you could gain an audience with him?' I responded, 'I am certain I could.' And that is what got several of our friends thinking perhaps we could procure a land grant if we would be willing to go there and cultivate it."

"Such groups are permitted to govern themselves?" Mary set down the rag she held to wash out a pot. "Do you realize how you become more excited each time you discuss this?"

"Do I?" William ran his fingers through his beard before saying more. "I did tell our friend that perhaps we should send Carver or Cushman to talk to the Virginia Council to see if we might be the type of group they desire."

Mary sighed. "And that is what has led to these plans now unfolding?"

William nodded. "I confess, that was the start of it. We spent the rest of that afternoon preparing a letter for Carver and Cushman to carry to England."

⁂

Carver and Cushman returned from visiting Sir Edwin Sandys with good news. The next time the community gathered, Robinson summarized their report. "It is encouraging news. The Virginia Company seems willing to grant us a patent to colonize. All that is needed is King James's approval, and they think he will give it."

First came gasps. People stared at Robinson, then at one another. A cacophony of conversation broke out in the sanctuary. Mary caught the woman next to her, who nearly fainted. Love and Wrestling started pulling on Jonathan's shirt. "Are we going to America?" asked Wrestling.

Everyone had heard stories about this strange place called America. Some were eager to go, others not so sure. Life in Leiden was hard, but here, they enjoyed the kindness of sympathetic neighbors. Wasn't the clarity of the known better than the uncertainty of the unknown? Mary held her tongue, but silently prayed this would be a passing phase and such talk would fade away.

Robinson was still talking, "There is one drawback we must overcome. Sir Edward requires of us a statement of the principles that will guide us in the New World. Here is the challenge we must overcome. We are required to include something about how we accept the king's authority."

He had barely uttered the last syllable when Bradford rose to his feet. Over the murmurs of those around him, he cried out, "That is precisely what drove us out of the king's reach to settle here!"

"I know, I know. Let me continue," said Robinson. "Elder William and I will pray for God to guide our quills as we write a statement that gives the king the homage he demands without sacrificing our freedom."

⁂

"This seems an impossible task." William crumpled another sheet of paper and tossed it on the floor. He and Robinson had been hunched over a stack of papers for hours trying to find the words to appease a power-hungry monarch while holding fast to their understanding of the nature and will of God.

Robinson agreed the criteria for the task seemed impossible. "What can we possibly write that would please this king's lust to control everything within his kingdom, even as he covets control of another, thousands of miles away?" Robinson stood to stretch his cramped muscles.

"Yet we must find a way that clearly states our conviction that ultimately, only the Lord God is sovereign over our lives," William replied.

"Though it seems impossible," said Robinson, "we do know that with God, all things are possible. How else could it be that we sit here today in this beautiful city?" Robinson walked to the window and gazed out over the street below.

He was still staring out the window a few minutes later when William asked, "What do you think of this?"

Robinson read the new passage: *We do hereby assert and acknowledge the sovereignty of the king's authority, if the thing commanded be not against God's word.*

Robinson nodded his head slowly. Hands clasped behind him, he walked around the table and back over to William, stopping only a few inches away. The afternoon sun cast long shadows across the room, bathing them in the November sunlight.

"I think that may be it, my dear friend. Read it again."

William read it aloud.

"Ah, yes. Good. Very good. We shall add that. Now, let us see what we have. But first, I shall have Bridget bring us something to refresh us. It appears from the slant of the sun that we have been long at this, and short on substance to sustain us. Bridget, my love, could I trouble you to bring us some ale, and perhaps a bit of cheese?" A few minutes later, Bridget Robinson arrived, carrying a platter of cheese, apple slices, and bread in one hand and a pitcher of ale in the other.

Robinson took the platter from her and set it on the table on top of a pile of papers. Bridget handed the pitcher to Robinson as William retrieved their empty tankards from the bookshelves where he had placed them hours earlier, in the only spot not occupied by books and papers. "Bridget, do sit a spell and see if you like our work this afternoon," urged Robinson. "We would have you hear it before we share it with the others." Bridget obliged, sitting stiffly on the edge of a chair at the end of the table. Long years of serving others made her uneasy sitting rather than moving around.

The men took turns reading the Seven Articles documents they'd finally finished. When Robinson reached the seventh article, he paused. "William, read what you have proposed as the end to our work."

William cleared his throat, and in a loud, clear voice, read, "We do hereby assert and acknowledge the sovereignty of the king's authority, if the thing commanded be not against God's word."

Bridget clapped her hands in approval. Robinson clapped his friend on the back. "Come, let us affix our names to this, and make it ready for Carver and Cushman to carry to Sir Sandys and the rest of the council."

The document, dated 12 November, 1617, went with Cushman and Carver to Sir Edward. When they returned from their journey, they brought an encouraging letter from Sir Edward, but also informed them that the matter required further discussion.

"I do rather think his signature "Your very loving friend" is a good omen. Do you concur?" laughed William.

Mary Brewster's hope the notion of relocating to the New World was a passing fancy faded fast. Now, two years and many conversations later, William was more enthused by the prospect than ever. She tried again to persuade him otherwise.

"Jonathan is still fresh in his sorrow over Suzanna and their baby," Mary pointed out. "It is true that Patience and Fear are old enough now, but the little ones still need a mother's guidance and a father's protection. How would I ever care for them properly in the wilderness? And where would Patience find a suitable husband? Is it not challenge enough for all of us that you must move from house to house to escape the clutches of the English enforcers? I fret so about your safety when I do not know where you will next seek shelter. Must we speak of such a drastic thing?"

William combed his white beard with long, bony fingers. He realized he would soon need to find shelter away from her and the children. Many families in their community had willingly hidden him as he dodged enforcers seeking to question him about his publishing efforts. William had friends who believed they served God by sheltering him, yet constant movement from place to place had its toll on them both, especially Mary.

Conversations about relocating to the New World grew in frequency and intensity. "We would not be the first. The Virginia Colony is now thriving. The tobacco they grow makes some quite prosperous. Remember the stories of how grandly Queen Anne received Pocahontas and her son Thomas when they traveled to England with Governor Dale and John Rolfe? Their visit did much to whet King James's appetite for further expansion in the New World. I heard that the Native woman was as enchanting as she was beautiful."

"Yes, I recall," said Mary. "I heard the poor woman died, leaving her son without a mother."

"The son was given a good English education. Surely God was watching over him. It is sad that she never returned home, but fortunate for the sponsors of the colony. Her visit sparked great enthusiasm for others to go."

Mary thought it a tragedy the Native mother had ignited so much interest in a place so far away from her home. Her voice was flat and cool when she spoke again. "I've heard the stories. Yet it is still a wild and unsettled land. Did you not also hear that of the five hundred who went to Jamestown, only a small number survived? And how would we pay for such a voyage?"

William combed his beard some more before answering. "We have friends and people who wish us well. Carver is quietly making inquiries on his trips back to England. I, myself, have had encouraging conversations with some of our fellow countrymen. For now, we are only exploring possibilities, but everything we hear is encouraging. Sir Edward Sandys reports the Virginia Colony is doing very well now. Mary, I am sensing more and more that we must be like Abraham and trust God to guide us, even if it means venturing to a place we have never seen."

Mary tightened her jaw and wrapped a strand of hair around her finger. She did her best to support whatever endeavors occupied William's attention, but there were days she wished he could better appreciate life from a woman's perspective. *How like a man to see only the possibilities and none of the problems.*

Normally, she accepted her lot in life as subordinate to the men around her—first a father, then a husband, and now, even her grown son—but this time, the risks seemed too enormous. Men always seemed energized by risk. A woman had to do what she could to avoid them for the sake of her children.

"I note, my dear husband, that the Holy Book says nothing about all the work that fell to Sarah when Abraham decided he must follow God's call." *I hope that did not sound too disrespectful.*

William smiled. Other men in the church community would have had a harsh word for a woman who spoke so boldly to her husband, but he rather admired her confidence to speak plainly to him. It made him believe that she trusted him, and he wanted there always to be trust between them.

"We would go as a group. You would have plenty of womanly companionship. As for our children, well, Patience is now a grown woman. Fear is already thirteen, not much younger than I was when I went to Cambridge. Jonathan grieves now for the death of his wife and the babe he never knew, but is doing well enough in his work. He will watch over our daughters. Love and Wrestling will go with us, and others in the community will help care for them, as they do even now."

"I am thankful that you are considerate enough to speak openly with me about these matters, and that you are planning on taking me with you." Mary tried to force a smile, and hoped it looked sincere. "But I do not think I could bear to leave half our children here! Nor would I want to be left behind, as poor Robert Cushman's new wife has been."

Mary made a clucking noise of disapproval. Her eyes turned moist, she wiped them with the back of her hands, standing up and stepping toward a cutting board covered with freshly picked green beans.

"Mary, we will do only as we believe God commands and calls us to do. No decision has yet been made, yet the idea does keep reappearing, much as the bird returns to the garden each spring."

✺✺✺

Several Separatist leaders in the growing community considered Leiden a convenient resting place from the turmoil in England, but not where they were destined to remain. Some of their young men became seamen due to lack of other ways to support themselves, taking them far from home months at a time. Younger children spoke Dutch freely, but struggled with their parents' native English tongue.

All of this kept Cushman and Carver travelling back to England, often in search of men who might finance this venture to the New World. "I would like to know what William thinks about all this," Robinson told Cushman and Carver after one of Cushman's trips back to Leiden to check on his family.

"I think our friend may have gone north for a bit," reported Cushman. "It would be like him to hide right under their noses near Doncaster while they scour all of Holland for him." Some of their fellow Separatists had stayed in the Doncaster area when Robinson and others fled to Holland. Though no one seemed to know for certain, it was commonly believed William occasionally returned to the area to seek shelter among family and friends who had sympathy for him—people who would not betray him to the enforcers.

"I believe his young apprentice, Edward Winslow, has a brother in Worcestershire. Perhaps he has found a safe place there for a spell," suggested Robinson. At that moment, William was in his own home, trying again to convince Mary that another emigration would be a good thing—possibly what God had ordained for them all along.

CHAPTER FORTY-SEVEN

LEIDEN – 1618-1619

Bridget Robinson and Mary Brewster sat in Bridget's sunny kitchen, snapping two large bowls of green beans—one for each family. They enjoyed talking away the afternoon over this chore while their husbands strolled along the canals, no doubt conversing again about how wonderful they imagined life would be for them all somewhere across the Atlantic.

"They all do that, do they not?" Bridget asked. "Men seem to think life somewhere else must be better than life where they are."

Mary placed some beans back into the bowl with others yet to be processed. Wiping her hands on her apron, she stood and stretched to loosen muscles sore from a long afternoon of repetitive action. Still standing, she asked, "Bridget, am I a wretched wife to doubt my husband? He sees God sending us out like Barnabas was sent to Antioch and Jerusalem. But Barnabas was sent to well-established places. How will we care for our boys in the wilderness?"

She looked over to the corner of Bridget's large kitchen, where eight-year-old Love and five-year-old Wrestling were playing with four tiny kittens. They sat so their legs formed a sort of human playpen and giggled with delight as the kittens romped and tumbled over one another within it.

Mary dabbed at her eyes with her apron. "I know I must be obedient to him. I would never want to be any other way. But sometimes, the immensity of it all does truly frighten me. I just cannot imagine how we will manage. Where would we sleep?

What would we eat? How would I ever make my sons new clothes when they outgrow these?"

She sat back down with a thud, resting both elbows on the table and propping her head in her hands. Without looking up, she whispered, "I just do not know if I can bear it. It will mean leaving a part of me here while another part of me travels there. I do not even know where 'there' is! How could I bear to be away from Patience and Fear?"

Her eyes now red and swollen, Mary looked up at Bridget, who reached across the table and took Mary's hands in hers. Biting her lower lip, Bridget began stroking the backs of her friend's hands. "I do not know, Mary. I simply do not know. God gave our men the duty of protecting us and our children. We must trust that they will do only what is right for us. We are so blessed to have such good men watching over us. So many women live lonely lives with too much toil and too little tenderness, but that is not our lot. If we go, I know God will go with us."

Mary nodded in reluctant agreement, wiping tears off her cheeks and picking up another handful of beans. She busied herself with preparing them. "I do believe you. And I do love him and trust him, though it overwhelms me at times. I am glad to have you here. You are a good friend to me."

❁

William and John Robinson sauntered around University of Leiden campus. They found great encouragement in their frequent walks and talks with one another. "Last night I was reading again the second letter we sent to Sir Edward Sandys two years ago, after we sent the Seven Articles," said William. More than once, it had proven beneficial to have a copy of what they'd sent off with their two ambassadors, Cushman and Carver.

"Here," continued William. "I brought it with me today. I thought it might strengthen our resolve in this matter if we reviewed it again." William pulled the old letter out of his pocket. "Let us sit under the shade of that birch. I would welcome a chance to sit a spell." He began to read, with Robinson interrupting often to finish the sentences he remembered so well. The document was becoming their own version of a creed of faith for their Separatist congregation. The essence of what they'd drafted was that:

  * They were loyal subjects to their king

* They believed the Lord Almighty was directing their endeavors

* They were well-weaned from the delicate milk of their mother country

* And used to difficulties of establishing themselves in a strange and hard land

* Which they had in great part overcome with patience

* Their people were as industrious and frugal as any company in the world

* They were now knit together as one body in a most strict and sacred bond and covenant

* Unlike other men, they would not be inclined to wish themselves home again should they encounter discontentments

William folded the document and returned it to his pocket. "Tell me, John, what do you think shall become of us? Perhaps we should stay in Leiden. You have done much good for our Lord here. You are respected among these halls as a teacher and a student. Our little flock has grown to nearly three hundred from our humblest of beginnings only a few years ago. Do you think we should leave, truly?"

Robinson stood and clasped his hands behind his back. He walked slowly along the path, back and forth in front of William. William remained seated on the grass, leaning against the giant birch. He looked up at his dear friend and spiritual guide in life, waiting for an answer that would settle the matter once and for all.

"I do earnestly pray that God will reveal to me, and to all of us, his intentions in this matter. You speak rightly about the numerous benefits and blessings God has poured out upon us here. Yet I wonder if this has not been but a much-needed place to rest and grow. Perhaps God has intended this to be a time of deepening our trust in His goodness; a time to gain a greater number of dear members who understand our desire to serve in the ways of those who first followed our Lord."

William stroked his beard for a moment before responding. "Yes, I see your point. Perhaps our Lord has only meant to prepare us here to go over to proclaim the gospel to those who have never heard of the wonders of our Lord's great love. Then our journey would not be for ourselves alone. It would be a mission like that of our ancient brother Paul, who went to Rome and Corinth and Ephesus."

"That is what I sometimes sense God is calling us to do."

The conversation was interrupted by a sudden shift in the weather. The wind was picking up, the birch leaves shivered, showing their lighter undersides, an indication rain was not far away. They decided to walk back to Robinson's home by way of the Golden Swan Pub. They entered to find Bradford and Carver already sharing a table, and joined their friends. Soon, the four were discussing their favorite topic: the advantages and feasibility of setting up a colony in the New World.

⁂

Letters back and forth between Leiden and England increased steadily over the ensuing months. The members of the Leiden congregation wrote with enthusiasm and conviction about their earnest desire to advance the king's wishes. The various men who received their letters held their fate in their hands. Back in February 1618, William and Robinson had sent word of their hopes of relocation to yet another person of influence. Sir John Wolstenholme served on the Virginia Council. On behalf of the king's privy council, he required yet another, more detailed accounting of Leiden's religious practices.

> *Dear Sir Wolstenholme,*
> *In response to your request to know more of the customs of our congregation at Leiden, we send you two declarations, and trust that you should know best which will most appeal to the privy council members.*
>
> *Yours, much bounded in all duty,*
>
> *John Robinson*
> *William Brewster*
> *Leiden, February 6 Anno: 1618*

When the letters were on their way north, Robinson explained to Bradford that they had sent one very short, vague declaration as well as one rather lengthy one reporting on such minutia as the fact that, unlike the ministers of the French Reformed churches, their ministers prayed with their heads uncovered. "We would minimize in the minds of the English authorities—and especially the mind of the king—the differences between our church and the Established Church of England," explained Robinson.

Yet another messenger was tasked with delivering the letter containing the two declarations. Sabine Staresmore carried the letters, which he had not read. Thus, when Wolstenholme asked questions about what Robinson and William had sent him, Staresmore had to improvise. "Who shall make their ministers?" asked Wolstenholme.

"The power of making ministers is in the church, to be ordained by the imposition of hands by the fittest instruments they have." Wolstenholme frowned. Staresmore improvised further. "The power of ordination must either be in the church or from the pope, and the pope is anti-Christ."

Wolstenholme frowned again. "Tis a pity these letters agree not with the Archbishop of Canterbury on the proper calling of ministers. I think it best not to show these letters to others, lest I spoil all."

Staresmore reported back to the congregation in Leiden that both the king and the bishops had consented to permit the Leiden congregation to colonize. He had met with Sir Edwin Sandys, and even had a meeting with the Virginia Council.

King James appeared to have Queen Elizabeth's tendency to frequently change direction. Initially, he seemed to like the idea of sending the annoying Separatists across the ocean, far away from his kingdom, where they could send money back to his treasury. The idea appealed to him greatly . . . until it did so no longer.

Much as Davison had been charged with delivering unpopular news to Queen Elizabeth, Secretary of State Naunton was tasked with informing the Leiden leaders they would now need to take up the matter with the Archbishop of Canterbury and the Bishop of London. Robinson was furious. "How they dangle us like puppets on a string."

Robinson, William Brewster, Bradford, and Carver had gathered once again to discuss their mutual dismay and frustration with this latest development. "Our hopes are dashed, but not gone," said William. "They would discourage us, but this only serves to strengthen our resolve."

"I do not think it wise to communicate with the bishops. How can they have our best interests in mind? Are they not the head of the very church from which we separated when we came here?" asked Robinson.

The others nodded in agreement. Bradford added, "Truly, this dampens our hopes."

Carver sighed. "Since we are in opposition with the English bishops, and have not the king's express approval, I fear the very foundation of our efforts to emigrate is crumbling. Perhaps we should not have tried to win the king's approval for our noncon-formist church."

"If God is with us, who then can persevere against us?" asked William. "I say we proceed with our plan."

"Perhaps the king does not truly object, but declines to give his approval in public," suggested Robinson.

"I agree," said Bradford. "Should we even have sought the king's favor? How will we know that he has kept his word?"

"Aye," agreed William. "He does change his mind as often as the winds change direction."

Messengers from Leiden to the Virginia Council were frequent passengers on the many ships sailing from Holland to England in 1618 and 1619.

One evening in late 1618, William wrote in his journal.

How much the present resembles the past. Davison and I once awaited word that Her Majesty Queen Elizabeth had consented to some favor; and now I wait here with my friends for word about King James. The names and places change, but the waiting continues on, seemingly without end. How long, O Lord? How long? Surely not as long as the Israelites spent in the desert! Yet it begins to feel as long. I must petition my Lord to grant me another measure of patience.

Yet how much better we are faring than Sir Walter Raleigh. With Queen Elizabeth, he was a hero, and greatly admired. Now he stands accused of treason, and in danger of being executed by King James. How much his situation reflects that of Davison when the queen betrayed him!

How is it that fools so often ascend to places of power? The good they could do is undone when their appetite for power goes unchecked. Why must he go so far as to undo the good already done by others? Now he has declared the people should be permitted to partake in sports, and even dancing on the Sabbath—the day the Lord set aside for worship and rest.

I do not think we shall have true rest until we govern our own affairs. As kind as our Dutch friends have been to us, they, too, dishonor our Lord with their games and frivolities on Sunday. We must continue to seek a patent to establish a place of our own.

❦

In the spring of 1619, the Leiden men again discussed how they should ever finally get the patent needed to relocate to the New World to establish their own self-governed community. Cushman labored in London, negotiating with the Virginia Council to obtain the patent that would grant them permission. They had before them a letter reporting the disastrous outcome for some of the Ancient Brethren they'd known in Amsterdam.

"'Tis shocking to read," said Robinson. "It saddens me greatly that so many souls were lost." He referred to the plight of Elder Francis Blackwell, who had led members of the Amsterdam Ancient Brethren to apply for their own patent to establish a colony in the New World.

He led them like lambs to the slaughter, wrote Carver. *One hundred and eighty set sail. Blackwell, along with all but fifty of them, died on the crossing. Even the master and some of the crew were gone to our Maker before they landed.*

"If that is what follows the bishop's blessing, happy are we that have missed the same," said Bradford.

Carver replied, "Cushman claims he would be glad to hear how this news will discourage us. He wrote, *I see none here discouraged much, but rather, a desire to learn to beware other men's harms and to amend where they have failed*. Do you agree?"

In unison, the other three shook their heads, an emphatic no. "I think perhaps I ought to join our friends in London to see what I might do to help our cause," said William.

Robinson agreed, so William began his time of separation from his beloved church and family. Mary was often at Robinson's home with news from her husband. Often, Robinson had news of his own to share with her.

When Mary had not heard from William for many weeks, she spoke with Robinson to learn what he might know. "I think he may not write us for fear of revealing where he is hiding. I know our Lord is watching over him. You must trust, Mary. All is unfolding according to our Lord's good and perfect plan."

Mary wished the Lord would find some way to provide that did not force her to manage without her husband quite so often. "We must trust both your father and our Lord to know best," she told the children when they again inquired how long they would have to wait to see their father again.

Pastor Robinson sent word to his congregation to gather for a day of discernment. It was a solemn day, devoted to asking the Lord for direction about how they should proceed. Robinson selected a passage from the Old Testament about David's men being afraid to go against the Philistines. Robinson read from I Samuel: *David asked counsel of the Lord again. And David found courage, and went. And the Lord delivered the Philistines into David's hand.*

The group agreed, that day, to make haste to find a way to leave. Though William was still in hiding in London, Robinson announced that William would accompany part of the congregation to the New World to serve as their spiritual leader. "He will do for you there all that I do for you here now, except he will not administer the sacraments. I will stay here with some of our members, and we shall join you as soon as we are able. In this way, you will be there to welcome us when we come. And should any who go now decide to return, we will be here to welcome them back."

The congregation decided that about half their members would go, and half would wait. Now all they needed was financing for the voyage across the Atlantic. As they awaited word from London that they were finally clear to go, a group of Dutch traders approached Robinson. They offered to take some of the Separatists to a Dutch trading post on Manhattan Island. "What they are suggesting is good," explained Robinson to the others. "They are offering us free passage, cattle, protection for as long as we should need it, and the right to self-govern with regard to internal affairs."

Bradford kept a journal of the events as they transpired.

12 February, 1620. Our Amsterdam merchants requested that two military warships accompany our members for protection.
11 April, 1620. The States-General denied the request.

Meanwhile, agents of the congregation met in London with Thomas Weston, a London entrepreneur who had shown interest in the industrious Separatists. He was also interested in ways to enrich himself, and never turned away from a prospective means of improving his financial lot in life.

Robinson greeted Weston on behalf of the congregation when the man traveled to Leiden to explore the possibility of backing their plans. Weston suggested, "Never mind about the Dutch, and do not depend too much on the Virginia Company. Should they fail you, I have friends who would provide the financing you need for this venture."

After so many months of waiting and wondering on the part of the Separatists, and looking for a sign that they might actually be ready to move forward with their plans, Weston said, "I will, of course, require something in writing of your intentions to show my fellow investors in England."

The leaders sent Weston back to London with their proposal. Mary, William, and others designated to be part of the first group to go began selling what they would not be able take, including their homes.

Mary added a plate for Jonathan to the dinner table. "Soon, we will part for a little while, so we must be together now all we can. My son, I know you will watch over Patience and Fear. Love and Wrestling, how you will gladden your father's heart when he sees you again. Soon, this test shall end. We must resolve now to do all we can to ease the worries of those charged with making arrangements for us."

Though she still hoped this might not come to pass, it did seem as if the hand of the Lord was guiding them. *Patience and Fear shall be welcome among the Robinsons. Jonathan will continue to do well with his ribbon-making. He shall be reunited with us soon enough. I must focus on what lies before me, and leave to God what will happen tomorrow.*

The following Sunday afternoon, Robinson announced good news from London. "Weston writes they have formed a joint stock company of seventy investors who put up seven thousand pounds each. He is confident they shall see a profit from the hunting and fishing we will carry out. Half the profits will be ours, and half shall be theirs. Carver and Cushman are continuing on in London. Our brother William is surely there, as well, but he must remain hidden until it is time to depart. Now our friends are busying themselves with making arrangements for the money they received from the Adventurers. I have advised them not to exceed the bounds of their commission."

It sounded too good to be true! The years in exile were finally coming to an end: the months of messages back and forth, and the promise of a future in a new land withdrawn time and again. Now, it seemed that they could see the promised land just over the horizon.

Yet more challenges presented themselves. Weston told Carver and Cushman that the investors required a few modest changes to the arrangement. "The settlers propose that they work five days a week for us, and take two for their own needs. We will need them to work all seven days for our benefit, since we are providing the funding that will allow them the freedom to work in a new land. Also, the settlers propose that the houses they build and the gardens around them should be their own. We must insist that these be the company's, in common, for the duration of the first seven years. Then we will divide them according the number of shares each of us holds."

Carver and Cushman conferred. "Pastor Robinson has given us no permission to agree to this!" exclaimed Carver.

"But if we do not, they will surely withdraw their support. We shall never see the new land," pointed out Cushman.

"We surely deserve better treatment than this! These terms better suit thieves and bond slaves than honest men. We are being asked to work for seven years without wages, as indentured servants. Why should we plan to take servants with us when this agreement makes us all servants?"

Cushman responded, "Did not Jacob work seven years to earn the right to be with his beloved Rachel? Seven years is but a moment in God's time. We must ensure that those in Leiden agree."

Robinson, usually a mild-mannered and patient man, was furious with this turn of events. He wrote a scathing letter to his brother-in-law, Carver, challenging Cushman's assertions. *Cushman, though a good man of special abilities, is known to be most unfit for dealing with other men by reason of his singularity and great indifference to conditions.*

For his part, Cushman insisted that the Adventurers would have withdrawn their offer had they not accepted the terms. He wrote back, *In the matter of home ownership, the settlers should not plan to build valuable houses. The purpose is to build, for the present, such houses that may, with little grief, be set afire and run away by the light.*

Robinson was as frustrated as he was disappointed. William was away, still in hiding, and Cushman and Carver were being run over by Weston. "It all seems impossible, Lord," he pleaded one evening while alone in his study. "This is too great a burden. Some have withdrawn, and I am confident others would also have done so had they not already sold their very homes in preparation for our journey."

Perhaps to soften the new arrangements, or perhaps to prevent the Separatists from refusing to leave after all, Weston encouraged the leaders to go to New England on a land grant that came from the Virginia patent, separately from the government established there. William's former financial backer, James Brewer, was among the investors.

William learned of the plans and wrote in his journal: *More and more, I feel the Israelites leaving Egypt were kindred spirits. Though we now number far fewer, I am beginning to understand all that Moses had to endure to get the pharaoh to let his people go. Yet if this is God's will for us, all will unfold according to His perfect timing.*

Apparently, it was God's will—or at least it was not against God's will. For while William was in hiding, others debated the details and slowly made progress finalizing their emigration plans. He resigned himself to the reality he'd have to hide from the authorities in both England and Holland to avoid capture. Yet still he managed to meet with Robinson and others to work out how to obtain the patent. William sent one last letter to family in Scrooby to let them know their departure for the New World was imminent.

PART FOUR

The

Voyage

CHAPTER FORTY-EIGHT

LEIDEN AND ENGLAND – 1620

WILLIAM pushed a few more books and journals into his bag, looking up when Mary came in. She said nothing, but her eyes made it clear she did not like finding him packing again. "Sit a spell with me, Mary. I long to reassure you that all is well, and all shall be well."

"I would find that easier to believe if I did not find you once more preparing to leave us. Where will you go? When will I see you again? How am I to manage so much without you here by my side?"

"Mary, Mary, you worry about many things. But as Jesus said to Martha when she worried, only one thing matters. And that is to do the will of our Lord. That is what we are doing, darling. Please do try to understand. I must leave now so that I might soon journey with you and the children. Enforcers are all about. It is not safe for me to stay here. If I were to tell you where I am going, even if I myself knew, then you would be in danger, as well. This way, if the enforcers come calling, you will be able to truthfully tell them you do not know where I have gone.

"It won't be long now until we will sail far away to a new life in a new land. If the enforcers find me before it is time to sail, I fear it will not go as well for me as it did the last time. Just think of it, Mary. We shall build our own village. We will be free to worship as we believe God intends. With time and hard work, we will prosper soon enough—and then we shall be free indeed."

Mary folded her hands together in her lap and sighed. "I see the logic of your thinking, but cannot yet accept it could be God's plan to separate us when we have been joined together all this time."

William walked behind where Mary was sitting and gently stroked her hair. *I have words enough to fill volumes of books, yet I lack words now to comfort my wife. God help me, for I know not where else to turn.* "Mary, can you not see how in these past years God has so woven us into the fabric of a little community of saints; and that when one member is absent, others quickly fill in? Pastor Robinson and Bridget will ensure you have all you need in my absence. It will be only for a short while, perhaps just a few more weeks. We have already procured the services of the *Speedwell.* Soon, all preparations will be completed, and we will begin our journey."

Mary said nothing. She sat, twirling several strands of hair. Finally, she stood to face her husband of nearly twenty-eight years. She patted William's cheeks and pulled him toward her, then hugged him with her face firmly nestled in the crook of his neck.

"I shall endeavor to become more like my namesake, Mary, mother of our Lord. Now then, tell me, what more do you need from us as you prepare to depart?"

"My books, Mary. Next to you and our children, I count these as my most precious things. Please bring with you those that I am unable to take with me now."

William packed what he thought he'd need until they boarded the *Speedwell.* He walked out of the house without looking back and scurried to Jonathan's cottage behind Robinson's home.

"You must look after your mother, and do all that she needs now until it is time for her to leave. Patience and Fear will be tended to well by our friends, yet I would that you look after them as well, after your mother and brothers leave."

"I shall, Father. You can count on me."

"That I believe. Until we are reunited, be safe in the Lord's care." William offered his son a stiff embrace, and abruptly turned and walked through the cottage door without looking back.

His next stop was the Robinson's home, where he spent a few final hours in his friend's study—the study where they'd spent so many hours discussing what was now coming to pass. "I know we shall be united through our prayers until we are reunited in our new settlement. I pray the time apart will be short," William said, pulling his beard.

"Know, dear friend, that I will care for your loved ones as if they were my own. Indeed, in Christ, they are my family as surely as Bridget and our children. Travel safely with God. Get word to me whenever you can of how you are faring."

The two men embraced. William clenched his jaw and turned away from the man who had been closer to him than even his brothers. He pulled his shoulders back, took in a deep breath, and walked out the door and down the street. Robinson watched out the window until his friend was no longer in sight. William was off to England again to hide from those who would arrest him.

CHAPTER FORTY-NINE

HOLLAND AND ENGLAND – 1620

The *Speedwell* was a sixty-ton pinnace. The Separatists paid to have it overhauled, anticipating it would stay with them to serve as a fishing vessel. They would join a cargo ship, the *Mayflower,* in Southampton, England. The fact none of the members of their community had any fishing experience did not dampen their enthusiasm. They assumed if it was God's plan to pay for their passage by fishing, God would teach them how to do just that. After all, hadn't they learned new trades to support themselves in Amsterdam and Leiden? Certainly they could learn this trade as well.

"Captain Myles Standish will serve you well and defend you from all danger," Robinson said. Some were complaining, worried that they couldn't trust the strangers their financiers had foisted upon them. Robinson continued his praise for Standish. "He served admirably among the English troops when we were in Amsterdam. Remember how we often saw English soldiers here in the Low Country? I have heard he is even now packing weapons and ammunition for the trip. Though he is yet a young man of thirty-six, he has sufficient experience to serve you well."

Over the summer of 1620, Mary made final arrangements for her daughters. She had hoped Patience would be married before they left, but since she was not, Mary was grateful that the Robinson family would take in both daughters. Love, now age ten, and Wrestling, age six, were going with her. Jonathan would stay behind in his own cottage. With his work as a ribbon maker, he could take care of himself and look after his sisters. It was far from ideal. Mary often had to force herself not to dwell on the ache in her chest every time she thought about splitting their family apart.

Four additional children were assigned to three of the departing families. The arrangements were spelled out in a letter to the congregation from Robert Cushman.

Thomas Weston now has in his care four children who are without parents to properly provide for them. He has determined that they should travel with the others to the New World. They are to be sufficiently kept and maintained with meat, drink, apparel, and lodging. At the end of seven years, they shall have 50 acres of land apiece in Virginia.

Two of the children, Richard and Ellen More, were assigned to the Brewster family as servants. Jasper went with the Carvers, and Mary with the Winslows.

Carver and Cushman continued their negotiations in England, staying busy purchasing supplies for the journey.

On the warm Sunday morning of July 20, Mary Brewster and her children went to the Robinson's house for the last service they would ever attend there. Always ready with an encouraging word, Robinson urged his congregation "to be ready to receive any further truth God might reveal to you. Join with other godly ministers who may come to the New World and seek unity in the Christian church rather than division."

He also advised them to separate themselves from the distasteful title of Brownists. Edward Winslow and William Bradford diligently wrote down the words of instruction from their beloved leader so they could remember them and have them available to instruct the children as they grew to an age of understanding.

Shortly after the service ended, they smelled the culinary efforts of the Leiden women who were staying behind. "It is a feast fit for a king!" declared Winslow when he saw the tables laden with many delicious items lovingly prepared for those leaving by those who were staying.

Mary dabbed at tears between mouthfuls. Bridget sat with her. Both women wept at the thought that their frequent fellowship must come to a close, at least for some time to come. "I shall put a bowl out for you when I make preparations for our meal. I will pretend that you have gone only for a moment to fetch something, and will be back shortly to converse with me, as we have so often done."

Mary hugged her dear friend and wiped away more tears with the backs of her hands. At last, Robinson could bear the sorrow of his congregation no longer. He began singing one of the psalms they had often sung together. Soon others joined him, and before long, they were all distracted with their singing.

"It was the sweetest melody that ever mine ears heard," Winslow would often say on their journey across the ocean.

❧

Mary woke the children before dawn. "Hurry. We must get to the canal and get on the boat that will take us to Delft Haven." Patience, Fear, and Jonathan went with Mary and the younger boys, accompanied by many of their friends from the congregation. They dreaded the final moments when they would have to divide into the group that was going and the group that would stay behind. Even a few friends and former neighbors from their Amsterdam days met the Brewsters at Delft Haven where the *Speedwell* was anchored.

Many women carried baskets of food to send off with their departing sisters and brothers. Robinson gathered his congregation one more time for a farewell prayer. He dropped to his knees and poured out his heart on behalf of those who would be on their way in just a few more minutes. One by one, the others did the same. With a lump in his throat the size of a Brussel sprout, Robinson pleaded with God to grant them safe passage. When he looked around, he saw that all of them were weeping—the only variation being how hard.

Those destined to stay behind walked with the departing group to the ship, but could not speak for the tears that overcame them. Mary wept openly as she hugged Jonathan, Patience, and Fear one last time.

"Come, sisters, we must leave Mother and our brothers in God's hand." Jonathan pulled on his sisters' arms and led them away. "Let us get on the canal boat and return to Leiden. God will watch over them until we meet again. We must be strong. That is what Father would want of us." The sisters reluctantly followed, but they looked back even as they slowly walked away.

Mary stood on the deck of the *Speedwell* with Love and Wrestling on either side of her. She kept her eyes fixed on the spot she had last seen Jonathan and her daughters. She looked in that direction until the land became a blur and the spray of the salt water made her eyes sting.

⁂

Bradford found a place to sit on the deck of the ship and pulled out a journal. Writing was difficult with the ship's motion, but he wanted to capture the moment. *Truly, it is as when the Israelites set forth across the parted Red Sea. We have left that goodly and pleasant city that had been our resting place for nearly twelve years; but we know we are pilgrims, and so we dwell not on those things, but lift our eyes to the heavens and our dearest country. This quiets our spirits.*

CHAPTER FIFTY

SOUTHAMPTON, ENGLAND – SUMMER 1620

"Look, Love! See, Wrestling! The masts of that ship, there. Soon, we shall see Father again and begin our crossing," said Mary. She pressed against the railing of the *Speedwell*, willing the ship to pull into the dock faster. "There. Look over there. Do you see Father?"

The Brewster boys stood on their tiptoes, straining to see their father. The dock was so crowded that neither they nor Mary could spot William. When the *Speedwell* docked and the passengers stepped onto the dock, Mary saw Cushman and Carver, but no sign of her husband. Her heart sank like a stone in a pond. She wanted to ask someone if they knew where he was, but didn't know who to approach. With one arm around the shoulder of each of her young sons, she slowly made her way through the crowd. Still, no sign of him. Now her heart was racing. *What if the enforcers found him? I won't sail away to a strange land without him. But we have nowhere to live if we go back. And how would we get back? This ship is going to America. I must find out where he is—but how?*

Mary concentrated on speaking calmly so as not to alarm her sons. She told them with a conviction she could only pretend to possess, "It is very crowded here. I'm sure he's looking for us as much as we are for him. It will only be a little longer."

The passengers recruited to voyage with them began introducing themselves. Mary overheard a few of them arguing with raised voices. She snapped her head toward them, thinking perhaps William was there, but in trouble. Still no sight of him. Holding on to her sons by their hands, she inched her way through the crowd.

The voices belonged to Bradford and Winslow. They were yelling at Cushman and Carver to join them. They brought with them Tom Weston. Skipping any civility, Weston launched into his demand. "You must accept the terms we laid out to you through Cushman."

"That we cannot and will not do," said Bradford. In the absence of both William and Robinson, Bradford shouldered enormous responsibility on behalf of his group. He pulled Carver and Cushman aside for a hastily convened meeting with Winslow.

"Perhaps, if we offer to extend the contract another seven years, if our first seven prove not to be profitable to their liking, that will mollify them," suggested Winslow.

"Perhaps it will," agreed Cushman.

It did not. Weston informed them, "Not one more penny shall I provide you if you will not adhere to the terms I am compelled to carry out on behalf of the London Company."

The men found themselves caught in an economic trap. They could not return to Leiden, for they'd already sold everything they had that was not in the hold of the *Speedwell* or ready to load onto the *Mayflower*. In addition, they had just come through heart-wrenching farewells with those they had left behind.

"We must press onward somehow. But how?" asked Carver. "Even if we pull together all that we have, it will not cover our fees to depart from this port for both the *Mayflower* and the *Speedwell*." Reluctantly, they agreed that they must determine what they could sell to raise sufficient funds to continue. They got busy selling what they thought they could best spare: their surplus of butter.

Carver approached Mary and whispered to her that he would take her to where William was hiding. She clutched his arm. "You know? He is safe? I have been so worried."

Carver removed her hand from his arm and reassured her. "He is fine. It is still dangerous for him to be out. We will bring him aboard when we can hide him in the midst of many of our group. He is well, and most anxious to see you and the boys. Follow me."

When Mary saw William, she leapt into his arms. She was too overwrought with relief to speak. The boys hopped up and down with excitement as their parents clung to one another, until William turned his attention to them. He ruffled the hair on each boy's head and led them to the tiny room that served as his hiding place. "You must tell me everything about the trip. What impressed you most?"

Now that their parents were together again, the boys began to talk with great animation, both at once. William laughed. Mary sat on the edge of the bed and wept—this time, tears of relief and joy at having at least this much of her family together again.

As the afternoon shadows grew long, William told Mary she must take the boys and return to the ship for the night. There was no room for them in his tiny room, and he could not risk traveling with them. "I will come aboard when opportunity presents itself; but I shall remain out of sight, even on the ship, until we are out to sea and I am away from those who still hunt me."

※

Their final preparations were underway. Local farmers cut hay for them to take aboard. When they arrived, they would mix the hay with mud to make their first homes. Workers plucked apples and pears from trees and packed them into barrels. The ship crew loaded barrels of beer, water, flour, jerky, and grain into the holds of the ships. "It is a challenge loading enough food for two or more months," groused one of the sailors as he wrestled with another barrel.

"We cannot count on finding food where we go. I do not relish the idea of dying out there for want of food," said the other, pointing in the direction of the Atlantic.

Meanwhile, John Alden supervised the men who were dismantling their shallop. They planned to store it in four sections in the Mayflower's hold. Alden was one of the men the Adventurers insisted join them. His skills as a cooper would have to double as carpentry skills. Other workers stored gardening and building tools wherever they found space.

"Glad this ain't where I'll be on the crossing," said one of the sailors.

His mate groaned under the weight of the barrel they were rolling into place in the hold. "Think I'd rather be tossed overboard than cooped up down here with all them little ones."

Daylight gave way to dusk. William cautiously made his way to the dock and slipped a few coins to a quartermaster to ensure his things ended up on the ship. Then he stood in the shadows near the dock pub, watching and waiting until he saw several people preparing to board the ship. He quickly slipped in among them, and, pressing as closely as possible, followed the group up the gangplank.

After months and years of praying, discerning, hoping, and planning, the group was now close to leaving. By this time tomorrow, they would be out in the open sea. William did not want to be snatched away in these final hours before they sailed, yet he feared that if the ship tarried much longer, the enforcers would find his hiding place. Would Mary and the boys be trapped into sailing without him? If so, how would she manage on her own with no home to return to?

Therefore, it was better to hide somewhere on the *Mayflower*. He'd already told Mary to cling to Strangers who were sailing on that ship. Most of the Separatists would travel on the *Speedwell*, but since the *Mayflower* was bigger, William thought he could more easily hide there.

Once on board, he quickly made his way to the first hold and explored until he found the perfect hiding place. It was a small closet where the crew stored the sails. Should anyone approach, he could easily hide under the sails. Confident that he would be safe there, William left to find Bradford to give him a message for Mary. "Tell her I am on board and safe. I will find her when we are at sea, and I am confident I am out of reach of those who would take delight in arresting me."

✠

Some of the Separatist men gathered with the Strangers sent to them by Weston. They were all eager to work out the details of how they would govern themselves during the long voyage. The Separatists had already determined that William would be the head of the congregation if no minister from England was available to travel with them. The Adventurers had not found an ordained minister willing to make the trip, so Elder William would assume the role as their spiritual leader, as they'd arranged back in Leiden. He carried with him a letter from Robinson to read to them when he thought it safe to come out of hiding. Robinson sent the letter to him via Bradford.

Evidently, Robinson was worried about what would happen when he was not with them to teach, correct, and lead them along the path of peace and harmony. William had read the letter so often, he had it nearly memorized. In it, Robinson urged the people to live together in peace, both with one another and with the Strangers. Like it or not, their fates were interlocked. William read the letter again by the light of a lantern he'd found hanging on a hook near a brick oven where bread was baking. His throat constricted as he poured over the familiar handwriting. He could almost hear his friend speaking to him, and willed himself not to feel remorse over what could not be changed.

> *You are about to become a body politic and no one among you is of special eminency, so ask God to guide you as you choose those persons most prepared to promote the common good. Once you have chosen men such as these, give them all due honor and obedience in their lawful administrations.*

William folded the letter and tucked it away. *As soon as we are safely at sea, I must read this to them, and we must pray to discern who should assume these roles.*

As it turned out, Christopher Martin, one of the Strangers sent by Weston, became governor of the *Mayflower* group. Cushman assumed that function on the *Speedwell*. Martin took the role quite seriously, proving himself a strict disciplinarian. Cushman was more concerned about his failing health than the duties of governorship.

The two ships set sail from Southampton August 5, and problems erupted almost immediately. The *Speedwell* began to leak only a week after leaving Southampton. The two ships turned back to England, docking at Dartmouth. While waiting for the ship to be repaired, Cushman wrote of his anguish to a friend in London.

> *What to call it I know not, but it is like a bundle of lead, as it were, crushing my heart more and more these fourteen days. The Speedwell is open and leaky as a sieve.*

Cushman also poured out his frustration about Martin, who began to act as if he were their king rather than a stranger pushed upon them at the last hour. *He will give no account for our money that he has spent on provisions. He is so insulting to our poor people, and acts with scorn and contempt, as if they were not good enough to wipe his shoes. He will not even tolerate that they should go ashore, lest they run away.*

<hr>

Separatists and Strangers alike became increasingly frustrated, as one day followed the next and fair winds blew without filling their sails. William was torn. He wanted to be with Mary to assure her all would be well, and that God would tend to them, yet he still worried that one of the crew could betray them, as had happened during their first attempt to leave England so long ago. The boys were still so young. He dared not let them know where he was, for fear they would give him away in their youthful innocence and excitement.

Bradford kept him supplied with food and information about what was transpiring, and delivered William's words of encouragement to Mary. Adding to William's consternation was the news that Martin had already managed to alienate the sailors when they were not yet out of sight of England. Bradford, Carver, and Cushman all did what they could to mitigate the situation, which grew more dismal each day they remained stranded.

On August 23, the *Speedwell* was again ready to set sail. However, before the sun set that day, the ship began to leak again. They anchored at Plymouth. The ship repair crew pronounced the ship unfit for an Atlantic crossing. Bradford confided to William, "Perhaps the crew has brought these problems upon us on purpose, to avoid the passage and to be relieved of their promise to stay a year in the New World."

William replied, "I pray that is not so. In either case, it matters not. We must rearrange our plans and be grateful the *Mayflower* has proven seaworthy." The *Speedwell* passengers resigned themselves to that which they could not change, and began the arduous task of moving all their supplies and belongings from the *Speedwell* to the *Mayflower*. When it became obvious that the *Mayflower* could not contain the passengers of two ships plus all their supplies, twenty people decided to stay in England. Robert Cushman, eager to reunite with his new wife and son, was one of them.

On September 6, the *Mayflower* at long last sailed away from Plymouth.

CHAPTER FIFTY-ONE

THE ATLANTIC OCEAN – FALL 1620

Grateful to at last be sailing away from England, William turned to his journal. He took the lantern he'd found hanging on a peg in the galley, along with the stick used to light it, and, seeing no one, lit the stick from the flames of the ship's oven. Light flickered through dozens of pinprick holes in the lantern's tin frame. It wasn't much, but it was enough light to see. He set the lantern on the floor and secured it between his feet. Using one of his many books as a lap desk, he wrote:

> *7 September, 1620*
> *Now in my fifty-third year, I again leave an old life behind to begin a new adventure. Scrooby and the people of my youth seem so long ago and far away. I can scarcely recall the young men I met at Cambridge, but how fortunate was I to have that time of intellectual nourishment.*
> *Even more, how fortunate was I to have such adventures with William Davison. What value I gained from my association with him and the events I witnessed. Even though it ended sadly, I am grateful for the experience. When I left Holland after his disgrace, I did not think I should ever see that country again. Now, I leave the land that has been home to me and my dear family these past dozen years. I shall never again see the place of my birth, nor shall I see the place I have most recently called home. I feel a twinge of sorrow at the thought, yet our Lord calls us ever forward, and I must follow.*

Whatever transpires now is truly in the hands of God Almighty. I pray I shall be up to the tasks presented by this new land. Into God's tender care I commit myself now.

While William was writing, Governor Christopher Martin was reviewing the passenger list with Master Christopher Jones. "Are you sure you've given me an accurate count, Governor?"

"Of course, I have." Martin's face turned crimson with anger at being challenged. "If it will give you assurance none here are cheating you, we shall go over it again. Not counting you and your own crew, we are a hundred plus two passengers. Thirty-three are children; maybe a dozen of them are old enough to be of some help. The rest young enough to be trouble if I don't stay after them—which I shall. They shall stay out of your crew's way, or by God, they will wish they had. I urge you to make haste crossing. Three of the women are with child."

"Bloody bunch of rebels. Too bad they weren't all on the *Speedwell*, that leaky excuse for a ship. The *Mayflower* wasn't built for so many. Usually, it's me and my crew and barrels of wine and dry goods, not womenfolk with noisy brats and dogs. Do I look like a tavern or a boarding house? What sort of a man brings a woman with child on a trip like this?"

"Weston paid you well, nearly a pound a person, plus what the Virginia Company gave you. I overheard the deal myself. So no more of this. Do your part, and deliver us to the New World."

Master Jones puffed out his chest and straightened up his five-foot six-inch frame to its full height. "I'm in charge now. We're on the open sea. You can call yourself governor if you please, but I will be the one calling out the orders here, not some flatlander who knows nothing about being on the sea. Tell me, who was that old man I saw sneaking about?"

"You must speak of William Brewster. He is one of the rebels who fled England some twelve years ago now. I know him to be over fifty, though by how much, I cannot guess. I'm told he's the main troublemaker among the Leiden group. The others readily agree to whatever he tells them. He's been hiding from the English and Dutch authorities nigh on a year now. He is a felon, but somehow, his group managed to get their grant to leave. I suppose King James had enough of them. If you saw him, he must think it's safe to come out from hiding now.

"How many of these rebels come from Holland?"

"I count forty. But I missed William because he was hiding. With him, forty-one of them, and sixty-one it pleased the Adventurers to send over. They are freemen, servants, and hired hands. I think the Adventurers worried the religious rebels would not know enough to start a settlement, so they recruited more folks to work and make them a profit. Someone said four of the children are orphans. Or maybe their parents saw a chance to be rid of them. I heard talk of such. Weston passed them off as servants, and split them up among three families."

Master Jones swore and grunted. "Go over your list again. Let me match it against my book." They finished matching lists of names.

Governor Martin concluded, "The Adventurers hired a few to work as crew for the settlers. They recruited Myles Standish to protect them. Captain Standish said he plans to make an army out of the men before we see land again. I say he won't have much success, but he is welcome to give it a go. That makes a total of fifty adult men, nineteen adult women, and thirty-three children. And there might be thirty-four children aboard if we don't cross in good time."

Master Jones growled, "Damn fools to take young ones so far."

"They would say they are full of faith. In any case, you get paid the same, regardless. Are we in agreement, then?"

Jones sighed and said, "We are. You tell all of them to stay where they belong. I will not tolerate children running wild and troubling the crew."

"I can assure you, they shall all do as they are told or very much regret it."

❦

Mary told the boys they could see what some of the other children were doing. She looked about, trying to tidy up the small space they'd established in the tween deck as their home for . . . who knew how long? Maybe eight weeks? Maybe less, if the winds were favorable. Longer, if not. She leaned against a section of the thirty-foot shallop. Before sailing, a few men had put the dissembled shallop near where they stored the cannons. The cannons ensured protection should they encounter pirates along the way.

Once they reached the New World, they planned to put the shallop back together and use it to explore.

This is hopeless, thought Mary. *How can I make any order out of this? There is no place to put anything. I can cross from end to end in less than sixty paces, and not even thirty to cross from side to side. Even if there were a place to properly store our things, how long would anything stay put with this constant rolling and pitching? When will William think it safe enough to come out of hiding and help me?* She bit her lower lip to keep from crying in her exasperation.

Mary visualized her large fireplace where she'd prepared so many meals for family . . . and friends who always seemed to show up just as she was setting out food. She pictured the bed she and William had shared, and felt a palpable ache that made her wince as she realized how little privacy they would now have for weeks and weeks on end. She let her mind wander up the stairs to the garret and printing press . . . the room that had caused the trouble leading to the current journey.

Mary tried not to imagine Jonathan, Patience, and Fear because thinking about them hurt with a pain akin to that of labor. Nonetheless, images of them floated by as if they were actually present. She rubbed her upper arms to chase away the shivers that consumed her. Mary's chest ached with longing.

I cannot endure such sorrow for all the days of this journey. I must do what I can to make this as pleasant as possible for William's sake. She focused her thoughts on him, and prayed that God would soon bring him out from hiding and to her side. Mary dusted imaginary lint off her skirts and walked over to a group of children busy in an imaginary world of their own making.

⁂

"Love? Wrestling? Where are you? Come out now. You boys, come to me at once!" The small space they shared with the others was too small for the boys to be out of sight for long . . . yet she could not find them. *If they tried to go up to the main deck, the crew would surely have chased them back down.* A growing sense of worry began to overtake Mary. *Have they gone to the galley? They are always hungry. Perhaps they thought the cook would take pity on them and give them something to eat.*

Muttering a complaint to William, who wasn't there to hear it, Mary started for the ladder, holding her skirts up with one hand and cautiously climbing one rung at a time with the other. Halfway up the ladder, she heard a gruff voice cussing.

"Get out o' here 'fore I feed you to the fish. Ain't I got enough problems trying to fix food in this hellhole of a galley without you snooping around? Where's your ma? Where's your pa?"

Mary raised her head high enough to see what was happening and gasped. "Love! Wrestling! You come here this instant! What has gotten into you?" She finished her precarious climb and stood at the edge of the galley. "Didn't I tell you to stay where I could see you? You cannot, you simply must NOT wander off. It is too dangerous. I said, Come here! Have you gone deaf?"

Love took Wrestling's small hand. Looking down at their feet, they inched their way toward their mother. They couldn't decide which was the more threatening adult at the moment . . . Mary or the angry man with the apron and unshaven face. When her children were within a few feet of her, Mary heard another voice coming from below the ladder she had just climbed.

"There, there, Mary. Do not be too hard on them. I believe they were looking for me." William finished his ascent up the ladder and stood next to her.

"William!" she exclaimed. "And are you satisfied now that it is safe to come out of hiding?"

William noted an edge to her voice that wasn't usually there. *We've barely begun our journey and I fear she is already pushed to the limits of her patience.*

The cook waved a long-handled ladle in the air as if he were getting ready to launch a slingshot of hot something at them. "Get outta here! The lot of you. I got work to do, and you ain't helping. Outta here. Now! And stay out of my way unless you want to be food for fish."

William grabbed his boys, one under each arm, and twirled them around before setting them down. He instructed Mary to descend first. Then he put Love on the first rung and followed. He called for Wrestling to come last.

"You heard the gentleman," said William. "Down you go, now, and don't be causing your weary mother any more trouble with your shenanigans. We shall talk when we're out of this kind man's way."

When they were all back on the tween deck, Mary gave William a quick hug and then they huddled together between the curtains Mary had somehow managed to hang around the small spot she had designated as "home" for now. They sat on their sleeping pallets and exchanged accounts of the past few days. William began combing his beard with his fingers. "What is it, William? What thoughts are going through your mind?"

"I must gather our congregation. I have a letter from dear Pastor Robinson to read to them. And we must thank God for bringing us safe thus far. We must never allow ourselves to take God's mercy and providence for granted. Mary, will you speak to the women and gather them all in this bit of open space in the middle? Here, I brought you a lantern to provide a bit of light. I will find the men. Love and Wrestling, I am counting on you to help your mother now, and be no new source of worry to her. You will be trustworthy in this matter, won't you?"

The boys nodded, saying in unison, "Yes, Father."

"Good. Then I'm off to gather the men. We shall meet here for our first congregational meeting on the *Mayflower.* I suppose we shall have many occasions for others in the weeks to come."

⁂

Scarcely had the last member of their congregation found a place to stand when the men began voicing their concerns in rapid succession. "He's too strict," said one of the Leiden men.

"He will turn the whole crew against us all with his meanness," insisted another.

"He shows no respect for any of us."

In a matter of a few days, Governor Martin had alienated pretty much everyone on board. William listened as one man after another rendered his assessment of the situation. He stroked his beard as they spoke, eventually raising his hand high over his head to silence them.

"Although we had thought we would sail as one cohesive congregation, all of the same mind and purpose, God has willed it otherwise. It may be to our advantage that Governor Martin and the others are traveling with us. Whether it is for our benefit that we may have assistance in the wilderness or for theirs, that we may show them the true path of faith. That is for God alone to know. We must pray for God's guidance, and for his will to be done. As Pastor Robinson admonished us in his letter, we must work together and give all due honor and obedience to the lawful administration of our affairs."

He knelt on the wooden deck floor and bid the others do so, as well. Several grabbed onto one another to keep their balance as the ship continued to roll with increasing frequency and intensity. William offered his prayer and had barely said "Amen," when a bell rang, indicating they could come fetch their evening meal.

Mary went over to a group of children, where she found Richard and Ellen More. "Come with me and be quick about it. I have a bowl for you to share." She gave another wooden bowl to Love to share with Wrestling. With William finally out of hiding to help her, she told the children to sit on the sleeping pallet and wait until the two of them returned with food.

She and William slowly made their way to the galley where they held out the two children's bowls for the ill-tempered cook to fill. They each carried them to the children, and returned with their portions of the watery broth and hard biscuits that would have to suffice as the last meal of the day.

The ship rolled from side to side, up and down, making it difficult to get everyone situated. Space was at a premium, so the children sat together on a sleeping pallet against the wall of the hold. Mary tucked a blanket around the four of them, saying, "Now, stay here until I come for you." She hoped the rolling back and forth would have the effect of rocking them to sleep. When she heard their breathing slow and deepen, she determined it safe to turn her attention to William.

"Truly, I do not know how we will survive this! There is no privacy. Even the simplest aspects of daily life have become an enormous effort. Will we wear these same clothes until we see land? How shall I occupy the children day in and out?"

William stroked Mary's hair as they stood facing one another with feet wide apart, trying to stay upright. They were surrounded by the murmur of a dozen other conversations. "I know it's a hardship for now, dear wife. But it is a blessing to be free of worry about prison, where I might have been beaten and prevented from ever speaking of God's saving word. Though it is difficult now, it is a blessing to be crossing, at long last, toward our Promised Land. The discomfort of this wretched ocean now is worth it for the wonders we shall see on the other side. This shall pass soon enough. We shall build a fine new home. We will build a meeting-house where we can pray, and never again fear interference from those who would take us into bondage. Mary, just trust a bit more, and a little longer. It shall all be well. All will be well."

Mary sighed and leaned into her husband, more because she had lost her balance and pitched forward than because she felt any affection at the moment. "I shall try. Honestly, I shall try."

Days passed, one as tedious as the next. The monotony was broken once or twice a day when one of the two dogs on board tried to steal someone's unattended food or when bored children got into a ruckus. From time to time, someone ventured too close to one of Master Jones's crew members, only to be promptly chased away with a string of expletives that caused the mothers to cover the ears of any children nearby.

Martin routinely lashed out at passengers for some offense, real or imaginary. William, Bradford, Carver, and the other Leiden men did what they could to smooth things over. As often as he could, William found a place to read or write in his journal. Space and privacy were rare commodities with 102 passengers crammed into spaces usually used for cargo. Day by monotonous day, they sailed further from the familiar, into the unknown.

Chapter Fifty-Two

The Atlantic Ocean – Fall 1620

"Are you Mr. Brewster, sir?"

"I am. What is your name?"

"William Trevore, sir. Hired to serve under Shipmaster Jones. That is why I come to you, sir. Master Jones wants to see you in his cabin. Now. He seemed quite eager. Follow me."

William followed the young man he guessed to be about the age of his daughter Patience. He entered the master's quarters and stood between the door and a wooden desk covered with maps, a compass, and other nautical items. Master Jones's stout physique showed the effects of many pints of ale. He was standing on the other side of his desk with a green-tinted window behind him letting in a stream of sunlight. Jones clenched the top of the desk chair and, with a scowl, looked William over from his white hair to his leather shoes.

"You are Brewster?" His question sounded more like a bark than an inquiry.

William nodded.

"Let me give it to you straight. Here on the sea, I am in charge. No one but me makes the decisions about what happens and does not happen. You understand?"

"Yes, Master Jones, of course."

"Then tell me, by whose authority do you—not even a pastor, nor one even authorized—dare to preach on my ship?"

"I was appointed spiritual leader of our congregation in the absence of our pastor, John Robinson. He stayed in Holland to tend to the others who will join us as soon as Providence permits."

"Renegades. All of you. It's not right for a man to disrespect the king and the one Established Church."

William said nothing as Master Jones continued to glare at him. William wondered if he was deciding what to do with him now that they were several days out to sea. *Surely, after two delays, he will not want to turn back now.* "Master Jones, as I think you must know, many of our people are sailing for the first time in their lives. Some are quite sick from the motion of the ship. It comforts them to hear a bit of Scripture and reassurances that we shall soon reach our destination."

"Enough!" shouted Jones. "Not my problem a bunch of bloody landlubbers cannot take to the ocean. My problem is keeping order on this ship. My men do not expect to hear preachers—or anyone pretending to be one—blabbering on and on about this and that. They've enough to manage to keep us sailing west."

"We are so confined, for many long hours every day. These poor people only seek a word of comfort now and then. What would you have us do to avoid presenting a further burden to your crew?"

Jones chewed on his lower lip, staring at William a moment before speaking again. "I forbid you, or any of your ilk, to speak treason to the others who have not rebelled against my king. Not on my ship. I have to worry about the well-being of all passengers and the crew. I will not have you poisoning people with your rebellious talk."

"If we speak only among ourselves? Would you permit that?"

"No way I can keep you from speaking, unless I gag all of you."

"Then we may speak freely to one another, so long as we are careful not to impose ourselves upon those who do not share our beliefs?"

"No way I can stop you, short of tossing you all overboard. I will not do that, so long as you keep it to yourselves and do not corrupt the others, or keep my men from their duties with your confounded singing.'"

"There we may have a problem, Master Jones. Yesterday, when I was reading scripture and prophesizing, I could not prevent those who were not among our congregation from expressing curiosity and listening."

"I think I have made myself clear on this, Mr. Brewster. You will not be bothering my crew or the others with your heretical ways. Now, off with you."

⁂

After William had been dismissed by Jones, he searched out Bradford and urged him to follow. Miraculously, they found a spot out of earshot of the others where they could speak plainly for a few minutes. "Master Jones has forbidden me—or you, or the others—to meet for worship. I fear if we cross him, great harm will befall some of us."

Bradford pulled on a lock of hair and rocked back and forth on his feet. "I believe they will come to understand our ways, with time. We will need to be more cautious in our gatherings, and perhaps wait until a later hour in the day, when the crew is occupied with other matters."

"Perhaps so," agreed William. "As for the strangers among us, I pray we will win them over in time."

The loud, insistent wailing of Samuel Eaton interrupted their conversation. The poor little boy, not yet a year old, was likely suffering the same seasickness as many of the others, but with no words to say what was bothering him.

Bradford sighed. "I suppose I should go to Dorothy. She seems to be suffering in both spirit and stomach. She misses our little son, and worries about him incessantly. It is of no comfort to her that the family we left behind is providing well for him. I fear that seeing the little ones among us has opened a sore than will not heal."

"And I should go to Mary. She grieves so for Jonathan and our daughters. I told her I could go ahead and bring her and all of the children over when we were settled, but she would hear none of it. Like the faithful woman she is, she reminded me of Ruth refusing to abandon Naomi. I am grateful for her companionship, but it troubles me how she struggles so to manage under these difficult circumstances. Love and Wrestling become bored so quickly, then pester her constantly. And now she also has the care of the More orphans assigned to us. Ah, my young friend, how grateful I am for your friendship through this."

"And I am grateful for your wisdom and fervent trust in the path we are taking." The two men parted to find their wives and settle down with them to wait.

Every day, one or more passengers leaned overboard to dispel the contents of their seasick stomachs. Others lay below, groaning in discomfort. They prayed for deliverance that did not come.

The children seemed to be faring best. For them, the primary issue was lack of stimulation. A few of the adults tried to conduct a semblance of school: teaching basic math or helping them read from a Bible. Some of the children from among the strangers taught them a card game they called "Maw." The children laughed and chided one another, often slapping their thighs if they lost.

The Leiden adults were not amused. "This is, in part, why we departed. These games are corrupting our children," declared Carver to William and Bradford. "Now, the very corruption we sought to escape travels with us."

"We cannot tolerate this," responded Bradford. "How shall we prevent it? We are confined to such limited space. So many parents clutching their stomachs and retching hour after hour."

"We must find a more suitable diversion," answered William. "We shall establish our own school onboard. We will set up a schedule taking turns." When the weather permitted, one or two of the Leiden adults gathered the children on the main deck for lessons in arithmetic, reading, writing, and theology. When the weather was foul, they crowded together wherever they could find room, and taught school there.

※

"Do you think today will be hot?" Mary asked William, directing the children through their morning ritual of dressing.

"I believe it will be. Hurry now, children, or all the warm porridge will be gone."

Mary sighed. "How far we have fallen when I am excited about waiting in line for porridge!" She found their bowls tucked beneath a growing pile of clothes, now filthy from the remnants of someone's seasickness.

William patted her shoulder and gently nudged her toward the ladder to claim their daily portions of breakfast. "We have more than our ancient ancestors did when they lived in the desert those forty years," he pointed out. As he spoke, a sudden lurch of the ship nearly knocked him off the ladder. He leaned in and wrapped his free arm around the back of it to maintain his balance. He looked up to see Mary sprawled out, her legs on the ladder and her upper body on the main deck.

He wisely decided that further commentary on their good fortune would best be saved for another time. They ate the lukewarm porridge on the main deck, seated with their backs against the side of the ship. The sky overhead turned pewter grey. Ominous clouds covered what sky they could see around the sails, masts, and ropes.

CHAPTER FIFTY-THREE

THE ATLANTIC OCEAN – FALL, 1620

Entry from *Mayflower* log:

Saturday, 23 Sept.: A sharp change. Equinoctial weather, followed by stormy westerly gales; encountered crosswinds and continued fierce storms. Ship severely shaken and her upper works made very leaky. One of the main beams in the midship has bowed and cracked. Some fear that the ship will not be able to perform the remainder of our voyage. The chief of the company perceived the mariners' fear the sufficiency of the ship (from their mutterings). They entered into serious consultation with the master and other officers of the ship about whether to return rather than cast themselves into a desperate and inevitable peril.

The ship's rolling grew worse. A cold breeze caused the travelers to shiver. They sat together in silence, watching sailors climb high overhead to pull ropes, adjust sails, and call out to one another. They appeared to be oblivious of the passengers, whose very lives were in their hands.

Some of the waves were so high they splashed the deck. "We better go below now," William told Mary. "The children will be frightened."

The wind howled at such a high pitch it was nearly impossible to hear what Master Jones was yelling to the crew. Jones was waving his arms in a wild arc, motioning for everyone to get below. The Brewsters returned to the tween deck to find most of the women and children either screaming or crying. The men were all shouting orders at once, making it impossible to decipher who said what. Two sailors tossed coils of ropes into the crowd. "Tie yourselves down. It's gonna get worse. Nothing we can do but ride it out. Go on, now—do it quick, 'fore someone breaks their bones."

A couple of the smaller children had already rolled from one side of the ship to the other as it pitched to and fro in the high waves. Mothers tied their children to one another, then to the ship's posts. The waves crashing against the ship sounded like a hammer pounding nails into a board.

Icy salt water poured over the railing and into the lower decks. The sailors tossed down more ropes, which the passengers stretched around poles and ladders for people to hold onto as they tried to move about. Next, they tossed buckets to the men. Though they could scarcely stand, even holding onto the ropes, they did as the sailors instructed. They formed a bucket brigade and began passing buckets full of water along a line to the open cannon ports. The men closest to the portholes pitched water back into the sea, and then sent empty buckets back. All the while, the pumps below ran at full capacity.

With great effort, the bucket brigade barely managed to dump water back into the sea as fast as more washed over the deck.

CHAPTER FIFTY-FOUR

THE ATLANTIC OCEAN – OCTOBER, 1620

Unlike the crew, who virtually lived on the ocean, the passengers were unaccustomed to the constant rolling. What little light they'd had at the start of the storm was gone now. William inched along in the dark, latching onto the rope stretched from one end of the tween deck to the other. He frequently lost his balance and bumped into someone—or something—as he made his way to Mary and the children. His throat was raw from calling out loudly enough to be heard over the gale-force wind. *I've never heard such loud wind. I can hardly hear my own voice. I must find Mary. She must be terrified.*

William eased along the rope, staggering like a man fresh from many hours and tankards at the pub. As he did, he prayed. "Lord, deliver us! Let us not have forsaken all to now be buried alive in this watery grave that surrounds us."

The roaring wind drowned out most of the wailing and screams from the terrified women and children who huddled together in the tween deck area. Some held ropes with one hand and placed the other on their bellies or covered their mouths, hoping to stave off discharging the contents of their stomachs.

Icy seawater, washing on the deck and then below deck, drenched everyone. Anything not tied down rolled back and forth, bruising anyone in the way. Some of the items sailors had secured earlier broke loose in the violent pitching. Crewmen seemed to be everywhere: some below deck trying to make things more secure, others lashing the lowered sails to beams. They latched onto ropes as they worked to avoid being tossed overboard. Master Jones was concentrating on keeping the ship aright until the gale winds and pounding waves subsided. The passengers had to fend for themselves.

Then their precarious situation got worse. The passengers all heard the loud crack, even over the roar of the wind and waves. It sounded like a clap of thunder. Everyone wondered what had happened, but none dared venture forth to find out. The rain was so heavy, they wouldn't have been able see anything even if someone had dared climb the ladder to the upper deck.

Sometime after midnight, the winds started to subside. The passengers soon learned from one of the crewmen that the noise they had heard was the cracking of the beam supporting the center mast. The stress from the relentless wind and waves had caused it to buckle. The crew surveyed the broken beam by the light of many lanterns. Meanwhile, the Separatist men gathered to assess their situation.

"We cannot turn back now!" said Carver. "We must convince the crew to keep sailing west."

Bradford added, "Let us pray, pray, and pray some more that this will not end our plans."

Edward Winslow suggested that their prayers would need to be very specific.

"We must help the crew," said Carver. "Though they distain us greatly, they are in sore need of our Lord's help. We must pray that the Lord will come to their aid."

"Perhaps the cooper Alden can apply his barrel-making skills," suggested Bradford. Just then, the master approached.

"I heard you talking. The ship's my responsibility. I'm not looking for help from a bunch of bloody landlubbers."

Carver interrupted. "But Master Jones, we have with us a giant iron screw. We brought it to build our new homes. We thought perhaps your cooper here, young John Alden, might use it."

"Where?" bellowed Jones.

"Below, with the other tools and provisions we've brought."

Alden was quick to add, "And I know how to use it, for I was a shipbuilder in the Southampton yards before I hired on to sail with you, sir."

When the storm and the crisis of the cracked beam passed, Master Jones recorded the events in the ship log: *There was great distraction and difference of opinion amongst the mariners themselves. They would do whatever needed done for the sake of their wages, having now crossed nearly half the ocean. On the other hand, they were loath to hazard their lives too desperately. Most favored turning about so as to only have half the ocean to sail instead of an ocean and a half before seeing England again.*

In examining all opinions, the master and others affirmed that they knew the ship to be strong and firm under water; and, for the buckling, bending or bowing of the main beam, there was a great iron scrue (sic) the passengers had brought out of Holland which would raise it into place. That being done, the carpenter and the master affirmed that a post would be put under it, set firm into the lower deck and otherwise bound to make it sufficient. So, we resolved to proceed.

⚅

A few weeks later, the ship had another first. Elizabeth and Stephen Hopkins had been talking incessantly about their concerns that they would not make landfall before Elizabeth's child was born. "Four weeks! We are four weeks behind our intended arrival. We were supposed to be there now, preparing for our first winter. We should be well on the way to having suitable shelter built, but here we sit, in the middle of the ocean with no idea where we are or when this shall end!"

William and the others did what they could to reassure the couple, but their talk gave little comfort. Elizabeth spent hours each day walking about the crowded tween deck area. She frequently went to the cannon portholes to try to breathe in some fresh air. Now very large with child, she no longer attempted to climb the ladder to the main deck.

One cold, grey November morning, Elizabeth began to moan and rub her back. The mothers around her suspected that this was the start of labor. Mary told William to shoo the men as far away as possible. Delivering babies was women's work. Some of the men went up on the main deck, while others gathered on the far side of the tween deck. Priscilla Mullens begged the cook for hot water, which he reluctantly provided.

Several women collected sleeping pallets and put them together to make as comfortable a bed as possible. Soon, Elizabeth's birth pangs started in earnest and her cries filled the ship. Women took turns wiping her forehead and supporting her back as she pushed her baby forward to the start of his life. After several hours, Stephen was summoned to meet his new son. Elizabeth, exhausted from the effort, but relieved that her time of waiting had ended, beamed. She clutched her infant son to her breast, asking, "What shall we call him? Stephen, perhaps?"

"No, I think not. I think we should give him a name suitable for the circumstances of this birth."

"*Hmm,* I agree. What do you suggest?"

"What do you think about Oceanus?" asked Stephen.

Elizabeth repeated the name slowly before nodding her approval. "Oceanus it shall be." Stephen took the infant from her and held him high for all the others to see. William approached and asked the parents if they would like him to offer a prayer of thanksgiving.

Master Jones noted in the ship's log: *Mistress Elizabeth Hopkins, wife of Master Stephen Hopkins of Billericay, in Essex, was delivered of a son; who, on account of the circumstances of his birth, was named Oceanus, the first birth aboard the ship during the voyage. A succession of fine days, with favoring winds.*

Chapter Fifty-Five

The Atlantic Ocean – November, 1620

With the damaged beam repaired and baby Oceanus safely delivered, the passengers began to smile again. No one could resist cooing at the babe, trying to coax a smile from him. The Leiden passengers thought perhaps this baby was the Lord's way of assuring them they had His approval, and all would be well.

Mary Brewster hoped this was the case, but had her doubts. She and many others started to have tender, swollen gums that bled easily. This was but one of several challenges. The cramped and stinking tween deck made tempers short, dimming the resolve of the passengers.

William provided what comfort he could by quoting comforting words from Scripture or discussing what life would be like when they could again walk on solid ground.

Another challenge was the sheer tediousness of it all. Day after day, the passengers saw nothing but the swells of the sea against grey skies. More days than not, it was hard to see where the ocean ended and the sky began. The wind turned colder. They had long since given up trying to wash their clothes, wearing as many layers as they could while still retaining the ability to move.

Children huddled together at night to share body warmth. Husbands and wives cared little about romance, but clung to one another under whatever they could find for cover to try to stay warm enough to sleep. A community-wide depression settled in as all they saw was grey ocean and sky.

"I thought surely we'd at least have passed an island by now," commented Bradford to William one dreary afternoon.

They often passed the long hours talking. Bradford wanted to absorb all the wisdom and calm he could from this man who was like a father to him. "I worry about Dorothy. She grows more sullen each day. She never utters a word of complaint, but I can tell she wishes she had never come aboard. I thought leaving our son behind was the best choice, but I did not account for how much sorrow that would bring her. I do not know how to console her."

William smiled, not at Bradford's predicament, but at how similar his own wife's response had been to this adventure. "I think Mary often thinks the same thing. But she has the children demanding her attention, and so has little time for bouts of regret or concern. And, of course, she also has many more years' experience dealing with the predicaments life delivers."

"How do you tend to Mary?" Bradford asked. He was sure William would have some suggestion for making things better.

William laughed. "I do not. I let her be herself, and go about with my reading and planning for arrival."

"Does that work for you?" Bradford raised his eyebrow in surprise at the ease with which William overlooked Mary's discontent.

"I suppose it does. We have been thus for some thirty years now. My young friend, I think it works best between a man and woman if they do not try too hard to understand one another. How can a man know what it is like to be a woman, and how could a woman know what it means to be a man? The Lord must have had reasons for deciding we should be created as one or the other. I think it best to tread with caution when attempting to know how it is for another."

Bradford scratched his head and decided to talk with William no more of his domestic concerns.

❋

Meanwhile, at the other end of the tween deck, Dorothy sought comfort and advice from Mary Brewster. "How do you stand it?" she asked. "Hour after hour of nothing to do, no privacy even to . . ." she paused and pointed to the bucket designated for the contents of the passengers' bowels. "I sometimes think I cannot endure it a moment longer! And I fear this is not the worst. What will happen if we ever do manage to get off this wretched ship?" She hung her head, clenching her hands into fists.

Mary noticed a damp spot from tears on Dorothy's apron and patted her back. "You dear girl. You are so young. A bit older now than when you married William Bradford, but you are still very young. You have been so brave; do not despair now. We surely must be approaching land soon. I have heard the crossing usually takes eight weeks. We are nearly at that now. I suppose the storm set us back some, but even so, land cannot be far away." Dorothy sniffled and wiped her nose with her apron.

Mary continued, "I cannot begin to know the mind of God that He would ordain that we must serve our husbands, even as it falls to them to protect us. After all these years with William, I have learned to trust that our Lord has good reasons. It is easier for me when I trust, and do not fret much about things I cannot change. I have heard of women who go about as if they were men—one who wrote poetry and even dared publish a book! I do not understand why any woman would want to do such a thing."

Dorothy looked up. "I suppose I shall survive this terrible time, as long as I can come to you now and then for comfort."

Mary put her arms around her young, distraught friend and pulled her into a hug. "We shall survive this together. We must. And we will. I have heard and seen for myself how you have been so patient in tending to the needs of poor William Button. Samuel Fuller has had to become the servant to his servant boy since the lad became so gravely ill. I just left the young lad a few minutes ago. I think a visit from you would cheer him considerably. Dorothy, it has been my experience that as we give comfort to others, we receive for ourselves the comfort we provide."

⁂

The Button lad had hardly left his pallet since the frightening night the main beam cracked. Every woman among the Separatists had administered what healing remedies she could to the poor boy. Dorothy decided Mary was right. Caring for children seemed to keep Mary's emotions on an even keel. She decided tending to someone in need of comfort might help her own dour spirits lighten a bit. If she couldn't have her own little boy with her, she could tend to this little fellow. She found a lantern, and with a bit of effort, managed to light it. Dorothy made her way to the dark corner where Button lay, not knowing if it was night or day. He seemed to be growing worse.

As Dorothy came closer, she heard some commotion. "Look! Look closely. Do you see what I found on the deck above?" one of the passenger boys was asking. "It's a bird! A bird! True, it is dead, but this must mean we are getting close."

William overhead the boy. "We must gather soon to pray. This is surely a sign of land. May I have the bird?" He held out his hand, confident the boy would relinquish it. William took it to show Bradford and some of the others. Bradford asked to hold it. The poor thing was still and cold, but it was definitely a bird, similar to many they'd seen back in England and Holland. "I suppose it was blown far out to sea by one of the storms and landed on our ship to rest."

"I say we give the poor thing a decent burial at sea and thank our Lord that we must now surely be near land."

Before they could finalize plans for a sea burial, someone came up from the tween deck with terrible news. "Young William Button lies dead upon his pallet. Sam Fuller is sitting with him." No one spoke. They looked west and wondered how much longer.

❧

November 9 brought a fog that reminded the passengers of similar days in England. They could see only as far as the length of the ship and mist chilled passengers and crew alike to the bone. William walked about, rubbing his arms and breathing on his hands in hopes that might lessen the ache that seemed always with him. Mary sat with knees drawn up to her chin, one son on either side of her. The two More children huddled together behind her.

❧

In his cabin, Master Jones lay wide awake and fully dressed. He knew he should tend to the burial of young Button, but his mind was focused on reaching land within a day or so. He had not spoken a word to anyone on the entire ship about the deal he'd made with Weston.

Weston had paid the shipmaster handsomely to take the *Mayflower* off course so the passengers would be out of the jurisdiction of the Virginia Company. This would enable him to establish his own colony and reap all the rewards for himself and his partners. Soon, all the passengers would realize they'd been misled. Master Jones wondered what they would do about it. Mutiny? Worse?

As the master pondered his immediate future, the passengers stood on the main deck in the brisk, misty morning air. They were gathered around the corpse of William Button. The crew had wrapped his small body in a sack and placed it on the bulwark. Now they were waiting for Master Jones to carry out his duty with a proper burial at sea. The passengers prayed and waited.

Finally, Bradford spoke. "We could just finish the deed, but I don't dare rile the shipmaster."

Fuller, hugging himself against the damp cold, asked, "Why does he not he come? He will not tolerate us bury the dead, and yet he does not do it himself."

Bradford responded in an icy tone that matched the numbness taking over his hands and feet, "He wants to lord it over us that he is in charge. Though we pay for his services, he shows us not an ounce of respect."

William nodded his agreement with Bradford's assessment of the situation, but, as always, he encouraged the congregation to show tolerance and patience. "Soon enough, we shall be free of this ship, and we shall again have say over our affairs."

The passengers' frustration with Master Jones was interrupted when the sailor at the top of the tallest mast yelled out, "Land on the horizon. Land!"

First Mate Clarke repeated the announcement down the poop deck so Master Jones could hear it.

"Land!" Several of the passengers cried out together. Those closest to the hatch yelled down to the deck below. Soon, there was a chorus all over the ship as people repeated the word they feared they might never live long enough to hear. "Land!" Seldom in the course of history had one word carried so much relief, hope, and sheer joy.

There erupted such an outburst of crying, shouting, hugging, and even dancing and singing that at last the crew ordered the passengers back down into the hold so they could manage preparations for the day they would anchor.

Sam Fuller turned away from the commotion and noticed that someone had pushed poor deceased William Button to his final resting place. Whether an accident or intentional, it had now been done. *Well, there is nothing more to be done about it. God rest his young soul. We go to our new home without him.*

PART FIVE

The

Encounter

CHAPTER FIFTY-SIX

CAPE COD HARBOR – NOVEMBER 1620

What Master Jones lacked in diplomacy, he more than com-pensated for with his skills on the sea. He instructed the crew to take the *Mayflower* north. An hour later, he had them reverse course and head south. This allowed the ship to hug the coast with minimal danger. When he saw the coast curved toward them, he instructed the crew to slowly sail southeast by south, and they approached the area they had first sighted. His instruments told him the depth was eight fathoms beneath them, and perhaps a mile to the shore.

Alone in his cabin, Jones smiled, then frowned, then smiled again. In spite of two false starts and a gale that nearly capsized them, he had brought his ship where Weston had paid him to guide her. They were now at the Cape he'd seen on John Smith's maps. He'd studied them every day of the voyage in preparation for this day. Smith's new detailed maps had guided him and many other shipmasters along this jagged coastline. Smith labeled this area north of the forty-second parallel "New England."

Jones had a copy of Smith's book open on his table: *A Description of New England: The Observations and Discoveries of Captain John Smith in the North of America*. He'd done it. His first voyage across the Atlantic and he'd sailed the *Mayflower* one parallel above the forty-first, the northern most boundary of the Virginia Company's charter. *Weston will smile when he learns of it*, thought Jones. *But what will these men think?*

By his calculation, the mouth of the Hudson River was a good four hundred miles to the south and west. The instructions he'd received from the Virginia Company would not be fulfilled on this trip. With increasing concern, Jones realized the part he had agreed to play in a plot to deceive his unsuspecting passengers. Shrewd capitalists had sold Virginia Company shares at a high price when they figured out another shipload of settlers would soon bolster the struggling remnants of the Virginia colony. Jones paced in the confines his cabin, playing out in his mind how to tell this to the passengers expecting to arrive in the Virginia Company territory.

That dog Weston convinced his fellow merchants to advance the money to hire me and the Mayflower to set up a colony at the Hudson. Then Weston sold off his shares and bought shares in the Plymouth Company. He must have figured old King James wished to get another colony going in the cold north. The original investors though expect to get their money plus a handsome profit from barrels of salted fish.

That fox. Even if the settlers fail, Weston's gotten his fortune from the exchange of shares. Heave ho to the riffraff, and good riddance to them anyway for their rebellious ways toward the church. It is not right. He got all that, and paid me the pittance of a hundred pounds to do his bidding. Well, it's too late to turn back now. I got them here. What happens next is not my concern, but they won't long be fooled. Some of them have more learning than a man ought to have. I shall have to confess what has happened, or somehow blame it on the storm. I've got to find a way to convince them that this is the best outcome.

As Master Jones thought through his strategy to convince the passengers to accept their fate, the passengers crowded on the main deck to see land for themselves. They didn't stay long. The cold November wind chilled them in a matter of minutes, and they gladly returned to the tween deck, away from the wind and mist.

"I believe this is the most beautiful sight I have seen since we left the gardens of Leiden," Mary said to William.

"I believe you are right," he agreed.

For the most part, however, the women were content to let the men and the more adventuresome children survey the sight. Love, Wrestling, and Mary's two additional children begged to stay on the main deck, but she feared William would get involved in another long conversation and not keep an eye on them.

"Away with you all, now," she told them when her teeth started chattering.

The ship sailed slowly down the coast. Cold waves crashed on either side as they made their way through the narrow channel. On Friday, November 10, Master Jones called the group's leaders to his cabin. William, Bradford, Carver, Mullins, Martin, Winslow, Fuller, and Hopkins all crowded together in the tight space. "Gentlemen, I do not know where we are, and cannot know until I have seen a great deal more of the coast."

Jones caught Bradford looking at the book of maps lying open on the table. He quickly plopped down on top of them so Bradford could not figure out for himself where they were. He wasn't ready to let them know that just yet. "We cannot continue to sail south with the sea churning up such a dangerous commotion. I can tell you the Hudson lies to the south, but I cannot tell yet how far. We don't have many hours of light left. If we're caught in these conditions in the dark . . . well, I would not frighten you unduly, but it would be most hazardous. We must reverse our course and head north again, away from these agitated waters."

The men exchanged puzzled looks, but no one knew how to protest. Master Jones continued, "I saw earlier this morning that we were passing near what appears to be a good bay. We'll head back that way and be there about dawn. It's a protected cove just on the other side of the land we passed today. Then we can put down anchor out of the worst of the rough seas. You can use my longboat to take a look around. Maybe you will come to fresh water and firewood. Our supply of both is nearly exhausted."

They all liked the sound of that, and readily gave Master Jones their approval.

※

The sun was slipping away in the west. A sunset over land was a vision William had seen only in his mind's eye for nearly four months. He paced back and forth along the deck, offering his own prayer of gratitude. Thinking about King Solomon and his prayer for wisdom, he added for good measure. "You have brought us this far. Soon, we shall be on our own, free of the rule of Master Jones.

I pray you will grant me the wisdom I shall need to guide your servants in this strange new land."

Several passengers crowded on the main deck to watch their first sunset over land in months. William asked them to kneel as he led them in their first prayer within sight of the land. Gathering Carver, Bradford, and the others who'd been in the master's quarters earlier, he said, "My friends, soon we shall be away from this ship. We are beyond the boundaries of the Virginia Company. We will soon be away from the dictates of the master. Perhaps we should give consideration to how we will govern ourselves once we are on land and have established our new settlement."

"Good idea," agreed Martin. "And remember, some of us did not sign on to be part of your ideas about how church ought to be. Now that it seems we find ourselves beyond Virginia Company territory, some of our people think they are free to do as they please. We all need to have a say in how things go, and that goes double for Standish. He may not be one of you, but he is the only one among us with any real military experience."

Carver joined in. "We need to put some thought to that this evening. I propose that in the morning we each present an idea or two for what we believe are the essentials for how we shall govern ourselves."

"That seems like a solid approach," confirmed Bradford. "Shall we meet here shortly after sunrise and work out details?"

"I think we must. We need to know how we will govern ourselves before we try to build shelter and establish a new community. Are we all agreed?" asked Carver.

Everyone nodded. Being too dark by then to see more than shapes, they headed down to the tween deck to spend what they hoped would be one of the last nights they'd have to do so. How wrong they were about that.

CHAPTER FIFTY-SEVEN

From the *Mayflower* log:

> *Saturday, 11 Nov. Let go anchors three quarters of an English mile offshore because of shallow water, sixty-seven days from Plymouth (Eng.), eighty-one days from Dartmouth, ninety-nine days from Southampton, and one hundred and twenty from London. Got out the longboat and set ashore an armed party of fifteen or sixteen in armor, and some to fetch wood (having none left), landing on the long point or neck toward the sea.*

Bradford, William, Carver, and the other leaders of the Leiden contingency worked to finalize their document. They determined that every man on board would sign or put his mark on it. This would guide the way in which they would govern themselves since they were not going to be under the governance of the Virginia Company.

The Leiden leaders were nervous the Englishmen Weston sent with them at the last hour might revolt and refuse to do their part to ensure survival. They gathered on the main deck in the sunshine, which, for the moment, made the November weather tolerable. William sat on a crate and used another one as his writing table. He wrote bit by bit, stopping every few sentences to read what he'd recorded. One or another of the men then suggested other wording.

"I object to saying we are 'the Loyal Subjects of our dread Sovereign Lord King James.' Did we not we endure enough suffering in getting away from that tyrant?" asked Winslow.

"You speak rightly, but if we do not put that in, he has the power to cut us off completely, and then we will surely perish, as other settlers before us have done."

Carver suggested that since, whether by deceit or Providence, they were now anchored beyond the jurisdiction of the Virginia Company, which had financed their voyage, they needed to insert, "Having undertaken to plant the first colony in the northern parts of Virginia."

William interrupted, "I think young Bradford speaks rightly. We need to acknowledge the sovereignty of King James, even as we loathe the way he has treated us. I propose we write, 'Having undertaken, for the Glory of God, and the Advancement of the Christian Faith . . .'" he paused. "His Sovereignty did like the idea that we would advance the Christian faith."

William tugged on his beard, looking up toward the heavens. "Let us add this: 'and the Honour of our King and Country, a Voyage,' and then what Carver suggested."

They went back and forth all morning, finally all agreed. They now had a document that would work for them in their new settlement. "Now that we are agreed, shall we affix our signatures? And if a man does not know how to write, we will witness him putting his mark on it?" asked Carver.

"So, it must be, but I do not think we can expect the hired seamen to sign. And some seem too ill to even affix their mark," pointed out Bradford.

"Surely God will have mercy on us for making these few exceptions," suggested William. Eventually, through a combination of cajoling, explaining, and pressuring, they obtained a combination of signatures and marks from forty-one men. "Now," William continued, "I propose we name John Carver as governor in our new settlement for a period of one year."

Carver responded, "If that suits all of you, then I shall be pleased to serve you faithfully in our new adventure." With that settled, they parted company and proceeded down to the tween deck.

Later that day, William stood on the main deck watching sixteen younger men climb over the side of the *Mayflower*, down a rope ladder, and into the ship's longboat. They headed to shore to make their first inspection of the land. *I long to be in that boat, but at my age, I can ill afford the exertion. Instead, I shall pray they return to us safe, and with good news.*

Captain Standish led the group. They wore what armor they had and carried their muskets, afraid of what or who they might encounter. They were uncertain as to whether the people already living on this land would befriend them or murder them. They did know there would be no friendly greeting party to welcome them to this wilderness. No one had yet spotted any signs of life on shore.

When they returned, Standish announced some encouraging news. "The ground is sandy, much like the dunes in Holland, but better. There is good topsoil, too, as deep as a spade. As for the trees, there seems to be an abundance of oaks, pines, junipers, and others we did not recognize. The logs we brought back for the stove are from the junipers. They will sweeten the smell of the cabin."

"Did you see anyone?" asked William.

"No, not a single soul, nor any signs of anyone living here," answered Standish.

From the *Mayflower* log:

Sunday, 12 Nov.: At anchor in Cape Cod harbor. All hands piped to service. Weather mild.

William began the Sunday service with a long prayer of thanksgiving for their safe arrival at this harbor. Since that harrowing night in the gale when the ship's beam cracked, Master Jones seemed to have had a change of heart about their worship services. He still displayed a gruff, distasteful personality, but was now prone to turn away when the Separatists wanted to sing their psalms or hold prayer services. William told Bradford, "See how our Lord worked good out of the calamity of that night?"

The chilly November weather left most of William's congregation wishing he would express his gratitude with a little less enthusiasm and fewer words. William preached a sermon that covered the ancient Israelites safely crossing the Red Sea, Joshua bringing down the walls at Jericho, and Jesus keeping the devil at bay for forty days in the desert.

They spent the rest of the day quietly making plans for what they would do the next day. Working was out of the question. Other than the sixteen men who'd gone ashore with Standish the previous day, no one had stood on firm ground. All were eager to change that, but not on the Sabbath.

Carver explained, "We have several crucial tasks before us. We must restore our shallop. It is useless until it is repaired. We must organize another search party to explore the area further. Our food and water are nearly gone. Master Jones told me he would not risk the lives of his crew by sharing his remaining supplies. He needs them for the return voyage."

All men who were healthy and strong enough to work organized into teams to tackle the tasks Carver outlined. The women rounded up their clothes, looking forward to a wash day on land. Mary didn't know which excited her more: the prospect of cleaner clothes, or standing on firm ground again.

※

Monday, November 13, the crew and some of the younger, stronger men hauled sections of the thirty-foot shallop out of storage. They dragged them to shore behind the *Mayflower's* longboat. John Alden assessed the damage incurred on the voyage. "I reckon it will take a couple of weeks to get her seaworthy," he announced after he inspected all four sections.

"Work as quickly as you can," instructed Carver. "We can't explore far without it. It is no good for much this way except to light a fire."

Mary Brewster and the other women bundled up dirty laundry and made their first trip to land, wading to shore through chilly, shallow water. "Oh!" exclaimed Mary as she felt soft sand under her feet. "I began to wonder if I should ever walk on land again," she said to Elizabeth Hawkins, Suzanna White, and Dorothy Bradford. With their arms full of clothing, they trudged across the sand to the freshwater pond the expedition party had discovered on Saturday. Several men with muskets went with them in case there might be anyone unfriendly nearby. Excited to be away from the cramped confines of the ship, the women set to work washing clothes.

"Children, you are free here, as long as you stay where you can see us and hear me when I call to you," Mary said to her four charges. "Go stretch your legs on this beautiful, soft sand." The children chased each other, thrilled to be free to run without someone constantly shushing them.

Chapter Fifty-Eight

Cape Cod Harbor – November 1620

Wednesday dawned with fair weather and sunshine. Carpenters continued rebuilding the shallop as Myles Standish led an armed group of sixteen men along the west coast of the Cape Cod arm. The group included Stephen Hopkins, who had previous experience in this strange new world, as well as William Bradford.

"We'll explore inland for a day or two," Standish announced. "We shall see if there is anything useful here."

"I hope we find a place to establish our settlement," said Bradford.

"Or at least a decent place to take shelter from the cold," suggested Hopkins. "Elizabeth and Oceanus cannot stay out in the cold through the winter."

During the voyage, Standish had tried valiantly to make an army out of these men. They had fumbled with their firearms and bumped into one another when he attempted to train them to march. Now he had them march away from shore in single file, each armed with a musket and sword. He insisted they wear a protective layer of corselet. "It will keep you warmer. You will be thanking me if an arrow comes your way," he said when they complained about the additional weight.

※

Back on the ship, Isaac Allerton, John and Eleanor Billington, and Robert Carver groaned with food poisoning. They and others had eagerly consumed the clams, oysters, and mussels the explorers found along the beach on the first trip ashore. Now, they regretted sampling the seafood. Others were getting sick from lack of fresh food. Those not stricken with food poisoning tended those who were.

On Friday, those aboard the *Mayflower* saw the explorers' fire, signaling their return from a two-day search for a place to establish their settlement. Master Jones and several crew took the longboat to shore to meet them. The explorers eagerly climbed in for the short crossing to the *Mayflower*. Though no stranger to hard physical work, Bradford could not remember ever being so sore and exhausted. Two days tromping over uneven ground in the cold had left him too tired to talk. He sat in silence as the crew rowed to the ship.

The explorers found a large cast iron kettle and brought it with them in the longboat. With great effort, several men labored to get it up to the main deck. They'd barely set their feet on the deck boards before curious passengers swarmed them with questions.

"How far did you go?"

"Did you see any savages?"

"No? Then any signs they might be about?"

"What sort of wildlife is there?"

"Did you find more drinking water?"

When the questions slowed down, Standish made his report. "We saw five or six savages. We followed them for maybe ten miles before we lost them."

Hopkins added, "We did find several springs of fresh water, and we drank it with as much delight as ever we drank in all our lives."

"We saw deer and waterfowl," added Bradford.

Standish added, "We came to a place where a house used to stand, and found a kettle which had come from a European ship and a buried basket full of corn. See, we brought some of it back with us." He pointed to the kettle, which was still on the main deck.

"We shall be sure to pay the savages for their corn, if ever we should meet up with them," assured Bradford when he saw William frown at this news. "And their kettle, as well, if we see them."

Hopkins, eager to prove his superior knowledge of how things were on this new continent, told them about what had happened on their second night out. "It was raining, and we and our muskets were soaked through and through, but we kept marching. Then we saw a young sapling bent over next to a tree. I knew it to be a deer trap," he bragged.

Hopkins pointed to Bradford, whose cheeks were turning red, and continued, "But William Bradford here didn't know it. Before I could warn him, he stepped right on it. It gave a jerk up and caught him by the leg." He laughed out loud at the memory of Bradford's naivety about the ways of the woods. Bradford hung his head and averted his eyes. He had hoped that incident might remain a secret.

Carver thanked them for their efforts, instructing two seamen hanging around the edges of the crowd to take the kettle below and make arrangements to store the corn for planting in the spring.

⁂

A week after they first dropped anchor in the bay, the carpenters were still working to reassemble the shallop. "It is taking more effort than we first calculated," Alden reported to Governor Carver and the other leaders.

"Well, there's nothing to be done about it but to do the work," sighed Carver.

William turned to his journal that evening:

After so many days at sea, we had hoped we might, at long last, be working on our shelter. Instead, one tedious day after another unfolds, while all I can do is wait with the women and children while others tend to mending our shallop or trudge around in the freezing weather in search of some place—anyplace now would be a tremendous relief— to set our feet firmly upon this new ground. I must implore God to forgive me for my impatience, but I have grown so weary of the waiting . . . and, truth be told, the wondering about what shall become of us. Many now lie sick on their beds. Master Jones has made it clear that he has no charity for our plight, and wishes only to be on his way back to England, though I did catch him taking some beer to some of our sick ones. I think beneath that gruff exterior, there may actually lurk a bit of tenderness.

I must continue to trust that God will not abandon us. Have we not come safely through the tempest of the sea when we thought for certain we were sailing in our coffins? I must continue to trust, not only for my own sake, but for the sake of the others, as well. I must have faith and trust sufficiently for us all.

The group's second Sunday in the cove included another Sabbath service. Again, William led them in prayer and expounded on stories from Scripture about Jesus turning a few loaves and a couple of fish into enough food to feed thousands. "See how even now, our Lord provides for us. In our want, we have found food, water, and fuel for our fires. How well we are cared for by our Lord, who is faithful to us even here in this place, so far from all that is familiar. Our surroundings are unfamiliar to us, but to the Lord, this place is as familiar as are the faces of our loved ones to us."

The crew had had more than their fill of the Separatists' religion, and went ashore to see for themselves what this place provided. The temperatures dropped as the day wore on. Everywhere they saw evidence that they had landed not in the fall, as planned, but at the start of winter. The longer nights and colder days meant that there was no prospect of growing food for months; this greatly concerned them all.

A new week began with carpenters continuing their efforts to make their shallop functional. Master Jones complained about how inconvenient it was to go back and forth to shore all the time. "We can only cross at high water, unless we wade." Many did wade, up to their knees, in the cold water. Some already suffered the consequences, sick from exposure. By the Wednesday of their second full week at anchor, the temperatures dropped even more; the weather turned stormy. Most were reluctant to go to ashore.

By Saturday, the end of their second full week at anchor, the carpenters declared the shallop seaworthy, but still in want of a few more repairs. The younger men prepared to set out on a longer exploration trip starting on Monday. Master Jones showed increasing levels of frustration.

From the *Mayflower* log:

Sunday, 26 November: At anchor, Cape Cod harbor. Third Sunday here. Master notified planters that they must find permanent location, and that he would keep sufficient supplies for ship's company and their return.

The would-be settlers grumbled amongst themselves. "He dare not leave us here with no shelter, no food, and no way to provide for ourselves!" said Winslow.

"I fear he might," said Bradford.

Standish stood tall and put his hands on his hips. "We bloody well outnumber him and his men. We can force them to stay, if it comes to that."

"He is correct, though, that we need to find a permanent place," said William. "I pray this next exploration shall locate a place where we can build shelter for ourselves."

"We will set out again tomorrow," assured Standish. "Now that the shallop is ready, we can really explore. Surely there is somewhere in this barren wilderness suitable for us to make a camp for ourselves on land."

"I pray you shall have success," assured William.

CHAPTER FIFTY-NINE

PATUXET NATION – NOVEMBER 1620

A KKOMPOIN tapped Corbitant on the shoulder. They were standing with four others in a grove overlooking the bay formed by the northern tip of Cape Cod. Akkompoin spotted it first, bobbing in the water about a mile off the beach. The massive wooden vessel gently rode up and down in the high tide, its tall poles tipping slowly back and forth against the early morning salmon colored sky. A long canoe-like boat hung over the side.

"I think it means trouble," said Akkompoin. "I have heard of these things. Many men will come ashore. Some will want to trade, but others will steal and kill if they do not get what they want quickly enough … but I've never seen one of their giant boats here before."

"I, too, have heard about white men who travel two and even three moons in this way," answered Corbitant.

"Tisquantum was in their land for many seasons. Now he speaks their tongue. I heard some of what he told Massasoit Ousa Mequin about their ways."

"The Massasoit believes they have an evil god who sent the killing sickness with some who came before." The Natives crept closer, peering out across the bay for a long time before withdrawing for the night.

"We must watch what they do," said Akkompoin as they walked away.

"And be ready for action," responded Corbitant.

Two days later, they watched again. This time, they saw a dozen or more men climb into a long canoe and row to shore across the bay. The men climbed out of the boat and waded through frigid water up to their knees until they reached the beach. A short man with hair the color of old strawberries seemed to be in charge. He pointed and gestured to show the others how to put their long fire sticks over their shoulders, and all began walking in a single line.

"They will never find a deer or bird that way! Don't they know anything about how to stalk prey? Maybe they think their fire sticks will get them something to eat, but they'll scare away any living thing, the way they tromp around," laughed Akkompoin.

"It looks like they plan to stay! The men in the boat are rowing away. Maybe they are hunting for us," Corbitant suggested.

"I think they saw us. They have nothing with them except those strange outfits and their fire sticks. I do not think they can stay long. How will they get back to their floating house? I would die before getting on it with them. Tisquantum warned us," said Akkompoin.

Hidden from view, six Natives stood silently watching the *Mayflower* men march stiffly along the shore. With their weapons over their shoulders and some sort of heavy vest covering the top half of their bodies, they approached within a few hundred yards of where the Natives stood. After they passed, the Natives signaled to one another that it was time to leave. Without a sound, they moved deeper into the woods, walking east toward the open ocean side of the Cape Cod arm. When they were sure the strange visitors could no longer see or hear them, they discussed what they should do.

"Massasoit Ousa Mequin needs to know about this," said Akkompoin.

"It is a long way to him, but I agree. We must let him know," replied Corbitant.

"Let's return to the homesite and rest. Then we will gather food and more arrows for our quivers," said Akkompoin. "We will start when the sun greets the new day."

At dawn the next day, they set out to alert Massasoit Ousa Mequin about the men they spotted on the shore.

Massasoit Ousa Mequin invited the messengers into his long-house. The fire was welcome after a long walk in rain that had occasionally turned to snow. The two men warmed themselves while describing what they'd seen. With additional people inside and a crackling fire, the temperature soon rose to a comfortable seventy degrees. The messengers gratefully accepted some venison stew offered them.

"This does not please me," Massasoit Ousa Mequin said as they lit their pipes. "You saw them digging through graves?" He was incredulous.

"One of them. He looked like the youngest one. He was poking around where some who perished from the Great Dying were buried. Then he pushed some earth back over the graves, and they left."

"I do not understand why they would do such a thing," said Massasoit Ousa Mequin.

"They carried nothing with them except their guns," pointed out Corbitant. "I think they were hoping to find food. I wonder if they know how to catch any for themselves. They were thin. No meat on them. They were dirty, too. All of their faces were hairy."

"Do you think they found what people left behind when the Great Dying came?" he asked.

"We will look when we go back," offered Akkompoin.

"I want you to do that. Tomorrow, I will send a runner to find Sagamore Samoset. He speaks some of their language. We may need him. I will ask him to stay close as we wait to see what they do," said Massasoit Ousa Mequin.

"What if they want to trade with us? It is winter. We have little to give after so many have died. What should we do?"

Massasoit Ousa Mequin drew in a long draught on his pipe and slowly blew out the smoke, letting it swirl around his face. "Maybe you should scare them a bit and see if they will go away. I will not let any more of them steal our people. Tisquantum told me all about how that Englishman kept them in the stinking bottom of the ship for many weeks. I must think about this more, and consult with the elders and other sachems. For now, return to your own homesites in the morning. Return to me if more of them come, or if it appears they plan to stay."

When the moon was high in the night sky, the guests settled in among the others in the longhouse on sleeping mats under thick fur covers. They all sang for a while, but then, gradually, gentle snores replaced the singing. Massasoit Ousa Mequin stared at the embers of the fire for a long time. Sleep eluded him.

It is not enough that the sickness fills communities with the bones of my people while the people to the west constantly threaten to take our fields and make trouble. Now we must add to our worries what these white ones will do. Tisquantum may yet prove himself useful. I do not trust him, but we may need him. I will speak with him tomorrow and warn him that we need him to stay nearby.

CHAPTER SIXTY

CAPE COD HARBOR – LATE NOVEMBER 1620

From the ship's log:

> *Monday, 27 Nov.: At anchor, Cape Cod harbor. Rough weather and crosswinds. The planters have determined to send out a strong exploration party, and have invited the captain of the ship to join them and go as leader. He has agreed, offering nine of the crew and the longboat, which were accepted.*

Twenty-four of the passenger men and another ten of the crew, including Master Jones, headed toward shore in the longboat and the newly repaired shallop. The wind became so strong they had to abandon their plans to sail across the bay, and instead headed to the nearest shore. The wind sprayed a fine mist of seawater, drenching their clothes. They waded through knee-high water to the beach, and in spite of snow blowing all around them, did not return to the ship.

On board the *Mayflower*, Susanna White sent her young son, Resolved, to fetch Mary Brewster and whoever would come with her.

"Mama says to come now," pleaded the six-year-old as he tugged on Mary's sleeve. "She says now is the time."

Mary rounded up Dorothy Bradford, Katherine Carver, and Elizabeth Hopkins. "We must go to Susanna right away. Dorothy, tell the cook we need hot water. Do not leave until he obliges you.

Then come straight away to the tween deck. You shall know where to find us by the sound of poor Susanna crying out in birthing pains."

While the men shivered and shook their way along the winter shoreline, the women tended to Susanna as best they could. After a few hours of crying out and gritting her teeth, Susanna delivered a healthy baby boy. When her husband returned from the exploration, they decided to name him Peregrine.

"He is the first child born in this New World," said Susanna as she proudly carried the newborn around to let the others admire his ruddy complexion and silky black hair.

On Tuesday, the crew who remained on the ship cleared six inches of snow off the main deck. Below, the passengers huddled together under whatever blankets and other items they could collect to fight the cold. The cook threw extra logs on the fire, and, in a rare moment of generosity, offered hot tea to everyone.

Due to their ages, William and Carver stayed on board. Now they sat off to the side from the others, sipping tankards of beer. The two elder leaders were engrossed in a passionate discussion about their situation. "I rather think we have no recourse but to be patient and wait," said William.

"I know you speak truly, but it is difficult to plan when we do not know what we are planning for and when. Perhaps Master Jones's attitude toward us will improve now that he is traveling with our men," mused Carver.

"God does rather work in ways we, with our limitations, are unable to fathom," replied William.

"We must continue to pray, and hope they return safely and with good news. Surely, it is a sign of God's providence toward us that another baby has been born just now. It does seem a goodly omen, does it not?"

"It does," agreed Carver. "So, we wait. But the waiting now seems an even greater affliction than the crossing through the storm that nearly ended all our lives."

On Wednesday afternoon, Master Jones and fifteen men returned to the *Mayflower*. They brought with them ten bushels of corn they'd found in their explorations of the area. The other eighteen men stayed on shore to look for a suitable place to establish their colony.

"After a long march, we came to two creeks where we saw many wild fowl. That is where we also found more corn and these beans," Jones told the passengers, who had gathered to welcome the men back. Though relations between passengers and the master were often strained, they shared in common a growing need for additional food and a way to end this trying time of waiting. Adversity had lessened their disdain for one another.

※

The next day, the master sent some of his crew off in the settlers' shallop with more supplies for those who had stayed on shore to continue exploring. They all returned at dusk with a stash of baskets, pottery, and other things they took from graves they encountered in their explorations. "The ground is frozen at least a foot down," said Standish. "The graves were shallow, and it took great effort to obtain this little. There was not much we could accomplish. Besides, the men need food, rest, and warmth."

On Saturday morning, Love and Wrestling ventured up to the main deck. "Look!" exclaimed Love. "See—just there." He grabbed his brother on either side of his head and turned it. "Look!"

"Whales! I see whales!" exclaimed Wrestling. He ran to the opening that led down to the tween deck. "Mama! Mama! Come see. Whales!"

Mary found William buried in a book, as usual, and insisted he go up to the main deck with her. She grabbed Richard and Edward More, and they all scrambled up the ladder. Soon, two dozen others had gathered on either side of the main deck to watch a pod of whales playing around the ship.

Standish grabbed his gun and told one of the servant men to grab his, as well. Fortunately for the whales, the servant man's musket blew apart into pieces, serving only to alert the whale closest to the ship to swim further out to sea after giving a loud slap of its enormous tail, which sent a spray of water over the people closest to it.

Master Jones smirked at the group's ineptitude in accomplishing anything to secure their own food. He ordered those standing closest to him to take the longboat ashore to fetch more firewood and water. "I do not know what is to become of any of us if your men cannot figure out where you will establish yourselves. I will not sit here with you forever. We need to head home soon."

For their fourth Sunday in the harbor, William focused lengthy prayers on petitions for relief from the hacking, coughing, and groaning that had become part of life onboard. Many were too worn out from constant coughing to make it to the service. Those who weren't sick had exhausted themselves tending to those who were.

Master Jones called Standish, Carver, William, Bradford, Hopkins, and a few other men to his cabin. "You must decide. My men and I must return to England. How much more plainly can I speak to you? We cannot stay here for bloody eternity. Get your men out on that shallop, and sail around until you find a place to get your cargo out of my hold. This is turning into a floating sick-room. I am sick myself. Sick of your keeping me and my crew here."

The men filed out of his cabin in silence. As they made their way back to the tween deck to report on Jones's most recent edict, they passed one of the seamen on his way to the master's cabin. "Master Jones, another one of them died. Edward Thompson."

"Who is he?" barked the master.

"Servant, sir."

"Servant? To who?"

"I think William White, sir, the one with the new baby."

Master Jones groaned. "Go fetch one of them to come back here."

The seaman left. The first passenger he saw was Standish. "Master wants to speak with you. Now."

"Now what? I just left his cabin."

"Best he tells you himself," said the seaman, quickly darting off to tend to his chores.

When Standish entered the master's cabin, Jones greeted him with a scowl. "Tell your people they need to take poor Edward Thompson to shore for a decent Christian burial. He can have the honor of being the first among you to have his final resting place in a proper grave."

Standish nodded, and left to deliver the news. The master performed the service. He begrudgingly granted William permission to pray over the corpse before others lowered it into the longboat to take ashore.

⚜

Most of the passengers who hadn't gone ashore to explore were too sick to do much of anything. It fell to the healthiest among them to empty chamber pots overboard and deliver food to the sick. Morale was dropping as quickly as the winter temperatures.

On Tuesday, Francis Billington provided some diversion from the monotony and drudgery of life at anchor. The young lad, no doubt bored and desperate for adventure, took his father's fowling piece and went where he thought no one could see him. He was oblivious to the people huddled together nearby in a futile effort to keep warm on the cold, overcast day. The boy stopped a few feet away from an open barrel containing gunpowder. He carefully situated the long-barreled weapon against his shoulder and pulled the trigger.

Within seconds, crewmen appeared. One snatched the weapon from him while two others tamped out the sparks that threatened to burn their only shelter out from under them. After a thorough cussing out from the crew, the boy slinked back to where his family had staked a claim in the crowded quarters. When Master Jones got the news, he slammed his fist on his table and reached for a bottle of whiskey.

From the *Mayflower* Log:
Wednesday, 6 Dec.: At anchor in Harbor. Very cold, bad weather. This day died Jasper More, a lad bound to Governor Carver. The second death in the harbor. The third exploration party got away from the ship in the afternoon in the shallop, intent on finding a harbor recommended by the second mate, Robert Coppin, who visited it on an earlier voyage. Captain Standish in command.

Seventeen men joined Standish: ten of them passengers, two of them seamen hired by the passengers, and six of them from the *Mayflower* crew. They carried with them the corpse of the latest causality of harsh conditions and an inadequate diet. After they buried the boy, the group struggled to row far enough away from the tip of the Cape to reach open water so they could, at last, hoist their sail and head out to explore what lay on the far side of Cape Cod Bay.

Chapter Sixty-One

Cape Cod Harbor – Late November 1620

AFTER Bradford left with the others on the third exploration trip, Dorothy approached Mary, who had just wrangled a cup of hot tea from the cook and was sitting quietly in the tween deck, sipping. She asked Dorothy if she'd like some. Mary thought she looked tired, thin, and discouraged.

"Tell me how you are faring, Dorothy. Your William is working so hard on our behalf. You must be very proud of him." When Dorothy only stared in response, Mary continued. "I do hope they are successful this time. We have been anchored here nearly a month. We can't stay here forever!"

Dorothy's eyes were red. Mary wondered if it was from crying or from the onset of an illness affecting more people each day. "I hope so, but I fear we shall not fare much better when they do find a place. How are we to survive? How many more will die before this ends? Even if they should find a suitable place for us to settle, what will they use to build us shelter? And how many will be strong enough to do the work?"

Mary let out a long sigh. "I know. This is all testing my patience more with each passing day, but I must trust that God continues to watch over us. How else could we have come safely through the trials we have endured? Surely God has not allowed us to come so far, and through so much, to now let us all languish and die here."

Dorothy wrapped her hands around the pewter cup to let the warmth of the hot tea penetrate her cold hands. She shivered and stared into the cup. "Truly, I know not how you manage, Mary.

Your man seems always off somewhere with a book or pen. Your boys climb all over the ship. All around you, people are throwing up, soiling themselves, or hacking. Yet you sit reposed and calm. How? How can you do this day after day?"

"I cannot say, my dear. I suppose it is just that I have lived a great many years. I have found that most troubles sort themselves out if we just tend to what we can, and leave the rest for God to manage."

Dorothy handed the cup back to Mary. She wrapped her arms around herself and rocked back and forth on legs folded beneath her. "I do not think I can do that. I cannot stop worrying about what is to become of us. Truly, I am frightened about the future. But I thank you for the tea and this time to talk." With great effort, Dorothy pushed herself into first a kneeling, then a standing position. "Good day, dear friend."

Mary felt great sorrow for the young woman. She was barely out of her teens and had already experienced more difficulty and deprivation than women many years her senior. *She must worry constantly about her little boy back in Holland. It must tear at her heart to see the children and not be able to hold her own son. And she is right. We cannot stay as we are. There is no shelter for us on land. Our food supplies are growing low, and more succumb to sickness every day. How many more are destined to die from the lack of food and an abundance of cold?*

✳

A flock of birds squawked as they flew overhead. Water lapped against the ship below. The cook was in the galley, stoking a fire and humming as he peeled the last of the potato supply to put into a kettle of boiling water. Other than these few background noises, an eerie silence had settled over the *Mayflower's* main deck. The children were playing some sort of card game on the tween deck, content for the moment. Most of the women were sitting with needle and thread, mending clothing. Others were busy mopping the brows of those in the area designated as the ship's sickbay—or napping.

It was four in the afternoon; it seemed a blanket of fatigue covered everyone. Most of the men were still out exploring the coastline in the shallop. Other than William and Carver, many of those on board were in the sick bay. The waiting hung heavily over everyone.

One of the seamen on the main deck was inspecting ropes when he heard a loud splash, and rushed to the rail to see what had caused it. It was a woman—a young woman. She flailed her arms about and bobbed up and down in the water like a cork. She had ingested saltwater, and was trying to spit it out. "Man overboard! Man overboard!"

A half dozen sailors came running. One grabbed the long hook they used to haul up nets of fish. He and another sailor handed it down to the woman. She reached for it, but lacked the strength to latch on. The weight of her wet, heavy woolen skirts, combined with the waves, kept dragging her under. Each time she almost had her hands on the hook, another wave pushed her away from it. Then she quit reaching. The men tried desperately to ensnarl her in their hook, but without her helping on the other end, their attempts were futile. They watched in horror as Dorothy Bradford went under and did not come back up.

⁂

"How could she just fall overboard in the calmest water we've seen the whole journey?" Susanna White asked. She tightened her hold on Peregrine and wrapped her shawl tighter around herself and her ten-day-old baby.

"Do you think she . . . I mean, she would not . . .?" asked Katherine Carver.

Mary Brewster cut her off. "We must not even think such a thing. I am certain it was an accident. I knew a woman back in England who drowned in only a few feet of water because her wet skirts got so tangled up around her legs, the poor dear could not walk out of the pond. Poor Bradford. He will be beside himself with grief."

"And, I think too a fair amount of guilt for bringing such a young wife on this treacherous adventure," said Susanna.

"I know the poor dear struggled with all the deprivations foisted upon her," said Mary. "But she truly loved him. I think she gladly made the sacrifices for his sake. She surely knew how much this all means to him."

Katherine said, "Do you ever wonder whether women have the harder lot, following their men wherever they lead? Or if the men have the more difficult role, leading us away from the injustices and cruelty they see in places we rarely go?"

Mary responded, "Perhaps God has designed us in such a way that we struggle in different ways, so we can better encourage and support one another. Truly, we are bound together by our Lord, who knits us together. When each part is working properly, the body of Christ grows and builds itself up in love."

Katherine said, "When the men return to us, we must insist that Master Jones conduct a service for poor Dorothy, even if she is already resting in her grave below in the sea. I know your husband could do it, Mary, but we dare not incur the wrath of Master Jones while we remain in such a precarious situation."

The women sat in silence for a while, each lost in her own thoughts. Then, one of the men in the sick bay began crying out in delusion from a fever. They got up and busied themselves tending to the needs of the children and the sick.

CHAPTER SIXTY-TWO

POKANOKET NATION – DECEMBER 1620

Massasoit Ousa Mequin rose while the moon was still visible in the predawn sky. The others in the longhouse snored softly in their dreams. He picked up a thick bear hide from his sleeping platform, wrapped it around him, then felt around with his foot until he located his moccasins and slipped them on. He then picked up his quiver of arrows, just in case. No one heard him leave, because he made no sound as he did so.

I must consult with Manitoo. He walked a short time in the woods surrounding his homesite until he came to the gathering circle, one of his favorite places to ponder problems. Massasoit Ousa Mequin sat on a large white boulder facing the first light of the new day. As he did with each new morning, he gave thanks as the night sky turned a soft, warm red and morphed into orange. He repeated the prayer rituals his father had taught him, sitting motionless as the sun gradually inched higher, turning the sky light-blue.

The responsibilities he carried for the thousands of people looking to him for wisdom and guidance felt especially heavy today. *More and more of the white ones are coming. Tisquantum would be as dead as all in his village if they hadn't taken him away. Now he lives here, and I wonder if I can trust him. Sometimes, I think "Tisquantum" describes him well. "Divine Rage" seems to suit him. He is a sly one. He talked his way into the home of a merchant. He talked his way back to his homesite. His tongue is slippery.*

I must be alert for the trouble our enemies to the west can bring us. Why do they not die from the strange sickness, as so many of our people have? At least, so far, we have kept them from trading with white men.

My people tell me these strange men take the corn and items from the villages littered with the bones of our dead. Manitoo, tell me: should I allow them to continue to do that? If I don't, they will starve. They don't seem to know how to hunt or fish for themselves. If I do, does that encourage them to stay? What will happen to us if they do?

Massasoit Ousa Mequin returned to his longhouse with no clear answer about what to do about any of it. He decided he'd keep a close eye on Tisquantum, and wait for more reports from messengers with news about the strangers in the bay. He would consult with others. He went to call on several of the Pokanoket Sachems: Iyannough, Namepashmet, and Ohquamehud. And Annawon, the leader of the esteemed Pineese Warriors. And Hobbamock. He could always count on these men for wise council and support. Each agreed that it was best to wait and watch—for now.

The Sasumeneash (Cranberry) harvest celebration had been an important time to gather and celebrate the strength of community. Pau Wau led them in prayers of thanksgiving for a sufficient crop of sasumeneashes to supplement their diet until spring. They had shared a community meal and danced and sang while some kept the beat with rattles. For a moment, worries about the pale people were forgotten. The mushroom harvest was over as well. The first snow had fallen. It was time to move to winter hunting camps and begin story time, when they would gather to remember the community's history.

A few days later a messenger reported, "We have seen them where Tisquantum lived before he was taken away. All day, they work at cutting down trees and making a dwelling for themselves. They row back and forth from their big boat to the shore. They have women and children with them." Massasoit Ousa Mequin rubbed his hands together, saying nothing.

The winter passed with little more to report. The community stayed mostly inside, making and repairing clothes and getting tools ready for spring planting. Outside, the wind howled for hours at a time, dropping snow flurries to blanket snow over the land.

As the daytime temperatures began to increase and the days grew longer, they checked to see if the maple sap was running. Many days brought rain, snow, or sleet. Messengers who visited Massasoit Ousa Mequin reported the strangers seemed to be suffering from some sort of sickness.

"They bury their dead in the sand. The ground is like stone now. It is impossible to make decent graves. We see them carry away one or two every day." The messenger continued his report, informing Massasoit Ousa Mequin how the strangers worked at building a shelter. "Almost every day, they bury another one of their dead. They go back and forth in their long canoe, but one day in seven, they do not work. On that day, the ones who cut down the trees and bury the dead do not come ashore. Others come, but they do not work. They wander in the woods. They carry bottles with them. When they drink from them, they laugh and carry on."

Massasoit Ousa Mequin sent messengers to Sagamore Samoset. "Tell him I have need of him. Tell him to come as quickly as he can." A few days later, Sagamore Samoset and a few warriors arrived in Massasoit Ousa Mequin's village. He welcomed them, and the Sagamore presented Massasoit a gift of wampum to communicate his respect for the powerful leader. Some of the elder men accompanying Sagamore Samoset danced and sang to show their appreciation and gratitude for the welcoming prayer and the food Massasoit Ousa Mequin had provided to welcome them.

When they were all seated around the fire, Massasoit Ousa Mequin turned to Sagamore Samoset. "We must go to these new arrivals. My messengers report they have seen them take giant fire sticks to their wood house. They can cause us much trouble. We must learn more about them and their plans. I think they plan to stay. They have built their big house. My messengers say now that they are working on building smaller ones."

"I have seen this before," answered the Sagamore. "A few come and build shelter. Then more come. Some are friendly, and only want to trade. Others—well, as Tisquantum knows—they are not happy only to trade."

"You speak their language. You must go for me. We will offer friendship, but I will send many men. If they do not return friendship, we will be ready." The Massasoit and Sagamore agreed that as soon as the earth was soft again, Sagamore Samoset would make a trip to visit these new neighbors.

CHAPTER SIXTY-THREE

POKANOKET NATION – SPRING 1621

A week later, Tisquantum found the Massasoit walking through the woods and approached him. "You will visit the English?"

"How do you know this?" Massasoit Ousa Mequin was always suspicious of Tisquantum. He seemed to show up when not expected, and often knew things Massasoit Ousa Mequin wasn't sure he wanted him to know.

"I was fishing at the creek. I saw Sagamore Samoset leave your village. He told me."

"He speaks the truth. It is time we meet these people, the ones you call 'Englishmen,'" responded Massasoit Ousa Mequin.

"I will go with you," said Tisquantum with a sense of certainty that annoyed Massasoit Ousa Mequin.

"Why?"

"I know many more words of their tongue than Sagamore Samoset. I lived with them. I know their ways. I can help you find out what they want." Massasoit Ousa Mequin thought this over. Sagamore Samoset knew enough words to make a trade, but he had never lived with them. He had never even seen where they live. Yet there was something about Tisquantum that irritated him. He wasn't sure exactly what, but he sensed it best not to divulge too much information to this man.

"Tell me again what you know about these white men. Tell me everything, from the beginning. I must better understand them." The two men walked together back to Massasoit Ousa Mequin's longhouse. They settled around the fire, and Tisquantum told about the day he and his companions had been out hunting all through the part of the story about the horrible sea passage.

"And how did you escape to make your way back here?"

"I told you. Why do you keep asking me this?"

"I want to hear it again. It helps me understand their strange ways." *And it helps me decide how much I can trust you.*

"Some men with brown robes came to us. They talked to us in words we did not understand, talking about a man they call Jesus. They said Jesus saved us, but we know it was they who did so. They gave us food and clothes and somewhere to sleep."

Massasoit Ousa Mequin nodded. He'd heard others talk about Jesus of the white people. This Jesus must know many people, because many white ones talked about him.

"They make no sense. If he is going around letting people out of prisons, how can he also be dead and on those branches? They go to this big place to visit a man who is not really a man, but a piece of wood made to look like a man? And they hang him on two logs tied together to form a cross?"

"Yes. That is what I saw."

"This I do not understand," said Massasoit Ousa Mequin. "What else?"

"Sometimes, they tie someone to a pole and build a fire under him and cook him alive. But they do not eat the person. They just burn him."

"Why?"

"I do not know. I heard them say things like 'heretic' and 'traitor,' but I did not understand what they meant."

"What you tell me disturbs me. They sound crazy. How do they get their food?"

"In the place they call London, they have houses that aren't really houses. They call them shops. In these, they sell many things. Some sell fruit or vegetables. In some, they hang the carcasses of hogs or chickens or geese upside down by their feet. People give the carcasses to others when they give them little round pieces of metal. Then they take the carcasses away with them."

"Have they no fields to grow food?" Massasoit Ousa Mequin scratched his forehead, where a mosquito had recently found its meal.

"They do, away from the place they call London. Sometimes, they attach a horse to a wagon and go out to fields. A few times, they took me there to pick things for them."

"I will make plans to visit them."

"I will go with you. I can help," Tisquantum assured the Massasoit.

The Massasoit didn't answer immediately. He knew Tisquantum's knowledge of their tongue would be helpful, but still didn't completely trust him. But if Sagamore Samoset went too, Tisquantum would have a hard time deceiving him. "I will let you know. I must go now to discuss with the elders how we want to respond to these strange people."

CHAPTER SIXTY-FOUR

CAPE COD HARBOR – DECEMBER 1620

The men who volunteered for the third exploration party climbed into their shallop. They were eager to sail instead of row, and confident that second mate Robert Coppin would guide them to the spot he claimed was suitable for a new colony.

"I know it was over there, just across the bay. I think it might be twenty or so miles if we can sail straight across." Captain Standish assumed he was in charge. Bradford often led, but whenever they ran into situations requiring the use of muskets, Standish took over since most of the men were still novices when it came to all things military. But then, Second Mate Coppin was the one who thought he remembered where he'd previously seen a good place to settle, so Standish tried to not show too much authority. It was a hard task for a man used to telling others what to do and expecting them to comply without question. In the end, it all sorted itself out in the shallop.

Coppin took his place in the front so he could keep a sharp eye out for anything that looked familiar. Standish took a place near the aft and watched for any potential trouble. The rest were simply pleased to be finally making a little progress while not rowing. True, it was cold, windy, and pretty uncomfortable, but then, that had been their lot for weeks. Misery while sailing was a considerable improvement over misery while walking through wind, rain, or even snow over uneven ground.

The men had barely sailed away from land when the winds picked up. The crewmen insisted they stay close to shore. "We most certainly do not want to be out in open water in a boat this size if that wind gets any stronger," Coppin insisted.

They made little progress on their first day out, and spent a chilly Wednesday night, December 7, near where they started hours earlier. The men huddled together for warmth and covered themselves with blankets.

They set out again on Thursday, heading south along the west side of the Cape's arm. This route would take three times longer than simply sailing across the bay, but the experienced crewmen insisted they stay closer to land in case another storm rolled through. Standish and Bradford reluctantly agreed—neither wanted to be held responsible should they get caught far from shore in such unpredictable conditions. They found a little protected cove on the north side of the cape's east-west portion, and rowed in for the night. Once ashore, they built a fire and devoured two waterfowl Standish shot.

Friday started out cold, cloudy, and windy. The men were rounding up their supplies when they heard a loud whoop from over a hill. They all dropped face-down on the sandy beach. Hundreds of arrows came whizzing past them. They waited. Five minutes. Ten minutes. When nothing else happened for another five minutes, Standish rose and fired his musket into to air.

Bradford challenged him. "Do you think that wise? It could make them more determined. We do not know how many they are, but from the number of arrows, there must be many."

"I was just letting them know we are not helpless." Standish glared at Bradford, but reluctantly pointed his musket down. "Well, we must find out what's what. Get up, men, and get your muskets ready." He told Bradford, Winslow, John and Edward Tilley, and Hopkins to come with him. "The rest of you stay here, but keep your weapons ready."

As quietly as they could, the men slowly made their way toward the hill. The rough terrain challenged the former Leiden residents, accustomed to cobble stone streets and fields. They marched cautiously up the hill. Several slipped and fell; progress was slow. When they reached the top, they gawked. Not a trace of humans anywhere. The only sound came from birds jockeying for space on tree branches.

The group went back to the beach, gathered their gear, and sailed west toward the mainland. The wind picked up momentum. By early afternoon, conditions were reminiscent of their night of terror on the open Atlantic. First, the shallop's mast split into three pieces. Then the sail fell overboard into the choppy sea. Finally, the rudder hinge came apart. The men were all soaked through and through. The shallop was bouncing up and down like a cork, and death seemed imminent. Over the roaring gale, Coppin shouted, "I think I know where we can take refuge."

"Where?" yelled Standish.

"Row that way!" He pointed west. Bradford's muscles quivered with the effort, but he joined the others and strained against the waves. He couldn't see, and his eyes were stinging from salt water splashing about. His teeth chattered. Coppin held his hands on his forehead to shield his eyes as he studied the coast.

"I do not see the place," he finally admitted. But they were closing in on a small island.

"Over there!" yelled Standish. "We shall spend the night there." The island offered no hospitality, food, or shelter—or even any decent firewood to dry themselves out if the rain let up.

"At least we can be sure we're alone here," said Bradford. "I, for one, will sleep better without wondering when the next arrow will fly my way."

The sun started to set and the rain turned to snow. The explorers hunkered down in the shallop, huddled together for warmth. Bradford tried to recall the last words he said to Dorothy.

"I say we name this island Clarke's Island," suggested Hopkins. "Coppin here missed the mark in getting us to safe harbor, so it seems fair enough we should name this one after Master Clarke."

"Agreed!" said Standish. The group passed around blocks of cheese, tried to get some sleep, and prayed that the next day would prove more productive and less exciting.

On Saturday, they finally made progress. They rowed around the bay and into an area between two long sand bars. They pulled the shallop ashore and climbed out, eager to explore. "Look ahead, there," said Hopkins. "Looks like a savage village to me."

As they drew nearer, they could see it was abandoned. "Looks like it must have been dozens or more living here at one time. It does not appear anyone has been here recently, though," said Standish. They found a stash of corn, pottery, and some sort of unfamiliar tools, and took them to the shallop to take back to the *Mayflower*.

"Is this the place you were seeking?" Standish asked Coppin.

"I think this is it," said Coppin. "It is hard to be sure. The last time I was here, there were people everywhere. Over there, they had a garden. See? Some of the corn stalks are still standing."

"What do you think happened?" asked Bradford.

"I suppose the same as what happened in the other places we saw. Some sort of disease must have gotten them," Coppin replied.

They found enough wood to start a large fire, and dined on hard biscuits, dried fish, and beer before camping on the beach for the night. As the fire died down, Hopkins pointed to the western sky and called out, "Look over there. Do you see it? Smoke rising."

"There must still be savages around here," said Standish. "Men, sleep with your muskets handy. I'll stay awake as long as I can, and then I'll tap one of you to take over the watch."

Bradford was so totally worn out, he managed to fall sleep with men all around him snoring, coughing, and snorting. It was still dark when Standish tapped him on the shoulder. Bradford remained on watch as the first light of dawn greeted Sunday morning. He decided to walk up and down the beach, staying within sight of the others should anyone appear. It was difficult to walk on the sand, but the quiet time to think made it worth the struggle.

Solitude is a welcome experience after so many weeks of never being alone. My God, what unknown things yet lay before us? If the savages can live here, surely, we can as well. If only we could finally be off that foul-smelling, noisy ship! We could build a common house at first, and then our own homes.

Home . . . oh, how I long for a home where Dorothy and I could be alone, together at last. Who knows? Perhaps this time next year, we might even have our little boy with us. Or, he thought, smiling at the prospect, *another baby. I thank you, Almighty, Immortal, and all-wise Lord, that you have brought us to this place so full of potential.*

When Bradford returned to camp, the others were moving about. They stretched and twisted to get some of the kinks out of their sore muscles before discussing what to do next.

"If we were aboard the ship, Elder William would be leading us in our fifth Sabbath here; but without him, I do not see that we have any recourse but to use our time to explore," suggested

Bradford. "I am comforted knowing that those on the ship will certainly be praying for us."

"He's right," said Standish, jockeying for status as the official leader of the small group. "We're low on supplies, and we don't know if we'll find anything else here, so we'd best make good use of daylight and clear weather."

Coppin responded, "As I recall, there is a pond of fresh water over in the woods."

"What about the savages?" asked Winslow.

"We'll have our muskets at the ready," answered Standish. "If any of them come around again, we'll be ready for them."

The group set out to explore. The more they saw, the more they dared hope they had, at long last, found a suitable place to establish their plantation. Hopkins said, "I think this is the place John Smith names Plimoth in his maps."

"I think the savages call it Patuxet," said Coppin.

"Plimouth sounds like the perfect name for it. I say we make our way back and tell the others," said Bradford.

"Since we have heard savages around us once already and our supplies are very low, we should head back. We will need more men to defend us before we can do much more," announced Standish, as if Bradford hadn't already suggested it was time to return.

Coppin nodded approval. "Without our sail, it'll be hard work getting back, even if we do not have to fight the waves so much."

"We cannot repair it?" asked Bradford.

"Not without some tools—and even with tools, it would take a spell to make her right again. But the winds seem to be in our favor. We can take turns rowing, so it should not be such a bad lot."

They climbed back aboard the shallop. Bradford wondered which was the worse challenge: the possibility of a storm on the open water, or savages attacking them on land. They stayed close to shore, slowly rowing their compromised shallop back to the *Mayflower*. That night they again camped on shore, but close to the shallop. Exhaustion defeated fear. Standish tried to establish watches, but he did not succeed. They all slept soundly until early morning.

On Wednesday, they finally returned to the *Mayflower*. Everyone was excited to see them, and eager to hear all about what they had found. William approached Bradford and gently put one hand on his shoulder. Those who had stayed onboard had already agreed that William should be the one to tell Bradford about Dorothy.

"Come, my friend. Come with me a spell and rest. Even a fellow as young as yourself must be fully spent from the effort of your explorations. The others can give the news of what you found."

Bradford moved along with William. "I must let Dorothy know I have returned. I am puzzled as to why she was not on the deck with the others."

William put his age-spotted hands on his young friend's slumped shoulders. "Though I have had many days to search out just the right words, none have come to me. I must tell you straight. Your dear Dorothy died the day after you left."

Bradford stared at his mentor and friend. His jaw dropped. Then closed. He stood like a statue.

"I am sorry, my son. She fell overboard. The crew tried to bring her back on board but she . . ." William had to take a deep breath before he could finish the sentence. "But she slipped away from them and drowned."

Bradford turned and walked away as if in a trance, his head toward the heavens. He spoke not a word. When he reached the small space he had shared with Dorothy in the tween deck, he sat, mute, for hours.

People came one or two at a time—people who loved him as if he were truly their own brother or son, wanting only to offer what comfort they could. He just stared at them until they gave up and left him alone again. Bradford cut off all human attempts at consolation, preferring to be alone with the shock and void. He was as alone as he had ever been in his life. There were simply no words.

CHAPTER SIXTY-FIVE

The rest of the explorers, unaware of the conversation between William and Bradford, stayed on the main deck. They were answering questions and describing their adventures to an audience hungry for every last morsel of news. They pushed and shoved to inch closer to these men who'd survived a week in the wilderness on their behalf. As for the explorers, they were so relieved and excited to be back among friendly, familiar faces, it didn't register at first that Dorothy and James Chilton had died while they were gone.

"And then our shallop washed up on the shore of an island," reported Tom English, one of the sailors hired by the English settlers. He held out his right arm and bent his elbow so that his forearm pointed straight to the sky. Then he curled his fingers around to form a backward letter C. "See this here," he said, using his left forefinger to point to the curved palm of his right hand, "This is where we have anchored these many weeks."

Then he slowly moved his left forefinger across the open space, down to point at a place on his side, midway between his elbow and shoulder. "And this, over here, this is where we come to the place Coppin was telling us about."

Standish pushed him aside and picked up the story. "It is a deserted village. Only we saw smoke some distance away the night we were camping there."

Coppin interrupted Standish, "But it does not appear anyone has lived there for some time."

Standish shoved Coppin aside and took over again, "English here did not explain it quite fully. We sailed down this way," he said, pointing to an imaginary map he was drawing in the air. "We sailed this way, and then that way, and then we got caught up in a terrible storm."

Clark cut in, "And we lost our mast, and had to pull our sail out of the water, but it was useless by that point."

"We saw where we wanted to be," insisted Coppin, "but the bloody wind kept us away on the island for the night. There we were—within sight of our destination but we could not get there."

Standish hurried to speak as Coppin took a breath. "We called it Clarke's Island." He pointed to seaman Clarke, who gave a sheepish smile in response.

Edward Winslow asked, "What happened to Bradford? Where did he go?" No one answered.

Standish didn't seem to notice the uncomfortable silence, so continued his account of their adventures. "Coppin said the abandoned village we found was called Patuxet by the savages."

Winslow murmured, "But where is Bradford? He should be giving his account of things."

Standish shrugged and went back to describing the place they'd found. Out of sight behind the main mast, Master Jones listened to their report. He was thrilled to hear that Coppin had led them to the very spot he'd decided they should settle. Four months dealing with these naïve, starry-eyed rebels had been more than enough. The sooner they settled, the sooner he could be rid of them and get back to London.

Jones stepped out from behind the mast and announced, "I know the place. I did not know exactly where it was, but I heard tell of others who found a place suitable for setting anchor. John Smith called it Plimouth on his map because so many ships heading this way set sail from our Plymouth—as even we ourselves had to do." A few of the Leiden leaders looked at Jones suspiciously. However, the joy of the excited majority dissuaded them from saying anything. "I'm going to my quarters. Bring your governor and any other men he would like to meet with me. We've got things to discuss."

William managed to persuade Bradford to join them. They found Carver, Martin, Winslow, Standish, Hawkins, and Alderman already crowded into Master Jones's cabin. "I've been a looking at these maps again. Seems to me as this is where your men found the place Smith calls Plimouth."

"Are you quite certain you did not already know that?" asked Carver.

"Impossible to be sure about a place one's never been afore," he replied without bothering to look up. "This is my first time across the Atlantic. Do you want to settle somewhere now, or dispute my ability to sail a ship? I'd like to see how bloody well any of you would have done getting her through that gale in the middle of the ocean."

No one dared challenge Jones's skill or integrity again. Having verbally beaten them into temporary submission, he continued. "I'll instruct my crew to prepare to sail again, just across the bay. Then I can finally get all of you landlubbers and all your possessions out of my hold."

> From the *Mayflower* log: *Thursday, 24 Dec.: At anchor, Cape Cod harbor. The colonists have determined to make settlement at the harbor they visited, and which is, apparently, according to Captain John Smith's chart from 1616, none other than the place he calls "Plimouth." Fetched wood and water.*

The next day, Friday, December 25, they pulled anchor and sailed across the bay to the place Coppin had led the explorers. The shallop, restored to sailing condition, sailed ahead of the *Mayflower*. Since the Separatists found nothing in scripture to justify the celebration of Christmas, December 25 was as good a day as any to commence setting up a new plantation. After so many delays and calamities, they were united in their opinion that getting established on solid ground was their top priority.

"Nor 'wester coming at us," yelled Coppin to Clarke. Clarke, in turn, reported the news to Jones.

"Can't sail into that," Jones determined. "Turn her around, back into the harbor we left." The shallop turned and headed back to the shelter of the cove that had served as their temporary headquarters for a month.

Once again, the crew and passengers spent the night in the safety of the Cape Cod cove. Mercifully, on Saturday, December 26, fair winds came and they were able to sail the short distance across the bay. After thirty-five patience-testing days anchored in the relative safety of the cove, they sailed the short distance to their new home . . . to what would become Plimoth Plantation.

With the shallop leading like a toddler anxious to show a parent some delight, they all finally reached their destination. "Let go anchors!" ordered Jones. "We reach the end of our outward voyage. A hundred and two days from Plymouth—one day for every one of these renegade passengers."

The crew dropped anchor. Below deck, passengers sorted their belongings into piles of what they wanted readily available, and what they would not need until they built some sort of housing. William and Mary stood on the land side of the main deck. Love, Wrestling, and the More children gathered around them. "Look, there," William said as they gazed the mile or so across the water. "Soon, we shall all be busy making a home for ourselves out of this wilderness. You will run and explore. Here, you will surely find plenty to do."

He turned to Mary and put an arm around her shoulder. "I confess that at times, I doubted. I wondered if we made the wrong decision in casting our fate with these brutal seamen and strangers—but now, Mary, now that we can at last see where God has led us, I doubt no more."

Mary was overwrought with a combination of exhaustion and relief. She leaned into William. Then, with glistening eyes, she turned to her husband and gave him a gentle hug. "Are we, at last, home? Are we truly now looking at the place where we shall spend the rest of the days God has granted us together?"

"I believe we are, Mary. We still know not the challenges that lie before us, but we have arrived, and here, we shall establish a place where we may worship free of fear that enforcers will find us. Do you see that hill over there, Mary? It reminds me of our Lord's promise in the psalms, 'I lift up mine eyes unto the hills, from whence cometh my help. My help cometh from the Lord, which made heaven and earth. He will not suffer thy foot to be moved: he that keepeth thee will not slumber. Behold, he that keepeth Israel shall neither slumber nor sleep. The Lord shall preserve thy going out and thy coming in from this time forth, and even forevermore.'"

Mary nodded. William stared out across the water until he began to shiver from the cold. He silently thanked God, saying, "It is finished. I thank you, Lord. I thank you."

CHAPTER SIXTY-SIX

PLIMOUTH HARBOR – DECEMBER 1620

From the *Mayflower* ship log:

> *Sunday, 27 Dec.: At anchor in Plymouth harbor. Services on ship. This harbor is a bay greater than Cape Cod, and is compassed with goodly land in the shape of a fish hook.*

William sat patiently as the others arranged themselves for their first Sunday service within sight of what was to be their new home. He stood, cleared his throat, and opened his Bible to the story about the Israelites finally completing their journey through the wilderness to arrive in the Promised Land. His listeners nodded their heads, murmuring, "Yes," "It is so," and "We have arrived." William closed his Bible and encouraged all who could to get on their knees. He offered a long, loud prayer, pouring out their collective gratitude that the Lord had, at long last, brought them to the end of the crossing.

All crew within hearing distance stood silent and listened. Usually, they went ashore when the passengers prayed, and if they stayed onboard, they delighted in mocking them behind their backs—sometimes even within earshot. But after weeks cooped up with these religiously fervent people, they were beginning to see a strength of character they'd not noticed initially.

"They sure have their own kind of fear. None of them knowing about sailing, and half of them tossing their guts over the railing at first. Some of them dead from scurvy and other pestilences. Yet here they are, praying and singing as if they were back in England."

"I'm still glad to be done with them," said another crewman. "But I must admit, they have some kind of spirit, that is certain."

When they were done with their service, Master Jones made an appearance and addressed the group. "I brought you a little something I set aside for the end of our outward journey. I thought you might be wanting to celebrate a bit." He pulled a bottle of rum he'd hidden in his coat and offered it to William. William was about to say they were not inclined to imbibe strong liquor on the Lord's Day, but then he realized that this was as close as dear, gruff old Jones was going to get to saying he was sorry for the foul treatment they had endured on account of him and his crew.

William replied, "It is a fine day, indeed. And I am sure it should please the Lord, who has brought us here to this promising land, that we accept your kind offer, Master Jones. I believe I speak for all of us." He waved his arm across the gathering of confused faces watching him. "All of us are, indeed, grateful to you and your crew for bringing us here. So yes, thank you. We would raise a toast with you."

One of the men closest to the hatch went down to the tween deck while William and Jones were talking. He returned with several mugs, which they then filled with Jones's rum, watered down with water.

Massasoit Ousa Mequin's runners looked out at the *Mayflower*. Trees hid them from view of anyone on the main deck who might be looking their way. "They do not come to shore?" one asked the other. "Why?"

"Who can say?" replied his companion, shrugging his shoulders. "How odd. They are close. Why do they not come on land?"

"Can you hear them singing? Tisquantum told Massasoit that once every seven days, they gather and sing. This might be the seventh day. It is strange though. This is a good day to find food, but they sing and do not hunt," noted the first runner.

"We must go now and tell Massasoit what we have seen." They left to deliver their report. Neither the passengers nor the crew had any inkling they had been observed.

From the *Mayflower* ship log:

Monday, 28 Dec.: At anchor, Plimouth harbor. The master of the ship, with three of four sailors and several of the planters, went on land and marched several miles along the coast. Made careful examination of locality. Found many brooks of fine water, abundant wood, etc. The party came aboard at night weary with marching.

Entries in the ship's log for the rest of the week gave similar accounts. Passengers and crew alike had settled into a new routine. A few of the men left each day to explore. Others stayed aboard to nurse the sick and dying as best they could, given that they lacked even the basics of fresh food and adequate bedding. Mary found William engaged in his favorite pastime, reading one of his dozens of books. "Dear William, how long until we sleep away from this wretched place? How I long to know again the pleasure of sleeping without rocking—to drift off to sleep accompanied by the sound of your gentle snoring, and not the sound of a dozen others, as well."

William put down his book and looked at his wife. He combed his fingers through his beard with one hand while reaching for Mary's hand with the other. "Though I am oft called upon to speak words of comfort or encouragement to our brothers and sisters in faith, I am woefully lacking in words to give you now. I remain resolute in my conviction that we have done nothing more than what our dear Lord has led us to do. That it has been such a burden to you troubles me often."

Mary dabbed at her eyes with the back of her free hand, but said nothing.

"Yet I know not what more to do than what we are doing. We pray that soon, the younger men will commence building shelter. I lack the strength of a young man, but I am not yet so infirm that I cannot do something of service."

Mary replied, "And I, too, will do all I can to assist those who groan and suffer with such poor health. I worry about poor Richard Britteridge. I see blood in his bowl when I clean it for him. This morning, when he tried to stand, he collapsed. We have seen so much death! Oh, dear William, what is to become of us?"

William pulled Mary closer and patted her back. "All shall be well. We must not judge the actions of God. It is not for us to know why some succumb to the sickness while others do not. We must trust that whatever God ordains is right. We must trust that his will is just, and for us. He leads us in the way of light. We have arrived here, have we not? And even though we are not yet settled firmly on the land, we can clearly see where we shall make our new home. Dear Mary, our God is all we need. He will preserve us."

Mary nodded. She pushed away from William, stood, straightened her skirts, and left to check on Britteridge, but received no response when she called out his name. She stepped closer and sighed. Mary stood over his cold, stiff body, offering the sort of prayer she imagined William would recite had he come upon the man's deathbed in her place. "The first to die in this harbor," was all Master Jones said when he heard the news.

Life went on as an endless song, even amidst lamentations. The day after Britteridge's death, on the first day of the new year, Mary Allerton gave birth to her fourth child, a son who died before he had a chance to live. "The third child born on the voyage; the first in this harbor," said Jones when one of the crew members told him. A storm kept everyone on board. A mood of quiet desperation settled in like a thick London fog.

CHAPTER SIXTY-SEVEN

PLIMOUTH HARBOR – JANUARY 1621

By Saturday, January 2, the storm let up. A small group took Britteridge's body to shore for burial. Men who were young and healthy enough to do the work went to shore and set to work felling trees.

On Sunday, one of Christopher Martin's servants, Solomon Prower, died. As was their custom, the Separatists gathered for Sunday worship. William selected a series of readings from Lamentations and Psalms, doing what he could to encourage his congregation. The service ended with a prayer for the men who had taken Prower's corpse to shore for another burial.

In his journal that afternoon, William wrote:

I will put my trust in my Lord, but oh, how it vexes me not knowing how to comfort these people when day after day they see only hardship and death. Our sixth death in only a month, and many more languish near death's door.

The men who returned from the most recent burial reported hearing the whooping of some savages. I have implored them to extend the hand of friendship, as I know others have not done so, but have instead sown seeds of fear and bitterness.

Yet even in the midst of our tribulations, some of our stronger men have begun to erect our first home! How this gladdens my heart. Perhaps by next Sabbath, I shall lead them in worship in a proper space. It will have to suffice for our church, our shared home, our storage, and our fort, but it will be on solid ground.

Following Massasoit Ousa Mequin's instructions, a group of twenty Natives had whooped and hollered from a distance far enough away from the tree-fellers to be out of range of their muskets. When their efforts didn't dissuade the white men, they returned to their own camps and debated what to do next.

"We will tell Massasoit what we have seen. He is wise. He will know what to do."

But Massasoit Ousa Mequin did not know what they should do next other than keep a watchful eye on their progress. "I have prayed to Manitoo. I have talked to elders. I only know I must be vigilant and watch them from afar," he said to his brother, Quadequina.

"It is all you can do for now. They do not seem to want to trade with us. It looks like they plan to stay. I think they are very weak. I hear they are burying someone almost every day. Perhaps they have the same Great Dying that carried away so many of our people. If that is so, we can easily defeat them when we are ready."

"Do you forget the power of the iron sticks they carry everywhere? They need only a few to overcome all of the men we could gather from the farthest corners of our land. No, we would not win if we engaged in war with them. We will have to find another way."

Quadequina nodded. "I suppose you are right. For now, then, we wait. We watch and wait."

※

Mary Brewster took a kettle of hot water and supplies for making tea to Mary Allerton. "You must try to get up. I can understand how your heart must ache with grief, but your other children need you. Little Mary is barely beyond being a baby herself. Your daughter Remember is scarcely old enough to take your place. Come, now, I've made you tea. Sip some. It will strengthen you for what must be done."

Mary Allerton pushed the cup away. She pulled her knees up and wrapped her arms around them. Without looking up, she said, "I am not as strong as you are, and Isaac is hardly like your William. He is gone half the time. I am left with all the work of tending to two small children, and now . . . and now . . ." she stopped talking and pointed to her abdomen, where her stillborn baby had been less than a week ago.

Mary's heart wrenched when she heard the woman's sobs, and she put an arm around her shoulder. "Would you like me to fetch William to pray with you?" When Mary Allerton didn't respond with permission or refusal, Mary quietly slipped away to find William.

"She is overcome with grief and dread for the future. If she will not even sip a bit of tea, I fear we will soon be tending to her burial. And then what is to become of poor little Remember and Mary?"

"I will do what I can, but I do not think there are any words, either in my heart or in our sacred texts, to console her. Remember how Rachel wept for her children and could not be comforted."

William went to Mary Allerton. She reluctantly conceded to allow him to bring her young daughters closer, but showed no inclination to get up and care for them. Mary visited each day and eventually got her to eat a little. However, Mary Allerton showed no interest in getting well or accepting responsibility for her daughters. Hour after hour, five-year-old Remember and four-year-old Mary sat beside their mother. Occasionally, she would acknowledge their presence, but only got up when nature demanded it. From time to time, Mary Brewster or one of the other mothers took the little girls by the hand and led them away to distract them for a while. Eventually, they were spending more time with the Brewster family, bringing to six the number of children who looked to Mary for their daily bread.

In spite of the bitter cold, all men who were well enough to do so worked on construction of a community house during the day. At night some returned to the *Mayflower*, while others kept watch over their building site in case more Natives came calling. Though they frequently heard Natives singing or saw fires in the distance, they had not yet made direct contact with their neighbors, friendly or otherwise.

Violent storms rendered working conditions impossible. As the group neared completion of the common house, they laid out a plan for the rest of Plimouth Plantation. "We'll run our main street up that way," said Carver, pointing up a hill set back from the shoreline. "Then one cross street halfway up."

"We need to build a platform for our cannons first," insisted Standish. "We are not safe as we are now. With so many falling sick and dying, we need to secure ourselves, and we need the cannons for that."

"I see the need for it," agreed Bradford, "but our families clamor to be off the ship and settled in their own places. We must at least show them where their future homes shall be."

"We have enough men to do both," said Carver. "But we need to keep working while we still can."

Master Jones began making daily visits to William. The two often shared a beer, usually in the master's quarters. "I've been thinking," said Jones during one of their afternoon conversations. "I don't know that we have enough provisions to get us back to England, now that we are so delayed by the weather. I was hoping you would all be in your own places by now, and my crew and me halfway to England. With the rain, snow, and sleet stopping your men from their work nearly every other day, well, it does not seem as though we can leave now."

"That news cheers an old man," said William. "And if you can wait a bit, perhaps we could send you off with at least some fresh meat or some dried fish, and certainly a goodly supply of fresh water."

"Exactly what I was thinking," said Jones, "seeing as how you still need my ship for sleeping, and with so many of your kind likely to die before you get proper houses built—well, it just seems as though we ought to plan on staying now, at least until the weather warms up a bit."

"I am thrilled to hear you say it," said William as the two finished their beer. William left Jones to his maps and thoughts, and went to tell the others.

"That is one worry less, then," said Governor Carver. "Perhaps we shall yet overcome the lamentations that God has set before us."

"He will not give us more than we can bear. That is His promise, yet I do sometimes wonder how much more we must endure."

⚛

The old year ended on the Sabbath. While William gathered the Separatists and others willing to participate, Jones gave the crew permission to go ashore. In the prayers of the day, William thanked God for Master Jones's good will toward them, and petitioned God's comfort for the many who still languished in their sickbeds. The new year began with yet another death.

"Only in his forties, and now gone. How we shall miss our brother, Degory Priest," said Bradford when he received the news.

"All of the men strong enough to take his remains to shore are already working on the Common House. His burial will have to wait until tomorrow."

The next day, the men returning from construction work reported seeing a Native fire, but there was no sign of anyone. The ship crewmen onboard said they had also seen the fire.

William stressed again, "We must offer them friendship. We will fare far better if we can be in good relations with them." Carver and Bradford nodded in agreement.

"But we must also be ready to defend ourselves," insisted Standish. "We do not know if we can trust them. They have already shot arrows at our men once."

"I suppose they have good reason to be frightened of us, if they have been mistreated by others who have come before," William responded. "We must show them that we mean them no harm. It is the only way we will survive. We are not numerous enough to overcome them, should we engage in battle. And, I would remind all of you, that is not what God would want. Have we not been instructed to welcome strangers? Are we not told to love one another as He himself has loved us?" Many of the men disagreed with William's approach, but none wanted to challenge him.

William routinely occupied himself reading a word of Scripture or praying with the sick. He played with the children when they passed his way. And he had managed to make friends with Master Jones—a miracle some ranked as great as the parting of the Red Sea. On the next exploration expedition, Standish took five men and went looking for Natives. They found several more abandoned Native homes, but no trace of humans.

By the end of the first week of the new year, Christopher Martin appeared to be coming down with the sickness. "Best tell Governor Carver to come back on board," William whispered to Roger Wilder, Carver's manservant. "There are things he'll be needing to know." Martin lay back on his pallet, gritting his teeth to temper the pain and wiping blood away from his lips.

Carver spoke softly to Martin. "What troubles you, friend?"

"I think it will soon be my turn to leave this earthly journey. I have more troubles than I can count, but the thing that most disturbs my rest is the fact that there are things you must know, for the good of all who will survive all this." He was propped up against the side of the ship, with several blankets pulled up to his chin. With considerable effort, he raised his hand and waved it to indicate the entirety of the tween deck.

For the next hour, the two men discussed the financial affairs of their group. When it appeared that Martin had no energy left to go on, Carver left. By Sunday morning, it seemed obvious this might be his last day alive. Carver and William sat with Martin for a long time that Sabbath afternoon. Periodically, Martin would recall another detail of the company's affairs he needed them to know.

Elizabeth Martin sat with her husband all through the night, anticipating that each breath he took would be his last. He finally did take his last breath on Monday, and a pall fell over those on board. Though he'd often caused them considerable consternation, he'd also procured most of their provisions for the journey and handled their financial affairs. William insisted that out of respect for his deceased soul, they refrain from recounting any of his errors.

While people focused upon Martin's final hours, Mary Allerton slipped away into death. Isaac Allerton was on shore with the men hunting for food. Mary Brewster and Priscilla Mullens found her two little girls, Remember and Mary, shaking their mother's still body, trying to wake her and pleading with her to answer them. Mary Brewster gently pulled Remember away and prompted Priscilla to do the same for little Mary. The women held the girls close, rocking them back and forth until their father returned to the ship.

The mood on board improved when the hunters returned with three seals plus a large cod. As they were discussing the delight these additions to their diet would bring, they saw young Francis Billingham and one of the crew returning to the ship. "Young master Billingham saw rightly," reported the crewman. "He told us he saw a great sea from a tree he had climbed, and he was right. We found it."

"And savage houses!" exclaimed young Francis.

"Yes, and houses—but all abandoned. There are two great inland seas. This is surely a good place to establish your settlement," concluded the seaman.

Tuesday was a mix of sorrow and hope. After the funerals for Christopher Martin and Mary Allerton, a burying party took their bodies to shore to add their graves to the many others already buried at the new settlement. The cold made the ground nearly impossible to penetrate with their meager tools, so the community buried their dead as best they could in the grassy sand. They tried to bury them well, and didn't mark the graves. If any Natives were watching, they didn't want them to realize how many of their community had already died.

⁂

The building project slowly progressed in spite of all the deaths. Members of the community were ready to draw lots for the locations of their new homes and gardens. The Brewster family lot would be at the crossroads of the village, with a garden extending down to a small creek.

"Even as we mourn the deaths of our loved ones, we also rejoice at the new opportunities," said William. He and Mary were standing where their new home would soon be located. "Our common house is nearly finished. All that is lacking is a proper roof. Perhaps even by this Sabbath, we shall be able to gather to thank our Lord for the first time on the firm foundation of land."

"I pray you are right, William. I pray you are right," said Mary.

CHAPTER SIXTY-EIGHT

From the *Mayflower* log:

> *Thursday, 11 Jan.: At anchor in harbor. A fair day. Party ashore from ship and coming off at night, reported Master William Bradford very ill. Many ill aboard.*

"Mary, I fear our dear friend now also appears to have the sickness," reported William. I shall go offer whatever comfort I can. Kindly see if the cook will provide you with a bit of warmed porridge to bring to him. I do not think he can abide the cold gruel we had today."

"Not William! This scourge spares no one. How many more?" Mary sighed, taking the wooden bowl William handed her. "I will bring him something with all haste." Mary found the cook stoking the fire in the stove.

"Your men do not bring sufficient wood. Look at that sorry mess of a wood bucket—all bark and twigs. I cannot start a decent fire from that. What's left now will not last more than an hour, if that long." The cook slammed the cast iron oven door shut and locked it closed, turning to the heavy kettle on the stovetop. With his thick, calloused finger and thumb, he pulled the top off and scowled. "Not enough water in here, either."

Looking at Mary for the first time since she'd approached, he barked, "Fetch me some water over there, and be quick about it. I don't have all day to heat something for the Master Jones." Mary thought about protesting, but decided that perhaps if she got him what he wanted, he might be in a less sour mood when she asked for something hot for Bradford. The cook took the water bucket from Mary, and, without a word of acknowledge or appreciation, poured it into the kettle. He handed the bucket back and pointed toward the water barrel. Apparently, he now assumed she was there to assist him.

When she returned from hanging up the bucket, she cleared her throat, sucked in her breath, and stood as tall as she could manage before speaking. "If it pleases you, sir, is there enough heat to perhaps add a bit of warmth to one serving of porridge?" She held out the wooden bowl she'd brought to fetch something for Bradford. "A little warmth might settle a man's innards when he's not well, do you think, sir?"

The cook harrumphed without bothering to look at Mary. "I do not see why any of yours ought to get special treatment. Can't do it. No, ma'am, I just cannot do it. Tell your men to bring me more wood! That's what is needed if my cookin' don't please you."

Mary left to return to William and Bradford. As she approached, she overheard them talking. "You must recover, my dear friend. We all look to you for guidance. Carver and I are approaching the end of our time when we will be able to lead all of you. Master Martin, God rest his soul, has already come to the end of his own. You are the logical one to carry us forward."

Bradford pushed himself up a little straighter against the side of the ship where he was resting, letting his head fall back with a gentle thud as he pulled his blanket up around his shoulders. "I just do not know if I can." He paused to take in another breath, rubbing his elbow and trying to push away the pain in his joint. "It burns and throbs so," he said, now rubbing his knees. "They all do."

Mary approached, carrying only a bowl of cold porridge and a mug of beer. "The cook says he lacks sufficient wood to make a decent fire this day." She sat next to Bradford and across from William. Both men groaned their disappointment. "I will go ashore today and work with the others. It is not right that I should stay here with the women and children while others subject themselves to cold, hard work day after day," William announced.

"But William," protested Mary. "We all count on you to give us courage. I could not bear it if you became so weak you could no longer tend to us. I need you. We all do."

Bradford whispered, "She speaks rightly, dear friend." He struggled to take in a deeper breath. "You . . . are like . . . a father . . . to me." He paused, coughed, and continued. "You serve us . . . best . . . here—" he was interrupted by another coughing spell that lasted several minutes. When he had finished, he wiped his mouth with his sleeve and pushed himself up a little higher against the ship wall. "See? You must not get this sickness. Go now. I will rest a bit. Perhaps tomorrow I shall feel better." Bradford closed his eyes to dismiss them.

❧

William gently pushed his friend's hair back off his face, patting his shoulder before pushing himself into a standing position. He steadied himself by holding one hand against the side of the ship. "I shall go ashore, but will not tax myself with heavy work. Perhaps I can do something to help the others. And I shall have Mary try to bring you something warm later. It may be that after he has his meal, the Master Jones will be in the mood to let our cook prepare something decent for you."

As they walked away, William said to Mary, "Perhaps I can ask Master Jones to have one of his men take me to shore to fetch more wood. That would not tax me unduly. The boys can come with me. They are big enough to fetch firewood, and that will save a man or two from that task to work on completing the common house."

"Please take them. They get so restless. I worry they will fall overboard, yet I worry, too, that if they go ashore, the men are so busy with their work, they cannot properly watch them. What if they run away and get lost, or worse?" She looked down.

❧

A dozen Natives moved silently through the woods, hiding behind centuries-old maples and oaks. From there, they could watch the white men work. They saw young boys wandering around searching for shells, eels, and driftwood. An old man walked along with them, calling out to one or another from time to time. Two dozen men were busy building a structure. They kept moving in and out of the building, and all looked pretty much alike from their vantage point, so it was hard to count them.

The Natives stood observing the Englishmen until the shadows grew long, the birds circled overhead in search of evening perches, and the wind blew away the warmth of the late afternoon sun. As silently as they'd approached, they left.

When they were safely out of earshot of the white men, one man said, "We could easily snatch one of the young ones. Then we would have a ready defense if they bring us trouble."

"The Massasoit says no. No killing. No capturing. We just watch and wait."

"It would be just. They captured Tisquantum and many others."

"Sagamore Samoset told Massasoit it was other white men who took Tisquantum. Not these. For now, we watch and wait."

⁂

The next morning, Mary found the cook in a better frame of mind. Apparently, the secret to pleasing him was sending boys to fetch wood for him. He seemed to actually enjoy having Love, Wrestling, and the More children hanging around, pestering him with their questions and regaling him with tales of what they'd seen on the shore. He actually said thank you when little Richard More handed him a large conch shell. The lad held it up to his ear and then handed it to the cook. "Try it. Can you hear it? Don't it sound just like the sea?" He agreed it did, and handed it back.

When Mary handed Bradford's bowl to the cook, he filled it with steaming porridge and offered a mug of hot tea to take to her sick friend. Mary called for little Remember and Mary Allerton. The sorrowful girls stayed always near Mary Brewster these days. "Help me now to carry these things to Master Bradford." As they approached, Mary told the girls, "Now, go tidy up where you slept. I shall come and inspect soon. We will move some of our things to shore this week, so you must gather up your things. Now, off with you."

Shortly after midday, the heavens released torrents of rain. Those who had gone ashore to work were wet through and through. They returned to the ship to dry off as best they could. It was impossible for them to work under such conditions. As they looked around, they realized two were missing. "Did you see Goodman or Browne on the shallop?" asked Allerton.

"No," answered Hopkins, "But with all the rain, I could not see much of anything. They must have known we were all climbing aboard."

"Last I saw either of them, they went into the woods in search of a deer or rabbit—or anything to add to our diet," said Fuller.

Standish took it upon himself to organize a search party. He sent half the men to the tween deck to see if they had slipped down there unnoticed. He told the other half to spread out over the main deck.

They all reported back to Standish half an hour later. No one had seen either of them, and the temperature was dropping as the rain shifted to snow. Everyone agreed there was no point in going ashore now; soon, it would be too dark to see. William offered to pray for the safety of John Goodman and Peter Browne. The others kneeled on the slippery deck under the protection of a sail stretched over them. William prevailed upon the Lord to protect the missing men and keep them safe until they could mount a search.

⁂

Saturday dawned with a layer of ice covering everything as far as an eye could see. Women wrapped their children in every available piece of clothing and bedding. In spite of the frigid conditions, Governor Carver asked for volunteers to go in search of Goodman and Browne. Twelve men came forward. Carver started coughing so badly he couldn't speak. "Go to your bed," suggested William. "These men know what to do. It will not do for you to catch your death of cold on this venture."

Reluctantly, Carver turned and left. Those who had volunteered to form the search party were soon crossing the mile from the ship to the shore. They returned many hours later with more firewood and fresh water, but no sign of either of the missing men. "We saw many footprints around the common house, and it looked like they might have built a fire in the fireplace, but we looked for hours, and saw no sign of them," reported Standish.

It was a solemn congregation that gathered for the Sabbath meeting the next day. No one wanted to suggest that they may never see the missing men again, yet that was all anyone could think about. William stood before them and opened his Bible. He read them the story of Elijah, worn out and weary with defeat, who had run until he collapsed. He read to them how God had sent an angel with food and water, not once but twice, to comfort the defeated prophet. Then he asked the people, "Do you not believe the Lord will also send angels to watch over our brothers? We must pray for them, and trust that God is watching over them. Come now, let us improve our dispositions with a song." With a strong, sure voice, William began singing the first lines of one of their favorite hymns. Soon, everyone joined him.

From the corner of his eye, William noted that Master Jones was watching from the poop deck. When he looked around at his congregation, he thought he saw a few of the seamen watching as well.

⁂

Two Native scouts spotted the two white men wandering around in circles in the woods, leaving footprints in the fresh snow. "They will die from the cold," said one. "We should take them to our fire. They look as helpless as children."

"No, I do not think so," said the other. "The white men will think we have captured them. They will repay us with those iron fire sticks they carry."

"I know what we should do. Put a pile of fresh firewood in the big house. They can build a fire to keep warm."

The two carefully crept up behind the common house. "No tracks. They have not yet found their way back.

"Look how big," said one as he gazed up at the thatch roof.

"Bigger than any longhouse," agreed the other.

The common house was nearly complete, and had even been covered with fresh thatch on the roof. It would have been finished if the planters had not been compelled to stop work at midday when the rains started.

The Natives inched their way around to the front of the common house and stopped to listen. All they heard was the sea washing against the shore and some birds far away in the woods. They carefully stacked the wood next to the fireplace, then left, covering their footprints as they retreated.

⁂

Browne and Goodman were worn out from searching for an animal or bird to shoot, and thoroughly drenched from the rain. After hours wandering in circles in the dense forest, they finally found their way into the open area and the common house, stopping when they saw that the shallop was gone, and the others with it. "They left without us," said Browne. "We are stranded here alone."

"Not completely alone," answered Goodman. "See? The common house is under cover now, and look—there is a stack of wood ready to make a fire. We can start a fire and dry ourselves." Gradually, the men's hands and wet feet turned warm and dry. They wrapped themselves in their bedrolls and sat on a blanket next to each other. Covering themselves with another blanket, they settled in for a bitter cold winter's night.

"Perhaps we should take turns sleeping, so we will be ready if any savages come around," suggested Goodman.

"I think we are safe enough in here. It is so cold, I doubt they will venture out this evening."

The two men spent the night sleeping sitting up, as was their preference. Each kept his musket lying across his lap, just in case. Morning came, but rescue did not, and hunger eventually drove them back out to find something—anything—to eat. Neither had anything left from the lunch they'd brought when they had left the ship the day before. They had nothing to help them fish, and no boat to venture into the sea. At about midday, they went into the forest again, this time being careful to lay a trail by kicking away leaves and twigs as they went so they could find their way back. When it was nearly sundown, they finally spotted a large rabbit in the thicket. Content to have something to cook for dinner, they made their way back to the common house. They froze in their tracks when they saw dozens of fresh footprints all over the area. "Natives have been here," said Goodman.

"Looks like maybe a dozen or more," agreed Browne.

"Let's move that work table inside. We can push it against the door in case they come back."

"At least we have something to eat!" Browne pointed out.

Neither man slept much their second night on the shore. More than once, one or the other jumped up with his musket and went to the door to listen. The men woke with a start in that eerie time after the moon disappears from the night sky and before the sun peeks over the horizon.

"Fire! Fire!" yelled out Browne.

"It's the thatch. A spark from the chimney must have set it on fire. Quick! We must do something!"

"Aye, but what?"

They worked frantically to move the work table away from the door as the smoke was starting to fill the house. Browne helped Goodman climb up on it, and then Goodman pulled him up. With great effort, using the tips of their muskets, they pushed the burning thatch off the roof and onto the ground outside. Jumping down from the table, the two men grabbed shovels they found propped against the wall and dashed outside, working frantically to push the smoldering thatch away from the house. They beat out the last few sparks with their shovels, stomping on the cinders until they were sure they were out.

The embers in the fireplace were still glowing, so they rounded up pieces of thatch that lay on the common house floor, and soon had a good fire going to warm themselves. Fearful of being attacked by Natives or wild animals, they stayed inside the common house and waited. Whether they were waiting for rescue, an attack, or to freeze to death, they did not know.

"That was close," sighed Browne as he sat down on a blanket to rest.

"That it was," agreed Goodman. "Do you think they will see the smoke from the ship and realize we are here?"

"I pray it is so," said Browne. "It is the Sabbath. This is my prayer for today. That they see it, and come for us."

✦

The next morning the night sky gradually turned to rose, yellow, and orange streaks. The seaman on watch on the *Mayflower* strained to see better. "Fire on shore!" he cried out. "I see a fire!"

Several other seamen rushed up the rope ladders to see for themselves. "My God! It is their new house."

"Fetch the master. We must get ashore. Go tell them below. Tell them to come quickly!" A quarter of an hour later, two dozen men were stomping their feet to keep the bitter cold at bay and discussing their situation.

"Savages must have come in the night," declared Standish. "I warned you we could not trust them. We should have left a watch behind, as we have done every other night."

"We do not know that, Captain Standish," pointed out Hopkins. "Maybe Goodman and Browne started a fire to signal us."

"The tide's low. Nothing we can do until it comes in a bit higher," said Master Jones. For nearly an hour, they alternated between pacing back and forth around the main deck, going down to deliver updates to those below, and cursing the Natives for undoing what they had labored so hard to achieve.

Finally, the water was high enough to allow for the short crossing. Browne and Goodman waved at them from the common house, but did not venture down the beach. Both were shivering and clinging to each another to keep themselves from falling down. When the men got to them, Browne and Goodman nearly collapsed from relief. Gathering in the Common House, the group surveyed the situation. They could see black soot where the fire had destroyed a portion of the roof, but overall, it appeared there was little damage.

The two men who had been left behind told their tale. "We would have frozen for sure without the wood you made ready for us," said Goodman, pointing to the fireplace.

Everyone in the rescue party looked at one another. Finally, Hawkins said, "We did not leave you a fire setting. It was raining so hard when we left, we just got into the shallop and went back to the ship. We thought you were with us, but the rain made it hard to make out anything."

Goodman and Browne stared at them. "Then who? It was all set, ready to go," said Goodman.

"And we let it keep burning while we tried to sleep in the cold. That must be what set the roof on fire," said Browne, pointing to the burnt thatch remains overhead. The men looked up, then around at one another again.

Not knowing what to make of the strange tale Browne and Goodman were telling them, Allerton changed the subject. "Elder Brewster was sorely disappointed that we could not come ashore for the Sabbath meeting today," he said.

"Next week, for certain," said Fuller. "We shall get the roof repaired. Then we can move some of our sick here, and at least get them off the ship. Now that some of us can stay here, we can build a proper fire to warm them and cook for them. Bradford and Carver are both down with the sickness now. Those of us who are able need to keep going."

"Some of us should start in on a shed, so we can keep some of our things here," said Hawkins.

As Hopkins was talking, Browne fell to the ground with a thud. He sat up and pulled off his stockings, wincing as he did so and rubbing first one foot, then the other. "It feels like someone's been using my feet for a pincushion."

Sam Fuller stooped down to inspect his feet, now bare. "Too red, my friend. I think you have frostbite. Mr. Goodman, let me see the state of your feet."

John Goodman reluctantly sat down on a blanket and pulled off his stockings. He, too, winced as he carefully peeled them over his red, swollen feet. Sam Fuller pulled the hat off his head and began gently rubbing each man's feet one at a time with the woolen garment. "If we can get some warmth into your feet and get you back to the ship and into dry clothes, perhaps you will not lose any of your toes. Your feet are paying for the time you spent in this cold."

With one man on either side, Browne and Goodman slowly made their way the short distance to the shallop. The other men pulled the boat far enough onto shore that both of them could climb in without getting their feet wet again. Several of the party opted to stay on shore and do what work they could for the rest of the day.

Chapter Sixty-Nine

From the *Mayflower* log:

> *Sunday, 21 January: At anchor in Plymouth harbor. Sixth*
> *Sunday in this harbor. Many ill. The planters kept their meeting*
> *on land today, for the first time, in the Common House.*

The common house, measuring some twenty by twenty feet, served as temporary communal housing. It provided even less privacy and room to move about inside than the ship, but it didn't rock all day and night and between the fireplace and thick walls constructed of wood, it was possible to actually experience warmth occasionally. The builders used rocks and mud to fill in gaps between the wooden planks. The men had completed it in less than a month, which, they all agreed, could only have happened with the Lord's grace. They often commented what a miracle it was to meet inside their very own place. One end served as a sick bay for those in need of nursing.

Some people still slept on the ship at night, but almost everyone now came ashore during the day if it was neither raining nor snowing. The women and children who did sleep on the ship relished having more room to move about, since nearly all the men slept in the common house. The ship's crew stayed busy repairing the wear and tear the ship had suffered in the long crossing. They were thrilled that the Separatists, with their incessant Scripture-reading and praying, were out of earshot on the mainland for most of each day. They could now cuss and drink to their heart's content without disapproving glances or comments from the passengers.

Life settled into a routine. Master Jones convinced his crew that it was in their own best interests to stay with the planters a while longer. "A couple of our men have already died along with the planters. We must repair the ship before heading back to open water. Also, we have to get in some more food. Now that the planters have their common house, they can help us restock our larder. With them working on it, we shall sail out with a full hold if we wait a bit." The men grumbled as Jones continued. "If we head out now, we'll be running into more storms. It's settled. We stay until the spring thaw. Now, get back to work. And don't let me hear you complaining. I will have none of it."

Much as they were ready to be done with these religious zealots, especially the women complaining about the way they talked and children always underfoot, the sailors accepted their lot. They knew Master Jones would see to it that they would suffer even more if they did not do as he said. They spent their days working on the ship or going ashore to hunt. The women took full advantage of the fireplace in the common house, occasionally surprising the sailors with freshly-baked goods. It seemed the animosity between the crew and the passengers was thawing, in contrast to the frozen ground.

The Monday after their seventh Sabbath in Plimouth Harbor and the second Sabbath meeting in the common house, the fledging colonists suffered yet another death. Myles Standish, always on high alert for any danger, was incapable of protecting his wife, Rose, from death. She died in the common house sick bay, tended to by several women who eased her discomfort as best they could.

Edward Winslow sent his servant, Elias Story, to fetch Myles. He came and stood by her corpse, clasping and unclasping his hands. William approached and led him away.

"I told her to stay behind. I told her it would not be safe for a woman to come to this wilderness. I always thought it would be some other danger that would take her from me. I never counted on it being the sickness. What am I to do?"

William invited Standish to take a walk outside. "You shall do as all the others have done. You will carry on. You know the women will see to it that you have ample food. You are used to being gone long days, and now you will just go on. That is what we all must do. We must go on."

Standish gazed over at William and nodded. "Would they think me less of a man if I did not dig the grave myself? I've dug so many. I don't think I can do one for Rose."

"I think you should go hunting for something we can cook. Then we shall honor her with a proper meal after we have the service for her."

Standish walked a little taller as he headed off into the woods to see what he could find. The others got to work digging yet another grave. January ended a couple of days after Rose Standish died. The total death count for the month was ten: eight among the planters, and two among the crew.

CHAPTER SEVENTY

February opened with a bit fairer weather, though frost was still a frequent companion. Those who chose to sleep on the *Mayflower* went on shore by day, if they were able. Mary Brewster sometimes sent her children ashore with William, but preferred to stay on the *Mayflower*. Between nursing the sick, watching over several young children, and tending to her own family's daily needs, she was busy from the moment she awoke each morning until she dropped into exhausted sleep each evening.

William spent more time on land now, so it was rare for the two of them to have extended conversations. When he was on the ship, he told her about progress in the building of the first houses. In response to his reports, she said, "I can scarcely remember when we had a home. Leiden seems so far away, and Scrooby Manor is like a dream I once had."

"You will again know the comfort of your own home. This is the end for which we labor. We trust in the living God, Mary. First Timothy 4:10. Let us cling to that."

The crew liked seeing the ship's hold gradually beginning to empty. Boatload by boatload, the settlers moved their things to shore. This meant the *Mayflower* was closer to leaving for England, yet the lack of ballast concerned them. On their eighth Sunday in Plimouth Harbor, the wind kicked up. Driving rain kept those on the *Mayflower* on board, while those in the common house were forced to stay on shore. The wind increased to gale proportions, tossing terrified passengers from side to side until they were forced to latch onto a post or railing. Children screamed, women called out for men who weren't there, either because they had taken refuge in the common house or were in their graves.

Without the tonnage of the planters' possessions, the ship rode high in the harbor and nearly tipped over on her side. When the winds died down sufficiently, Master Jones surveyed the scene. To the women, he said, "All the more reason you need to be moving off the ship and into your own places." To the crew, he said, "We need to get more ballast on board. We're going to need tons of it before we try crossing the Atlantic. I don't want to see any of you coming back from shore without bringing ballast with you."

That week Master Jones shot five geese. In an amazing change in attitude, he instructed the cook to prepare them and then personally distributed them among the sickest of the planters. A few settlers came upon a dead deer in the woods, presumably killed by the Natives. Settlers heard, saw, and found evidence of Natives everywhere, but even after weeks in this strange land, they had not yet been close enough to actually meet even one of them.

The settlers also came upon a wolf tearing into the deer carcass. As they approached, it growled and bared its teeth. Hopkins fired his musket over the animal's head, and it turned and disappeared into the thick underbrush. The venison, added to the geese Master Jones had shot, filled many a grateful belly that day.

⁂

By the ninth Sabbath in Plimouth Harbor, the weather had cleared but still remained cold. Master Jones had extended his stay in the harbor many weeks beyond his original plans. Now that the weather was turning toward spring, he again pressured the settlers to finish their houses and move the last of their belongings out of his hold. The three groups—the crew, the Separatists, and the Strangers foisted on the religious refugees by their financial backers—forged a fragile friendship founded upon desperate circumstances. However, this friendship did not alter Master Jones's determination to return to the open sea soon, leaving the others to their fate.

So many were deathly ill, it took most of those who weren't sick to nurse them and keep a supply of clean clothing and bedding available. They also had to forage for food. The situation was desperate. No one wanted to predict how many might still be alive to plant a garden in the spring.

Master Jones put mounting pressure on his former passengers to clear off his ship. However, the cold temperatures, combined with rain or frost, resulted in slow progress on construction of houses. In a combination of desperation and determination, the men kept chopping down trees, making the lumber into planks, and building their homes, which progressed plank by plank.

Each family drew lots to determine where their house would be built within the newly defined layout of the plantation. Each family was supposed to build their own house, but few families had the means to do so. Both the common house and the ship continued to serve as lodging for those too sick to work. The few who had miraculously dodged the sickness hunted for food, cared for the sick, and worked on houses. By mid-February, the sickness was claiming nearly a life a day.

Elder Brewster often commented how similar the earliest Christian community was to their own. "Those who had shared gladly with any who had need, and they praised God heartily together. Our brothers and sisters of the ancient church stood out because of the uncommon way they took pity on the sick and tended to them. So it is among us now."

※

One day, Standish and Francis Cooke went hunting in the woods in search of something for the women to cook. Standish heard a sound first. He put his finger to his lips, signaling Cooke to be quiet. Off in the distance, they spotted a group of Natives. "Must be ten or twelve of them," whispered Standish.

"Looks like they're marching straight for us," Cooke whispered back.

"From the sound of it, there's many more not far away. We must warn the others."

Standish and Cooke ran as fast as they could over the rough, frozen forest ground, calling out to alert others as they went. "Savages! Savages in the woods. Run!"

Others hunting nearby heard their warning and ran to the common house.

Once inside, Standish barked, "Have your muskets ready!" The men all stood, muskets pointed toward the door. Behind them, the women gathered into a circle with all of the children inside it. Some of the women cried out in fright. Standish shouted, "Quiet! I gotta listen to hear how close they are."

They waited. Five minutes, ten minutes, fifteen minutes. The only sound heard was their own uneasy breathing, and a few children and women crying softly.

"We must go see where they are," announced Standish. He signaled for Hopkins to come with him. They walked back into the woods where Standish and Cooke had been a half hour earlier, but, as had happened so many times before, they saw no one. "But they have been here. In our haste, we left some of our things right there." He pointed to a fallen log. "They stole our things and left."

With the threat of attack over for the moment, Hopkins took several others with him to deliver more wood and water to the *Mayflower*. Some of the crew told Hopkins they too had seen smoke from a fire. Comparing notes, they decided it must have been a fire from a Native village not far from their own common house. When Hopkins returned with this information, Standish organized shifts to keep watch though the night.

The next day, Saturday, February 17, Standish decided he had to get all the men, even those in their sick beds, organized and prepared. "'Tis only a matter of time before they come back. Sooner or later, we must meet them. Might as well be prepared." Since it was obvious the Natives were very close by, no one challenged Standish.

"When you do see them, you must not shoot! You simply must not!" admonished William. "We must offer to trade with them."

Standish opted not to argue with Elder Brewster, but insisted that they establish some military discipline. Bradford was still feeling too sick to argue, and Carver was hardly much better. William checked with Hopkins, Allerton, John Alden, Sam Fuller, and the others. All agreed they needed to be prepared, and Standish was best equipped to organize them. They began practicing drills, marching four abreast back and forth, up and down the hill, with Standish calling out orders. On one of their marches, Fuller called out, "Look! Over there! Do you see them? Two of them at the top of the hill."

"Muskets ready!" ordered Standish.

"NO!" cried out William. "Not yet. Let us see if they approach."

One of the Natives waved to indicate that he wanted them to come closer.

"What should we do?" asked Allerton.

"We should go, of course," said Standish. "I'll go. Hopkins, you've the most experience. You come with me."

By the time the group had concluded that was the best plan, and Elder William had admonished them yet again to keep their muskets pointed down so as not to appear threatening, the Natives had slipped away into the woods.

⁂

Massasoit Ousa Mequin met with his advisors, Sagamore Samoset, Annawon, and Hobbamock, to discuss a strategy. "They carry their iron fire sticks everywhere. Two of our scouts saw them marching up and down, out in the open. Foolish. We could easily take some with our arrows before they even knew we were there."

Sagamore Samoset laughed at the image. "I heard the sickness is killing them. Perhaps by spring all of that will be left of them will be their bones."

"I heard that, too. Yet as long as they have their iron sticks and enough men left to march, we must be careful," said Massasoit Ousa Mequin.

"What do you think we should do? We will have to meet them one day. It may be better if we go to them."

"I think so. It is best for us to show courage and strength. You speak their tongue. Perhaps I should send you."

"I will go. If Annawon has the Pineese warriors ready to help if I need them. And I can take Tisquantum. He too speaks their tongue."

"We will see. We must make preparations. Tell your people to be ready. I will tell mine. When the time seems right, we will go find out what they are doing here."

⁂

The encounter with the Natives convinced the settlers they needed their cannon on shore. It was of little use on the ship. The Monday after their tenth Sabbath at Plimouth, they started moving the cannons. It took the joint effort of Master Jones, many of his seamen, and a half dozen of the youngest, healthiest, and strongest of the settler men to get the job done. Huffing and puffing all the way, some pulled with ropes while others pushed from behind. Exhausted from the effort, they managed to get their weapons up the hill. They mounted them, along with five other guns, on the platform they'd built earlier for defense purposes.

The group celebrated their achievement that night with a fat goose Master Jones shot, a crane Hopkins killed, and a mallard procured by Winslow, flavored with some dried ox tongue from the ship's larder. Settlers and crew alike feasted and celebrated the day's accomplishment.

The celebratory mood, however, changed as quickly as it had come. William Mullens sent for Carver in order to give his final wishes to the governor about the property assigned to his family. Barely able to speak, Mullens dictated his last will to Carver with two of Jones's crew as witnesses.

Both Mullens and William White died before the end of the day, along with two others—four in one day. Alice Mullens and Suzanna White joined the growing sisterhood of widows. Alice still had three young adult children, and Suzanna had a new baby and a young daughter depending on her. Those well enough to do so gathered around as Master Jones led the funeral service, this time encouraging Elder Brewster to do his part.

William wrote in his journal that day:

The deaths demoralize us all. The bit of good that has come from it all, however, is that bit by bit, the seamen who so cursed and berated us at first now see the wisdom of our ways. I see them pause often as I give discourse or read from the Holy Scriptures. Surely, the ways of our Lord are mysterious and wondrous to behold. Out of the deaths of so many—ours, and even some of theirs—new lives of faith sprout forth.

The month of February ended with seventeen more crew and passengers at their eternal rest.

CHAPTER SEVENTY-ONE

POKANOKET NATION AND PLIMOUTH HARBOR –

MARCH 1621

Friday, March 16 delivered a welcome and much-needed warm day. "It is time," Massasoit Ousa Mequin told his brother Quadequina. "I do not know how this will go. I will need many warriors. We must leave some here to protect our families."

"I will send some of my men to stay close, but out of sight. These white-skinned people still stay far away, by the beach?"

"Yes, they are building where Tisquantum's people died while he was gone. Others will follow. We must learn more about them to decide how we will deal with them."

Quadequina crossed his arms and nodded his approval of his brother's decision. "I sent runners to tell Sagamore Samoset. You return and tell your people. It is time."

"We will be ready."

When the Abenaki Sagamore and his men met with Massasoit Ousa Mequin, they discussed the best way to approach the white-skinned people. "You go to them first. Go alone. Do not take your bow or quiver with you. You speak their tongue well enough."

Tisquantum started to object, but Massasoit Ousa Mequin cut him off with a you-do-not-want-to-challenge-me look that stopped him from protesting. He turned back to Sagamore Samoset. "You go. My bravest warriors will stay near, but hidden. Tisquantum, you can go, but stay with the others. We will set up camp close enough so you can send runners if you need more help.

We will wait there for you to tell us what you find. Learn if they are good ones, or ones we must prepare to fight."

❧

The death toll among the English kept mounting. Everyone, from the crusty seamen to the smallest child, was grieving the death of someone. This, however, was a luxury reserved for their weekly Sabbath meetings or the funeral and burial services which had become as much a part of their routine as chopping down trees for houses and hunting for food.

Establishing governance for this fledgling settlement now demanded the attention of the group. Mercifully, both Bradford and Governor Carver were sufficiently recuperated to call a meeting. Since the sun was warm, they met outside the common house and stood in a circle. Each family had already drawn lots to determine where their house would be built. Now, they had to determine how to manage issues such as sharing from a common bounty of tools and resources and addressing any discipline issues that might surface.

In private conversation, William, Bradford, and Carver expressed their concerns about some of their group—most notably those the Adventurer financiers sent with them. "They do not fully embrace our values, and might yet undermine them. That would likely lead to our demise, with no one to notice or care," sighed Carver.

"And we have so many widows and orphaned children among us," pointed out Edward Winslow.

"My own household now includes four children in addition to our own Love and Wrestling," said William. "Nearly every family has buried at least one family member."

"We will have to assign those who are single to live with families," suggested Bradford. He sighed and spoke no further.

"You will stay with us again until you are in a position to have a place of your own," William told him. "Mary will welcome your cheerful demeanor at our table. Love and Wrestling do sometimes think you are their brother."

William and Bradford walked out in the sunshine with Carver, where Hopkins, Standish, Edward Winslow, John Alden, Isaac Allerton, John Billington, and Sam Fuller were conferring. Master

Jones invited himself to the meeting as well. "I need to know when you will be fully off my ship so my men and I can set sail."

They had barely begun talking when Standish pointed toward the top of the hill and yelled, "Look! There! See? One of them is approaching." Without thinking, he removed his musket from his shoulder and pointed it at the man.

Sagamore Samoset stopped. At the same time, Winslow, standing on Standish's left, and William, standing on his right, reached out and pointed his musket to the ground. "He comes alone. See, he has his arms stretched out—empty. He means us no harm," said Winslow.

Standish relaxed a bit, but kept a tight grip on his musket. The Abenaki took a few tentative steps forward. William pushed Bradford and Winslow forward toward him as well. "Go and greet him. Hold your hand out as he does, to extend him a welcome."

"Welcome, Englishmen," said Sagamore Samoset when Winslow and Bradford were a few yards away. The two Englishmen stopped and gawked at him. His face was painted with black and red stripes. He wore a deerskin breechclout, leggings and shirt, and ankle-high moccasins.

Bradford regained his composure first. "You speak English?"

"I know your tongue," the Sagamore confirmed. "Many others come—there." He turned and pointed across the bay to the north. "They make trade with my people."

Winslow turned back to the group standing outside the common house. They strained to hear, but the beating of the ocean against the shore muted the three men's conversations. "He speaks English!" yelled Winslow, his hands cupped around his mouth.

Master Jones told the group, "Many English have been here before we got to these waters. There are likely to be others that speak some English. Some of my crew have learned a bit of their language, as well."

William took a few steps away from the group and cupped his own hands around his mouth to call, "Bring him hither! Let us commence conversation."

Sam Fuller slipped away and went into the common house. A quarter-hour later, Samoset followed the Englishmen inside to find Fuller helping the women put together what food they could manage to offer their first guest.

Several of the Pokanoket warriors watched Sagamore Samoset go inside. They waited as the sun dropped lower and lower until it was hidden behind the trees. No one came out. "Should we go in?" asked one.

"No. We wait and watch. The Massasoit will want to know what we have seen," said another. They moved in closer, and as they did so, they could hear voices getting louder. However, the pounding surf made it impossible to distinguish any nuances.

The Englishmen were fascinated with this Abenaki, the first indigenous man they'd seen in person. Though his English was broken so they often guessed at what he said, they paid rapt attention. "We call this place Patuxet," he told them, pointing toward the area where they were building their houses. "All died not long ago. All dead but one. He was not here when Great Dying happened."

Over the course of the next few hours, the Sagamore explained how he'd heard that there was a large fishing vessel in the harbor. "We think, more white ones come to fish. Then we hear you cut down trees. Some of our people see you build this." He pointed around the village. "Very big. We are curious. What do you want? Why are you here?"

Bradford, Carver, Winslow, and William took turns trying to explain how they had come to be in this deserted Native village. The vast differences between their worlds, compounded by Sagamore Samoset's limited English, and their total lack of any Algonquin words, made any efforts to fully explain their situation impossible.

In frustration, William turned to the others and asked, "How can we possibly help him understand that some of our lives were in danger? We would have been arrested and likely tortured if we'd stayed in England. What would he know about a king who would kill his own people, or gladly send them a world away to die so he could add wealth to his treasury?"

"But then, by the grace of God, this opportunity to travel far, far away from the king and the chance to eventually become prosperous ourselves came to us," added Bradford. "How do we explain that?"

"Or the riches waiting for those willing to risk the hardships of establishing a good English community in this place of untouched abundance?" asked Hopkins. The Sagamore, bored with the Englishmen's chatter, got up and walked over to the fireplace. He nodded approval as he absorbed the heat from the fire and leaned over to smell what was cooking in the pot.

Governor Carver interrupted the conversation, "It grows dark. It will be night before long. We should invite him to stay on the *Mayflower*. It will soon be too dark for him to travel. Who knows how far he has come?"

Carver turned to their Abenaki guest. "You stay with us now?" He nodded, "I stay."

"We will take you to our ship. He pointed out toward the bay. "You stay there tonight?"

Sagamore Samoset nodded his consent again.

Carver appointed Hopkins, Standish, Bradford, and Winslow to escort the Sagamore to the shallop. They were barely settled in when the wind picked up and turned what had been a placid harbor into a treacherous whirlpool of swirling waves and foam. That, combined with the low tide, led them to change their minds.

"I will take him to my house. Though it is not yet finished, it is far enough along that we can sleep there," offered Hopkins.

※

The Natives watched Sagamore Samoset came out of the common house with several white men and get into their boat. A few minutes later, they watched them come to shore and all climb out again. They saw one of the pale men point to a house. Another put his hand on the Sagamore's shoulder and urged him to follow that man. When the Natives saw that the Sagamore didn't seem frightened, but rather willingly followed, they went way back to their own camp for the night.

On Saturday morning, Sagamore Samoset rose early and disappeared back to the Native camp before any of the settlers realized he had gone.

Chapter Seventy-Two

Plimouth Harbor – March 1621

THE English gathered in the common house for their fourteenth Sabbath meeting since anchoring at Plimouth Harbor. The women sat on one side with the younger children, and the men and older boys sat on the other side, muskets nearby. William closed his Bible after reading the Matthew text about giving food and drink to the hungry and thirsty, clothing the naked, and visiting the imprisoned. He was a few sentences into his thoughts about the text when the door opened. The Abenaki Sagamore Samoset walked in, accompanied by five other Natives.

Startled by the interruption, William signaled that the visitors should find a seat. Whether they did not understand or did not wish to comply, the men came up front where William was standing instead. The all held out their hands. "See, no weapons. Taniska. Greetings. Aquene. We come in peace."

"Yes, of course. We, too, desire 'aka-key-knee,'" responded William, doing his best to repeat the word he assumed meant friend. "Friends. That is what we also want. Please, sit with us."

Again, the men ignored the invitation to take seats. Sagamore Samoset pointed to one of the men with him, who handed the Sagamore a sack. "We bring good things. You look. You see. Furs. We make trade, yes?"

"Friends, you are welcome to share our food and spend time with us, but we cannot make trade with you."

Puzzled by this reaction, the Sagamore asked, "You do not like what we bring? We have more."

"No, no, but this is the Sabbath. We do not toil on the Sabbath," William told them.

"Sabbath? What is that?"

William sighed, and turned to Hopkins and Standish for help. "Can you explain it to him?"

Hopkins tried first. "One day in every seven, we do not work. Trade is work."

"No trade?"

"No, not on this day."

Baffled by this but determined to stay, Sagamore Samoset and the others moved to the back of the area and watched as William went on with their Sabbath meeting. After a Sabbath worship service, much shorter than usual, the English invited their guests to speak. Instead, the Natives started singing and dancing. The English were equally shocked and intrigued by the performance given by their guests.

After a while, as though he'd just remembered he had them, one of the Natives opened up another bag and pulled out the tools Standish and Cooke had left in the woods the day they thought they were being attacked.

After several hours, the settlers rounded up a few trinkets for the unanticipated guests, hoping that would inspire them to take leave. The Natives laid some of the furs they'd brought on the dirt floor near the fireplace, and started for the door. As they approached it, Sagamore Samoset let out a loud groan, bent over, and wrapped his arms around his stomach. He switched from moaning and groaning to making gagging noises, and hurried out the door to some nearby bushes. He appeared to be vomiting. After his companions left, the Sagamore came back into the common house, standing tall and looking quite fit. He looked around until he made eye contact with Hopkins. "I stay with you now, yes?"

Hopkins wasn't sure how to react to this. He, Carver, Bradford, and William murmured among themselves for a couple of minutes. "If you are willing, perhaps it will advance our situation to forge a favorable friendship with him. He seems to want our friendship," said Carver.

Sagamore Samoset spent another night with his reluctant host.

The next day, the women got to work in their gardens so they could sow seeds as soon as the nights stayed warm enough. They did the same the next day as well. Fewer people were getting sick now, and some who had initially been too ill to help were starting to recover. Sagamore Samoset wandered about, inspecting their gardening efforts and observing how they went about constructing their houses.

By Wednesday, they'd had enough of his company. As politely as they could manage, given the language barrier between them, Bradford and Carver suggested it must be time for him to return to his people. He walked a short distance from the settlement and retrieved the bow and arrows he'd partially buried under a fallen log. He turned to wave at them, and was soon out of sight.

Bradford conferred with William and Carver. "We still must tend to the matters of how to govern in our new settlement and approve the military orders Standish proposes," pointed out Carver.

"Perhaps, now that spring planting is getting underway, our visitor will report to his people that we are not a threat. Let us finish the meeting we tried to have a week ago," suggested Bradford. William offered to round up the other men. They gathered in the common house to discuss business. An hour later, one of the *Mayflower* crewmen interrupted them to announce that the Native was back with a few others, and they appeared to be preparing to attack.

The men all jumped up and dashed outside to see for themselves. Always ready for action, Standish grabbed his musket and called to Hopkins, who was nearby and ready to go with him. Two seamen from the *Mayflower* joined them. Master Jones sent one of his officers, Master Williamson, the *Mayflower* treasurer, and one of his seamen, since both spoke a few words of Algonquin.

The four marched toward the Natives with their muskets ready to fire. The Natives responded by pulling out their bows and arrows into shooting position. After staring at each other for a few minutes, the Natives turned and left. Standish and Hopkins returned to the common house to give their account of the standoff to those who had opted to stay inside. "Perhaps we offended them on the Sabbath, when we would not trade," suggested William.

"Maybe he was angry we asked him to leave," suggested Bradford.

"We must do more to assure them we mean them no harm," said Carver.

"I believe our future depends on that," agreed William. "We must pray that God will have them return to us in peace to give us that chance."

Standish scoffed, but didn't offer a rebuttal.

They discussed their next move in the cat-and-mouse game in which they almost, but never actually, got acquainted with their Pokanoket neighbors.

❧

Fuller had been tending to the sick on the ship, and approached the others with the bad news. "I fear we are two fewer this night. Goodman and Cooke never really recovered from the frostbite. I did what I could, but it was not enough. They died this afternoon, within an hour of one another."

"True friends to the end," said William. "I will alert Master Jones. He will want to have a service for them before we find room for them in the graveyard."

❧

Sagamore Samoset found Massasoit Ousa Mequin talking with his brother, Quadequina. "Tell me all you have seen and heard," the Massasoit instructed.

"First, they offered me food and drink. They were going to take me on their big boat." Massasoit Ousa Mequin frowned at this.

"I was not afraid. They were very friendly with me. But the wind made the water too rough, so I stayed with one of them in his house."

Massasoit Ousa Mequin raised his eyebrows at this news. "They did not try to hurt you?"

"No, not at all. I did not understand many of the words they use. They are new words to me, but they were kind. I left early the next day to tell my men. They camped in the woods to wait for me. I needed to let them know I was not hurt. They said they saw me go into the house, but when all was quiet, they decided not to come for me."

"You were gone many days. Did you stay with them all that time?" asked Massasoit Ousa Mequin.

"No. I took a few of my men with me the next day to trade. I thought they wanted to trade, but they do not."

"No trade? That is odd."

"They sit on benches. One of the old men talked, and the others listened. They put their women and little ones here, and all the men here." He pointed to first one side of Massasoit Ousa Mequin, then the other. "When we displayed the many furs we brought to trade, the old man said they could not. He said that one day a week, they are not allowed to trade."

"How strange," said Quadequina.

"I think this is how they worship their God. The old man talks much. Then they stand and sing something. Then they get on their knees." Sagamore Samoset dropped to his knees the way he'd seen the English do. "The old man talked more. They stood and sang some more. When they start to get up and move around, we showed them how we worship."

"That is why you were gone so long? You stayed with them?" asked the Massasoit.

"My men wanted to leave, but I wanted to stay, so I pretended to be sick. After my men went back to camp, I stayed in the white man's house again for two days. I watched how they garden. They do not know how to plant so things will grow. They don't put fish in the soil to feed what they plant; they plant some seeds too early. They don't put in poles to let their plants climb to the sun. I also saw how they build their houses. They are sturdy. They work hard, but it takes them days to do what our people can do in a few hours."

"Hmm. It is good you have learned so much. I like much of what I am hearing," said the Massasoit. "So, you made friends with them."

"I thought so. But then some of them came to me and said I must leave. They did not tell me why. So, I went back to our camp. We took our bows and arrows and went back to let them know they are on our land and we can protect it if they make trouble for us."

"Good. Did you fight?"

"We were ready. They came to meet us with their iron fire sticks pointed at us. We stared at them, but we decided it was best to come and tell you. We were not numerous enough to do battle with them. We need more men."

Massasoit Ousa Mequin didn't speak for a few minutes. Then he said, "I will go now to talk to Manitoo and consult with Annawon and Hobbamock. They must tell me what to do next." He got up and left. The others encouraged the Sagamore, and those who'd gone with him, to tell them more about the English.

CHAPTER SEVENTY-THREE

PLIMOTH PLANTATION – MARCH 1621

The weather was balmy the next day, Thursday, March 22. The *Mayflower* crew focused on final details to ready the ship for her return voyage, especially more ballast to replace the weight of the passengers' cargo. Then they'd be ready to sail.

The few women not nursing the sick or caring for babies worked in the warm spring sun planting gardens in long straight rows, as they'd done years ago in England. The house builders were nearly done with their backbreaking labor. Families settled in their own homes; every family household included at least one additional widow, widower, or orphaned child.

Many languished in sick beds, on the ship or in the one house designated to their care. Their common house now functioned as intended: a gathering place for meetings and worship. The death toll slowed a bit after the deaths of Goodman and Clarke, and some of the sick were starting to feel better.

Bradford and Carver called the men together again to continue discussions about managing the business affairs of the new settlement. An hour later, Tisquantum approached. "I know your tongue. I come to you with message. The great Massasoit is nearby."

The English gaped at this new Native who came to them talking in English and telling them more of his kind were nearby. William whispered to Bradford. "Surely, this must mean God has answered our prayers to live in peace among these heathens."

"He waits. With his brother, Quadequina. Massasoit Ousa Mequin says he wants meet you," said Tisquantum. After several frustrating attempts to explain he expected the settlers to come with them to meet the Massasoit, the settlers followed Tisquantum outside.

⁂

The Massasoit and Quadequina watched the settlers come out of the common house. "We will ask them to send us an ambassador," said Massasoit Ousa Mequin.

"You think they will?" asked Quadequina.

"Who has wisdom to know what they will do? We will send six of our men back with Tisquantum," he continued.

"So many?"

"Yes. They send one. We send six. That shows we come in peace. We want to make them understand we are good. We want them to be our allies. We need them to help us against the threat from the Narragansett. They have many more warriors than us now because they did not have the Great Dying we did. My runners tell me they have seen the English bury many, too. They need us. We need them."

Quadequina nodded. "If they understand we will help them, they will want to help us against our enemies. That is the wise way."

"So, we send six of ours for one of theirs. Then they will see we come in peace. There is too much bloodshed already. Peace is better, but we must be careful. Some of the white ones are crafty and wicked. They trick and deceive. Tisquantum knows this. We must be careful. Maybe they taught him to deceive, too."

Quadequina pointed toward the common house. "Look, here they come. With baskets. Now they are ready to trade, I think."

⁂

The settlers looked toward the hill and saw the Native brothers poised at the top of it. A shallow brook ran through the area about halfway between the common house and the base of the hill. Even from a distance of a couple hundred yards, the majestic brothers looked like royalty—like two kings surveying their kingdom. Each wore a deerskin cloak covered with painted designs and adorned with feathers. Sixty or more other Natives stood behind them. Tisquantum told the settlers to stay where they were while he returned to the Massasoit. "I will tell him you will meet him, yes?" he asked.

Carver assured Tisquantum his people were eager to finally meet this great man and his people who had eluded them for months.

William added, "Assure your leader we want only peace."

Tisquantum came back a few minutes later to report. "He wants one of you come with me. Only one."

The settlers looked around at one another, wondering what they should do. "Clearly, we are outnumbered," said Bradford.

"They must also seek peace," said Winslow. "Often, they have seen our people alone, or only two or three at work and fowling. They did no harm when they easily could have done so."

"That is so," agreed William. "We must let them know we want only peace. We must let him know we trust him."

"I do not," declared Standish.

"We must establish peace, and perhaps trade with them," Carver said, looking pointedly at Standish.

"Though we are fewer, we have our muskets." Standish held his up to emphasize his point. "And there . . . we didn't drag those up here to sit idle." He pointed at the cannons sitting on the platform nearby.

For the next few minutes, it was Standish versus most of the rest of the settlers in a debate about whether to send one of their men alone, or show their strength. Tisquantum watched, turning his head from one to another like spectators at a javelin match. One at a time, each man made his point. Edward Winslow ended the debate when he shouted over the others, "I will go."

"We are all in your debt, Master Winslow. But before you go, let us put together some food, drink, and gifts to take to them." Carver turned to Fuller. "Ask the women to put together a basket of a biscuits and butter. Oh, and a jug of strong water." Next, he turned to Bradford. "What have we to present as gifts?"

"I have some knives, and some jewels they might like," said Bradford.

"Good. We will send that too," said Carver.

"This is good," said William. "For surely they are hungry and thirsty after traveling to meet us. It is exactly what our Lord commands us to do. We will show them by our deeds how great is our God. Perhaps God has brought us here for the very purpose of converting them to the true faith."

While all this transpired, the Massasoit and his brother, along with all the others, watched from the hilltop. The settlers kept an eye on them from below. Carrying the assembled gifts, Winslow followed Tisquantum up the hill.

"Assure them that we seek peace," William called out after them.

Tisquantum turned and called back, "He wants peace. He does not want war with the English. We have plenty of enemies. No need for more."

⚇

Winslow turned to look back frequently to verify his friends were still there, waiting to see what would happen. "Look." Tisquantum told Winslow. "No weapons."

As Winslow and Tisquantum made their way toward the Massasoit, the great leader and twenty of his men walked slowly toward them. The Natives stopped about halfway between the top of the hill and the brook. Seeing they did not carry bows, arrows, or hatchets gave Winslow little comfort. His stomach was twisting and his armpits were soaking through his shirt under the protective armor he wore. He bowed to the Native brothers and waited with quivering knees as Tisquantum and Massasoit spoke in Algonquin.

Winslow gulped and fixed his gaze on a fallen tree trunk a few feet behind Quadequina. Of all the ways he thought he might die on this adventure, being left alone among these strange-looking men was not one of them. He'd had nightmares about being attacked with arrows while out in the open, or trapped inside the common house while sleeping as the Natives set fire to the thatch roof. He'd envisioned one of them sneaking up while they were hunting, and chopping them to pieces with their hatchets. He'd also worried a wolf might devour him ever since Standish came upon one tearing away the flesh of a dead dear in the woods.

This situation terrified him more than anything else he thought might have been his fate. *Well, here it is. If putting my life in their hands is what allows us to establish friendship, it must be God's providence. Did not Jesus say it is the greatest form of love to lay down one's life for a friend? And have not these dear people been true friends to me since I first helped Elder William with his printing business in Holland?*

Winslow closed his eyes and tried to imagine he was back in Leiden. When he opened them, he was face to face with reality. Though he had done his best to bring greetings of peace and goodwill from King James to this king, Tisquantum's interpretative skills didn't convey the message as intended. Tisquantum held Winslow's arm with a vice-like grip. Painted faces examined him like a rare specimen. He could not understand a single word they spoke as they looked him over.

Tisquantum turned to Winslow and repeated what the Massasoit had told him to say. "You stay here, with him," he said, pointing to Quadequina. "The Massasoit will go now. I will go. I talk for him."

Winslow looked over his shoulder toward the common house. No one was walking toward him. No one.

"I will stay," Winslow said. Tisquantum released his grip.

⁂

Then the Massasoit, accompanied by Tisquantum, Annawon, Hobbamock, and twenty other Natives, proceeded to the brook separating them from the English. About halfway there, he stopped and selected six of his men to go on with Tisquantum across the brook to meet the English. The settlers waited for them. Massasoit Ousa Mequin instructed his men to hold out their empty hands to show they carried no weapons. Tisquantum and the six Natives crossed the brook to reach the waiting Englishmen.

Tisquantum relayed Massasoit Ousa Mequin's message. "He says, 'Six of mine. One of yours.' He will talk with you now."

The settlers were confused. *Mayflower* mate Williamson repeated Tisquantum's message. "Their chief says he is leaving six of his men with us in exchange for Winslow. He wants us to meet him at the brook and talk. He is afraid of you. Years ago, Master Hunt took this one," he said, pointing to Tisquantum, "and twenty more like him. They do not forget. They will keep Winslow in case we try to hurt any of their men and send us these to show us they come as friends."

Governor Carver, Bradford, William, and Captain Standish, escorted by Tisquantum, slowly moved toward the brook to meet this great leader, leaving the other settlers with the six Natives Tisquantum had just delivered to them. Williamson stayed with them and the six Natives to interpret if needed.

After Tisquantum led the others to within a few yards of the brook, the Englishmen nodded their heads at the Massasoit. "Taniska. Aquene," he said, stepping across the brook. Annawon, Hobbamock, and the others followed him. None of the Natives were armed; all of the Englishmen were. "Taniska. Welcome," said Massasoit Ousa Mequin.

With Standish on one side and William on the other, the Massasoit proudly advanced with his men toward the set-tlers gawking at the scene from where they waited outside the Common House. With Tisquantum and Williamson translating, they talked. Hobbamock would stay with the six Natives chosen as an exchange for Winslow. Tisquantum would go with the others as their interpreter. Leaving Hopkins and Hobbamock in charge, the others made their way toward the new homes.

※

Hopkins examined his charges. All had their faces painted and stood as still as tree trunks while their English guards discussed their appearances. The Natives' expressions remained as still as stone, revealing nothing of what they might be thinking. The lan-guage barrier precluded the two groups trying to talk. Instead, the English scowled at the Natives; the Natives stared back. Finally, Hopkins suggested they should move these six Natives to an empty house and post guard.

CHAPTER SEVENTY-FOUR

PLIMOTH SETTLEMENT – MARCH 1621

William and Mary Brewster had finally moved from the ship and common house into their own home, along with six young children and two single adults. After Priscilla Mullens's family died in February, Mary and William took in the young woman. Bradford, a widower after Dorothy drowned, also lived with them. Since he'd lived with their family in Leiden before marrying Dorothy, it seemed right that he should stay with them now.

With neither rain nor snow, the fifty-degree March day actually felt warm if standing in the sunshine. Mary shooed all the children outside to make traps to catch eels like Samoset taught them to do.

Priscilla was helping Mary unpack things and decide where everyone would sleep. The options were limited. This home was certainly better than their accommodations on the *Mayflower*; nearly anything short of the open air on a rain-soaked night would be. And this was better than when they had been crowded together in the common house where dozens of people vied for a place close enough to the one large stone fireplace to enjoy a bit of warmth. Still, such a small house for so many people made challenging logistics.

"Oh, dear, look at this!" Mary said, clasping her hands to her chest. "I'd forgotten this. My family gave this to us when William and I married. Oh, my, it's been nigh on thirty-five years! I could not bear to leave this, though I know it hardly seems like something we would ever need here."

The item she'd pulled out from among the more practical household items was a beautiful large green silk floor cushion, with braided trim all around and a gold tassel tied to each corner. She gently pulled the delicate pillow free from the candles, cooking utensils, sewing items, and fabric she'd packed for the trip, clutching the pillow to her chest. Priscilla thought she saw a tear or two escape.

"Ah, well, sentiment will not get us settled. Here, put these things over there by the fireplace. We'll have to get one of the carpenters to make us some shelves, or a table." Priscilla piled the things against the stone wall of the fireplace. "Oh, dear, what am I to do with all of these?" Mary exclaimed as she opened a barrel containing dozens of books William had deemed too important to leave in Holland. "Did you ever know a man who could read so many words?"

"Has he truly read all of these?" Priscilla asked in awe.

"I believe he has, and probably more than once. He does have a love for books."

"Well, we are the benefactors of that love," said Priscilla. "I have not heard many preachers, but enough to know not all are as eloquent as your husband in their application of Scripture to the situations we must face every day."

"Yes, I suppose you speak correctly. Well, I simply do not know where I shall place them. For now, it is enough that they are off the ship and safely in our own house." Love and Wrestling came charging through the door just then, as if chased by the devil himself. "What is it, young masters? Slow down! You shall knock something over. You must calm yourselves now, do you hear me?" The boys stopped running, and instead began hopping from foot to foot. "Mama, you must come. The brown people are coming here! Father and Governor brought them! You must come and see it."

Before she could collect her thoughts, William came through the door, though at a considerably slower pace than the boys. "There is to be a parade to welcome our esteemed guests and then a meeting. Hopkins and that Samoset fellow are with six of their men. In exchange for our dear Edward Winslow. It appears their chief wants to talk to some of us about a treaty."

William spotted the cushion Mary had just unpacked. "You brought that? How dear of you. It will always remind us of when our lives were simpler, and less of a challenge every hour of the day."

He picked up the cushion and turned it over to carefully inspect it. "This will be the perfect thing for our meeting this afternoon. We lack a proper chair for their supreme leader, but at least we can offer this elegant pillow. I shall watch it carefully, and assure you it shall return to our new home. You and the children stay here now. We have agreed to talk, but I do not know how this will go or whether we are yet safe. It appears we are, since we have six of their men under guard in exchange for our own brave Master Winslow alone at the top of hill, surrounded by them."

William left Mary and Priscilla to do what they could to set up a decent household in the midst of the wilderness. The boys were incorrigible in their excitement. After giving them firm instructions on how to behave, Mary reluctantly let them go. "You must not make any noise that would attract attention. I am counting on you now to be as quiet as mice hiding from a cat."

Outside, they could see the Natives, their faces painted in bright colors and their bronze skin glistening in the sun. They surveyed the new settlement, accompanied by a dozen settlers wearing armor and carrying muskets.

✠

Mary and Priscilla jumped when they heard the first drums beating only yards away from the house. They dashed to the door to watch. "Dear Lord, it is a parade!" exclaimed Mary. Twenty of the Pokanoket men marched with that many Englishmen. Together, they marched up and down the open areas between the new homes of Plimoth Plantation.

Governor Carver, beating out a rhythm on his drum, led the parade. On either side of him, two other settlers blew trumpets. Sam Fuller carried the Brewster's green pillow. Several others followed, two carrying a large green carpet and four others carrying more cushions. William and Bradford walked along on either side of Massasoit Ousa Mequin. His men followed the settlers up and down the street until they entered an empty house. Hopkins and one of his servants followed them, carrying a basket of food and a jug of strong water.

Mary and Priscilla waited until the drum and trumpets were silent and all the men were in the house. Then they strolled over to determine if they could hear anything through the oiled paper covering the window. Mary signaled to her boys to come to her side. She put her finger to her lips to silence them. The boys giggled and pressed near to listen.

Mary could smell the sweet aroma of tobacco, but try as she might, she couldn't catch enough of the conversation to make sense of it. "Look, there, see?" Priscilla whispered while peeking through a gap between the oiled paper and the window frame. "There's room right inside the door. We could slip in and listen for ourselves, could we not?" asked Priscilla.

"I think not, my dear. They would surely see us, and the distraction could cause them to overlook some necessary detail that might prove crucial. And who would then watch over the children? I do not trust these children to be still in such excitement. No, we must trust our men to make a good treaty for us. How grateful we should be that William has experience in diplomacy from his service to Secretary Davison. Even now, the Lord provides for us in this matter."

Priscilla sighed in the disappointment that comes when youthful enthusiasm encounters the objections of seasoned experience. "Then what are we to do while they spend the afternoon talking?"

Mary laughed and patted her young friend on her shoulder. "Why, dear young friend, we shall do as women always do. We shall tend to that which is in need of our attention. First, we had best round up some of the children and put them to some task that benefits us and prevents them from doing mischief on such an important day."

"I see," agreed Priscilla.

"With nearly half our people now gone to meet our Maker already, we must rely upon anyone who is well enough to stand up to do what they can," Mary explained. Priscilla stared down at her feet, wiping away tears that suddenly wet her cheeks. Mary put her arm around Priscilla's shoulder and gave her young friend a hug, but the lump that caught in her throat prevented her from speaking for a moment.

After several minutes, Mary said, "I know, dear. I know. We have witnessed too many deaths, your own dear parents and brothers among them. I pray our dear Lord will strengthen and comfort you." Mary turned so she could look into Priscilla's face. "I wonder if perhaps God has spared us in order to help those who have survived. It falls to the few of us now to prepare their meals, wash everyone's clothing, tend the gardens, care for the littlest ones, and nurse the sick. I am weary even thinking of it, but the work must be done. How grateful I am that God has spared Suzanna, Catherine, Elizabeth, and Constance. Truly, we must trust that our Lord shall not give us more than we can bear."

"If only we spoke a few words of their language," said Priscilla, pointing to the house where Natives and settlers sat negotiating their mutual future. "I should think their women could teach us much about this wilderness."

"Ah, I wish it too. I thank the good Lord that we have Squanto and Samoset, but what do they know of women's ways?" laughed Mary. Mary and Priscilla walked slowly toward the common house. Inside, a handful of women were busy preparing the next meal. They looked up when Mary and Priscilla joined them.

"What news have you?" asked Suzanna White.

"We could not make out what they were saying. They seem engaged in good talk. I am sure they will be pleased to have food to fill them up when they finish. How is everything here?"

"It seems that we barely finish one meal before it is time to tend to the tasks for the next one. To speak plainly, I wonder if perhaps those now laying sick in their beds are not better off than the few of us left to tend to them," said Catherine Carver. "We must work out a plan for how we will manage if we are to have any hope of keeping up, with so few of us and so much to do."

"Let us send the older boys out to catch lobsters and eels," Mary suggested. "The older girls can watch the little runabouts so they don't get hurt. Priscilla, dear, can you manage to take nourishment to those in the sick house?"

Priscilla nodded. Mary hoped the errand would distract her from her sorrows for a bit. "Good. Then the rest of us can focus on our tasks here so we will be ready whenever they finish their talk. They will surely be very hungry after so much talking." All the women laughed at that and settled into their tasks, but struggled to concentrate. It seemed the meeting would never finish. One hour passed. Then another. Tension mounted as the women in the common house waited to learn the outcome. They all realized how much their futures depended on what the men were doing in that house.

CHAPTER SEVENTY-FIVE

PLIMOTH SETTLEMENT – MARCH 22, 1621

The treaty-making was tedious, for both sides had a great stake in achieving a clear understanding between them. Neither side wanted to offend. The lack of language fluency posed a barrier every bit as great as the ocean that had separated their two cultures. The settlers assumed the Natives lacked any modern form of government and worshipped as pagans. Tisquantum did not know enough English to explain the complicated English system of royalty, courts, secretaries, and the hierarchy of the Established Church the Separatists had so desperately wanted to escape.

The language barrier was not their only challenge; the English settlers arrived in the Pokanoket territory with two very different motives. "First and foremost," insisted William, "we must be free to worship as the early disciples did. We cannot, and shall not, tolerate any effort to impose the excesses of the Established Church here." He looked pointedly at Billington.

Billington sometimes liked to make a sport of challenging the way William led Sunday worship and study meetings. He rarely actually did more than hover around the back of the group, yet he was quick to critique, and slow to actually assist in any helpful way.

"That is all well and good," Isaac Allerton pointed out, "but do not forget, we are not truly free men. Weston and his partners expect a return on their investment. They do not care one wit how we pray, so long as we pay them. We have seven years of cruel labor before we are truly free of the scoundrels."

As the Separatists and Adventurers debated among themselves, Massasoit Ousa Mequin conferred with Annawon and Habbamock. "They seem weak and confused," observed Habbamock.

"That is good for us. We can make a good treaty now," pointed out Annawon.

Governor Carver kept passing around baskets filled with meat while Bradford did the same with jugs of drink. Massasoit Ousa Mequin nodded, and one of his men passed around a mixture of tobacco juice. As they exchanged treasures from their traditions, Governor Carver and Massasoit Ousa Mequin worked out the details of the treaty.

"Neither I nor any of my men will do harm to any of their people," Massasoit Ousa Mequin told Tisquantum to tell the settlers.

"And we shall do no harm to any of his," agreed Governor Carver. "And if any of ours do harm to any of his, that one will be sent to him, that he might punish him," he added, pointing to Massasoit Ousa Mequin.

William wrote down the terms of the agreement, and, with Tisquantum and Williamson taking turns interpreting, read back to them what they'd agreed upon with regard to how they would live as neighbors.

"If anyone took away anything from any of theirs, he should cause it to be restored; and they should do the like to his," William read. He checked his notes and continued. "If any waged war unjustly against him, they would aid him; and if any did war against them, he should aid them." Then William said, too quickly for the Natives to interpret, "It seems there are other Natives close enough to be a threat to us, as they already are to this group. Do you see how God uses even enemies to work his will so that we have help in our time of need?"

William returned to his notes, speaking slowly so the interpreters could translate. "He should send to his neighbors confederates to certify them to this, that they might not wrong them, but might likewise compromise in conditions of peace. That when their men came to them, they should leave their bows and arrows behind." Massasoit Ousa Mequin nodded his approval when he heard the translation.

William continued, "And our men will leave their weapons behind when they visit, as well." The treaty-making progressed back and forth through interpreters all afternoon.

When the negotiations were finally complete to everyone's satisfaction, the men stood, stretched, and left the house. William retrieved the cushion Mary had unpacked earlier and went to locate her. He found her handing a bucket to their son with instructions to fetch more water. After Love left, William summed up the details of the afternoon for Mary. "And our men agreed to leave their weapons behind when they visit them?" Mary asked in astonishment.

"That was a hard point to concede, but it was necessary. We told them that our King James would esteem Massasoit as a friend and ally."

"What about Winslow?" asked Mary.

"Governor Carver is taking Massasoit and his men back to the brook just now. Then his men will send Winslow back to us. When Winslow is back, Captain Standish and Hopkins shall return to the brook with their men. Bradford said they will make camp in the woods tonight. Squanto wants to stay here in the village."

"We have a treaty? There will be peace?"

"We have a treaty. And I pray to God that all will abide by it."

While William was talking to Mary, Governor Carver went with Tisquantum and Massasoit Ousa Mequin back to the brook. The Natives who'd been sent to the settlement as good-faith hostages stayed behind in the house where they'd been guarded during the negotiations. Carver had expected to bring Winslow back with him, but he returned to the settlement alone.

Quadequina did not release Winslow. Instead, he sent Tisquantum back to the settlement with a message, "Tell the white men I will come to visit them. Say to them, no guns. We will put down our bows. They will put down their guns."

Reluctantly, the settlers put their weapons away in an empty house. Then Quadequina sat down with them. With the assistance of Tisquantum as interpreter, he learned for himself the terms of the treaty and agreed to them. When Quadequina was satisfied that both sides had made the treaty in good faith, he returned to the far side of the brook and released Winslow.

CHAPTER SEVENTY-SIX

The sun slipped below the tree line in the west as the six Natives walked away from the village to join the others across the brook. William went with Bradford to let the crew and the few settlers still on the *Mayflower* know what had transpired that day.

"That is good. Very good," said Jones when the two men told him the details of the treaty. "My men and I must be heading back soon now. I will sleep better knowing there is to be peace here. I know it is not always so in new settlements."

"We shall all strive to live together as good Christian men among those who are ignorant of God. Perhaps in time we will be able to show them the ways of faith," William replied.

"Our women have made everything ready now for those who lay here in their sickness," said Bradford. "If your men will help us, we can remove the last few of our people to shore now."

"It shall be so," said Jones. He left to give the orders to his crew to assist the settlers in any way they might require.

Mayflower Log, Friday, 23 Mar.: *At anchor. A fair day. Some of the ship's company went on shore. Some of the savages came again. Captain Standish and Master Allerton went to see the king, and were welcomed by him. This morning, the savages stayed till ten or eleven o'clock, and the governor, sending for the king's kettle, filled it with peas, and they went their way.*

Making ready for sea. Getting ballast, wood, and water from the shore. The planters held a meeting and concluded military

orders as well as some laws, and chose Master John Carver as
Governor for the coming year. He was "governor" on the ship.

The next day passed pleasantly enough. Men sorted through the
last of the cargo delivered to shore by Master Jones's men. Women
split into teams: some tending the sick as best they could, others
supervising the smallest children and preparing another meal.
The *Mayflower* crew worked on final preparations to sail back to
England. Everyone seemed optimistic now that they'd seen the
Natives up close and knew the details for a peaceful coexistence.
Tisquantum and Samoset seemed intent on staying with them.

"I think they are curious about our ways," suggested William. "I
see no harm in them watching what we do. Perhaps they will come
to understand our God, and will become Christians themselves."

Carver and Bradford weren't so sure. "Maybe they are here to
spy on us and report back to their king," suggested Carver.

"Well, I think we must show them hospitality. If we are concerned about something, we can write of it to one another. They
surely cannot understand our written words."

"An excellent point," agreed Carver.

⁂

Massasoit Ousa Mequin and Quadequina walked away from the
others. "Do you think we can really trust the white people?" asked
Quadequina.

"I do not know. I am more concerned about Tisquantum. I do
not trust him. I worry he will let them know too many of our worries about the Narragansett and how we manage our community.
It is true that we are stronger and more numerous. Look how thin
they are! I think the sickness has been a cruel enemy to them. But
they have their fire sticks. If they decide to turn on us, we will
suffer greatly."

"What should we do then?" asked Quadequina.

"We will go home now. We will make our fields ready, and
continue to watch."

The two brothers returned to the others, who were packing up
and getting ready to head home. As they approached, they saw
two white men approach, carrying a large kettle hung on a pole
balanced on their shoulders. "What is this?" asked Massasoit Ousa
Mequin.

"Their men said to send our kettle to them. They filled it with peas from far away. We will plant these, and have more food. Tisquantum stayed to show them how to add fish to their seeds to grow strong food for themselves."

"This seems good," said Massasoit Ousa Mequin. "Now, we go home. We have done what we must do for now."

⚜

The next day, Edward Winslow found William sitting on a blanket, leaning against a maple tree with a book perched on his knees. "Greetings, Master Edward. What do you think of our new settlement now?"

"I bring sad news. My dear Elizabeth passed on to her eternal rest this morning. She was pleased to finally be in our own home. And now she goes on to her heavenly one."

William put down his book and stood up. He put his hand on his friend's shoulder. "I am truly sorry, my friend. You have been so brave when we needed you. I had so hoped your dear wife would be spared, and recover from this dreadful sickness. The Lord giveth, and the Lord taketh away. We must not question the ways of the Lord. But I am sorely sorry to learn of this."

Winslow nodded and closed his eyes, trying to contain his tears. When he opened them again, he said, "Master Jones told Mr. Bradford that many of his crew lie sick on the ship, as well. When will this scourge come to an end?"

William moved to stand beside his friend. "Let us go to her and prepare her for her final resting place. Shall I ask Master Jones to officiate at her funeral?"

"Must you? Are you not now our official spiritual leader? Can you not do what must be done?"

William pulled on his beard as he thought about the best option. *Soon enough, there will be no Master Jones to consult on such matters. And it is true that we are now on our own and well settled here. Yet he is still here, and I suppose it would put him in a better position to come to our defense when he returns the ship to the investors void of any cargo they might have sold to make a profit on their investment. I must think about this some more.*

"I will consult with Governor Carver and Master Bradford."

⚜

"If you are willing, Elder Brewster, I think it would soften the hearts of our investors to receive a kindly report of our struggles from Master Jones," said Bradford. "The master does seem to have warmed in his opinion toward us in the many months we've suffered together." "I rather agree. They will not be pleased he returns with an empty ship, with half the crew left behind in their graves. If this one last act of respect toward the old seaman could benefit our future, I think we must at least approach him on the matter."

Crusty old Christopher Jones performed his first land funeral for Elizabeth Winslow, and his final one for the passengers. William wrote in his journal that night:

> I am confident I did see a tear slip down his wrinkled, bearded cheek. How mysterious are the ways of our Lord. How very mysterious, indeed.

※

> Mayflower log, Thursday, 29 March: At anchorage. The master offered to take back any of the colonists who wished to return to England, but none desired to go.

> Mayflower log, Saturday, 31 March: At anchorage. Settling up rigging, bending light sails, etc. Getting ballast and wood from the beach and island. The colonists have lost thirteen to death this past month, which makes half their number in all.

By the end of March, half the passengers and more of the *Mayflower* crew were dead. The deceased among the *Mayflower* crew included the cook, a master gunner, the boatswain, three quartermasters, and a third of the general crew. Master Jones reported to Carver with a considerable understatement. "Been a bad voyage for the owner, Adventurers, ship, and crew."

William wrote in his journal on Sunday, April 1:

> It is the sixteenth Sunday our ship has been anchored in this harbor. So many deaths. I cannot help but wonder if we have truly followed our Lord, or perhaps we have run away, as Jonah ran away from Nineveh. Have we been faithful or foolish in our

plan to establish for our God a new congregation far away from
the corruption and contention of the Established Church?

I must not allow myself to doubt, but rather pray that the Lord
shall give me the strength and wisdom necessary to embolden the
spirits of these dear men and women—aye, even little babes—to
be firm in our resolve to establish here a place that is pleasing to
our Lord, who has brought us so far from home.

The last official task requiring attention before the *Mayflower* sailed away from the fledgling Plimoth Plantation was the preparation of the will of Adventurer William Mullens. Carver copied the will carefully onto a fresh parchment, reserving the original copy for Priscilla's keeping. Master Jones and one of his crew witnessed it, then rolled it and secured it with a ribbon.

"Master Williamson and I shall be sure that it will be properly recorded for probate upon our return to England. We shall also deliver the many letters and keepsakes your people have already given us," Jones said, extending his hand to shake hands with Carver.

For the last time, Carver made the short trip across the bay from the ship to the shore. Most of the ship's crew gathered on shore to bid farewell to the settlers. The chronic challenges of sickness, deprivation, and death had served as sandpaper to rub away the animosity that festered between them only a few months earlier. The seamen climbed into the longboat after Carver stepped out, and returned to the ship.

※

William and Mary, along with their sons and fostered children, stood with the other settlers able to leave their sickbeds and watched the crew working on the ship that had been their home for so long. One hundred and eleven days after entering the harbor, the *Mayflower* crew pulled anchor at full tide, set the ship's colors, and gave the planters a final salute with the ensign and ordnance.

The community stood silent, each absorbed in their own thoughts as the *Mayflower* grew smaller and smaller. They watched until the ship was but a dot on the horizon . . . and then was seen no more.

William reached for Mary's hand and led her away along the sandy beach. "We pledged for better and for worse, in sickness and in health, and truly, we have had ample portions of all of that," he said.

"We pledged it with no idea of what that could possibly mean," countered Mary.

"And we have arrived in this strange and wonderful new world at last. I cannot imagine what shall come of this, darling, but I am grateful you have accompanied me on this journey. Truly, I thank you for your faithfulness. I pray that I may be so faithful to you and to our dear Lord, who watches over us all."

"Where you go, I will go with you," Mary replied. Looking away from the sea that had been their perilous home and toward the new buildings recently completed, the Brewsters walked forward into the new life unfolding for them at Plimoth Plantation.

EPILOGUE

U<small>NDER</small> Shipmaster Christopher Jones's skillful seamanship, the *Mayflower* completed the return voyage to England in thirty-one mostly uneventful days. The treaty Massasoit Ousa Mequin negotiated with the settlers held until 1675. Jonathan Brewster joined his parents the following year when the *Fortune* sailed into the Plymouth Harbor with more members from Pastor John Robinson's Separatist congregation at Leiden, and more pioneers seeking fortunes in the New World. The Brewster daughters, Patience and Fear, were reunited with their family in 1623 with the arrival of their ship, the *Anne*. Patience later married the widower Isaac Allerton.

Due to a combination of age and illness, John Robinson never joined the settlers in the New World. Elder William Brewster never saw his dear friend and mentor again.

Though forty-five of the *Mayflower* passengers died before the ship began her return voyage, Plimoth Plantation survived, and eventually thrived. The General Society of the Mayflower estimates there are some 10 million US citizens who are descended from the 102 passengers on that ship, and as many as 35 million people worldwide. Estimates for the Pokanoket community are more difficult to determine, but there are an estimated 30,000 descendants of those who survived the Great Dying that wiped out an estimated 70% of their population.

The Pokanoket and English shared many collegial moments in the early years following the day of the treaty. William Brewster and Massasoit Ousa Mequin forged a friendship, and visited with one another often. Edward Winslow personally tended to the great

Massasoit when he was gravely ill. The Pokanokets responded in the fall of 1621 when they heard the English firing their weapons. Thinking they were in trouble; they honored the treaty by going to render aid if needed. It turned out the English were celebrating a successful fall harvest. The two groups ended up celebrating together in an event that is commonly known today as the first (it wasn't) Thanksgiving celebration.

However, tensions grew, and problems erupted as more and more English immigrants arrived to establish settlements up and down the Atlantic Coast. New arrivals did not see the wisdom, need, or value of honoring the treaty. They broke it twice in the years leading up to King Philip's war.

The Pokanoket people suffered horrific losses in King Philip's War that erupted in 1675. Many of those who survived were sold into slavery, often in the Caribbean. After their defeat, when the English forbid them to speak their own language, practice their own rituals, or use their own name to refer to themselves, some Pokanoket people regrouped as the Wampanoag people in order to try to get along with the English. A remnant of the once strong and proud Pokanoket people lives on today, with the nucleus living in the Rhode Island area.

When the war came to a bloody end in August 1678, hundreds of the region's Pokanoket were dead, captured as slaves, or executed as a way to discourage future efforts to preserve their ancient ways and use of the land where they'd lived for thousands of years. The percentage of deaths from that bloody conflict exceeded the percentage of casualties in the Civil War. The English claimed victory, but also suffered devastating casualties. The Pokanokets not only lost their way of life, but also any remaining hope for peaceful engagement with the Europeans.

But *that* is the subject of another book.

ACKNOWLEDGEMENTS

I T takes a village to publish a book. In the case of this book, it's taken multiple villages. One is Scrooby in Northern England where the Brewster story begins. Another is in Holland where the Separatists lived before sailing to a new world. I walked where many of the Separatists did four hundred years ago and spent an informative afternoon at the Leiden American Pilgrim Museum, opened and operated by Dr. Jeremy Bangs. In Plymouth, Donna D. Curtin, Executive Director at Pilgrim Hall, and Darius Coombs, Director of Wampanoag & Algonkian Interpretive Training, Research & Community Recruitment at Plimoth Plantation graciously filled in important historical details. I am also grateful to Chris Newell at the Akomawt for enlightening me on a variety of seventeenth century Native customs.

In my search for Natives to review the text, I met Po Wauipi Neimpaug (Winds of Thunder) William Guy, Sagamore of today's Pokanoket Nation; Po Pummukoank Anogqs (Dancing Star) Tracey Brown; and Po Menuhkesu Menenok (Strong Turtle) Donald Brown, Pokanoket Tribal Historian. I am deeply indebted to them for correcting some of my details about the first encounters between their family and mine. All three are descendants of Massasoit Ousa Mequin.

Each author cited in the bibliography contributed to the story through their extensive research for their own books. I am particularly indebted to authors Sue Allan and the late Mary B. Sherwood for their enlightening research into the lives of William and Mary Brewster. I am also grateful for the books on the topic published by Caleb Johnson, and his detailed website: mayflowerhistory.com.

Additional insights were provided *The Elder Brewster Press*, edited by Gregory Evan Thompson. I found the American Museum of the American Indian a valuable research resource.

Authors do not write in a vacuum. I am thankful for the support of the Houston writing community, especially Sandy Lawrence, mentor and colleague at Perceptive PR, for her consistent guidance through the worlds of publishing and promotion. Special thanks and appreciation to Dr. Roger Leslie and the Rev. Larry Johnson for their professional editorial coaching and insights, for Trisha Lewis for suggesting multiple helpful edits, and Sophie Bonifaz for diligent research assistance.

This book exists in part due to the encouragement of Steve Eisner, founder of When Words Count Retreat in Vermont. He urged me to finish the manuscript and enter it in one of WWC's pitch week competitions. There I met six new writing sisters who provided welcome feedback. Thank you, Karen Kaiser, Renate LeDuc, Sally Newhart, Stephanie Schorow, Elizabeth Splaine, and Jamie Taylor. At WWC I met Dede Cummings who agreed to publish the book through her Green Writers Press, along with Marilyn Atlas and Ben Tanzer, whose professional wisdom helped shape the final version of *Mayflower Chronicles: The Tale of Two Cultures*.

And finally, but hardly last or least, thank you family for bearing with me as I've spent more time in the sixteenth and seventeenth centuries than I have in our own. Thank you for accompanying me on the research trips to England, Netherlands, Germany, and New England. Thank you for patiently listening to details about events four centuries ago. I come from and claim as family amazing people, for which I am profoundly grateful.

BIBLIOGRAPHY

Allan, Sue. *William Brewster: The Making of a Pilgrim*. United Kingdom: Domtom Publishing, Ltd., 2016.

Ames, Azel. *The Mayflower and Her Log: July 15, 1620 – May 6, 1621 – Complete*. San Bernardino, CA: Filiquarian Publishing, 2017.

Bangs, Jeremy Dupertuis. *Strangers and Pilgrims: Travellers and Sojourners: Leiden and the Foundations of Plymouth Plantation*. Plymouth, MA: General Society of Mayflower Descendants, 2009.

Bradford, William (Paget, Harold, Ed.). *Of Plymouth Plantation*. Mineola, NY: Dover Publications, 2006.

Brooks, Lisa, *Our Beloved Kin: A New History of King Philip's War*. New Haven, CT & London, UK: Yale University Press. 2018.

Bunker, Nick. *Making Haste from Babylon: The Mayflower Pilgrims and Their World*. New York, NY: Alfred Knopf, 2010.

Carpenter, Edmund Janes and McHugh, Michael J. *The Mayflower Pilgrims*. Arlington Heights, IL: Christian Liberty Press, 2004.

Demos, John. *A Little Commonwealth: Family Life in Plymouth Colony*. London, UK: Oxford University Press. 1970.

Dunbar-Ortiz, Roxanne. *An Indigenous People's History of the United States.* Boston, MA: Beacon Press, 2014.

Fraser, Rebecca. *The Mayflower: The Families, the Voyage, and the Founding of America.* New York, NY: St. Martin's Press, 2017.

Heath, Dwight B., Editor. *Mourt's Relation: A Journal of the Pilgrims at Plymouth.* Bedford, MA: Applewood Books, 1963).

Johnson, Caleb. *Here Shall I Die Ashore: Stephen Hopkins: Bermuda Castaway, Jamestown Survivor, and Mayflower Pilgrim* USA: Xlibris Corp. 2007.

Johnson, Caleb. *The Mayflower and Her Passengers.* USA: Xlibris Corp. 2006.

Kupperman, Karen Ordahl. *Indians & English: Facing Off in Early America.* Ithaca, NY: Cornell University, 2000.

Mann, Charles C. *1493: Uncovering the New World Columbus Created.* New York, NY: Vintage Books, 2011.

Mann, Charles C. *1491: New Revelations of the Americas Before Columbus.* New York, NY: Vintage Books, 2011.

Niles, Judith. *Native American History: A Chronology of a Culture's Vast Achievements and Their Links to World Events.* New York, NY: Random House Publishing.1996.

O'Brien, Cormac. *The Forgotten History of America: Little-Known Conflicts of Lasting Importance from the Earliest Colonists to the Eve of Revolution.* Beverly, MA: Fair Winds Press. 2008.

Philbrick, Nathaniel. *Mayflower: A Story of Courage, Community, and War.* New York, New York: Penguin Group, 2006.

Russell, Howard S. *Indian New England Before the Mayflower.* Hanover, NH & London, UK: University Press of New England, 2014.

Sherwood, Mary B. *Pilgrim: A Biography of William Brewster.* Virginia: Great Oak Press, 1982.

Ulrich, Laurel Thatcher. *The Age of Homespun: Objects and Stories in the Creation of an American Myth.* New York, NY: Alfred A. Knopf, 2001.

Wilbur, C. Keith. *The New England Indians.* Guilford, CT: The Globe Pequot Press. 1996.

Winslow, Edward. *Good Newes from New England: A True Relation of Things Very Remarkable at the Plantation of Plimoth in New England.* Bedford, MA: Applewood Books, 1624).

Zophy, Jonathan W. *A Short History of Reformation Europe.* Upper Saddle River, NJ: Prentice-Hall, Inc. 1997.